MW00324780

Eternal Service

By Regina Morris

Silkhaven Publishing, LLC

Jesika,

All my best.

Regina Morris

Silkhaven Publishing, LLC

ISBN: 978–0–9888222–1–4

Library of Congress Control Number: 2013900069

Copyright (c) 2012, Regina Morris.

(V3) September 8, 2013

All rights reserved. No part of this book may be used or reproduced in any manner without the written permission of Regina Morris with the exception in the case of brief quotations embodied in critical articles and reviews.

Printed in the United States of America.

This is a work of fiction. All of the characters, organizations, places and events portrayed in this novel are either products of the author's imagination or are fictitiously used. Any resemblance to actual persons, living or dead, business establishments, events, or locales is entirely coincidental.

Silkhaven Publishing, LLC does not have any control over and does not assume any responsibility for author or third–party Web sites or their content.

The scanning, uploading, and distribution of this book via the internet or via any other means without the permission of Silkhaven Publishing, LLC is illegal and punishable by law. To obtain a copy of this novel, please purchase only through authorized electronic or print editions, and do not participate in or encourage electronic piracy of copyrighted materials.

Adult content within. Sex, nudity, violence, and language. Suggested audience is 18+ years of age.

Vampires exist among us.

They can be our neighbor, best friend, our child's teacher …

They alter their aged appearance based upon the amount of blood they consume. They move to a new area, drink a lot of blood, and appear young. Slowly they limit their intake of blood and age, right in front of our unsuspecting eyes. After decades, they fake their death, move, and do it over and over again.

Most live quiet lives in an effort to blend in.

Some however want power and control.

The Colony is an elite group of vampires sworn to protect the President of the United States from these rogue vampires.

~ One Page Teaser ~

Raymond smiled at Alex. It was a beautiful smile, not fake or forced. You can always tell when a smile is real. His black colored eyes held the smile, not just his luscious, full lips. Alex noticed his hair remained a bit damp, probably due to a last minute shower on his way over. His hair parted on the side tonight, and a curl of bangs hung lopsided onto his forehead. It gave him a Superman appearance. She always did like Superman.

Alex knew her pulse sped up as she took in the visual strip tease in her mind. She thought back to their earlier conversation. Humans and vampires could have sex together. Sex. She swallowed hard. She hadn't thought of having sex with a man in a long time. Her heart sped up even faster. She wondered if he could hear the beats. If he did, he didn't show any reaction. He just sat sipping his wine, looking sexy as hell.

Her hands still held her wineglass, so she took a gulp of wine hoping to squelch the heat she felt within her. Instead, the drink fueled the flame. Would sex with a vampire be different than with a human? If there were a difference, she was betting it would be better. The sexual relationships she had in the past, if she could remember that far back, were moderately satisfying. Definitely not romance novel, page turning, steamy … but satisfying.

Blinking a few times, she realized she was staring at his crotch. Could she be more obvious? She knew in her heart that she was going to take this promotion. She couldn't start a romance with a team member, it wasn't professional. She wasn't that type of woman. Plus, there was no guarantee that he was interested in her such a way. He had treated her with nothing but respect.

Then again, she couldn't deny her overwhelming attraction to him. His dark raven hair, soulful teal colored eyes, strong muscular jaw ... they beckoned her. She bit her lip imagining the vampire shirtless, or even better, nude.

"Alex?" Raymond asked.

Alex looked up, making eye contact. "What?"

"Are you okay? You've been quiet for several minutes."

Reviews (Amazon & Goodreads)

**** *"I will say that I love, love, love this author's style and would put her up there with Lynsay Sands."* – Candy G.

***** *"I loved every minute of this book and what's even better is that there are more to come!! ... Definitely a 5 Star book and a must read!"* – The Sub Club Books

***** *"This story was really a great adventure and romance all rolled into one. I recommend this first of the series and intend to read the rest of the series as they are released."* – Janice H.

***** *"I love the new twist that Regina has used with the vampires in this story. It is unique and very refreshing. I love all the characters and am looking forward to learning more about each one as the series progresses."* - D. Thomas

***** *"I absolutely loved this book! She pulls you in and captivates you with her characters! I highly recommend this book! Total awesomeness!"* Laura L.

**** *"Eternal Service was a wonderful paranormal romance. Regina Morris knows how to draw you into a story and keep you begging for more."* – Book Maven

**** *"Regina Morris creates a world of vampires that is fascinating."* – T&K Book Reviews

**** *"Hilarious! I can't wait for the 2nd book in the series..."* – Twinsie Talk Reviews

***** *"Amazing book!"* Salli B.

***** *"I loved the twist the author had on her vampire world. ... Very unique!"* – Pennie B.

CHAPTER ONE

Raymond recoiled from the sight of the woman's blood on his hands as he struggled to keep the exhausted blood–soaked forger pinned to the cold hard ground. "You son of a bitch," he scowled. The crisp dried leaves crunched beneath his prey. "That woman had a life. She had a family who cared for her – and you killed her like she was nothing."

The subdued forger shrugged, unwilling to make eye contact. "Collateral damage. Nothing more."

The cool night breeze blew the scent of the woman's blood into Raymond's face, causing him to grimace. He shook his head in disgust. The secluded spot where he held the forger down intensified the darkness of the evening, but he could still easily make out the faces of his men.

One of the shadows separated from the darkness. Agent Ben knelt down next to Raymond, his dark skin and stocky, muscular build contrasting sharply with Raymond's tall, marble–like perfection. Ben callously crushed the forger's hands as he digitally scanned his fingerprints.

"Aargh! Son of a bitch! Look, I'll make a deal with you if you let me go."

"You don't know who hired you, so you have nothing to bargain with," Raymond said dismissively as he watched Ben finish his task and pocket the scanner. Next, Raymond glanced over at his son, Sterling, who was checking the vampire's belongings.

"I've got everything I need," Sterling mumbled as he tossed the backpack to the ground.

1

Raymond pulled a dagger from his boot. He wondered if the forger would show any remorse or fear now while facing his own death, but none came. Sterling moved to hold the captive's feet down in preparation for the end.

"I can pay you. I can get you gems, gold, blood … whatever you want."

Raymond didn't bother to acknowledge the forger's bribes. Instead, he showed him the cold steel blade as his answer.

"C'mon, everybody's got a price. What do you say?"

"You breached the perimeter of the White House in an effort to kill the President," Raymond accused.

"I did a job, but I wasn't sent to kill anybody."

Raymond studied at the man in disgust. "Tell that to the guards you attacked and the pregnant woman you killed as you fled."

The forger's eyes widened, as if thinking of anything to say to save his life. After a moment, he finally blurted out, "I tried to plant bugs. I also had to deliver documents. That's all!"

"Name the target." Raymond growled.

An answer squeaked out, "The President."

"What about the documents?" Sterling asked.

The forger eyes darted over to Sterling. "The drop didn't take place. No one showed up at the appointed time."

"Perhaps you were expendable," Ben chimed in. He glanced over to Raymond. "Or, the documents were no longer of use."

"The documents are fine," the forger barked out with pride.

Raymond looked over to the backpack. "We'll be taking those *fine* documents off your hands." Moving the dagger so the blade reflected the dim moonlight, he added, "There's also a price to pay for the lives you took." Raymond plunged the dagger into the vampire's heart. Instantly, Raymond's knees sank into the dirt as the vampire disappeared beneath him. A cloud of dust scattered across Raymond's fatigues and the once shiny blade now lay stained in a dusty mound on the ground. The last remains of the captive.

Ben knelt down beside Raymond, "We'll have to list him as an enemy killed in action," he said as he collected what was left of the EKIA for DNA.

"We need to inform the Director and Homeland Security about this breach," Raymond said as he stood and shook the dust from his pants.

Nodding, Sterling took out his phone, "Dixon, we need to meet. McGregor's Pub. Give us an hour."

****

McGregor's pub sat on the outskirts of the suburbs – the type of place with a back lawn as a parking lot, beer (not Appletinis) filling the taps , and a bartender always ready for you to bend his ear. The lit neon beer signs shined through the window and glass door, so Raymond led the team in.

They strode past the long bar counter, with its many empty stools sitting in a row. The few tables in the place were clustered together. Booths and pool tables took up all the room in the way back. The older place remained kept up, at least to the point where you could sit down and not worry about sticking to the chairs. They found

3

Dixon sitting in his usual back corner booth drinking a beer.

"Dixon, good you could make it here so fast," Raymond said as they approached the older man.

The waitress eyed the three handsome men as soon as they entered, and bustled to the booth to take their order. As she approached, she eyed each one as though sizing them up. Each stood well over six feet in height, and offered her various flavors to choose from. Raymond, towering over the others and striking with his dark hair and pale, flawless skin, sat down next to Dixon. The other two men squeezed their large frames into the other side of the booth. The shorter of the two, with his long blond locks and playboy appearance managing to look like he was lounging even in the small space, seemed to have tempted the waitress, as did the cocoa brown skinned and powerfully built muscles of the other. Of course, each one was her senior by over a century, but that was undetectable. "You boys want something?" She winked over at Ben as her chosen favorite. Obviously, nothing was wrong with a little brown sugar in her sugar bowl tonight.

Raymond searched deep into her eyes and willed the human to obey him. "Quickly finish closing. We'll lock up when we're done here." As he compelled the waitress, Ben rose with his usual military precision to contend with the bartender. At a stern glance from his father, Sterling slouched over to each of the few patrons in the place. The pub cleared within minutes. The men helped themselves to drinks and gathered around their table.

"OK, I'm guessing this has to do with what happened earlier tonight on the south lawn of the White

House," Dixon said, scratching the gray whiskers of his five o'clock shadow. He then added, "The guards are fine. The hospital released them a short while ago. Naturally, the media frenzy is still going on. The incident has been classified as a random attack with the assailant having been captured. We used a classified, random picture to represent him to the media, and they seemed to have accepted it."

"Has the President been briefed about the event?" asked Raymond.

"Yes. He was unaware of the breach at the time. He is still safely tucked away in the residence quarters, probably asleep by now." Dixon raised an eyebrow. "Nobody suspects anything, but am I correct in assuming the man was a vampire?"

"Yes." Raymond nodded towards Ben. "Show him."

Ben shrugged the backpack off his massive shoulders and handed the satchel over to Dixon, who opened the bag and studied its contents.

"These forged documents are damn good copies of the invite to the President's state dinner." He continued to scan the bag. "And, four security passes and paperwork as well. Christ," Dixon cursed.

"The forger is an EKIA. He gave us quite a chase. He planned to ditch us in a park outside the city, but we got him." Raymond sighed. "He also took a pregnant woman hostage at the start of the chase. She didn't survive. By now, her body has been discovered." Raymond glanced across the table with saddened eyes at his team members. The pain of the loss hung in the air.

"There was no way to save her." Ben then shifted gears, pointing to the forged documents. "With the

5

dinner still days away, there's time to get new passes made."

Dixon didn't comment on the death. They all knew she'd become another unsolved murder, just like all the others. "I'm sure you did what you could." Dixon studied the evidence in his hand. "At least these passes contain pictures. Should be good for some facial recognition software … might get a hit in the FBI, CIA or police databases. Obviously the people on the IDs will try to infiltrate the state dinner next week. The President is in grave danger." Setting the IDs aside, he asked, "Any idea what might be on the memory cards?"

"Probably backups of these documents," Sterling tossed out.

"If we're lucky, possibly Intel about the leader. This vamp was a good forger, and he may have given us a good chase, but he wasn't the brains behind the operation," Ben added.

Sterling pointed his gloved finger at the backpack, "I didn't sense anything off the docs or the tech stuff, but I got a reading off the backpack. The forger seemed to be a loner and did this job only for the money. He didn't know and didn't care about any bigger plan."

The team was well aware of Sterling's ability to acquire information from inanimate objects, and Dixon was no exception. He brushed his fingertips against the fabric of the bag. "We'll need to find out who hired him. I'll make sure the Director of Homeland Security gets access to these findings, including that the assault was committed by a vampire."

"We'll provide what information we can from the tech pieces," Raymond offered. "With the forger now dead, whoever hired him may suspect immortals to have taken him out, since humans couldn't have dispatched him so easily. If the leader is also a vampire, they'll be taking their game up a notch when this vampire fails once again to show up with the passes. We'll need to be more careful."

Dixon nodded. "Right." He shifted in his seat and drained his beer.

Raymond carefully observed his old friend. "So what's bugging you tonight? I can feel your thought patterns, and I can tell you're anxious about something."

"Yeah, I've wanted to talk with you boys about something for a while now." Dixon took a deep breath. "I'm going to retire. I've pushed off retirement as much as I could, but the years are getting to me now. It's time to hand the reigns over to the next Director for you boys."

The men at the table were deadly quiet now as they studied Dixon's face and took a good look at the man they had known for decades. "Are you sure?" Raymond asked. "I mean, we've had a lot of Directors in the past, but we see you as part of our team. Are you really that old?"

"You know my age, Raymond. I'm not old, but I'm also not young anymore," he sighed. His face suddenly appeared more aged to Raymond.

Only the President and a handful of people knew about the Colony and its immortal vampires who worked for the federal government. Once you left the inner circle your memories were erased. Raymond had performed the memory wipe many times and the process was always complete, decisive, and permanent.

"I've been reviewing possible candidates and I think I have the perfect replacement. Raymond, I'd like for the

7

two of you to meet so I can see what you think of the Captain. How about this Friday at 8 a.m.?"

"Whatever you need," Raymond agreed. He suspected Dixon wanted to talk more, but the late hour didn't afford them the opportunity. With the unspoken language most old friends seem to have, Raymond looked over at Dixon, tilted his head slightly, and lifted an eyebrow.

Raymond was happy the message was received. Dixon nodded, "Let's put everything in motion, just like we talked about." The exchange wasn't noticed by the other team members, and the response seemed cryptic enough so only Raymond understood.

"Does anyone want more to drink? I'm buying." Dixon pulled out his phone to transfer money to an account the bar owner kept.

"No. Go home, Dixon. The night is late and we have a lot of work to do tomorrow." Raymond smiled at his friend as he watched him pick up the backpack and start to leave. "I hope you're happy with your decision."

Dixon completed the money transaction and put the phone back in his pocket. He then pulled a worn key off his key ring and placed the tarnished item on the table. "Make sure to lock up." He stood up from the table and walked out.

"Man. Didn't expect that," Ben said, as he slid the key over to Raymond. "But, if you two will excuse me, there's a lovely lady I stood up this evening, and I plan to make it up to her tonight"

"Ben," Raymond touched his friend's arm, "if you're talking about the secretary from this afternoon, did you notice the ring on her finger?"

8

"Yes, but she doesn't seem to be a fanatic about it. Plus, her husband is out of town. See you later."

Overall, the trist wasn't any of his business, but it still bothered Raymond that the secretary was a married woman. His empty bottle indicated it was time to go.

Sterling finished his drink and walked out with his father. As Raymond locked up, Sterling announced, "See ya at home tomorrow."

"Where are you going?" Raymond asked.

"I have a date," he said, hopping into his red Ferrari.

Raymond tried to bite his tongue, but failed as usual. "With whom?"

Sterling cocked an eyebrow and a devilish smirk appeared on his face. "I don't know yet."

Raymond had to collect himself once again as he dealt with his only child. "Sterling, I don't understand why you insist on this reckless lifestyle of dating any human that crosses your path. I can't say anything to Ben since he isn't my son, but it bothers me when you behave like this. We have blood at home, so there's no reason to go looking for your next meal."

"Blood isn't what I'm after."

"Yeah. I know." He shook his head. "A wife would be …"

Sterling cut off his father. "We're not having this conversation again, Dad."

Raymond raked his hand through his dark, thick hair. "I just don't understand."

Anger flashed across Sterling's face. "Because unlike you, I don't like to sleep alone. Mom's dead. Stop loving a ghost." He then drove off, his license plate, 'LOVR4U', fading into the distance.

9

Alex Brennan entered her therapist's office, and folded her long, lean body into her usual spot on the couch. Vanilla fragrance hung in the air from the candle on the windowsill and assaulted her nostrils, leaving a sick feeling in her stomach. She hated the smell of vanilla since the fragrance always reminded her of this room. For a distraction, she mentally reviewed her long list of things to do that seemed to never get done. A dentist appointment topped the list. Sighing, she thought how much nicer a teeth cleaning sounded. Checking her watch, she realized she arrived early for the session. Damn. She hated therapy, and definitely didn't want to appear eager for her sessions.

She stared at the spot on the wall where the calendar charted time. She had seen three different calendars hanging over the years and would prefer not to see a fourth one. She glanced at her watch and readied herself to hit the stopwatch feature. She was paying for 50 minutes of therapy, and she always made sure she got her full time.

Dr. Micki O'Neil entered and closed the door. Alex appreciated that Micki always arrived right on time. She dressed in her usual button down blouse and slacks at every one of these sessions, and it pleased Alex that Micki was a civilian therapist and didn't wear a military uniform. She suspected that she opened up more to the doctor when she thought of her as perhaps just an old friend, rather than a military officer. Micki sat in a chair adjacent to the couch. Overall, everything from the wing backed chairs, the paisley pillows with tassels, on down to the throw rug on the floor seemed designed to give one a sense of calm in this room. Perhaps such decor did work for many people, but Alex's anxiety–wrung hands told a different story.

"Good Morning, Alex. Happy belated birthday."

Alex's eyebrow rose questioningly, but she composed herself quickly. She had given the therapist a fake birthday due to security reasons, but had forgotten until this very moment. Her birthday was actually weeks ago. She smiled at the woman and said, "Thanks, Micki. My birthday was earlier this week."

Micki pulled out a pen. "What age did you turn this year?"

"Thirty–eight." She was really thirty–nine.

Micki smiled at her attractive, well put–together client. "Well, you appear much younger – probably due to all the workout and training you do."

Alex felt her cheeks flush as she flashed a smile. She brushed her shoulder length auburn hair behind her ears. "Thanks Micki. And thanks again for meeting me so early this morning."

"No problem," Micki smiled. "Last week when we met you seemed a bit anxious about your age and the passing of time in general. How was your birthday?" Micki thumbed through the folder she kept with the details of the years of therapy she conducted with Alex.

Alex cleared her throat. Growing older always worried her. She thought back to her birthday. "I'm slowly dying alone. I'm shriveling up and I'm lonely. So in every respect, my birthday remained the same as all the other days, except the day came with a Sara Lee individual, frozen, fat–free cake at the end of it." Alex's tone saddened as she played with her fingernails. She hung her head and avoided eye contact with Micki.

"Why don't you tell me a little about the day itself," Micki suggested as she moved the box of Kleenex closer to her client.

"There's nothing to tell," Alex said, settling deeper into the couch. "I'm getting older, and the few men I do attract are immature boys."

"Uh huh," Micki studied her client's folder, flipping back several pages. "Alex, try to remember how far you've come," she said as she put down the folder and looked into Alex's eyes. "Only a few years ago you were afraid to even date. Not only are you going out, you have had several dates this past month alone."

Alex glanced away. The increase of dates was directly proportionate to her birthday weeks ago. "I don't think any of those guys count as real dates. In fact, one seemed more interested in my X–Box than he was with me, and believe me Micki, that isn't a euphemism."

Micki leaned in, "Alex, you chose to date those men. You said 'yes' to their invitations to dinners and movies, but then you rejected the one who wanted to have sex with you."

Alex sighed and thought back to that moment. If she had eaten breakfast, it would be coming up right about now. Alex raised her voice in protest, "I don't want to settle. I want a real man."

Micki nodded, "You've told me in the past what a 'real man' is for you, but I'd like for you to tell me again now that you've started dating again."

Alex rolled her eyes. "I don't know," she asserted, but mentally she thought back to the man she had been dreaming about as of late. She couldn't completely make out all of his features, but the name Adonis came to mind. Her heart rate sped up just thinking about him and his dark hair, but she repeated, "I'm not sure what I'm looking for."

"Somewhere deep inside, you do know. And you also know why you went out on dates with those other men as well."

Alex crossed her arms and looked away from Micki, "I don't want to talk about dating."

"All right, we can postpone this discussion for a few minutes. However, we will still need to address your dating choices. I can't help you unless you're open and honest with me."

"I don't want to talk about it."

"Okay. We can come back to that later." Micki picked up the folder and flipped through more pages. "Looks like over the last few years your career took off. You had two promotions ... and now you're up for another one. If you get the promotion, it will make you ... ?"

"'Security Chief' is the unofficial title," Alex said, giving the woman an ambiguous job description. If she did accept the promotion, she couldn't afford to allow a therapist to know exactly what she would be doing. It wasn't as if she didn't trust the woman; she just didn't know her more than their therapy sessions. And even then, any personal information shared could be open to future blackmail. Even after all this time, Micki never even knew Alex's real last name – and she always paid in cash. "I'd be responsible for the security teams that guard state officials," she added, not wanting to mention that the state official would be the President of the United States. "The position is a good career move, even if it does sound like a mountain of paperwork."

"Fair enough," Micki replied as she studied her client. "You don't need to share with me the exact title or duties, but I do want to know how you feel about this promotion and what it means for your career?"

Alex grabbed one of the pillows from the couch and, while she played with the tassels along its edge, she reflected upon her career. If she wanted something career–wise, she got it. She had always positioned herself strategically so she could command the best opportunities that were available. "I put my career above everything else. It's what I do, but at least I can control what direction my career takes me," Alex grimaced. She pulled at the strings of the tassel, carefully straightened them, and then moved to the next one in the row.

Micki wrote in the folder as she commented, "Control is very important to you."

Isn't it to everyone? After a pause, Alex admitted, "At least I can get what I want."

"And how is that working out for you? Is it making you happy?" Micki asked.

"Ugh!" Alex threw the pillow aside. "My career is great, but what I really want is a passionate relationship. I want a family. Where are all the real men?" She glanced over to her therapist, "I mean, I have this unclear picture of who I want. He's perfect. He's a Mr. Butch Manly … I just can't seem to find him."

"Alex, you're a top level security specialist. Your accomplishments at this young of an age can be intimidating to some men."

"To all men, I guess." Alex said, "Except for the socially inept or the mama's boys." Alex bit her lip, looked down to the floor, and added, "Or the crazy stalker types."

14

"Men come in many sized packages, Alex. But it's what's on the inside that counts. A small–framed, computer nerd who loves playing games can be a wonderful catch. You need to get past the wrapping."

Wiping away a tear, Alex confided, "It's … it's not the wrapping, Micki. I never get to know a man well enough to even get to the inner layers of who they really are."

"I know, and you're doing a great job working on that. You are approaching your 40th birthday in a couple of years. The big ones tend to get people thinking about where they are in their life and what they are doing. We've had this discussion many times in the past, Alex. You want a passionate romance with a 'Butch Manly' type of guy, but you select men who never quite fit that bill, then you only go on one date with them. You force yourself to be emotionally flat in these relationships in an effort to protect yourself from being vulnerable." Looking at her client she asked, "It's been a long time since we discussed it, but you did just mention it. Do you want to talk about the stalker that attacked you some more?"

"Hell, no! I just wonder where all the heroes are." Alex peeked at her watch and realized 45 minutes remained.

CHAPTER TWO

The scent of freshly made coffee invited Raymond into the kitchen. His bare feet barely made a sound on the tile floor as he walked over to the long counter filled with coffeemakers. From French presses, machine drip and even percolators, he had many choices. He preferred whole beans freshly ground over the pre–ground, tasteless variety stored in cans. He considered a French Roast, but instead settled on the already made Texas Pecan flavor.

While he poured himself a cup, he noticed his sister Sulie sitting quietly at the kitchen table working a crossword puzzle. She seemed blissfully unaware of the mountain of dishes piled up in the sink, on the counter tops, and even on the stove top. Raymond checked his pocket watch. The time was after 8am, so the mess resulted from Jackie getting her two kids off to school. Counting all the wineglasses laying about, he realized the dishes had not been done in some time – obviously the kids were not drinking wine.

"Good morning, Sulie." When she barely nodded a hello, he asked about the mess in the kitchen.

She shrugged dismissively. "We had to let the maid go."

Raymond looked over the dishes. Pregnant vampires, and children who had not reached their transitional year, ate human food. Actually, by the amount of dirty dishes, they ate a lot of food … or perhaps the maid had been gone for several days and he had not noticed.

"Let me guess," he began, "Sterling took an interest in the maid and then he compelled her to leave after she visited him upstairs in his bedroom."

"Stop," Sulie chided him. She glanced up from her crossword puzzle. "We did our best in raising him. He's a good kid."

"Hardly a kid," Raymond said. "Boy's nearly 180 years old, and still acts like he's a horny teenager."

Sulie brought her hand up to stifle her chuckle. "You need to lighten up on him. Life is hard when you don't have your mother. I did the best I could to help you raise him, but it's not the same. Besides, the maid left because of something else, *this* time. She had been compelled a little too often to ignore empty blood bags and syringes lying about. Her mind couldn't take the erasing anymore. She suffered migraine headaches so I let her go."

Since the vampires received free room and board from the Government, they had also negotiated a maid come with the deal. It was a smart move on their part, especially since none of them knew how to operate any household appliance more advanced than a coffeemaker.

"Regardless, Sterling is out of control. We worked late last night. Afterward he ran off to find a date. I heard him come in a few hours ago."

Sulie looked up at her brother. Her eyes seemed a bit more tired and her face more haggard looking than normal. Her short normally coiffed hair was unkempt. He noticed she still wore a fuzzy blue robe and house slippers. "The kids kept me up, then you woke me, then Sterling came home and the noise woke me up again."

"I'm sorry, sis." When moving into the mansion, which they called Fang Manor, Sulie had selected a bedroom on the first floor next to the kitchen. The mansion had twelve bedrooms, scattered among three different floors. The walls were thin, but surely the other bedrooms not so close to the kitchen were quieter. If any had been vacant he'd suggest she switch bedrooms.

"Do you want some coffee?" he asked.

She stood up from the table and shuffled in her slippers to the cupboard to get out a wine goblet. She then poured blood from a medical bag into the cup. "I'm good." The back doorbell sounded. Raymond knew who the visitor was, and he arrived right on schedule.

The beeps sounded as Sulie disabled the high tech alarm system and opened the door. "Hey, Karl. Nice to see you. We've had a busy day today at the hospital," she suggested, looking into his eyes and compelling him to see the images she laid out for him.

His expression instantly changed and his eyes became distant. "Hello, Dr. Smith. I have this week's supply of blood for the hospital. Can you please sign here?"

"Gladly Karl," she said taking the clipboard. "Please bring in the blood. You know where we keep it." Karl obeyed, wheeling in carts of blood for the mansion, or as it was classified by the government, "Colony Private Military Hospital."

"Kind of early for wine this time of the day, isn't it?" Karl asked.

"I'm coming off the night shift, Karl. This is my nightcap."

"Ah, well I can understand late night hours. I used to work them myself for a while." He busied himself with storing the blood in the walk–in cooler.

"She'd offer you a glass Karl," Raymond began, "but trust me. You wouldn't like this vintage."

*****

Alex stepped into the office belonging to Matt Dickson and Brandon Wyatt. She had worked very little with the pair, but they were always good for a comedy relief in an otherwise routine afternoon.

Matt stood the taller of the two, standing at a lengthy 6' 5". He wore Burlington store brand suits, not designer or even tailored fit ones. Overall, he always appeared clean and pressed, even if the quality seemed a bit off. Today he wore a single-breasted suit, light heather in color. The pink tie threw off the assemble but matched in an odd way. About 80% of the time, Matt acted as rock solid as any other agent. That is, when his sidekick, Brandon, didn't pull him down some rabbit hole looking for a white rabbit, or more likely, a white *alien* rabbit.

Alex gazed over at Brandon, who had still not noticed her enter the room. He kept himself busy by listening to his chest with a stethoscope. Man, she really didn't want to ask about that one. Brandon was probably doing his best to confirm that an alien had probed him during lunch or something – which was not a conversation she wanted to listen to. When he turned to face her, Alex noticed that Brandon could take fashion lessons from Matt. Brandon's black suit jacket didn't match the dark navy blue pants, not even in the dim light of this office. Of course, who would notice such a horrid combination with the fluorescent green tie the man wore?

"Hello, Captain," Matt said while standing up. "Is there something we can help you with?"

Alex noted that Brandon stopped the personal medical exam when Matt asked his question, and also stood. If she did get the promotion, these two would report indirectly to her. A scary thought indeed. But then again, she'd love to read Brandon's personal file. He had to be an idiot savant, a member of Mensa, or at least suffer from Einstein Syndrome. He acted too quirky just to be an idiot. "Here, I brought you the files of the new kitchen hires. I need security checks done on all of them."

"Sure. We can get right to work, Captain," Matt said with a smile.

She observed Brandon give Matt a look. The glance was like he was checking to see if he should say something. Whether Matt agreed or not, Brandon blurted out, "Have you heard anything about a second security team?"

"What do you mean by a second team?" she asked.

Brandon took a deep breath. "For some time now, we have felt …"

"You. *You* have felt," Matt corrected.

The correction was met with a stern glare from Brandon. "*I* have felt that there might be a secondary team who …"

Alex had heard that Brandon could be a bit paranoid, but to see it up close was very off–putting. This little ditty smacked of the same paranoia that last week's 'lizard men live in our sewers' did. She allowed Brandon to prattle on for a few minutes, but then had to stop him. "Riddle me this, Batman. What would be the point in having two teams do the same job? To waste taxpayer money? To ensure redundancy in case the first team proves to be incompetent?" she asked.

20

"You're in denial," was his answer.

Alex needed to get back to real work. She watched as Brandon reached for the folder she had placed on Matt's desk; his face twinged as though in pain.

"Captain, did I give you a security file yesterday regarding some broken glass found near the Beast?" Brandon asked before she could leave the room. Again his face cringed in pain.

She turned to face the man. Taking a deep breath she said, "No. I don't recall any such file. What glass near the President's limo?" she asked, worried that leprechauns might be involved in this story.

Brandon rubbed his temple. "I can't find the file. Matt said I went to Dixon's office and gave it to him, but I can't remember."

Alex took a step closer into the room. "If there is a file missing ..."

Matt cut her off. "He gave the file to Dixon. I saw him walk the paperwork down to Dixon's office. Everything is fine." He tossed Brandon a bottle of Advil from his desk. "He's been suffering from headaches lately. I think they're affecting his memory."

"Probably a tumor from mind control," Brandon said reaching for some water to down the pills. He took a sip, tilted back his head, and took the medicine. He then quickly added, "Oh, on an internal channel last night I overheard something."

"Internal to the White House?" Alex asked.

Matt shook his head slightly, but Brandon continued. "Someone was playing World of Warcraft last night. I swear the noise sounded like it was coming from the Oval Office."

She studied Brandon for a moment before she left the office. There is a thin line from crazy to brilliant. She could guess which side of the line Brandon straddled.

CHAPTER THREE

Raymond and Sterling arrived at FBI headquarters to check on some domestic terrorist suspects. The federal government received hundreds of threats monthly endangering the lives of military and political leaders; they also received many bomb threats on historic buildings. Sterling usually came by the headquarters, but today's threat was from a man on a case that Raymond had been working on. A case that was practically tied up with just this one loose end.

Everything from the humans' microwave lunches, the stale recirculated air in the building, to the blood coursing through the humans' veins hit their nostrils the second the two vampires entered. This building belonged to the human team's turf and Raymond knew Sterling hated coming here. It wasn't that Sterling didn't like humans; Raymond knew far too well that Sterling liked one of their genders considerably. He suspected Sterling's hatred for the place was that he didn't like smelling human food and spending time with the lowest of the low in the human gene pool. At least that was why Raymond avoided it. This building tended to have the worst scum imaginable.

Using an alias, Sterling flashed his presidential badge at the security desk. He dressed in a suit and looked like any FBI or CIA operative in the place. Raymond knew his son hated wearing a suit and a tie. The material always felt itchy against his skin, and gloves always seemed odd with a suit. Sterling had no choice though; the gloves protected him from flashing on every object he touched thanks to his special ability.

As they approached the security station, the guard requested that they sign their names and then walk past the security scanner.

"Disable the metal detector," Raymond compelled. The guard obeyed and turned off the unit. They passed through with his personal armory of weapons. No alarm sounded.

It wasn't long before a lieutenant named Gallendar came to collect them from the front desk. He led them towards the interrogation rooms. "We picked up a Mr. Raul Medina this morning for a substantial threat to the Pentagon. We also have two others, one of which may have been working with Medina."

"Medina was the mole we had. But he turned bad, just like the rest of them," Raymond explained to his son in the vampire high-pitched voice that humans could not hear.

"Let's start with Medina," Sterling suggested to the lieutenant.

The door to the room opened. Sitting in the center of the room was a heavily tattooed man with bulging muscles and a sneer on his face. Actually, the word "Godfather" came to mind when Raymond looked at him. Across from Medina sat two CIA agents. "Leave," Raymond commanded. The agents and Lt. Gallendar obeyed the simple command, closing the door behind them.

As soon as the vampires entered the room, they knew they were dealing with a human. Vampires rarely got this far inside an interrogation room. They would never allow themselves to be held by humans and normally would compel their way out of any situation. Of course, it all depended on the suspect's evil agenda.

24

"Yo, you and I are going to talk," Sterling said to the thug.

"Fuck you, pretty boy!"

"Now that's not a nice way to greet someone," Raymond said.

Medina spit his reply.

"Your attitude is only going to piss me off. Trust me; I can eat thugs like you for breakfast. I really can." With his gloved hands, Sterling grabbed Medina's head and forced him to stare into his eyes. "You are going to cooperate with me and these agents. Do you understand?"

Medina's skin paled and his eyes went dim. *"I understand."*

"You'll answer every single question they ask of you."

"Answer questions."

Sterling removed his gloves and touched the man's clothing. Next he compelled the man to remove any jewelry, and he began touching that as well. Finally, he touched the man's skin. Raymond watched. He had seen his son in action many times, and was proud of how he used his ability – especially since Sterling's skin would become itchy, and migraines usually formed because of it.

Sterling sat back down and put on his gloves. "I got security codes, dates and names," he said to his father in a matter–of–fact tone. He glanced back at Medina. Hell, Sterling had some time. "You're also not going to leer at any female guards while you are in custody. You will treat them with respect."

Raymond rolled his eyes. Leave it to Sterling to be the champion of the damsels in distress.

25

"No leering. Respect only," Sterling said. "And I want to hear some 'please' and 'thank yous' from now on. Use your manners,"

"Manners," Medina meekly said.

"You'll volunteer information about prior crimes you committed to these agents," Sterling said with a smile.

"Crimes."

"And you'll rat your buddies out on their crimes." Sterling added.

Raymond jumped in, "If any innocent lives are in jeopardy by you doing this, you will tell the guards immediately."

"Rat out buddies. Save innocent lives."

Sterling shrugged his shoulders in response to his father's input. "That's a good boy." Sterling said to the thug, handing him a tissue. "Clean that up!" He pointed out where he had spat on the floor. Sterling then opened the door to let the two detectives in. Next Raymond, Sterling and Lt. Gallendar went to the next of the three rooms to have similar conversations with the other two men in custody.

CHAPTER FOUR

Friday morning arrived quicker than expected. Raymond looked over at the alarm clock which would go off any minute now. He stretched to wake up his muscles, and then his phone chirped at him. He knew who the text came from.

He partially sat up in bed and reached for the phone. Suddenly his palms became sweaty as he held it, and his heart began to race. The message was from exactly who he thought it would be, the Vampire Council. Last night, after he told Sulie about Dixon's retirement, she begged Raymond to make a request to the Council to have Dixon turned. She need not have bothered with her plea; he planned to make the request on Dixon's behalf anyway. Being turned is what the man wanted. Raymond held his breath as he opened the message.

"No."

No other explanation was given. Nothing else but the one word.

"Christ!" Raymond threw the phone back onto the nightstand. He lay in bed for a few minutes mad at the Council, but also rethinking in his mind how to break the news to Dixon.

The alarm clock sounded and brought him out of his concentration. The answer was what it was; with nothing else to be done. He hit snooze on the alarm to give himself a few more minutes to think of anything else other than Dixon.

He heard the house come alive with activity, even from his bedroom on the third floor. The snooze was hit two times before he finally rubbed his eyes, awakened, and decided to start the day. He looked at the wall across from his bed where a small portrait of his wife hung. He had commissioned an artist to paint it well after Wilma died, using Sterling's adult face and Raymond's description of his late wife as a guide. The result wasn't an exact image, but reasonably close. When he first saw the completed artwork, he was disappointed the artist couldn't quite capture Wilma's true beauty on the canvas. Now, after all these years, the image on the wall was what Wilma looked like to him. He smiled at the portrait and murmured, "Good morning, Wilma."

With dread, Raymond removed himself from his bed and donned his robe to cover his nude body. Like all the occupants of the house, Raymond's bedroom had a small refrigerator. He kept his morning breakfast of two syringes of blood chilled. Other than a couple of syringed meals, the fridge was empty.

He placed his breakfast in a warm water bath. He loved the little device. Its main purpose was to warm cold baby bottles, but the device warmed up blood in syringes very quickly — and to the right temperature.

He stretched to wake up and heard the timer on the warmer beep. He reached for his breakfast, and while still lying down in his king–sized bed, he slowly injected the contents of the first syringe into his arm. The warm sensation tingled as the blood traveled up his forearm. His eyes closed and he concentrated on the feeling of fresh blood once again running through his veins. His mouth slightly opened and his fangs extended. His heart raced and his body surged with energy.

Raymond had fed himself this way for decades – ever since bagged blood became easy to transport and use in hospitals. The feeding was quick but felt nothing like the real thing. For Raymond, feeding off a fresh vein and feeling the flesh against his fangs was a foregone delight. He didn't wish to be near a human woman, and definitely didn't want to feed off a male of the species. The only human woman he wanted to feed from was dead. And even when he had had his wife at his side, he was too young to partake since his fangs hadn't come in yet.

He took the second of the two syringes and slowly injected it into the same arm where the first crimson delight had traveled. His heart rate sped up and his body renewed itself. Cells were regenerated. The few gray hairs he had turned back to their dark brunette color, the slight wrinkles around his eyes ironed themselves out, and his skin glowed with the healthiness of youth. Each drop was a taste from the fountain of youth. Raymond aged back from his mid thirties to his early twenties — nowhere near the 199 years he had actually lived.

Raymond concentrated on the feeling of the blood. His body became replete and he felt alive and new. Now, blood lust set in. Sometimes he hated being a vampire.

His body responded, yearning for a woman's touch. Wilma died ages ago in childbirth and there was no other woman he craved. His length hardened and demanded attention. He wanted to ignore his arousal, but the blood lust insisted he satisfy his manly urges. Thirst overcame him as well and he felt his fangs extend. Now two of his body parts wanted a woman, and he was alone – all alone.

More blood sat in the fridge, but he dare not indulge himself. More blood in his body would keep him sexed up all day. It would just add more fuel to the fire once the lust came to him. Christ. He didn't need that. He licked his lips; his tongue brushing against his fangs. He had never partaken of Wilma's blood during their brief year together since it was before he had transitioned into an adult vampire. He craved her touch, and now her blood. God. Drinking her blood and making love to her at the same time was a joy stolen from him long ago.

The Vampire Council, with all of their antiquated laws, managed to do one thing right. Forbidding love between humans and vampires resonated soundly within him. The folly of it all. Humans were weak and frail. Of course, Wilma was an angel that touched his soul like no other woman had. How could he not fall in love with such a creature? The year he spent with her as her husband was the best year of his life. She had also given him a son as she died in his arms — a beautiful son who looked just like her. If he had only turned her before he impregnated her she'd still be with him. If only.

He pushed the images of Wilma's death aside and thought of her as she was in life. So warm, so giving, so sexy. Reclining on his bed, Raymond reached between his thighs and parted the robe down the sides of his hips. With the beautiful image of his wife in his head, he focused on nothing else but her. In his mind's eye, he saw her naked on their marriage bed, her arms calling out to him. Touching himself, and remembering his cherished past, he made love to her.

CHAPTER FIVE

Dixon had just poured himself a cup of coffee when a knock sounded at his office door. Opening the door, he noticed not only Raymond, but also Ben. "Good idea," he said. "Ben can mellow the mood of the room." Dixon stepped aside and allowed the two gentlemen into his office.

Dixon closed the door briefly. "Captain Brennan is my top choice. On paper, the Captain walks on water. I need you to check on the immortal weird stuff. Ben, your ability to alter moods may prove handy." He took hold of the door handle. "Go ahead and take a seat at the table. I'll get the Captain. The mugs are for you and there's a fresh pot in the corner." He left closing the door behind him.

Raymond nodded towards the table. "Leave the chair next to me empty for the captain to sit. This way if the thought patterns are hazy I can touch the man." Hazy thought patterns. Sometimes a human gave off clear patterns, and others appeared hazy. Raymond never knew which it would be. In any case, touching would ensure a good reading.

Ben filled the two mugs with the steaming coffee. It wasn't so much the coffee the vampires were after, but the warming steam of its heat as the temperature permeated through the ceramic mugs to warm their hands. They liked feeling warm, and if humans mistook the transferred heat for body warmth, so be it. It was a win twofold.

Raymond hated touching humans. Just absolutely hated it, and did it as little as possible. It thrilled him when the "knuckle touch" became popular, but of course at the White House it would be another frickin' handshake. Raymond took the mug Ben offered and a tiny clank sounded as his wedding ring hit the porcelain. He switched the mug to his right hand and warmed it up. It would not take long to give his hand "body warmth."

The door of the office opened and Dixon stepped in, followed by the captain. Raymond and Ben stood up to meet the man. When Captain Alex Brennan walked in, she surprised them by being a woman.

She walked into the office, and Raymond noticed her smile lit up the room. He sensed self accomplishment and pride radiating from her mental patterns and knew instantly that accepting this promotion pleased her. She wore her hair professionally up and the style revealed a supple, beautiful neck. Her hair was put back in a bun but tresses of wavy auburn hair on each side framed her 'girl next door' face. The few freckles she had on her face added to her appeal; they made her look fresh and innocent.

Raymond stared back at Dixon and prayed this was a mistake. Oh, this was so not what he wanted or needed. His heart sped up and anger grew within him. He felt set up. In today's age there were of course female officers in the military, but Dixon omitted the little detail of Captain Brennan's gender. *Alex?* That was a man's name. Of course Raymond assumed the new director would be a man. The director was always a man.

Raymond took in a deep breath to calm himself. Was that perfume? The scent smelled light and feminine — not what he wanted at all. He kept his distance from humans, especially female humans. He didn't socialize with female vampires either. It wasn't an official vow of celibacy, but close enough to count since no one could compare to Wilma.

He studied Alex. Or was it really Alexandra? Maybe Alexi? She looked classically beautiful, just like his Wilma was. Her emerald eyes shone across the room and sparkled like gems. Her tailor made suit was feminine. Her outfit curved in all the right places, like an hour glass. With her long sexy legs, she stood in high heels that accentuated her muscular calves as she walked into the room. She embodied elegance with a Greek goddess body.

Raymond's breath caught, his heart sped up, and he couldn't stop staring at this gorgeous creature. He needed to remember to breathe. He took in a deep breath and realized his palms now glistened with sweat, and it wasn't from the heat of the coffee. He listened to the clicks of her heels on the hard floor, and he watched the effect it had on her muscular calves as she walked in. This was the closest encounter he had with a human woman in decades.

Dixon closed the door, trapping Raymond in the room. "Captain Brennan, this is Raymond Metcalf and Ben Gatto."

CHAPTER SIX

Raymond watched as Alex walked across the room. The clicking of her heels echoed in the tiny space. "Good to meet you," she said, extending a hand to Raymond.

He shifted the coffee mug to his left hand, and quickly wiped his sweaty palm on his slacks before extending his hand out. He knew his hand would feel warm, so he shook her hand and made eye contact to see if the trick worked. It must have, her pupils didn't contract in surprise. Instead, her beautiful eyes remained glued onto his.

There was very little shaking considering this was a handshake. She held his hands, and stared at him as though reading his soul.

Closer up, the scent of her perfume was stronger, and he liked the fragrance. He noticed she took in a deep breath, swallowed, and then she parted her lips slightly and bit the lower one. He stared at her plump and kissable lower lip. He needed to say 'hello' back, but found he couldn't quite make the word come out.

Her eyes shifted slightly, and he took note as her temple cringed. He realized she thought she recognized him from somewhere, and was trying to place his face. A slight headache was forming because of her attempts to remember him. He was familiar with this look. Usually, he would dismiss it, but not today. Today, he regretted that his predatory nature had humans forget him unless they had direct contact with him. Obviously this woman had seen him in the background, but her mind had dismissed him. He felt sorry for her as her mind tried to process the holes.

He looked down at the marathon handshake. Her skin felt smooth. How long had he been holding her hand? Actually, she seemed to be the one still holding his. Could that be right? He swallowed hard as he realized the two of them had stepped much closer to each other as their hands touched.

She must have picked up on his awareness, because she immediately released his hand. Her cheeks flushed. Great, he probably embarrassed her in some way. She seemed flustered as she quickly offered her hand over to Ben.

Raymond took note of Ben's touch on her, and a bitter taste permeated his mouth. His grip tightened around the handle of the coffee mug, turning his knuckles white. He stared at the two of them as they greeted each other. Ben's age was currently in his mid fifties, and he looked quite distinguished in his tailored suit and shortened, grayed Afro. She probably liked tall and dark men. Of course, he was taller than Ben, but would she even notice? Maybe his pale white skin was unappealing to someone who sported a tan. Since he avoided the sun as much as possible, he looked even more pasty white than the average Caucasian man. His dark brunette hair and teal eyes would only accentuate his paleness even more.

She looked to be about thirty. Perhaps she liked older men. Raymond blinked several times to stop his train of thought. This was ridiculous; he just met the woman. Of course Ben's smile looked too friendly to him, but then their handshake ended – after a proper amount of time.

Why was he even thinking such thoughts? Women never mattered in the past to him, and neither did his appearance. When he glanced over at Alex and saw her smile, he knew she was not like other women. Was it getting warm in here? Normally he liked feeling warm, but this was downright uncomfortable. He scratched the back of his head, just to do anything other than stare at her. Touching his thick locks of hair he realized that he was back down to his base age. He had fed well this morning, and now looked the same age he was when he transitioned into an adult vampire – 22 years old. He closed his eyes. She must see him as a child, with Ben being the senior member of the team. She probably thought he knew at least ten different Pokemon names, carried Magic cards in his wallet, and secretly wished his car was a transformer. All of which couldn't have been farther from the truth. If it hadn't been for the young kids at Fang Manor, he wouldn't even know what those things were. He was an old geyser locked into a youthful body, and that package was probably someone she couldn't take seriously – even if Dixon ordered her to.

It was worse than that. Raymond realized that he had not even said hello to the woman when she shook his hand. OK, not only must he be young in her mind, he also didn't have manners. Great.

"Let's get started," said Dixon as he plucked a folder from his desk and took a seat between the Captain and Ben.

Once they all had taken their seats, Raymond glanced at Alex. He reached into her mind to compel her, and was surprised by how accepting her mind was to him. "Captain, please excuse us for a few minutes."

Her expression turned to stone as she froze in her seat; her eyes were expressionless. Raymond now glared at Dixon. "Sir? Seriously?"

"What? This is Captain Brennan."

Raymond looked in disbelief. "A woman? You chose a member of the fairer sex to be our director?"

Ben huffed. "Good Lord, Raymond. When was the last time you spent any time with a woman. 'Fairer sex' my ass."

Dixon interrupted. "Alex is well accomplished in martial arts, field training, and holds the highest sharp–shooter ranking the military offers. Not only does this woman walk on water with her credentials, but she'd skim across a lake and tear you a new one if you weren't immortal. Trust me. She's the one for the job."

Raymond studied the woman's 5' 8" strong muscular frame. Her body shape did not lie. "There was no one else?"

"There were plenty of others, only less qualified." Dixon glanced over at Alex. "She's the best. I just need your opinion if the team can work with her."

Silence hung in the room as Raymond fell deep in thought. "It's not that I have anything against women," Raymond defended himself. "My sister Sulie is very accomplished as a doctor and as a soldier for the team."

"Yes. She is," Dixon added. "And over the years I've seen your sister personally kill dozens of terrorists. She's gone undercover on numerous successful missions and never let the team down."

"She is one of the Best," Ben commented. "Personally, I don't like being on Sulie's bad side. She's like a tiger."

Raymond smiled. "Sulie's always been special like that."

"No Raymond. It isn't that Sulie is special. She's a woman. Quite capable of doing anything a man can do, and then some." Dixon pointed to Alex. "Now unfreeze the captain and give her a chance."

CHAPTER SEVEN

Once the captain rejoined the party, Dixon continued. "You have perfect credentials Captain. I will be retiring shortly and we're looking for a replacement as Colony Director."

Alex shook her head. "I'm sorry. I thought the position was Chief of Security."

"Oh it is," Dixon reassured her. "That's only part of the position. What is discussed in this room is confidential. I need for you to sign this non–disclosure agreement locking in your silence before we proceed." He slid the paper and a pen over to the captain.

"Of course." she noted as she signed the paper.

Dixon continued. "The security chief position is the generic term for what you would be asked to do. The job encompasses that, plus quite a bit more. Publicly, you will interface with the director of the Secret Service mostly for daily security protocols involving the President. At times you will work closely with the commanding officer for the Joint Special Operations Command, but only if a situation with JSOC calls for it. Your job will be to coordinate efforts between those two departments and a secret special op team you will be directly responsible for. As the director of this special team, you will report to the President and be his liaison to the team."

Alex straightened more in her chair as she tried to control the smile that threatened to overpower her. Opportunity wasn't just knocking; it was barging in and taking down the door. This was exactly what she wanted for her career.

Dixon continued, "The special op team is known as The Colony. The team is funded through the President's Black Budget, so even Congress is unaware of its existence. It was founded in 1866 as a direct response to the assassination of President Abraham Lincoln and works in conjunction with the Secret Service as presidential security. The Colony's responsibility has broadened to include assignments with other federal and military agencies, but at all times a member of the Colony is within the inner perimeter of security and works covertly with the Secret Service. Their strengths are many, including the capacity to work with biochemical elements, or in regards to specific 'cold–blooded' killers. For example, they were instrumental during the Anthrax scare a few years ago."

Alex appreciated the longevity of the team. Its history meant security and prestige for her career. "No doubt, unsung heroes," she commented.

"Indeed." Dixon continued, "The men and women who form the team are unique. Their existence was discovered by a Union lieutenant and personal aide to President Lincoln. One of the founding members of the Colony served under this lieutenant. Another founder was a freed black slave who fought beside him."

Alex wasn't a Civil War buff, but the story fascinated her. So far, the interview seemed right on track and heading to the town of successful–career–move.

"Those two Civil War soldiers, and founding members of the Colony, are the two other men in this room."

Her train just got derailed. "I'm sorry, can you please repeat that?"

CHAPTER EIGHT

Raymond watched the captain as strong mental patterns washed over her. Her cool demeanor had changed from all business, to being confused, and even a little angry. He glanced over at Ben and saw him deep in concentration as he adjusted her moods with his special ability. After a few seconds, Raymond felt the professional, polished edge emanating from her once again. Raymond nodded towards Dixon to have him continue.

"The two Civil War soldiers are Raymond Metcalf and Ben Gatto," Dixon repeated as he pointed to the other two men at the table.

Silence.

She laughed. "Oh ... yeah, right. I'm guessing you must be vampires and live forever, right?"

We have a winner, Raymond thought. She couldn't have zeroed in on the truth more if she tried. He watched as Ben concentrated even more. The fact that Ben remained so focused told Raymond that Alex's moods were hard to control. If he understood the colors correctly, Ben was washing her aura over in a yellow to mellow her out.

"Yeah, what a great joke fellas. Now really, what is the promotion?" She glanced over to Dixon, but the man's look was stoic and no laughter followed. She gazed over to Ben, who was too focused to notice.

Raymond cursed inwardly. Of course she'd look over to Ben for any guidance during this interview. Raymond's youthful appearance made him look like a joke, instead of the team lead. Raymond waited until she shifted her eyes in his direction, then he bared his fangs to show her there was no joke. Ben followed suit, and bared his fangs as well.

Alex practically jumped out of her chair, her eyes wide in fright. Ben focused even more, mentally painting gallons of yellow paint over her aura. To Ben's credit, Alex slumped back into her chair. Her response was very calm indeed. Alex's eyes bulged in her head as she shifted in her seat. Next she pointed at Raymond's fangs and asked, "Are those real? Can I touch them?"

"No, you can't touch them!" Raymond exclaimed. He glared over at Ben to have him tone the mellowing down. Bright canary yellow wasn't the best color for an aura anyway.

Ben turned down the aura paint job and she reacted in a way more in line with someone whose world had been turned upside down.

"Whoa, whoa, whoa" she insisted as she held up her hands.

Raymond easily read her thought waves now. They were a roller–coaster of emotions. So many thoughts pummeled him that he became dizzy himself. Thankfully, Ben was at the helm of her mental carnival ride and prevented Alex from panicking.

Raymond felt sorry for Alex. She woke up this morning understanding the world. Now everything was torn apart. As her thoughts subsided and calmed, Raymond nodded to Dixon to continue.

"Immortals, vampires ... whatever you want to call them. They go by either name. They live among us. Their numbers are small. The Colony itself has less than a dozen members.

Alex examined Raymond. "Vampires? OK. So next you're going to tell me that werewolves and leprechauns exist? What's next? Should I worry about running into a mermaid when I go swimming? Or even a unicorn at the Bronx zoo?"

Alex paused as she caught her breath. "You appear human. … Well, except for the fangs. You live among humans?"

Raymond liked that she directed her question at him, and not Ben. Most Director candidates treated him as a zoo specimen at this point in the interview. The woman was either properly bred, or incredibly open-minded and brave. Either way, he appreciated her manners and it was a point in her favor. "We don't grow older, but we can alter our appearance by our blood consumption. The more human blood we have in our system, the younger we appear. If we consume daily amounts of blood, we can look to be in our 20s. If we feed once a week, we look in our 30s. If we feed every 6–8 weeks, we can look as old as the President himself. Of course, it depends on how much we consume at each feeding."

Her voice cracked. "You look well fed."

Raymond noticed she crossed her arms and leaned away from him. Her body language and thought patterns spoke volumes. She was scared. She remained under control thanks to Ben, but scared nonetheless. "I'm not hungry right now," he lied. Vampires were always hungry. He sensed her elevated heart rate, and had even stared at her jugular vein once or twice. Her blood type was A+. Sweet and delicious. He wondered if other parts of her tasted as delectable. Her lips certainly looked plump and inviting.

"So you can be 20 one day, and the next day 70?" She relaxed her stance. Whether it was her own choosing or Ben's doing, Raymond wasn't sure.

"In theory, yes," Raymond answered. "Aging that quickly in such a short amount of time usually means that we've been physically hurt in some way; maybe even dying. When hurt, we age rapidly and need human blood immediately. Under normal circumstances, we never change our age that quickly intentionally because the switch in our feeding habits, from young to old, can cause serious discomfort in us. Painful reactions, actually. Going from old to young is no problem at all. In fact, many times a vampire will relocate, appear to be in their 20s, then over the next 60–70 years they gradually allow themselves to appear to age so they can go undetected among the humans. After they look the age of 80 or 90, they fake their death and start anew in a different location."

Her mental patterns flashed like a strobe light. He noticed she processed the information quickly, with curiosity winning out.

"And you drink human blood." It was a statement, not a question. Her beautiful eyes traveled up and down his body, at least to the areas not covered by the table.

"Yes. Animal blood can't give us the nutrients we need." Raymond felt on display. It was an odd sensation to be scrutinized in such a way by a woman. Did she like what she saw? She certainly didn't act repelled. Her emerald eyes pierced his as if she were looking deep into his soul.

"You look young. Do you bite people every day?"

And there it was. Dietary needs were always the first issue of business. "No. The Colony is classified as a

44

private military hospital. We receive bagged blood courtesy of Uncle Sam every week. Enough for us to feed daily."

The refreshing breath and softer posture suggested a comfort level of probably knowing she was not Raymond's next meal. "So you blend into the human population by pretending to be human."

If she wanted to hit one of Raymond's buttons, she certainly did. His jaw tightened. "I don't pretend to be anything I'm not. You assume everyone you meet happens to be human." Scorn filled his thoughts, and in an accusatory tone he added, "I'm guessing you won't be doing that again."

"Probably not." Her tone seemed level and calm. He could tell he hurt her, not just by her mental patterns, but also by the fact she shifted those beautiful emerald eyes away from him and now looked down at the table.

Sounding more distant she asked, "You turn into a bat, Mr. Vampire?"

Damn. Her open–mindedness impressed him. She showed genuine interest in knowing who and what they were. Ben controlled her mood, but her questions were her own. She had done nothing wrong and he had snapped at her. Raymond kept his tone in check and calmly responded, "Chihuahua actually." Her confused expression was priceless to him. "No. Just kidding. We can't shape shift."

CHAPTER NINE

Dixon cleared his throat trying to resume the meeting. "Your duties, Captain, will be as a liaison between the Colony and the Secret Service, as well as other federal departments," Dixon explained. "You will spend much time with the vampires. Helping them with blood issues, security access, new aliases and such. Your primary responsibility is to protect their secret of existence at all costs."

She held up her hand. "Wait, you're telling me we use vampires to protect government officials from threats. Are you talking about vampire threats or human threats?"

Dixon was the one who answered. "Both. In my tenure as Colony Director there have been 91 breeches to White House security. That is what has been publicly announced. In truth, there have been an additional 15 breaches – all vampires."

"Fifteen. Fifteen breaches." Alex let the words sink in. "How many vampires exist in the world?"

"Enough to warrant our special op team," Raymond said. "We control our population so our existence can remain secret." Raymond's glanced over at Dixon as he was reminded of the Vampire Council's denial of his turning. Raymond pushed the memory aside. "The threats committed by vampires have been a few dozen over the last century and a half. Not many. The human team does most of the security for the federal government and we're backup in case of a vampire threat. At times, such as an anthrax scare, we're used when chemical dangers exist for humans."

Dixon removed his glasses and looked directly into the captain's eyes. "Captain, I know this is a lot of information. I remember all too well sitting where you are right now." He took a deep breath as he viewed her signed oath in his hands. "If you choose not to take the promotion your memories of this meeting can be wiped away. That decision will not negatively affect your career."

"Immortality and mind games." She peered down at the signed agreement. "I'm glad to see Hollywood does you justice." Rubbing her brow she continued, "I'm fine. I can do this job … I just need a minute to think everything over."

Dixon's eyes did a classic ping–pong match as he scanned the room from Alex to the vamps and back. Silence filled the room as Alex rubbed her temple. "Take a week to ask Raymond and Ben questions. They'll be happy to discuss everything about this job and about their vampire culture with you. If you do accept the position, your new assignment will be noted in the President's Daily Briefing and I will remain on staff to help you transition." He stood up. "Go grab some coffee and talk."

"Alone?" Alex squeaked out. "You want me to be alone with them?" She moved one hand to touch her neck, or maybe she reached for the cross necklace she wore. Raymond wasn't sure, but for someone who took the news that vampires walked among humans fairly well, Alex had now begun to panic.

"They won't bite you." Dixon paused, "No pun intended."

"But you don't want to come with us? What if I have questions they can't answer? What if … I don't know? What if I need something? Or …"

Dixon cut her off. "There's nothing I know that they aren't going to know. Go talk. Get familiar with one another and with the rest of the team so you can make an informed decision. This position is long–term, not something you take on for only a few months."

"For starters, captain, call us Raymond and Ben. No need to be formal." Ben said.

Alex visually sized the vamps up. "My first name is Alex. Please, feel free to use it."

CHAPTER TEN

Raymond watched as Ben escorted the captain out of Dixon's office. Just as he was about to follow, Dixon pulled Raymond aside.

"I hate that I even need to mention this," Dixon said in a hushed tone, "but Alex is off–limits."

Raymond turned so his back now faced the opened door giving them some privacy. "Off–limits?" he whispered back.

Dixon raised his eyebrow and repeated, "Off–limits. So make sure your son doesn't go after her."

Apprehension marred Raymond's face. He hadn't even thought of Sterling in this entire scenario. The first thing that boy would do is to make a play for her, and yes, he agreed, Alex was definitely off–limits to his son. He nodded to Dixon and stepped out of the office.

Once he reached the hallway, he picked up on a familiar scent. The smell of Irish Spring soap, crest toothpaste (the plaque reducer one), and Old Spice hung in the air. The scent remained strongest right outside the office, which could only mean one thing. He looked around and spied the pair – Matt and Brandon. God, those two were the thorn in his side more times than he wanted to count. He watched as the two men stood at the end of the hall, looking like they were having a meeting with the plants near the window. They couldn't appear more out of place if you paid them. The fact that their scents were strong right outside Dixon's office meant they had spent some time right outside the closed door. Spying, no doubt.

Raymond nodded over to Ben, who immediately caught sight of the two humans. "Please escort Alex to her desk so she can pick up her purse," he directed Ben.

Once he was alone, Raymond walked slowly down the hallway in the opposite direction of the two spies. Using his sensitive vampire hearing, he eavesdropped on their conversation.

"... Looks like they got to the captain too," Brandon said.

"Who? Who are 'they', Brandon? Nobody got to anyone. Dixon is one of the security directors for our division," Matt replied.

"Don't be so naive. Trust me; Mr. Teal Eyes is up to no–good." Brandon rubbed his temple. *"Do you have any more Advil?"*

Matt sighed. *"It's in my office. Let's go get it before we're late to our next meeting."*

Raymond kept walking slowly down the hallway. He knew when the two humans had turned down a corridor towards their own office, and out of earshot. This Brandon guy was more alert than the humans gave him credit for. Of course, his IQ scored much higher than the average humans as well, not that any of the humans would ever admit the fact. Overall, Brandon looked like a quirky idiot most of the time – which was to the Colony's advantage. The fact that Raymond had a nickname of "Mr. Teal Eyes," wasn't good. The nickname meant Brandon was remembering him more and more. He didn't want to have to silence Brandon, but would if needed. He turned on his heels and made a beeline to Alex's office.

"Where is she?" he asked Ben once he arrived.

Ben nodded over to the ladies room. "I picked up something in her aura when we left Dixon's office. Her aura went from all sorts of colors to sheer white," Ben said, pitching his voice to the higher octave that only Raymond as a vampire would hear.

He responded in the same pitched volume. "Her thought patterns would have knocked me over if I wasn't already sitting. She's panicking. I think she has her emotions under control, but she's terrified."

"She took the news of our existence well — better than others have in the past. Did you pick up what spooked her?" Ben asked.

"Not really. She's scared and I think her fear is more than of us being vampires." Raymond sighed. "It's hard to read panicked thought patterns. Nothing is ever clear at that point." Fear and rage. The only two thought patterns that felt like reading shredded documents. "I could have touched her arm to get a better reading, but I didn't want to scare her anymore than she already was."

"Yeah, that would have been bad." A brief pause in the conversation hung in the air, and then Ben broke the silence. "You know what else isn't clear? Your aura is lit up like a Christmas tree."

Raymond shook his head and shrugged his shoulders in response.

Ben narrowed his eyes in disbelief. "You've known me this long and you don't think I can see what's going on with your aura, Raymond? You normally have a gray professional aura with mood lining streaks of other colors. Today you are every color in the spectrum."

"A lot on my mind I guess."

"I'm only saying …"

51

Raymond eyes narrowed as he cut him off. "Your job is to read her aura, not mine. So stop it." Raymond turned towards the bathroom once again to see if Alex was returning.

Ben studied Raymond. "I think we shouldn't team up on her. You know, it's probably for the best if only one of us takes her out for coffee."

"She'll be fine. She's open–minded, intelligent, sophisticated … I think she'll do fine if we both spend the afternoon with her."

Again, Ben studied Raymond.

"Quit reading my aura!" Raymond demanded.

"I think it's best if you take her out, Raymond. Besides, I have other business to attend to."

"What business? I cleared your schedule for the day. I know you're free."

"Look. I don't think we should gang up on her. Two–to–one is not a level playing field. You take her out. She seemed to like you and your choirboy looks and charm." As Raymond smiled at that, Ben asked for the car keys. "Let her drive and be in control of where you go. That will calm her down. I'll catch you at home later. You two should go enjoy a coffee together."

*****

Alex needed a moment alone without the excess testosterone at her side. The empty bathroom seemed ideal for her panic attack, which she felt coming any second now. She splashed cold water on her face to pull her back to her senses. The water just made her face and shirt wet. She lived in la–la–land and would be heading out with two vampires, one on each arm.

52

She couldn't shake the feeling that Raymond not only looked so familiar to her, but that she knew she had seen him before. She had spied his gorgeous body plenty of times, but somehow forgotten about him. She loathed mysteries and suspected vampire mind games at work. If she accepted the promotion, she assumed any mind control on her would end. Actually, she'd make sure of that. She didn't want her mind mucked with, but part of her also didn't want to forget Raymond.

Vampires exist. It was a sentence she never thought she'd say in her life, at least not without it being in jest. Were they all bloodsucking monsters? Were they civilized, but misunderstood? How many of them were there? She took a deep breath. What else existed that she did not know about? That question had her rethink her opinion of the National Inquirer and other salacious tabloids. Maybe there was more truth in those pages than she gave them credit for. Her heart was pounding, so she closed her eyes and counted to ten.

Immediately after she said 'ten' in her head, she thought about Raymond. Other than not being human, he exuded her ideal man. Majestic eyes, statuesque build, gorgeous smile, and overall rugged good looks sized him up as the overall perfect manly package to her. Toss in his patriotism and he had a noble quality about him.

She couldn't stop thinking of his beautiful ivory skin, his dark hair, and piercing teal blue eyes. Gorgeous, simply gorgeous. His strong and lean body sent shivers down her spine, and she found his broad shoulders deliciously inviting.

Damn. She had to stop thinking of him in such a way. If she accepted the job she would work closely with him. Perhaps very closely. The idea excited and terrified her. She needed to keep a professional distance from him, and that wasn't going to be easy. She couldn't place it, but she knew Raymond. She had met him before somewhere. She couldn't identify where she had met him, but there was some connection. She'd have to figure the mystery out.

While in the bathroom, she examined her face in the mirror. Fear left her face haggard looking. A cup of strong coffee sounded good. Her headache from earlier could be from lack of caffeine, or it could be from the excessively tight schoolmarm hairstyle she wore. She dug in her purse for a hairbrush. It rested next to the sharpened pencils she snatched from her desk as she grabbed her purse before escaping to the bathroom. She brushed her long hair out and the stroking relaxed her. She left her hair down, reapplied her lipstick, and headed out of the bathroom.

As she walked over to the waiting vampires, she scanned their huge body size. They were big men ... er, vampires. She wondered how strong they were and where they were going for coffee. Was she really allowing herself to be alone with two men she knew nothing about? She noticed the two of them whispering and her heart skipped a beat, but not in a good way. She mustered her courage and forced her feet to continue towards them. They seemed nice enough in Dixon's office. Maybe this outing wouldn't be too bad after all. She did her best to smile back as she approached, what she hoped, were not bloodsucking monsters.

CHAPTER ELEVEN

Raymond felt Alex's thought patterns relax when he told her she would have only one escort for the day. He noticed she smiled when Ben excused himself and left the two of them alone in the hallway. He enjoyed watching her smile. Her emerald eyes twinkled when she did so.

She walked him to where her older model Volvo was parked. As she climbed in, and came into familiar surroundings, Raymond could feel her at a near peaceful calm. He captured her thought patterns, but she wasn't actively thinking about what had spooked her ... so he remained unsure of what had scared her. Of course, he could compel her or physically touch her, but that probably wasn't the best way to start this professional relationship with his new director. Her fear was in check, at least for now, and that's all that mattered.

"Where should we go?" she asked.

"Anywhere. Lady's choice," he replied, adjusting the seat all the way back. He tilted the seat as well and gave himself some extra headroom.

"Starbucks?" She suggested.

Her voice pitched higher than he thought seemed normal for her, so he scanned her mental patterns. "You okay?" He watched as she took a deep breath and told him she just wanted another hit of early morning caffeine. Raymond continued to feel her fear as she started to drive.

Naturally, since there's a Starbucks on every corner, they found one quickly. The place smelled like ground roast and cinnamon when they walked through the door.

"I love their pecan mocha latte and cinnamon buns. What do you like?"

Raymond heard her inhale deeply and enjoy the aroma of the place. But as she finished her last sentence her heart rate had sped up, and her stance turned more stoic. He softly replied, "I enjoy drinking coffee. It's one of the few foods that do have a taste. You assumed a blood exclusive diet?"

"That's what Hollywood and my nightmares would have me believe," she barely managed to squeak out.

"Relax. I won't hurt you." He listened to her heart beats slow down. "You dream of vampires?"

A blush came to her cheeks, and he realized it was more than her twinkling emerald eyes that captured his attention. She looked absolutely beautiful, and so damn flushed at the moment. Her loose hair framed her blushed cheeks. He started to reach out to her. He wanted to brush the hair from her face when she smiled, but she turned away from him.

"No. Sorry. Bad joke. I'm a bit nervous." She glanced at the menu board on the wall. "Nothing else has a taste?"

What was he doing? He nearly touched her face – in a very intimate way. Oh sure, he could justify touching her if it meant saving her from being hit by a car, or even offer first aid if she were wounded, but that wasn't the case here. He cleared his throat. "Everything has a taste. Most foods just taste like paste. Coffee is good and so is alcohol. A few other specific things taste good to me. But that's all."

She placed her order and spoke specifically ordering low–fat cream, a half shot of hazelnut, and a whiff of cinnamon. She obviously had a favorite from their varied menu selections. She then turned to Raymond. "What would you like?" she asked.

"Make it two," he said to the hostess. Raymond didn't care overall what coffee he drank, as long as it was coffee.

"Do you miss eating?" she whispered.

Raymond thought little of food any more, but the question mentally pulled forth a wonderful childhood memory. "My mother made these great honey cakes for special occasions. My father harvested honey from a nearby beehive. I can still remember the taste of those warm cakes. I've forgotten what most other foods taste like. So I guess I don't miss food all that much."

He watched as she reached into her purse, obviously to pay. He quickly touched her hand. "I'll pay, Alex." He handed some money to the cashier.

Alex's hand felt warm and soft. Damn. He told himself he wasn't going to touch her. He mentally cursed himself for such little restraint. If he were honest with himself, he felt grateful for the opportunity. He just didn't want to think about that meant right now.

"Thanks," Alex said.

She glanced down at the hand he touched. Raymond held no body warmth and he knew his touch felt cold. She obviously noticed. He carefully accepted the change from the cashier. After years of not touching humans he didn't want to add another one to the tally today.

The time was mid morning and the place ran in a reasonably quiet atmosphere. He saw a table that offered some moderate privacy for their talk. Raymond let Alex lead the way and they situated themselves for a long stay at the place.

Deafening silence loomed over the two as Alex quietly sipped her coffee. Raymond enjoyed her delicate beauty. She sipped her coffee and carefully blotted her lips with a napkin, soiling it with her lipstick. She shifted in her seat and crossed her legs, that's when he became aware he was staring at her. But it wasn't just her physical appearance which attracted him. She seemed intelligent as well. The whole package was a turn on. This outing transpired into the closest thing to a date he had been on since … well he couldn't even remember ever having a real date. Again he mentally reminded himself this was business. He wasn't ready to start dating anyway, so it should be a moot point.

"Why didn't you burst into flames when we walked out into the sunlight?" she finally asked, breaking the spell which had caught hold of Raymond.

He turned to look at Alex and answered, "Myth." She appeared almost embarrassed asking. Her adorable smile said as much to him. He could only imagine how awkward this conversation was for her.

"You look about 22 or so. And I know you fought in the Civil War. How old are you?"

"My 200th birthday is coming up soon"

Alex's mouth dropped open and a slight gasp escaped her lips. "That's a long time." She drank a sip of her latte. "I've seen you before, many times. I've seen you at the White House, at the Pentagon … I've seen you also at the FBI headquarters. Now that I think about it, I've seen you everywhere. And yet, I didn't remember you at all. How is this possible? I know I would have remembered seeing you, so don't lie to me. What is going on?"

"Your memories of seeing me are flooding back. We're predators, Alex. We slip into the background and are forgotten immediately. It's just part of our nature. Unless you talk with one of us directly, you won't notice us. Well, your short–term memory does, but your long–term memory soon forgets us."

Weird. Even from across the table he picked up on the fear from her thoughts. He wondered what caused such a response. He thought about touching her hand for a better reading, but as he put his hand on the table the fear intensified.

"Does garlic repel you?"

What an odd question. He expected a question about humans being turned into vampires. Even a question about his lack of body warmth seemed fitting. Garlic? Weird. "Garlic smells bad. Tastes even worst. But it does not repel us."

"What would repel you?" Her face turned white. Panic threatened to overtake her. He felt the wave of fear hit him like a tidal wave.

"Are you asking what would kill us, Alex?"

"No."

He sensed the lie as it radiated off her thoughts. "Why the falsehood? It's a valid question. The answer to which the director should know."

She cleared her throat. "OK. So how do you kill a vampire?"

He smiled and shook his head. "I respectfully reserve the right to abstain from answering that question until you officially accept the position. I'm sure you understand."

Her eyes narrowed and it took a while for her response. "OK. What if I were attacked by a vampire, what would help me escape? Holy water?"

Raymond shook his head. "Holy water would only make your attacker wet. If you accept the position you will be given weapons to aid you in subduing a vampire."

"Subduing? Not killing?"

"Again. That is for a later discussion." He noticed sweat forming across her brow. "Alex, are you afraid I will attack you?" Her silence was not reassuring. Hell, she didn't look like she was breathing.

She sat motionless until the coffee cup slipped through her fingers. Coffee splashed onto her lap and she jumped up in response. When Raymond offered to help her, she brushed off the offer. "I'm fine. Thanks for the coffee, but I probably should head out now. Can I drop you off someplace?"

"Alex, calm down. You're safe here with me. I'm sure you have more questions you want to ask of me."

"Baby steps. I need some baby steps here. We have a week. I want to review … ah, gather my thoughts. … I just need some distance."

Fight or flight response was in full effect. She needed to leave, and right this minute. "We should meet tomorrow sometime and keep talking. Maybe lunch?"

"Yeah. Sounds good. Maybe I can call you, or you can call me." She grabbed her purse and a handful of napkins.

"Alex, relax. You don't have to take this assignment if you don't want to. I'll call you tomorrow and we'll have lunch."

"OK. I'm fine. That sounds good."

60

"I can get my own ride home. Why don't you just go?"

"That works for me." She got up and quickly left Starbucks, leaving Raymond alone.

****

Her heels warded off her nearing panic attack by clacking quickly on the floor as she raced out of Starbucks. She could hardly breathe. Good Lord. If what Raymond said was true, she could take it two different ways. Either hunky, good–looking men did exist, but were invisible to her since she forgot them the minute she saw them. Or there were predators are all around her and she just didn't know it. Neither sounded good. Shit, maybe her attacker all those years ago wasn't human. It would explain his hulking size. Christ. Ignorance really is bliss.

Why did Raymond stare so intensely at her? He said he wasn't hungry. It wasn't like she felt like a slab of meat when his eyes glared at her, but the feeling was still unnerving. She wasn't even sure he ever blinked.

His eyes were so compelling and beautiful. That's probably how they control you. Hell. She should have made sure there were no mind games during their time together. Had she been controlled? She thought it unlikely. Why bother compelling when you are giving full disclosure? That wouldn't make sense.

He said he wouldn't hurt her. Of course, what else would she expect him to say?

His eyes never stopped looking at her. It would be flattering if she had been on a date, but this wasn't a date. She had never dated anyone as handsome as Raymond before. He was out of her league. Oh, that's right. He probably only dates vampire women. God. Why did it even matter? He was an immortal. A different species. A species that had the broadest shoulders she had ever seen, and sculptured muscles to match. Strong and masculine. Powerful.

She blinked her eyes to stop the daydream. Distance. She needed distance from these large, hulking men. She fumbled with car keys and was grateful to speed away.

Alex did not return to her office. Instead, she headed for the gym. She needed to run and get some adrenaline going. Her female–only gym was a sanctuary. She couldn't wait to get there.

CHAPTER TWELVE

Alex enjoyed working out at the gym. Exercise always empowered her. The running, the lifting of weights … she loved it. She worked out several times a week and her training showed. Many times she would grab dinner from the gym cafe downstairs before she headed home. Not only would the meal be healthy, but the already prepared food kept her from having to cook a single meal for herself.

The time was earlier than usual for her to be at the gym. She took her gym bag to the locker room to change. She grabbed a hand towel and refilled her water bottle as she entered the cardio room. Rows and rows of stair climbers, treadmills, bicycles, and every other piece of equipment lined the room. The back area stored the free weights, which she was also familiar with. The usual crowd had not arrived yet and she got on a treadmill without having to wait.

From the second she left Raymond at Starbucks, her mind raced with thoughts, ideas and images. Vampires. Who would have thought? Here in Washington D.C. Of all things, the government has known for ages. Alex began her run on the treadmill starting out on a warm up speed. A great government secret revealed to her, and she waited for someone to yell "April Fools." It just wasn't April, and Uncle Sam usually didn't have much of a sense of humor.

After warming up, she increased the treadmill speed. She thought of her attraction to Raymond. At the time of the earlier forgotten sightings of the man, she had wondered what department he had worked in, what his name had been, and whether he was single. And now she knew which department. She knew a lot about him already and there was so much more to discover.

All those sessions where she whined to Micki about wanting a real he–man, she had envisioned Raymond. She just didn't realize it at the time. She thought he had been invented by her imagination. "Butch Manly" was how she referred to him when she thought of what she wanted in a man. He excited her in so many ways. Physically, he was the measuring stick that all other men did not measure up to. She wondered if any man could be fairly compared with an immortal hunk like Raymond.

And, as always, you find a man and he has a flaw. Raymond was a dead, soulless vampire. A handsome dead soulless vampire that she had fantasized about for a long time. God. She could really pick them.

Not a problem though. She knew never to fish from the company pier. Plus, it wasn't as if he was attracted to her. Hot men usually didn't find her attractive and now in her late thirties she had resigned herself to a life of unmarried bliss, or at least she was trying to. She had hopes in her early twenties of finding Mr. Right, but the night of the attack changed all of that for her. Thanks to Micki's help, she could get past that dreaded stalker, and now she dreamed of finding a Mr. Butch Manly of her own, but one that wasn't a vampire.

She criticized herself for not being strong enough to ask him more questions while at Starbucks. She reminded herself she needed to be professional. Raymond and Ben were going to be team members and she had to leave it at that. It was bad enough to lust after a coworker, but just shameful to lust after dead ones.

The idea sounded crazy hearing it in her head. Maybe she needed to talk with Micki again.

She couldn't get the image of Raymond out of her mind. Alabaster white, flawless skin with piercing teal eyes. Dark hair that was just long enough to run her hands through. A strong, muscular jaw. And his lips, they looked soft and inviting. Her heart raced, and not due to the workout.

She usually worked a full hour of cardio and lifted weights while at the gym, but after a 30–minute run she decided to go home and Google vampire lore. She wanted to prepare for their next meeting.

****

Raymond walked into the dining room at Fang Manor just as his sister, Sulie, began unpacking a box of antiques she had recently bought. "What did you pick up for the house?" Raymond asked as he peeked into the box. He noticed a lace tablecloth, a vase, miscellaneous books, and a set of salt and pepper shakers. Other than a cursory glance, he paid the items little attention.

"Not much. The vase is nice. It's vintage and made of porcelain, I think."

Raymond shifted the tablecloth aside and found the vase. He lifted it out of the box and ran his hand down the side of the off–white stand. The vase felt heavy and the handiwork exquisite. The outside contained porcelain rosebuds along the base and he traced them with his fingertips. Fifteen little roses adorned the vase. Roses. Delicate and beautiful.

He swallowed hard as he looked away from the vase. Tears filled his eyes as he cleared his throat.

Delicate. Fragile little things wilting before their time — way before their time. So temporary in their existence. Without knowing what he was doing, Raymond's fist tightened around the vase until the porcelain shattered in his hand. Shards of the vase pierced his flesh causing his blood to drip onto the tablecloth in the box.

Sulie let out a surprised squeal, then grabbed the tablecloth and wrapped it around her brother's bleeding hand. "Let me help you," she said.

"Suzanne Leigh, leave me alone," he growled. Raymond noticed the coldness of Sulie's eyes when she heard him use her full name, instead of the nickname he had given her when they were only children.

In a stern voice she said, "Raymond, come with me. I want to wash you up." She looked at her brother, who no longer noticed her presence. "Raymond! Let's go get you cleaned up. Now." She gently put her hand on his elbow and led him into the kitchen to the sink.

As she worked removing porcelain shards from his hand, she asked, "How did you get home without a car?"

He blinked once, then again. "William was downtown. He picked me up, and then left to find Jackie and the kids."

She ran the water at low-pressure as she pulled his hand under the stream. Blood pooled around the drain and his hand healed as the shards were removed. She removed a large porcelain splinter from his thumb and he winced. "Where were you when William picked you up?"

"At the National Mall. Walking around."

"Were you with the new director?"

Raymond paused. "No. She left."

"Ben said she was nice. Did you like her?"

"Yes."

Sulie turned off the water and dried his hand. "Where did you go with her after Ben left?"

"Starbucks."

"Did you have a pleasant talk with her?"

"Not really. She left early."

"Why did she leave you alone at the coffee shop?" she asked placing a bandage on his nearly healed hand.

"I don't know. I guess we were done talking."

Sulie's eyes narrowed in on her brother. "You noticed the vase I bought. Did you like it?"

"It's nice. Beautiful roses. ..." He made eye contact with her. "I'm sorry I broke your vase, Sulie. I'll replace it."

"I don't want the vase replaced. Tell me about the roses, Raymond." When he didn't respond, she led him outside to the gazebo. The bandage was already not needed. His skin had already healed itself, but sometimes people need to see a wound to admit that one exists.

Once settled on a bench, she leaned over the side of the gazebo and picked a rose from the bush. She handed the flower to Raymond and asked again about the roses.

He stared at the rose in his hand. "They were beautiful red roses."

Something was wrong. The vase had yellow roses, and the one in his hand was more orange than anywhere near the color of red. "What is the significance of red roses?"

"They were her favorite."

"Who? Captain Brennan?"

67

He blinked. "No. Wilma. I planted them for her on her birthday. She was pregnant with Sterling."

Sulie shook her head, remembering the past. "Yes. You planted them in her garden. The flowers were beautiful. Tell me about the roses."

He caressed the petals of the rose. "She would pick the roses in full bloom and put them in a porcelain vase, and set it on our table for our evening meal. She loved the roses." He sniffed the rose in his hand.

"Raymond, why did you destroy the vase with the roses on it."

"I don't know." He glanced away from his sister. He could have blocked the guilt he felt from Sulie, but either didn't want to spend the energy or he felt too raw to hide his feelings from her anymore.

"Raymond, do you regret giving Wilma the roses?"

"No. Of course not. The rose bushes were a present for her," he looked at his sister in disbelief.

"Why do you feel guilty about the roses?"

"I don't feel guilty about the roses. They made her happy." He paused a long time before continuing. He took a deep breath. "I wanted to be a good husband to her." His eyes filled with tears.

"You were a good husband to her. She told me so herself." She gently rubbed his shoulders and back.

He smiled back at her with that acknowledgment. After a short pause, he admitted, "I'm attracted to Captain Brennan, and I don't want to be." He shook his head. "I really don't want to be attracted to her. I don't want to dishonor Wilma. My memory of her is all I have."

Sulie's eyes lit up to the confession. "It's healthy to see other women, Raymond. You've been alone a long time. You're young. It's only natural to have an interest in the opposite …"

"I don't need a shrink. I'm fine," he said, cutting her off. He started to get up, but she pulled him back down onto the bench they shared.

"People who are fine don't go around breaking vases." Sulie allowed that to sink in. Then she continued, "You've been in mourning over Wilma for way too long. It's okay to move on."

"Thanks Sulie. I know your heart is in the right place, but I don't want to discuss … moving on."

As he got up to leave, she quickly asked, "Are you afraid of replacing Wilma in your heart?"

Raymond stopped in his tracks.

"A heart can hold a great deal of love. You can have a relationship with someone else without the new feelings taking away from what you had with Wilma."

He turned and looked at his sister. "It's not that easy. Wilma meant the world to me. No one else could come close to what she means to me."

"Yes. She meant a great deal to all of us." Sulie stressed the word 'meant'. "No one will ever mean the same to you as Wilma did. She was a special individual, and your relationship with her is unique. A relationship with someone else would be different. It could be just as nice, just as wonderful … but it will be different. A new relationship should be different because this person is different from Wilma. You're a different person today than you were all those years ago." She paused as she noticed Raymond had played with the rose so much that several petals had fallen off into his hand. "But I want to hear more about this woman. 'Alex', right? Tell me about her."

He hesitated, but then broke the silence. "Alex is different. You're right. She's easy to talk to and I felt a connection with her the moment I laid eyes on her. It was the same feeling I had when I first saw Wilma. It's hard to explain. Like a door opened and I have to walk through it."

"That's good Raymond. You are entitled to find love. You've been alone a long time and raised a child on your own. I don't think a relationship with someone else could ever erase the memories and the joy you had with Wilma. Plus, you shouldn't forbid yourself love just so you can preserve the love you had with her."

He gazed down at the mostly destroyed rose in his bandaged hand and handed it to her. "Thanks for taking care of my hand." That was all he said before he left her in the garden and headed back into the mansion.

CHAPTER THIRTEEN

Raymond inwardly laughed. Alex had suggested a picnic at a park for their next meeting, and had insisted on packing herself a lunch since Raymond wouldn't be eating. Outdoors? Raymond needed to explain the dangers of the sun on his delicate vampire skin to her.

"Thanks for agreeing to meet me at the park." Alex came up to him with her bagged lunch. He agreed to meet her at the park because it was his job, but he found himself eager to see her today. He wanted to spend time with her, and his talk with his sister last night had helped. He noticed the sunlight radiating off her auburn hair. The light made her appear almost angelic, and beautiful.

He led Alex to a remote area so they could talk in private. He spread the blanket under a large tree with plenty of shade. He suspected she chose the park because it was such a public place. He remained uncertain of what had spooked her yesterday.

"Next time I'm picking the place," he said as he allowed her to sit down first.

"Oh, are you feeling weakened by the sun's rays?" She almost sounded delighted.

"No." He looked at her as he sat down. "Is that why you picked the park?" He wondered if she were testing some of the fake vampire lore the movies and TV shows were always spewing about. He hated the way the media depicted vampires, but he liked Alex's spunk. He had not expected it.

"I read something about vampires growing weaker in sunlight. I wanted to test the theory."

"You could have asked." He knew what she was up to, and his smile showed it. He liked this playful side to her; he just didn't like to sit in the hot sun and wondered what other lore she might test him on.

Alex took her sandwich out of her bag and fidgeted with the plastic wrap. Gaining her courage, she finally asked, "Are you dead?"

Boy, this was always the stupidest question people would ask. "No. Do you see me here in front of you? Can you hear me talking to you? This animated state is called 'being alive'. It says so in all the medical textbooks."

He sensed her nervousness as she nibbled on her sandwich. "I don't understand. Why vampires? What can you do better than humans who protect the White House and other agencies? I mean, I'm sure you can do more … I just want a list of what that is."

OK, let's bring on the list. "We have better hearing and sight. We're harder to kill. We have fast speed while running or hunting. Overall we have heightened abilities, like being able to see at night, hearing outside the normal human range, and such."

"What about sense of smell?"

"Yes, that too."

"Can you smell my blood type?"

He took an unnecessary deep breath for dramatic purposes, since he already knew her blood type, and had the second she walked into Dixon's office yesterday. "Yes. It's A+"

Alex smiled as her eyes widened in surprise, "Well, wouldn't that come in handy in a medical emergency?" She took another bite of her sandwich and a sip of water.

Raymond smiled at her. Just like yesterday at Starbucks, he found himself less lonely when she was nearby. He never would have guessed that talking to a woman would be so enjoyable and easy. She hadn't yelled for help or run away from him as if he were a bloodthirsty monster. Of course, he did notice her play with the collar of her shirt and cover up her neck a bit at his last statement. He sensed she was comfortable talking with him, but still a bit overcautious.

"Do you prefer one blood type over another?" she asked.

"I prefer A+." If he had to sit in the sun, she could take some friendly prodding herself, but it was obvious his comment didn't sit well with her. She squirmed on the blanket, perspiration dripped from her temple, and it wasn't that hot outside. Raymond felt bad for that one; maybe he shouldn't have made his last comment.

"The government also employs us because there have been vampire attacks on the White House and the President in the past. Some congressmen and senators have been targeted as well," Raymond said, bringing the conversation back to her last question. "We can sense when another vampire is nearby. It's our predator instincts. You also need a vampire to catch a vampire usually since humans are too easy to compel."

"Compel?"

Thought patterns shot out again in panic from her. He wanted to calm her down, and mentioning compelling was not going to do the trick, but he had already laid it on the table. "We can compel humans to do what we want."

Her eyes narrowed as she took a good look at him, "Am I being compelled right now?"

Raymond was tempted to flirt with her, but he was out of practice. He decided to just answer her questions and ignore his interest in her. "Of course I'm not compelling you right now. I wouldn't compel you." Taking a good look at her, he added, "You need to lighten up. You're tense. It's understandable, I guess, but I'm not the enemy. We can't compel you to do anything you normally wouldn't do. If you were a criminal we could get you to talk, but we couldn't have you step in front of a moving bus, for example, if you didn't already have suicidal tendencies."

She fidgeted with the buttons on her blouse. "Vampires in the movies compel women into their beds, against their will. Could you compel a woman to undress?"

The question embarrassed him – probably because he had never been asked such a question before. Maybe because the question came from Alex. He wasn't sure.

He considered his answer. "Depends. If she were an exhibitionist? Yes. If she believed her shirt had toxic waste on it? Sure. If they were already inclined to go to bed with me? … Well, there would be no need to compel her in that case." He cleared his throat and continued, "Women get undressed every day, Alex. It's ordinary for them. If I wanted a woman's shirt off, I see no reason why I wouldn't succeed." He realized his last statement sounded a bit off–putting, so he added, "Of course, it's a moot point unless I wanted the shirt off to begin with. Personally, I've never compelled a woman in such a way."

She appeared more nervous at his answer, so he smiled at her to look less menacing. Now he realized that all he could think of now was her shirt off, and the idea surprised him. Of course, she was a beautiful woman, and any man would want to see more of her incredible body, but he had not realized until this moment how much of an effect she had on him. He was actually aroused, and he had not felt that sensation in response to a woman in quite some time. He knew his eyes were pitching black in response, so he blinked several times and resisted his feelings.

"Something in your eyes?" she asked, as he continued to blink.

"It's nothing." He wiped his eyes and felt for his fangs with his tongue. No fangs produced themselves under his inspection; he was okay to look at her. "I'm fine," he said as he gazed into her emerald eyes again.

He watched as a squirrel came up to her. She tore off a piece of bread from her sandwich and handed the food to the animal. He found it odd that she didn't tear the bread and throw it onto the grass for the squirrel to pick up; she was hand–feeding it. "You should be careful, Alex. The squirrel could bite you."

She looked at Raymond. "I'm guessing one of the points of this outing is to prove to me that not everything that can bite you will bite you." She studied the vampire from head to toe, and then gazed into his eyes. "You don't sound so sure of that though. Are you sure I'm safe around you?"

She toyed with him, or so he thought she did. Was she flirting with him? Maybe she was serious. He chose his next sentence carefully. "I'll ask your permission before I bite you. I give you my word on that, Alex." As if a ton of bricks fell on him, he realized saliva pooled in his mouth. He wanted to know the taste of her blood. He wanted to feed from her vein. He swallowed hard and tried to dismiss his feelings.

Alex took a look around the park. The place was filled with families enjoying the sunny day. "Just in theory, why not create a super army of our own. Why always be on the lookout for human and vampire threats alone, why not create a threat for our side? ... In theory of course."

"Because we're living beings. We feed, breathe and have children. We're not robots ... and this isn't Nazi Germany and we're not a supreme race. Plus, the more vampires there are, the harder the secret of our existence is to keep. Eventually every rock star would want vamp bodyguards; hell, they'll want to be vampires themselves. Where would it end? The Colony is a small group. Vampires are not federally registered or on government reservations, they are scattered and, at least with the civilian vampires, they are relatively unorganized just trying to live their lives among humans."

"Don't say that word again." She appeared irked at his last statements.

Surprised by her tone, he asked, "What word?"

"'Hell'. You're in the presence of a lady."

Raymond's jaw slackened as he blinked a few times. "I apologize for offending ..."

"It's a joke Raymond. You need to lighten up." She smiled at him.

Raymond smiled back. He wasn't expecting her to make a joke. She had a softer side to her, he just knew it. Of course, there existed a tough exterior. She lived and breathed career military and now a top federal official. Putting vampirism on the table would cause anyone to be a bit edgy. But here she joked with him. Tit–for–tat. And wasn't that sexy.

Alex nodded as the information sunk in. "Can you have children?"

"Yes. Of course we can. That's how we get baby vampires."

"I thought vampires were all sterile."

He shook his head, "Only in the movies." Raymond hated the way the movies portrayed vampires.

She asked the next question in a hushed tone. "Can vampires and humans have sex?"

Boy, she went straight for the hard questions. "Yes." He uttered the word slowly and lingered on the 's' as he looked deep into her eyes and spoke in the same hushed tone. OK, now all he could think about was having sex with her. Damn. The breeze caught her scent and blew it towards Raymond. His nostrils flared instantly; she smelled so good. The sandwich smelled God–awful nasty, but she smelled great. His attraction grew, as well as an erection. He looked away and forced himself to concentrate on the smell of the sandwich.

"So humans and vampires can have children together?"

The intimate questions surprised him, but her curiosity in vampires as a people pleased him. He felt that he surely had no idea how attracted he was to her, or she wouldn't be asking these questions. "Vampire males can father children with human females but not the other way around," he answered, barely making eye contact with her. Before she could ask him why, he continued, "Human sperm, well, any human genes, can't penetrate a female vampire's egg." The discussion centered itself on topics that were intimate in nature. He

77

said the word 'sperm' to a woman he had recently met and instantly felt his age. The times had changed, and the world was more open with such topics. Or maybe it was just Alex being so open with him? He wasn't sure, but Raymond could not remember a single male director of the colony ever asking such questions. He concentrated more on the foul smell of her sandwich so he could clear his head.

"So a vampire man can father a child with a human woman?"

Raymond knew from experience the answer. After all, he had fathered Sterling with his beloved Wilma. "Yes," he answered looking back at her.

Her face focused in concentration. "The half–breeds have the same vampire qualities? Or are they human?" she asked.

Raymond's stare intensified as he looked at her. "My son is a half–breed," he said coldly. "I don't like the term. Please rephrase the question." His attraction to her took a step back, but then he had to remind himself that to her the term was not meant to be derogatory in any way. She simply asked a question and was genuinely interested in the answer.

"I'm sorry. … Ah, I'm sorry for the offense, not sorry that your son is a 'half … um. … OK. Let me start again."

Raymond had scowled at her half–breed remark, but as she tried to clarify her last sentence she looked horrified for the blunder. Many vampires used the term half–breed, but Raymond hated the term. The embarrassment made her look sweet, so he smiled back at her.

"Do the children produced with one parent being a vampire and the other a human take on human characteristics or vampire ones?"

"They're vampires. They have both human and vampire genes. Depending on who they choose to have children with, they could have children that are purebred vampires, more half–breeds, or even human children." He felt bad for snapping at her. "I apologize for my anger about the term half–breed. It was unwarranted. Please accept my apology."

She nodded and then finished her sandwich without touching the chips in her bag. "So your wife is a human."

It felt like a knife. "My wife is dead. And yes, she was human."

"I'm sorry. How did she die?"

"No. Ask another question." He didn't want to talk about his loss.

"Okay. Are your parents mixed?"

"No. My parents were both vampires. I'm a purebred."

Touching her neck, she asked her next question. "Can humans be turned into vampires? And if so, how is it done?"

Bingo! This question usually made it in the top five people would ask. "Yes they can. The vampire has to be fully mature, about 25 years old. That's when the blood is potent enough to turn a human. The human has to be fed a little of the vampire's blood which will stave off death temporarily. The human needs to bleed out, the vampire usually drains them. Then the human must drink more vampire blood to start the change. The change takes about 24–48 hours, they'll need human blood immediately afterward, but after that it's pretty much done. They are known as full vampires."

"And do full vampires have all the vampire characteristics that purebred vampires have?"

"Yes."

"Full, pure, and half … oh, my." She paused before her next question, "I know I'm one–fourth American Indian. Are there individuals who are one–fourth, or less, vampires?"

He shook his head. "No," He took a deep breath "A half–breed genetically has his father's vampire DNA. They are sometimes considered … ," he cleared his throat, "… considered a DNA copy. Their ability to reproduce with vampire women is limited, not only because of genetic limits, but also because our women shun them for being weaker and not good breeders."

Her eyes pierced him with curiosity. "So your son …"

He cut her off. "I'd rather not talk specifically about my son."

She nodded, and then her hand instinctively reached for the cross she wore around her neck. Alex looked around at the other people in the park, and then leaned in towards Raymond and whispered. "Have you ever turned a human?"

Raymond decided he had been grilled enough for right now, both by her and the sunlight. He leaned in towards her, and deliberately stared at her cross necklace. Her heart raced, and he knew he shouldn't tease her, but it was payback for the sunny day picnic. Once he was mere inches from her face, he gazed her deep in the eyes. "Have I turned a human?" He moved in even closer and whispered, "That's classified."

80

Remaining close to her, he pulled an antique pocket watch out of the side pocket of his jeans to examine the time.

She leaned back away from him, her face a bit white with fear. "What a lovely timepiece." Alex's shaky hand reached across to touch the watch, "May I?"

The chain was still attached, but they were sitting close enough that the time piece easily reached.

She held the watch. "It's beautiful ... and old."

"The watch belonged to my father," he said, counting the freckles on her face.

Alex looked at the back at the engraving; the initials did not match Raymond's name. "He doesn't miss it?"

Raymond took a deep breath and he removed the watch from her hand, never allowing his gaze to drop from her face. "He's dead."

"I'm sorry," she said, her eyes meeting his.

He could still hear her heart pounding, but didn't believe it was all because of fear. With the sandwich gone, all he could smell was her sweet scent. He wanted something to say, anything. Right now all he could do was look into her beautiful emerald eyes and wonder what her lips would feel like if he kissed her. He licked his lips and nearly leaned in to find out.

His phone beeped and broke him from his trance. He pocketed the watch and grabbed the phone. It was Ben with some routine business, but Raymond needed a break. He was enjoying his time with Alex a bit too much, and just needed a breather so he wouldn't do anything inappropriate – like compel her to remove her top.

"What is it? A bat signal asking you to return to the bat cave?" she asked.

It was as good an out as he needed. "Something like that," he chuckled. "I'll pick up at your place for dinner tonight."

CHAPTER FOURTEEN

Raymond met Alex for dinner at The National Mall. Alex had changed clothes and now wore a pair of tight fitting jeans and a plain white t–shirt. She styled her hair down and just tousled, like she didn't bother to put much effort into her appearance. Damn, she could look good in anything. Raymond always preferred women in dresses and skirts, but had to admit, Alex looked amazing in her tight jeans and t–shirt.

"Hi, Raymond. Sorry I'm a few minutes late. I just got done at the gym."

"Hi, Alex. Not a problem. I only now arrived here myself." In truth, he had arrived a few minutes early since he hated being late. Raymond stopped texting when she approached. "I need another minute. A random shooting just occurred at the Pentagon."

"What? Did anyone get hurt?"

"No. The Pentagon police caught the suspect. Appears that he acted alone. Ben is near Interstate 395 so I'm asking him to stop by and read the suspect's aura. My son will swing by FBI Headquarters later and read him as well." The human team, once again, had done a wonderful job in protecting government officials and the civilians. Chances were likely that no vampire had a hand in this, but the double check of his team comforted him. Once done texting Sterling, Raymond looked up at Alex. "All is taken care of. I thought we could walk around a bit before dinner. Maybe talk a little."

"Are you sure you shouldn't go to the Pentagon and check on the situation? Perhaps we both should go."

"No. The humans have everything covered. My team is fine with the checks so I don't need to do anything, and neither do you." He smiled at her as he pocketed the phone. "Shall we walk?"

"That sounds nice."

Her mental patterns remained calm with no signs of panicking, which was good. The exercising probably contributed to her mood; at least Raymond didn't feel like he should check her purse for any stakes tonight just in case that was the next theory she wanted to try out for vampire lore.

He sensed excitement from her. He'd have to touch her to be certain, but he sensed excitement about the promotion and what the new position could mean for her career. He decided to test if his reading was accurate. "You're excited about this promotion?"

"Yes. I really want to accept the promotion. It would be a great career move for me, and I think I would enjoy the work. Actually, I moved to D.C. so I could take my last promotion. I've sacrificed a lot for my career." She smiled at him. As tall as she stood, she still looked up to make eye contact. "You're a lot bigger than the average man. How big are you?"

How big am I? Raymond cleared his throat. "What?"

Alex looked up. "How tall are you?"

"Oh," Raymond took a cleansing breath. "I'm 6' 4" and 260 lbs."

"Is that average for a vampire?"

"For the men I guess. We grow during our Jahrling Year. The year after our fangs extend. For the males, we get broader shoulders, bulk up with more muscle, grow a couple of inches. Our females do the same during their time, but the change is a more feminine growth. They get the height and the muscles, although they don't bulk up as much."

The two of them walked as they talked. Raymond explained more about the Jahrling Year and that both of his parents were killed in a house fire after his transition had occurred. The two were lost in the discussion and had wandered down a remote path with little lighting.

"We need to turn back around." She turned on a dime and quickly walked back to where they came from.

"Wait, what's wrong?" Raymond caught up to her.

"Nothing." Her eyes said more than her voice did.

Raymond was horrified. "You're afraid I'm going to attack you!" Actually, this was the typical response when someone met a vampire – at least in the movies.

She hesitated briefly. "Maybe"

"I'm not going to attack you." He looked around at the place; he didn't want to attract attention to their conversation now that they were back where people walked about. "I'm not going to hurt you. The US government entrusts me with their President. I'm a trustworthy individual." He sensed she wasn't afraid of vampires in general, she was afraid of him. Of being alone with him. "Here, let's sit down a minute." He suggested a bench under a park light. The well lit bench was easily within eyesight of several people who passed by. After they sat down, he asked, "Why do you think I'm going to attack you? Have I given you any sign that I would?"

"No. I'm fine. … I'm just paranoid. That's all. I don't spend much time with huge men who I really don't know. And I use term 'men' very loosely in the current situation. It's only a silly fear."

Her fake smile told him it wasn't just a silly fear. He knew most fears were based on some past experience. "Alex, when I was a young boy I was in my parents' garden gathering vegetables for dinner for me and my sister. I was there with her and a friend of ours. As we were gathering food, I came across a snake hiding in the garden and it surprised me. Before I knew what to do, the snake struck my bare legs and pumped its deadly venom into me. The venom nearly killed me. My mother was cooking our dinner over the fire pit on the side of our house and my father was in town. I cried out partly in pain and partly because I was scared, but my mother was too far away to hear my cries. My friend ran to my mother for help while my sister, who is five years my junior, sucked the poison from my leg. My mother carried me into town so the doctor could see me." Raymond paused in the story to look Alex directly in her eyes. "It took me a long time before I could go back into that garden to gather food, because I was convinced for the longest time that a snake would be the death of me. Eventually I did go back, I had to. Fear can be crippling. I know. And the fear can last a long time. I'm a vampire, Alex. There is no way a snake could ever hurt me today, and yet I won't go near one, ever. I can't even look at one at the zoo. I guess there is a part of me that will always believe a snake will kill me." Raymond took a deep breath. He had never shared that story (or fear) with anyone else before.

Alex looked at the vampire in front of her. "I know it's a silly fear that I have."

"Fear is what it is. You have to do your best to get past it."

"Oh, I've been trying for years. Trust me. I've tried and tried to overcome my fear. I wish I could move on."

"Would you like help to overcome it?" He didn't like her being afraid of him. As they sat on the bench, he could tell she wasn't scared, just anxious. He wanted her to be comfortable with him, especially if she accepted the Directorship of the Colony. She said she had wanted the position. Plus, he wanted her to have it since her career, and especially this promotion, was important to her.

"Oh, I'm working on it."

Raymond didn't like to compel people. He often would compel a waitress or a store clerk to look the other way and not notice him, but he usually didn't interfere with humans in general unless they attacked the US government. But deep within him, he wanted to help Alex, and he knew he could by simply compelling her. "Look at me Alex." As she turned her head and their eyes met, he added, "I won't hurt you. You will be safe while you are with me. Do you understand?"

Alex's face went pale and her eyes dim. "I understand I will be safe with you Raymond." He hated to compel her, but he wasn't going to hurt her. He would take the compelling off her once she got to know him better. "How are you feeling?" he asked her.

"What? Oh, I'm fine. What were we talking about?"

"You were going to ask me another question."

She looked at him and said, "Can I touch your hand?"

What was he just saying about fear? "I'd rather you didn't" Raymond cursed himself for his lack of courage, because a part of him very much did want to hold her hand.

"Why can't I touch your hand?"

"I will allow it if you will tell me why you want to."

"Your hand felt warm when we first met. At the Starbucks counter the other day, it felt cold. I want to feel your skin temperature. Some websites say that vampires give off no body warmth."

He knew he should have mentioned the mental connection he would have with her, but for some reason he wanted to hold back on that little detail. He reached out his hand so she could hold it. She took his hand and held it gently in her hands. Sure, he shook hands all the time with women for business purposes, but this felt more intimate. This was almost like holding hands and a part of him wasn't ready for that, but he liked the way her fingers massaged his hand as she held him.

Once the touch was made, the mental connection grew stronger. Not just thought patterns but actual thoughts came across. The images of her thoughts flooded his mind. He fascinated her. She wanted to know more about him and his people. She was attracted to him and curious what he looked like with his shirt off. She was ashamed with herself for even thinking of a vampire in such a way. She thought of him as a monster. Vampires were monsters. ... Too much information obtained way too quickly. He dropped the connection and put his hand back in his lap.

Well that was an eyeful for Raymond. Shame. She felt shame for being attracted to him. She thought of him as a monster. "Alex, there's something I need to attend to. Could we maybe meet for lunch tomorrow instead?

CHAPTER FIFTEEN

Raymond and Ben sat in the Colony's operation's room. Raymond had taken his usual spot at the head of the conference room table. They watched as William walked in. The door closed behind him and immediately locked into place. The room resembled a tomb, which fit considering it was in the basement of Fang Manor. Each team member of the Colony had their own special seats at the table, but nothing had ever been officially assigned.

Raymond glanced up from his computer screen, and greeted William with a slight nod of his head. "Did the forger's real information get uploaded?"

"Natch! I took care of everything. In fact …" William took a seat next to Ben, and then typed on his computer to pull up a request order, "Looks like some dude hit the new data last night while you were out with the new director."

"Really? That was fast. What was the forger into?" Ben asked.

William typed on the keyboard and the smart wall directly across from the conference room table came to life. An image of the forger appeared with his physical stats. The info displayed next to the name of a Pennsylvania detective who made the request. "Look it — our man had a big–ass rap sheet. His prints were a match to an art heist last November, to some petty thefts earlier the year before, to a museum break–in a few years back, and a whole lot more." William pulled up the information for each of the cases as he read them aloud. "One case was still active, so this Pennsylvania detective could match his case's unknown fingerprints to him. Our man is listed as deceased, so the trail will end and the detective will be shit out of luck."

Raymond gave a wry smile. "At least we helped Rodriguez with his case, and possibly helped with the closed ones." Raymond cleared his throat. "I received information from the Vampire Council," Raymond said, which gained him the full attention of the other two vamps in the room. "The forger's DNA matched a rogue vampire from a coven up north. He has been independent for over 80 years now, with no ties to his coven. His bloodline has been verified and his family told of his death."

"Well, Goddamn! What was his family line?" William asked excitedly.

Owning a seat on the Council extended Raymond private information to many social covens, but his oath of secrecy prevented him from divulging all information to his own team. "His family wishes that information not be made public. The forger was older than I am and they want to protect their family name."

"If he's been independent for that long he probably didn't have strong ties to his bloodline, but it's understandable they wouldn't want this made public," Ben agreed.

William shook his head. "He did have an amazing talent. Shame he wasted his gift."

Ben held up one of the fake security passes. "Here is something odd I wanted to share with you, Raymond. The woman on this security pass is already an employee at the White House. She's an intern."

Raymond took the card from Ben. "What security clearance is on the pass?"

"All access. She was supposed to work yesterday but never showed up. Sterling was investigating the names on these passes. He just called from her apartment. It looks like she hasn't been home in weeks."

Raymond read the name from the pass. "Is Verna Foiles even her real name?"

"She checked out," Ben said as he posted his findings onto the smart board. "I reviewed her White House application forms, her college transcripts, birth records, everything. If Verna Foiles isn't her real name, she has been that alias for the last thirty years."

"Keep an eye out for her then. She's the only lead we have in the case." A text came in on his phone and Raymond quickly read the message. He gritted his teeth. "Something went wrong with the forger's evidence. What happened to it before you uploaded the fake info?"

"Did our human team find something that ain't right?" William asked.

Ben looked over to Raymond. "Our human team won't find anything. I scrubbed everything, including the bag itself. Not a single fingerprint or DNA remain on the forger's backpack or its contents. I made sure of that."

William added, "With no DNA to help ID that forger, they'll be pullin' up short on their end. As long as they don't ask for a body, we should be rockin' our way to easy street on this one. It'll just be an unknown forger who disappeared into the wind."

Raymond looked back down at the text. "Should be, but they're having issues with the evidence. What about the memory cards? Were those clean?" Raymond asked as he texted back a reply.

Ben furrowed his brow with concern. "I transferred the designs of the passes on to new memory cards. The original cards had other files on them. There was nothing specific to vampires on it, no bloodlines and no names. But there were some files that read like journal entries. The forger sure hated humans and was verbose and explicit in his writings."

William shot a concerned look over to Raymond. "Dude, it's all good. What's crawlin' up their asses about the evidence this time?"

Raymond read Dixon's email, "Cleanup needed – Tweetle Dee and Tweetle Dumb."

William looked over to Ben, "Who?"

Ben rolled his eyes. "You know, Brandon and his tall sidekick."

****

Raymond arrived nearly an hour later to Dixon's office for the cleaning. He felt sorry for Dixon the minute he entered the office – judging by the coffee mugs and the exhausted expression on Dixon's face, Matt and Brandon had been there for a while.

"Thanks Agent Smith for coming by," Dixon said. "Please continue fellows, and tell Agent Smith everything you've told me."

Brandon inspected 'Agent Smith' like he had ordered a ham on rye, but was handed a snail sandwich instead. Raymond watched as Brandon made some cryptic hand gestures over to Matt, but, because of the expression Brandon had on his face when Matt began talking, the gestures missed their mark.

"It doesn't add up," Matt began. Matt checked a database, once again, of all known federal counterfeit artists who had the skill needed to create such beautiful forged federal documents. "Every single one of them is either in jail or out of the country," he reported to Dixon and Agent Smith.

"We must have stumbled onto someone new," Dixon calmly explained.

"Agent Smith, you look familiar," Brandon said, slightly rubbing his temples. "I've seen you around quite a bit, but I thought your name was Agent Reese."

Raymond waved his hands to dismiss Brandon. "I'm confused for many people."

"I've seen you a lot, Mr. Teal Eyes," Brandon said, with emphasis on the code name. He looked over at Matt, who immediately had a new interest in who this Agent really was.

"Please continue telling the agent your findings, Brandon," Dixon urged.

Brandon held up the evidence documentation reported by the evidence team for the backpack, memory card and security passes. Looking defiantly at Mr. Teal Eyes, he waved the documentation in the air like a prized flag. "You know what doesn't add up?"

The only reaction in the room was Matt's widened eyes. Raymond caught it, and knew that Matt's memories were flooding back to him as well.

"It's odd that no file encryption was performed on the memory cards. They weren't even password protected. For as brilliant as the forger was, you'd think he, or she, would have protected their work," Brandon stated.

"You're assuming the forger owned the bag and cards. Maybe he, or she, was only a courier. Couriers sometimes don't know what they're transporting and

93

mistakes can happen," Dixon said, trying to calm the two.

"Maybe. But files like these you would expect to be protected in some fashion." Brandon eyed Mr. Teal Eyes as if he were the enemy.

"You know what else is odd?" Brandon said accusatively at Dixon. "You gave us the evidence to ship to the computer analysis team. We were wearing gloves, so of course we left no fingerprints on the bag nor the passes or memory cards."

"And?" Dixon asked.

"Your hands weren't gloved," Brandon accused.

Dixon remained quiet and shot a concerned look over to Raymond.

Brandon held out the evidence report. "There were no fingerprints found on the bag. Not even your fingerprints came back."

Matt stood up, and with a shaky voice said, "The report can't be correct. Brandon and I both saw Dixon touch the leather strap."

As Matt read the paperwork, Brandon continued. "It is weird. I'm sending in a request to view the evidence again, if that's okay with you, Dixon. I'm betting the filament tape on the inner container has been broken, or replaced. It's the only explanation as to why your fingerprints were wiped."

"No one else had access to the evidence but the teams who were supposed to," Raymond said. It was the truth, even if the two humans didn't know the vampire team had permission to view it as well.

"Well, when we get our hands on the evidence we'll see if there is a statement inside the packaging about anyone else who may have viewed the items," Brandon sealed the box.

"I doubt there will be any statement, Brandon," Matt said looking from Dixon to Raymond. He held up the evidence sheet. "I think this paperwork is forged as well."

Raymond had heard enough, he looked deep into their eyes. "Men, give me your full attention, and I'll explain this all to you."

CHAPTER SIXTEEN

Raymond decided an early lunch with Alex would be best for their next meeting. He suggested meeting at a restaurant. One benefit of an early lunch was to avoid the crowds and talk privately. Another benefit was to see her that much sooner. Thoughts of her consumed his night, and he felt like a child eager to see Santa on Christmas morning.

Oddly enough, watching her eat did not bother him. The sandwich in the park had reeked like garbage, but he had enjoyed watching her as she had eaten her lunch. It seemed nearly sinful how she had taken small bites, almost timid nibbles. She had dabbed at her mouth with her napkin, which had taken her lipstick off in the process as well as any food. Dainty. Very girly.

He assumed Alex had many questions remaining for him. It tantalized him that her questions were not all business related. You can tell so much about a person by what they ask of you and he wondered what questions she'd fire off at him during lunch today.

She chose a pizzeria since she would be eating alone and only her opinion mattered. He suspected the repulsion of garlic myth would be tested, but he didn't mind.

The quiet pizzeria felt quaint. Too early for the lunch crowd to arrive, so they had plenty of privacy for their conversation. Red tablecloths lay on the tables, with candles lit on each one. Italian wines lined the bar and the place also boasted a nice beer selection. Artwork hung from the walls featuring images of Italy and soft music played in the background.

Raymond smiled as he realized the place screamed as a date night spot. He liked the place. Restaurants like this didn't exist when he had courted his wife. He would have enjoyed taking her to such a place. Even though the food smelled awful to Raymond, he could tell by the enjoyment of the humans consuming it that the dishes were well prepared and delicious to them. Yes, he would have liked to take Wilma to a place like this. She would have looked beautiful with this candle light.

"A penny for your thoughts, Raymond." Alex smiled at him. "You're so lost in thought. What are you thinking about?"

Her smile lit up the room as they waited to be seated. She looked nothing like Wilma. Wilma had blond hair and had a much smaller frame. Alex was a gorgeous redhead with a more athletic build. He never thought about how attractive an athletic build on a woman could be, and he found he did like the look.

"I was thinking how times have changed. When I was young, restaurants such as this didn't exist. We cooked our meals over a fire pit in our yard. We farmed for vegetables and had livestock for meat. Much easier these days to just stop off at a grocery store or go out to eat at a fancy restaurant."

The hostess greeted them at the door and they chose a seat in the back of the restaurant in a separate room that resembled a wine cellar. When they neared the table, Raymond pulled out a chair for Alex.

"May I?" He smiled as he held the chair. The old school charm and manners must have surprised Alex since she stopped as she approached the table and looked at him. He suspected most women were not accustomed to this formality.

She smiled and took her seat. "Thank you, Raymond."

Her polite response melted away any lingering hesitations Raymond had of getting more acquainted. She was well mannered, beautiful, and full of life. What wasn't there to like?

As they waited for their waitress, Alex asked, "Where did you grow up, Raymond? Can you tell me more about your home and the fire pit you cooked on?"

Rarely did Raymond stroll down memory lane, but he did want to share. "My parents were well off financially. We lived in a small, one story home on the outskirts of town …" He chuckled, "… away from prying eyes and pitchforks." He shrugged his shoulders. "My childhood was typical, not much different than any human one. It was just my parents, my sister Sulie, and me."

The waitress came by with menus and rattled off the lunch specials. They each ordered a drink. Raymond only continued his story once the waitress was a good distance from the table. "We had land, so we grew crops for mine and Sulie's meals since my parents didn't eat. We had chickens for eggs. We weren't vegetarian, but we didn't eat too much meat other than chicken." He cleared his throat. "I went to school with the humans and had mostly human friends. There were three other vampire families that lived in the same town. I still hear from them every once in a while."

Alex smiled. "Like a Christmas card at the end of the year type of thing?" she asked.

"Yes. Sort of like that. I didn't stay in that town after my parents died. Sulie and I moved to a new location."

Alex tilted her head sympathetically. "The pocket watch. You said he died, but I thought you were all immortal."

"You asked me once what would kill us. Fire is one. Like I mentioned earlier, both my parents died in a house fire. Authorities said the blaze appeared accidental, but I wasn't sure. The deed may have been committed by an individual who had discovered what we really were. I packed Sulie up and we left. About that time, I became a widower. Sulie helped me raise Sterling. We wandered about from town to town, living several different lives. We befriended Ben decades later, and the four of us found a home with the Federal government. This brings us up to today."

The wait was not long, and the waitress came by with their drinks and asked to take their order.

"I'd like the personal spinach and garlic lover's pizza on thin wheat crust. Light cheese. Extra sauce," Alex said.

After jotting down the order, the waitress turned towards Raymond.

"Nothing for me. Thanks." Raymond handed the menus back to the waitress just before she left their table.

"I'm sorry about your family," Alex said. "Sounds like you had your hands full."

"Sulie is only five years younger than I am. And yes, it was challenging. I found myself in my early twenties, a young baby to tend to, a teenage girl in my charge, and I was transitioning into an adult vampire." His mouth formed a slight smile, "The transition is not an easy one. You generally feel sick for the entire year until you can properly process the blood you drink."

99

"It takes a year for the change?"

"Symptoms appear much earlier, but the dietary needs are the last to come ... and the most painful. It's hard to learn how to properly feed, how to compel humans — and basically to be what you are supposed to be when no one is there to help you. My sister and I went through it alone, but we did have each other."

The waitress returned with Alex's salad, and again asked if Raymond wanted anything to eat. Again he politely said no and dismissed her.

Alex rolled her eyes as the waitress left. "Did you see how she stared at you? She acted like I wasn't even here."

"Really? I must have missed that."

"Probably most women gawk at you like that. You're just used to it," she teased.

Raymond smiled and leaned in. "She'll forget me soon enough. They all do."

"Like I did the few times I bumped into you."

He wasn't sure if that was an accusation or merely a comment. It actually occurred to Raymond that Alex may even be flirting with him. "Yes," he answered. "Just like you always managed to forget me in the past."

Raymond studied Alex and felt mental patterns of genuine dislike for the waitress. Thoughts of jealousy and possessiveness were obvious as well. Even in the short time he had known Alex, Raymond knew he wouldn't want a man leering at her. No. That would never happen again in his presence. He'd make sure of that.

Alex picked out the croutons in her salad and placed them on a nearby napkin. "What happens when you eat human food?" she asked.

"Nothing. Food tastes terrible so we don't eat it."

"Does food pass through your digestive track? Or do you gag and throw up?"

Raymond chuckled. "You ask some of the oddest questions. I know it would taste terrible. Most likely I'd vomit based on that alone. But if I could consume it, then it would pass through my body. The food would probably cause stomach cramps since I'm not used to digesting food, and then I would probably pass it without my body processing it in any way. My stomach doesn't have any digestive acids, so I couldn't break down the food."

"So I'm guessing you wouldn't want to taste my salad." The blush on her face reminded Raymond of what he did eat. Her beautifully red, flushed face looked inviting. "So," she said, "other than your mother's honey cakes, is there anything you wish you could eat? Like chocolate or something?"

He forgot he had told her about those delicious honey cakes. "I've never tasted chocolate. ... Well, I tried the sweet once, after my transition, since everyone always raves about it. It tasted vile to me. That did cause me to vomit."

"Really? You've never enjoyed chocolate? Wow, that's my one true weakness."

He gazed at her beauty in the candlelight as the waitress served Alex her pizza. He watched as she shook spicy pepper flakes onto the melted cheese. She was so sexy and beautiful, and a bit naughty. "So spinach and garlic lover's pizza. Your favorite and usual pizza choice for this restaurant?"

"I've been meaning to try this combo for a while now. Will my eating garlic bother you?"

The minx! "I wasn't planning on kissing you this afternoon. So I'm fine if you have garlic breath for the rest of the day," he said testing her reaction to such a comment. She merely blushed a reply. A smile curled on Raymond's lips as he thought how cunning Alex was. Noticing her lips, he realized how much he wanted to kiss her. Why did he say he didn't want to kiss her?

"You seem to be testing out a lot of vampire lore. The sun from the picnic just made me thirsty, Alex. The garlic will have no effect. Trust me, asking me will get you the correct answer without having to always test it as a theory. I will tell you now though, if you are planning on checking whether a stake through the heart will kill me, let's just say I don't want to go through the pain. So please take my word for it and try not to murder me."

Alex blushed and looked away. "I believe I have enough control to stop just shy of the stake, Raymond."

"Great. I love truces," Raymond chuckled. "I won't kill you; you won't try to kill me. It all works out in the end."

He sipped his wine. "I would like to hear more about you. I know very little about the new director I'll be working with, and I'm curious."

There was that blushing smile again.

"You can ask me anything. Whatever you want to know."

Raymond wanted to know a great deal, but decided to warm up with simple questions. "Where did you grow up?"

"Omaha, Nebraska. Smack–dab in the heartland. Lived there and a few other places, including Europe."

It explained her lack of an accent. "Are your parents still living?"

Her smile faded. "My parents died years ago. I have a brother and a sister. We're close, but we haven't seen one another in years. It's mostly emails and an occasional call."

Alex was alone. Raymond could tell from her mental patterns she was lonely. "I'm sorry to hear that. What made you choose to join the military?"

"My father was career Air Force. I liked the lifestyle and wanted to serve my country."

As the questions continued she opened up more and more. He learned about her childhood, her family, her early years growing up in Omaha, and how she had traveled across Europe as a teenager. She lived a remarkable life and he enjoyed watching her smile as she told her stories. Her eyes sparkled at the joyous stories; and they teared up at the sad ones. The few that had her blush fascinated him. He could tell she was a private person. He wondered if she had ever shared some of these stories with anyone before. He found it sexy and desirable the way she opened up to him.

For the first time in ages, Raymond wanted a woman. He wanted to take her back to the mansion and make love to her. He grew hard and found his jeans a bit too tight for comfort. He fed just before meeting her, and that fueled his desire as well. He may still be slightly aroused by the blood coursing through his veins, but knew it was pure Alex that raced his heart rate.

His body tensed. Feelings and emotions flooded his thoughts. He had to have her. His body ached for her. If she picked up one of the thick, bread sticks glistening with butter, and started eating it, he was going to die.

Thankfully it looked like she tried to avoid bread and starches; she even left her pizza crusts behind on the plate. Thank you, Lord.

He watched her lips as she ate, watched them as she talked. Her passionate lips were round and full. She wore bright red lipstick and throughout the meal it slowly faded from her lips. He started thinking of her milky white skin – surely the skin that poetry was always written about. He imagined it to be soft and smooth all over her body.

Why was he even thinking about such things? He had heard it in her thoughts, he was a 'monster' and she felt shame for even being attracted to him. Shame. He felt bad for even thinking of her in any romantic terms since he knew how she really felt, but he couldn't help his newly aroused feelings for her. She was intelligent, caring, and goal oriented. He never would have thought that last one would be on his list of attractive qualities in a woman, but it was.

He made sure not to touch her and did his best to ignore any thought patterns that came his way. He respected her. Yep, you can't help the way you feel about someone. Her allure drew him like a moth to a flame though. He knew if he got too close he could get burned.

"… and I know … (giggle) it was the wrong time and place, but we still went ahead and walked onto the stage wearing the costumes anyway. (giggle). Isn't that insane?"

Raymond had stopped listening for the last several minutes; he was so glad there wasn't a test that would follow. He paid no attention to her stories; he was making up nasty little stories of his own in his mind. He

104

mentally undressed her and shifted in his seat as a growl left his throat. Fortunately, the restaurant noise covered his growl so she didn't hear the noise.

Mental note, next time he would not eat right before he saw her. Surely that would help. He looked at her as she laughed about a story she had just shared. He drank some of his wine. The beverage tasted sweet, but he could tell by the fragrance of Alex herself that she would taste even sweeter.

He hadn't planned his next question; it just sprang forth from his lips. "Alex, are you married?" He hadn't seen a ring but he knew that some modern women didn't wear rings, or at least he had thought that was the trend these days. He was sure many women no longer took their husband's last names, and he never did understand the hyphenation of last names. Whose name went first? Whose was last?

"I've never been married."

"Never? You're an attractive woman Alex. I would have assumed otherwise." She blushed, but it was a true statement. A woman such as Alex not being married made no sense to him.

Many people these days choose to have children out of wedlock so Raymond decided to ask his next question. "Do you have children?"

"No."

It was a short answer, very curt. Definitely some strong mental patterns wafted from across the table. "Do you want to have children one day?"

"That's a personal question, Raymond. … I guess if I found the right person, was married one day, sure. I would love to have children."

She played with her hair. He kept track of how many times she did so, and the count was over a dozen times since they first sat down. He loved watching her. Her hair appeared to be soft and he wanted to touch it. Even over the horrible smell of the pizza, he could smell her hair and the fragrance coming off her skin.

He needed to know something about her, and he needed to know the answer now. The question was not proper, but he didn't care. He wasn't sure what he would do if the answer to his next question was 'yes'. He prayed that it would be a 'no'. "Are you involved with someone?"

"Am I dating?" Her eyes grew wide.

"Yes. Are you currently romantically involved with someone?" He tried to phrase the question as nonchalantly as possible.

Visibly her guard went up. "That's another personal question. I don't see why you need to know the answer."

"It's standard procedure, Alex. When Dixon joined the team he was married. Trust me, security checked out his wife as is standard protocol. If you are romantically involved with someone, who may be at your home, have access to personal and private files about us … we would need to know so we could run a check on him."

She nodded and her expression softened. "No. I have not had a man in my life for quite a while now."

Raymond hid his smile by taking his napkin and pretending to wipe some wine off his lips. He liked the answer, it was the right one to him.

They continued chatting as Alex finished her meal. The waitress swung by the table to see if they wanted any desserts. "No. I think we're good. Thank you," Alex said.

Miss?" Raymond caught the waitress before she left the table. "An order of chocolate cake please. One fork." When the waitress left, Raymond added, "You can enjoy the chocolate for both of us."

CHAPTER SEVENTEEN

Dinner, Alex thought, now that she returned home – alone. Raymond had asked her out to dinner as they left the restaurant. Granted, his job was to answer her questions, but it still felt good to have dinner plans again this week with such a handsome man … er, individual. Of course, their time together centered around business. Otherwise, this would be considered speed dating. She'd gone out more with Raymond than any dates over the last few months.

"God, I'm helpless." Alex found it ridiculous to be attracted to a creature she would have run from only a few days ago. Why did he have to be so handsome and charming? Of course, many of the Hollywood vampires were gorgeous hunks as well. Women would flock to them in the movies. Those women were in their twenties, not knocking on the door of 40 in just a year. Plus, that was Hollywood, not real life.

Alex couldn't read Raymond very well. He joked about compelling her to remove her clothes, but then said he did not want her to be undressed. At lunch earlier he had looked spaced out, like he wasn't even paying attention to her. And, of course, she had rambled on about her boring life. Then there was the comment about garlic breath and not intending to kiss her. Yep, that was a decisive statement right there.

Men, and she guessed vampires as well, were never attracted to the older woman with the boring stories. Boy, she fit that bill well today. He didn't get a word in edgewise!

Admittedly she was very interested in a world where vampires existed. Honestly, they had always remained her favorite monsters when she was growing up. Mummys. Werewolves. Frankenstein. So many others. Yep, vampires were the monster she would most likely want in her world if given a choice.

She never liked the scary, ugly vampire stories. She preferred the sexier vampire stories. God, if Hollywood only knew how sexy and handsome real vampires were, they'd never be able to cast actors in those roles. No man could hold a candle to Raymond's good looks.

And he was good-looking. She had forbidden herself from falling for a coworker long ago. But that was before she met Raymond. Was it morally right to have the hots for someone she will be working with for decades?

She realized that his beauty would still exist decades from now. In her opinion, her looks had already faded. Her bubble burst. He didn't seem like the playboy type. He probably dated many women – and all at the same time. God. He probably has dated hundreds of women in his lifetime! She knew she'd pale in comparison.

She remembered his comment about being widowed. Thinking back to their meal, she had noticed a ring on his finger. Engaged. Of course he was taken.

Alex wished she had a girlfriend to talk to about all of this. Of course, she was close with her therapist, Micki. Alex sighed as she realized that she needed to schedule a session, and quick. She needed to talk things out and keep Raymond off-limits.

CHAPTER EIGHTEEN

Raymond checked the Jag's clock as he pulled up to Alex's single story red brick house. The well manicured yard had a large shade tree in front. A white picket fence outlined the lush grass and gave the home a charming touch.

He checked his pocket watch. Five o'clock sharp, right on time. The drive to the house was pleasant and she lived in a quiet neighborhood. Big trees lined the sidewalks and offered plenty of shade for taking walks. Shade was always good. He parked his Jag in the driveway, opened the white gate, and walked down the pathway circling the garden leading to her front door.

Before reaching the door, Raymond noticed a red rose bush in her garden. It bloomed with red flowers which shined brilliantly in the fading sunlight. Raymond paused mid–stride. Roses. Not only that, but red roses. Identical with Wilma's roses. He wasn't one to read into signs, but if he were, what would this be telling him? Should he not knock on the door? Or, did the sign indicate potential happiness again for him? He knew he was attracted to Alex. He wanted to spend more time with her and reminded himself that his being here wasn't a betrayal to Wilma. He forged ahead and continued up the walk.

The doorbell chimed setting off a barrage of noise. Raymond heard dogs barking, an alarm unit being turned off, the sliding of a chain lock and the chamber of a doorknob being unlocked.

"Hi, Raymond. I welcome you to my home." Instantly, three little dogs greeted him and the door

110

slammed in his face. Raymond heard her voice through the door. "Are dogs okay? Can you be around them without anyone getting hurt?"

Too late. Pain already radiated from Raymond's nose. Maybe he misread the sign of the roses. A bloody nose seemed to be another sign, a bad one, but he chose to ignore the potential omen. "Yeah, dogs are fine. I like dogs." Pain shot through his face and blood dripped down to his lips.

The door opened and she saw the mess that was now his face. "You're bleeding! I'm so sorry. I give you permission to enter my home. Come in while I get you some ice." She scurried the dogs from the door and back into the kitchen. She returned with an ice pack and towel to find him still standing in the entry way of her home.

"Here you go." She handed Raymond the ice pack and towel. "You can come in. I said it was okay." As he put the ice pack up to his nose, his eyebrow rose inquisitively behind it. "Don't you have to be invited in to enter someone's home?" she asked.

"No. We can go anywhere humans can go. I'm standing in your entryway because I don't want to bleed on your carpet."

"Oh. That's kind of you." Raymond noticed a blush overtake her beautiful face. She became flushed with embarrassment. "Here, the bathroom is right down this hallway." She led him past her bedroom and into the smallest room of the house. "I'll be in the living room. Let me know if you need anything else. Again, I'm so sorry." She closed the door and left.

Raymond had chosen not to eat this morning. Hunger pains tugged at his stomach as he lost more blood. This minor nose bashing was not a huge ordeal since he knew he would heal, but he hadn't expected to have to spend energy on healing himself right now. He appeared late twenties and knew he could fast much longer if needed. Feeding right now would bring on more urges, and his already aroused body didn't need any help.

He assumed her bedroom was the closed door they had passed when walking down the hall. He couldn't ignore what he had on his mind. He used the towel to wash himself. His nose healed by the time he finished washing his face. He placed the towel on the sink and headed out to meet Alex.

She eyed him from across the room, and before he realized what she was doing; she had crossed the room and stood mere inches from his face. She inspected his nose, amazed at the healing. "How fast do you heal?" she touched the bloodstains on his shirt.

She felt too close, or maybe not close enough. She inspected his bloodstains, and her hand on his chest excited him in such a way that made him catch his breath. Her body heat radiated towards him, and he enjoyed the heat. "The more blood a vampire has in their body the faster they heal. My current alias has me feed several times a day, so minor injuries like this heal quickly."

She stood even closer to inspect the blood. "It's red, but just slightly darker than human blood." Her body warmth radiated off her and her scent filled the air. Raymond became aware of her smooth skin only inches away. He wanted to draw her closer to him, but shed his impulsive thought and decided to explain to her the reason behind his slightly darkened blood color.

"Yes. I feed often. The color would be red for me. Very similar to the color of human blood, but slightly darker." She smelled so good, and a ringlet of her hair had fallen onto his chest. He wanted to reach out and touch it, but resisted. Temptation was not going to win this time. "My blood is close to human–red because I have fresh blood in my body. We don't have the luxury of producing blood ourselves, so we consume human blood and have that coursing in our veins. The less often we drink, the more our bodies must recycle the blood using it over and over again. That's why our cells age and we appear older. Eventually the blood turns to a dark purple, nearly black goo. When that happens the vampire is aged quite a lot. The blood stops circulating and the vampire will starve to death. My blood is just slightly darker than human, but still red, because I always have a fresh supply of blood in my system."

Being so close to her tortured him.

He watched her as she studied his face. Her emerald eyes focused on his nose, her hair gently cascading down her face as she pushed a loose strand behind her ear. She wrinkled her nose as she touched his, perhaps in sympathy as to what she thought he was feeling. He forced himself to think of sports, something from the multiplication table, old nuns … anything that would soothe his arousal to the beautiful woman mere inches from him. "You're looking older today Raymond. Do you feel different as you age?"

He cleared his throat. He felt like a coward and could barely speak. He knew he should have taken a step back to give himself distance between them, but he basked in her body warmth. "I feel the same whether I am 22 or 72. The more blood I have in my system, the younger I appear. When I've eaten a good, let's call it a meal, my body takes on the warmth and the blood courses through my veins. It feels better the more sated I am with blood. My body always aches for blood since I can't produce it on my own. I can keep the cravings down easier when I appear my youngest because I'm staying well–fed." Cravings? Hell, more like desperation right now.

"I see." She looked directly in his eyes. "You eat several times a day. How? I know you don't attack humans, but …"

He blinked his eyes and looked towards the ground. His eyes were going to be jet–black any minute with her looking into them like that. "We receive bagged human blood from the government. The bags are difficult and messy to eat from. I feed myself with syringes. I usually carry a couple with me during the day; I keep some in my car for emergencies." He looked up at her to see if her eyes were still focused directly on him. "You will probably have some emergency bags and syringes here when you accept the promotion. I know Dixon always had a supply for us."

Alex appeared a bit anxious on her next question. He thought it showed in the way she didn't make eye contact with him. "When you feed from a human, do you kill them?"

Raymond's eyes nearly popped from his head. "Alex, feeding and killing are different. I have not personally fed from a human in some time, but I can assure you I have never killed anyone while feeding. Now if you are asking about vampires in general, we are civilized creatures. We don't even feed ourselves on blood until our twenties, at which time we've adapted to living among humans." He took a cleansing breath. "We don't have to kill to eat. … But yes, if a vampire were dying, desperate for blood, they could drain a human dry. I'm sure it happens, but no one on my team has ever done so. … Even you humans have murderers, but humanity as a whole is deemed to be worthy."

Relief blew across Alex's face. "I see." She thought about her next question as she eyed Raymond from head to toe."So, are you hungry now?"

He closed his eyes slightly and looked away from her. His lips pursed and then he said, "I'm always hungry."

"But you can control your hunger? You can wait to feed if needed."

Christ, she looked nervous. "To a certain point, yes. I can ignore the hunger pains for a little while." She visibly relaxed and he felt her ease reflected in her thought patterns.

She studied him and finally asked, "Can I watch you feed yourself?"

It shocked him to hear such a question. It wasn't what he expected. Actually, he didn't know what to expect. In his heart he knew what he wanted his answer to be. His mind wrestled with his heart's decision. Ages had passed since he had been intimate with a woman, and having new blood in his system would be a catalyst into her bedroom. He pondered the question for a bit, and then asked, "Why do you want to watch me feed?"

"I'm curious. If ever there is a situation in the field where I have to give you blood one day, it'd be good to know how to do it."

Raymond ran her explanation through his mind a few times, and still wasn't sure what to make of it. Her thought patterns vibrated with curiosity. It wasn't necessarily a bad sign, but was it a good one?

Overall, what was the big deal? Dixon witnessed them feed in the past a few times. They normally tried not to feed in front of their food source, but Raymond didn't dismiss the idea. Business–wise it made sense. Romantically speaking, he was playing with fire. "Maybe after you have a bite to eat first."

The answer wasn't a yes, but also not a no. It left the door unlocked in case he wanted to open it or not. The temptation to change his mind and beg for her vein was great, until he smelled something foul emanating from the kitchen. Only one thing smelled that bad – human food. "You cooked? I thought we were going out."

She returned to the sitting area of the living room. "I figured there was no need since I was the only one eating. Plus, we'd have more privacy here to talk. I hope you don't mind." She sat down on the red chair next to the couch. Raymond took a seat on the couch a safe distance from her. He didn't mind at all for a little more intimate setting but wanted to take it slow.

As if on cue Alex's three dogs approached and sat at her feet in a defensive position. They were perfect little watchdogs. Their presence reminded him that they weren't alone. The smallest dog had scars on its body. "This is Luddy," she said picking the dog up. "He engaged in a fight with a much bigger dog and lost. His owner wanted to put him down and I was at the right place at the right time to save him. The big one is Tory." She placed Luddy down and now stroked the back of Tory's ear. "She's the youngest. Her owners no longer wanted her because they had a baby, so I took her in." Looking at the sheltie she said, "This one is Gracie.

She's the oldest. She's a good girl." She reached down and patted the little dog. "She has several health issues, but she's still here with me. I enjoy their company. It's nice to have another heartbeat around the house, plus they're great watchdogs for protection." She smiled at the dogs as they settled down on the floor.

Raymond was in awe. Alex held so much love in her heart for these little creatures. It reminded him of his youth when his mother would go to the hen-house to collect the eggs for breakfast. His mother would pat the heads of the hens as she took their eggs and she would talk to them. Alex was not only beautiful, but owned a heart to match. He enjoyed hearing her voice, seeing her beauty and learning more and more about her.

"Raymond, do you want some wine? I know you can drink it. I have red and white."

"Red wine is fine. Thanks." As she left, his eyes shifted down for a good look at her backside. Nice. She smelled sweet too, and not in any excessively perfumed way.

Alex brought back a Cabernet and poured two glasses. While she opened the wine, Raymond looked about her home. He appreciated the decor; his sister would love it. Raymond wasn't an expert on furniture, but would have guessed the pieces in her house were mostly antiques. He remembered furniture such as this from a few decades ago, perhaps the 1960s. The couch took up much of the living room. It was long enough even for him to be comfortable lying on. The coffee table and end tables matched, which added symmetry to the room. The red lounge chairs probably were a specific style, but they just looked like two comfortable chairs to relax in. The desk in the corner seemed sturdy.

117

Pop art adorned the walls with bookshelves on either side of the room. Planters with thriving plant life sat atop the tables and in metal wire stands throughout the room. Very few knick knacks cluttered the room, which he preferred. It was beautiful. Simply elegant.

"Here you go." She handed him one of the glasses of wine.

"You have a lovely home Alex. Beautiful belongings."

"This old stuff? My parents gave the furnishings to me when I moved out and went to college twenty years ago. Eventually, I want to update the entire look."

"Well, I like it. And my sister would love the decor. She enjoys antiques." He sipped his wine, hoping it would quench his thirst, but it didn't quite do the trick.

"That would be your younger sister, the one who saved your life when the snake struck you?"

"Yes."

"Any other family?

"Just my son, of whom you already know."

A smile appeared on her face. "You talk very formally. Doesn't that get you into trouble sometimes if you don't want people to know how old you are?"

She didn't know the half of it. Colloquial English was ever changing. It horrified him to discover the word mcjob made it into the dictionary. "Sometimes it is hard to keep up." He sipped his wine again. "This is very good wine, Alex. I like the taste."

They sat up talking for a while, and were on their second bottle of wine. She fixed herself a plate of some nasty looking and God–awful smelling pasta dish, but he supposed she found it savory enough as a human. He looked over her legs and was grateful that Alex

118

preferred to wear dresses, although she did look good in the jeans earlier. Her legs were shapely, but what stood out was she had a scar on her right one. Her perfect legs were flawed. Assuming it was an athletic injury, he asked, "How did you get that scar on your leg?"

He felt the thought patterns as they slammed into him. Insecurity, outrage, fears, and even guilt. She glanced away. Through her thought patterns, he sensed she was hiding within herself. He asked again. "Alex, how did you get that scar?"

She pulled her legs up on the couch, and her hand covered the scar. Raymond noticed the hesitation in her voice as she slowly began, "It's … it was a long time ago. … God. Well, I don't talk about it." She sat quietly for a moment, not making eye contact with him, and then added, "I was attacked three years ago this November."

Raymond's relaxed, easy–going attitude was instantly replaced by a predator–like position on the couch. "What happened?"

She shook her head as she now looked at him. "I was stupid. A stalker had been following me for weeks, and I wasn't very careful. I was in the wrong place at the wrong time. But, I'm fine. I had been on my way home. It had been a late night at work, like all my nights, really. I had stopped off at the commissary for some groceries. I never saw him coming."

She played with the cross necklace around her neck, took a deep breath, and continued, "He was an enlisted man that I had met briefly. He thought he was in love with me. That night he grabbed me from behind and forced me back into the bushes." She paused and looked up while taking a deep breath.

119

Raymond leaned over closing the space between them. He was close enough to touch her, but resisted the temptation. Her story would come out in her own words and her own time. Her thought patterns were strong, but her exact thoughts incomprehensible from a distance. He would not rush in to see what she may not want to share with him by touching her right now. ... However, he did want to put his arms around her to comfort her. His hands balled into fists to prevent him from doing so.

Alex's body stiffened as she crossed her arms. "He was a big guy. He had me pinned under him. He tore my clothes and ... well, I did get away. I escaped without being raped." She bit her lip, "But it was scary. The man had been in my home several times. He had pictures of me all over a wall in his apartment. It was eerie." She reached for her glass, and took a sip of her wine. "The police arrested him. He's undergoing psychic evaluations and will be locked up for several years." She tossed her hands out dismissively and said, "I don't have to worry about him anymore, but the idea that others like him exist ... well, that does scare me."

Raymond now understood all the locks on the doors and the guard dogs.

"After that night I signed up at the gym, started working out, eating better. I even took a self–defense class so I wouldn't be vulnerable again. I know I was so damn lucky. I know it. I couldn't date a man after that for a while. I just couldn't trust anyone. I guess in some ways I still don't."

Raymond listened to what she had said and tried to decipher the meaning of her words. She said she 'couldn't date a man after that for a while', did she date women? Raymond thought probably not, at least he hoped she preferred men. Her sentence suggested that she may be dating men again, but he knew she didn't currently have any lovers. Then it finally occurred to him why she was so scared earlier. "That's why you were afraid of me. You didn't want to be alone with me at all."

"Yes." She said as an awkward silence filled the room.

"I would never hurt you Alex." He wasn't sure what to say next, but finally added, "You do have a very athletic build thanks to all the workouts you do." He did admire it.

Alex laughed and poured herself another glass of wine as she continued to eat her meal. Raymond wanted to put his arms around her. Wanted to protect her. Wanted to chase away all the bad things in her life. He also felt the need to feed again, but knew that wouldn't be a good idea since he had wanted to touch her since he had entered her apartment.

Her eating was distracting and he relented to his surging passion and allowed his eyes to go black, and his fangs to extend as he watched her continue to eat her meal. He felt lost in the sensual way she ate. He watched as she lifted the fork to her mouth and engulfed the fork itself in her round luscious lips, consuming the contents that filled her mouth. He watched her swallow each bite, his body reacting with each swallow.

When she nearly finished her meal, she suddenly dropped the fork on the plate. "Your eyes are black!"

Raymond blinked and looked away. "Yes."

"Are you okay?"

"I'm straining not to give in to my hungers right now."

She set her plate down on the side table. "Can I feed you?"

He wasn't sure what this offer entailed, but his mind no longer wrestled with his heart. The decision was made. "Oh, God yes."

CHAPTER NINETEEN

He sounded too eager. Alex grabbed the cross at her neck as she put distance between them.

"I'm not going to bite you," he assured her. "Perhaps I should go."

He stood already half up before she stopped him. "No, no. Everything is fine." In her mind, she wanted everything to be fine, but she wasn't sure if it was. She felt like meat on a stick with how he had stared at her. She understood she would have to be comfortable around such things if she took the job though. She took a deep breath. She knew Raymond wouldn't hurt her. On some level, she just knew that to be true.

"Please. Sit back down. I can handle a little eye color change." She took a reassuring breath knowing that if he had wanted to hurt her, he had had plenty of opportunities by now, and still he had not attacked her.

He looked away as he sat back down.

"When did you last eat?"

"A while ago."

"Oh." She wiped her hands on her napkin and set it down next to her plate. "You don't look too much older."

Without looking at her, he pointed to his hair and eyes. "I have a few gray hairs now, the start of a few wrinkles here and there. Not much of a difference."

Alex noticed his lack of eye contact. "Do you have difficulty looking at me when you are hungry?" She took a sip of her wine, mentally trying to normalize the weird conversation.

"No." His head turned and his blacken eyes darted over to her. "I just thought it best not to look at you when I'm like this."

"I'm not afraid of gray hair, Raymond." she teased, lightening the mood.

He focused his eyes on hers. "My eyes turn black when a desire overcomes me."

His eyes resembled deep pools; pools she wanted to swim in. The way he had said the word 'desire' sounded sexier than anything else she had heard in a long time, if ever. Her fingers played with the rim of her wineglass as she watched Raymond sitting on her couch. He didn't just sit. He watched and studied her every move as if he wanted her in a physical, very passionate way. How many times had the last guy sat on this same couch playing video games to the early morning hours and had not even once glanced her way? But, she didn't want anything else from that man. She looked at Raymond. Yes, she did want more from Raymond.

The scene seemed familiar, like deja vu. The two of them being in her apartment felt natural. Perhaps this sensation came from her comfort level with him. Maybe it was the way he looked at her, like he was looking through to her soul. Either way, it felt right. She knew he wasn't looking at her to size her up as his next meal. No, there was more to it than that.

His gaze caressed her lonely body. His look sizzled with more passion than the heat she had experienced with any other man. But then, Raymond differed than her usual romantic interests. He exuded ruggedness. He wore a t–shirt tucked into a pair of what resembled spray–painted–on jeans. Ouch! The man sizzled in a suit but totally rocked the casual look as well.

124

What was the most attractive feature of all? He listened to her. For the first time, other than in confidence to her shrink, she shared the details of her attack with another person. He didn't try to fix the situation, he didn't dismiss her feelings, he didn't criticize her for her poor judgment ... he allowed her to tell him what happened, and he listened to her. She realized the term person seemed perhaps a stretch, but he was a living, breathing person, wasn't he? Not human, but a person nonetheless. She thought of the old saying, *"If it looks like a duck, sounds like a duck ... it's a duck,"* and wondered if whoever originally said those words would have applied them to vampires. Probably not.

She glanced over at Raymond. The man had a family, a job, and a body that she would definitely not claim as dead or soulless. So, he had a longer life span than most. A very long lifespan, but you never know how long you have whether you're human or vampire, his parents were a good example of that. Vampires weren't truly immortal, and probably feared death just as much as any human would when the end came. His parents' last thought were probably for their children ... just like any parents would be.

Raymond sat quietly on the couch, allowing her this quiet moment with her thoughts. He was a father, he loved his dead wife ... was being a vampire all that different from being a human? Sure, having black eyes seemed odd, but people wore colored eye contacts. It was a stretch, but she could live with a black eye color. Raymond was also a patriotic man, and a man who didn't shirk responsibilities. Honestly, how many men would raise a teenaged sister and a newborn on their own, all while trying to hide what they were from the humans, who would probably judge them and try to kill them just for being what they were? Raymond was a real man in her opinion. The type of man she longed for.

He smiled at her. It was a beautiful smile, not fake or forced. You can always tell when a smile is real. His black colored eyes held the smile, not just his luscious, full lips. Alex noticed his hair remained a bit damp, probably due to a last minute shower on his way over. His hair parted on the side tonight, and a curl of bangs hung lopsided onto his forehead. It gave him a Superman appearance. She always did like Superman.

Alex knew her pulse sped up as she took in the visual striptease in her mind. She thought back to their earlier conversation. Humans and vampires could have sex together. Sex. She swallowed hard. She hadn't thought of having sex with a man in a long time. Her heart rate sped up even faster. She wondered if he could hear the beats. If he did, he didn't show any recognition. He just sat sipping his wine, looking sexy as hell.

Her hands still held her glass, so she took a gulp of wine hoping to squelch the heat she felt within her. Instead, it fueled the flame. Would sex with a vampire be different from sex with a human? If it were, she was betting it would be better. The sexual relationships she had in the past, if she could remember that far back, were moderately satisfying. Definitely not romance novel, page turning, steamy … but satisfying.

Blinking a few times, she realized she was staring at his crotch. Could she be more obvious? She knew in her heart that she was going to take this promotion. She couldn't start a romance with a team member, it wasn't professional. She wasn't that type of woman. Plus, there was no guarantee that he was interested in her that way. He had treated her with nothing but respect.

Then again, she couldn't deny her overwhelming attraction to him. His dark raven hair, soulful teal colored eyes, strong muscular jaw ... they beckoned her. She bit her lip imagining the vampire shirtless, or even better, nude.

His black eyes beheld hers, and her breath caught. The glass she held suddenly seemed slippery in her hands due to her now sweaty palms. He was clean shaven today. The last few days he had a scruffy, rogue look about him, which was a great look for him. Today, with not a whisker in sight, he looked downright sinful. Actually, the blackened eyes gave him a mysterious quality. Maybe she could be that type of woman? Perhaps an exception could be made this one time. She stared at his lips, wanting so desperately to taste them.

"Alex?" he asked.

Alex looked up, making eye contact. "What?"

"Are you okay? You've been quiet for several minutes."

She shifted on the couch. "I'm fine. Just a lot to think about." She sat down her wineglass next to her empty plate, a clink sounded as the two touched. "Seems like I'm always eating in front of you. Sorry about that."

And there was his devilish smile again.

"You have to eat, Alex. I wouldn't want you to go hungry on my account."

Blood consumption. It was the only difference she could see between the two species. Well, he also had fangs, but that was so he could eat. She had only seen his fangs once. Were they always ready to strike a vein? Did they retract? She was supposed to ask questions, so

127

she blurted out, "Do your fangs ever get in the way of talking?"

"Am I slurring my speech, Alex?" he asked, revealing his extended fangs.

They were already out. Oh God. How long had they been there? They were huge! "No. You sound just fine."

"In truth, they're always there. They don't extend unless I have a hunger."

She nervously shook her head agreeing. "A hunger for blood."

"Sure. They do extend for blood." He sat with his hands folded in his lap. Alex assumed he did so to look as nonthreatening as possible.

"Do they extend if you feed yourself from a syringe?"

He licked his lips, covering up his fangs. "They do."

She mustered up her courage. The man was hungry, and he needed to eat. "Can you show me your fangs again?"

His mouth spread into a thin–lipped smile. "Probably not a good idea. Your heart rate is raised and you're sweating. I don't want to scare you."

"I'm not scared," she protested quickly.

"You're projecting some strong emotions, Alex. Nervousness, anxiety, fear … it's all confusing to me."

She pushed herself off the chair. Once standing, she held her chin high and strode over to sit right next to him. "I'm fine. Can I please see your fangs?" If it really was the only difference between the two, she wanted to see them up close. She wasn't sure if it was what she needed to draw that line in the sand with a concrete wall, or even if she could step over it. But the answer to their differences lay right here, and she wanted answers.

128

He leaned his head toward her and gave her a big, fangy smile. "I give you my word that I will not bite you."

*****

Raymond remembered how she had asked to touch his fangs a few days ago. Amazing how a few days could change your entire world. His voice sounded low and sexy, "I want you to touch me." Realization set in with that confession. He wanted Alex to touch him, all over. He shifted his body to face her. Taking in a deep breath, he opened his mouth wide and never took his pitch–black eyes off her as she leaned over to be closer to him.

Her soft warm eyes lowered themselves onto his fangs as she studied them with fascination. She leaned over his chest with her face mere inches from his. Her right hand braced itself on his left shoulder as she lifted her left hand to inspect his fangs. Desire soared through him as she touched his right fang and ran her finger down the length of it. His breath panted in reaction. His fangs were long and fully extended, and it wasn't the only body part of his in that condition. She ran her finger down the fang, letting out a soft breath that Raymond felt against his face. At the sharp tip of the fang she accidentally broke the skin on her finger and a drop of blood landed in Raymond's parched mouth. As she pulled her hand away, he snared her wrist and the blood ran down her finger. His action caught her off balance and she landed in his lap.

A breathy, "Oh God," escaped her mouth. Her reaction sounded as if it were fueled with passion, not fright. With his touch on her wrists, he could not only feel her thought patterns but could almost read her mind. His heart skipped a beat when he realized she was sexually aroused, and wanted him. Obviously she knew he was a vampire, and yet he not only listened to the quickened beating of her heart, but could smell her arousal. Taking in a deep breath, he realized how feminine she smelled.

He wasn't sure how to continue. His eyes had blackened due to an appetite all right, but it wasn't for blood. For the first time in a long while he wanted to make love to a woman. His tight jeans were now tighter with his erection straining against the zipper, and that was a sensation he had long been unfamiliar with. He said the first thing his mind came up with. "I swear I didn't bite you, Alex."

"You didn't. I was just not aware of how sharp they'd be."

He inspected the cut. Her blood ran down her fingertip. The small wound probably looked much worse than it was, but the cut seemed fairly deep. "Would you trust me to seal the wound?"

Her eyes widened, but she nodded her reply.

Raymond held her finger up to his mouth. "I will seal the cut, and it will be completely healed, but the process will require me to taste your blood. Are you all right with that?" After a moment of silence, he said, "I promise it won't hurt."

When she nodded once again, he wiped his tongue over the crimson elixir on her finger and never broke eye contact with her. The warmth of the blood caressed his dry parched mouth, oozing creamy delight over his tongue. The small wound sealed instantly, leaving no scar.

It was a mistake to have a taste. He needed more of her.

CHAPTER TWENTY

There was no pain involved. Alex thought the process would hurt, that his tongue would be rough, or at the very least she'd have a queasy feeling by what he had done. Instead, she wanted to melt into a puddle. She wasn't sure if a kitten could have licked her as gently as he had just done. A kitten sure wouldn't have excited her like this though. She felt his lick all the way to her very core. Liquid heat pulled between her thighs and she burned for his touch as she sat next to him.

"Are you all right, Alex?"

"Uh huh," she barely whispered. She wanted him to lick her again, in various body parts, and all she could muster was not much more than a grunt at this man? Her mind was made up. She could be this type of woman. She wanted to jump him right here on this couch, career be damned.

He still held her hand. "Are you still hungry?" she asked.

"Always."

A part of her wanted to know what his fangs are her neck would be like. She wanted to know, but then reality set in. That lick was probably the appetizer he needed to want her as a meal. It was stupid of her, but she'd do it again in a heartbeat. "You told me earlier that you always carry syringes with you. Maybe you should eat."

"I think I'll pass on dinner," he said, letting go of her hand.

She was already knee–deep in it, so she took another step. "I'd like to see how you eat."

"By a syringe."

"Yes. By a syringe."

*****

Disappointment crept in, but Raymond understood her answer. He barely knew her. Of course she wouldn't roll her head to the side and let him feast on her. He took out a syringe of blood from his pocket. The travel syringes differed from the ones they used while at home. These were encased in a thin metal covering. Alex took a deep breath and leaned in to inspect the syringe.

"The blood is cooled in this metal vial, by pressing this button the blood is warmed up in a minute." He explained, pressing the button. He reached out with his right hand and caressed the side of her neck. "The vial warms the blood to human temperature, so the meal tastes the way it's meant to taste. As if I took the blood from the source right here." He rubbed the veins on the side of her neck.

She leaned into him. "Sounds convenient."

The syringe timer beeped and startled him back to reality. His dinner was ready.

"I release the lid and I can inject it right into my vein by pressing here."

"Do you need an alcohol swab or something before you …?"

"No." He cut her off. "I won't catch anything. A few minutes after the injection, you'll see me visibly get younger." He hesitated while holding the syringe. Finally he said, "Perhaps this isn't a good idea."

She took the syringe from his hand. "Let me do it."

CHAPTER TWENTY–ONE

"Slowly. … Please give the blood slowly. … I like it like that," Raymond moaned.

Alex held his arm. Cold. It felt cold. She massaged his arm where the needle would go. She learned to prepare the skin and vein for injections from her vet, and she did the same for Raymond instinctively.

The last thing she wanted to do was to hurt him.

She watched as the needle disappeared into his arm. She then pressed the button and the blood shot into his system. He closed his eyes and hissed as it happened. While she removed the syringe from his arm, she asked, "Was that okay?"

He didn't open his eyes. He just nodded and moaned that it was fine.

The changes were slow at first. She would have missed it had she not been looking for them. The few hairs of gray slowly turned to a dark brunette color. His eyes closed, but even so the few wrinkles ironed themselves out. Overall his skin looked younger, more elastic and healthy. She watched until no more changes occurred, but his breathing grew heavier and heavier. She touched his shoulder, "Are you …"

"Don't touch me."

She sat back. Her breath caught in her chest. That's when she noticed his hands were in fists, his knuckles white. Thinking it was best, she scooted to the far end of the couch, but eyed the chair, or maybe even the kitchen, as a safer retreat.

In a blink of an eye, he moved from his slumped position on the couch to being next to her. He moved his hands up to her face in a fluid movement. He touched her cheeks on each side of her face and looked into her eyes. She should have been afraid, but all she could think of was the two of them laid out on her bed entwined in each others' bodies as they undulated in sweet release over and over again. She was nearly panting at such a prospect.

He slammed her back on the couch and shifted his weight so her legs curved under his hips, which she was more than willing to do. With his body flushed against hers, she closed the short gap between the two and kissed him deeply. Her tongue explored his mouth with eagerness and it brushed up against his fangs. It was more of an aphrodisiac than she could have guessed. She grabbed fingers full of his dark, silky hair, and pushed him more on top of her. She gasped in excitement as his hands found her thighs and his hands made their way up.

"I want to make love to you, Alex. I want you so much." He kissed her neck as his hands made quick work under her dress.

She felt dizzy, but in a good way. She had never been so swept away in a moment before. She wanted, no, needed, him. Her hands found the zipper of his jeans and fumbled with it. Before she realized it, she blurted out, "yes, Raymond … yes!"

He leaned up and helped her with his belt. It was barely unlatched when she pulled the zipper down and tugged his pants off. "You can even bite me if you want, Raymond. I completely trust you. I trust you."

As fast as he was on her earlier, he was off her, and sitting on the chair across the room. "No."

Her heart was pounding in her chest. She was half undressed and he reacted to her like she was the plague. "Did I do something wrong?"

He pulled up his pants, and looked at her. "My sister just called. There's an emergency needing my attention. I have to go."

Dizziness swept over Alex and a headache pounded in her head. She sat on the red chair looking at Raymond, who sat on the couch. The setting sun shone through the window and shined directly into her eyes. Strange. She hadn't noticed the fading sun until this very moment. Looking over at Raymond she noticed his more youthful appearance.

"Sorry. Sulie called. I need to leave." He held the now empty syringe in his hands. "So that's how we eat. Just an injection, we feel younger, and voila, we're fed."

Alex looked around the room. She couldn't put her finger on it, but something felt off to her. She noticed her plate on the coffee table full of pasta. Yes. She was eating dinner, but she wasn't hungry now. She saw the metal syringe in Raymond's hand. It was familiar and she felt like she had jamais vu, the opposite of deja vu. Looking at Raymond she noticed his teal eyes looking down at her as he stood up. His eyes were icy teal, she could have sworn they were different looking, and that … she couldn't put a finger on it. Was he sitting closer to her before?

"I have to go," he said as he headed towards the front door.

"I understand," she said as she got up. "We can talk another time."

*****

136

He opened the door to the Jag and jumped in. "Jackass!" he cursed as he sped down the street. How could he be so stupid? He had picked up inconceivably erotic images from her, of sensual passion wanting to be tapped; he also picked up on serenity. She was thinking how much she felt safe with him and secure.

Damn it to hell! He thought. Of course she felt safe. It was exactly as he had compelled her to feel just yesterday. As bad as he felt, he felt worst when he realized that he was no better than the animal that attacked her years ago. Actually, he was worse. He undid the first compelling of her feeling safe with him. Then he had to compel her a second time to forget their evening tonight. Damn it.

While she was no longer being compelled this last time, he had asked if she was ready emotionally to make love to him, and her answer was 'no'. It was 'no'. He pulled the Jag over and punched at the steering wheel. She wasn't ready for this relationship and he did such a wicked act of nearly compelling her into his bed.

To top it off, during this second compelling he had her believe a lie that his sister had called with an emergency. He was twisting this love affair into a pretzel and it hadn't even started yet.

His body still ached for her. He wanted to make love to her tonight. He wanted to feel her shudder under him as she called out his name. He looked up to the heavens and thanked God that he only fed on one syringe.

CHAPTER TWENTY–TWO

Raymond drove around aimlessly as he calmed himself down, but the car found itself back at Fang Manor earlier than expected. As he pulled his Jag into the garage, he noted the few cars that lined up in a row. Not to many team members were here for the weekly poker night. He let out a slight smile. Playing poker would be a good distraction from the evening's disappointment, plus the game was his favorite pastime.

He grabbed a cold beer from the refrigerator and headed to the poker table to embarrass the team in utter defeat once again. He rested the beer on the green fabric as he took a seat next to Ben.

"I wasn't expecting you to be home so early," Sulie said.

"It was just dinner," Raymond said as he dismissed the unasked question. Trying to change the subject, he added, "Dixon, William, and Mason are still tracking down Verna Foiles. She was the intern on one of the fake ID badges. They'll probably not make it for tonight's game."

"Well I'm glad you could make come. We were only getting started." Sulie counted the chips and placed the correct number at each place at the table. "So we only have four tonight? We can't play with just four of us. Maybe Jackie is available."

Sterling was already sitting at the table. "She's helping the kids with their homework. We'll have to make–do." He shuffled the deck.

"We 'make–do' a lot around here." Sulie glanced around the house. "We need to hire a new maid."

"Don't we have one?" Sterling asked.

"Uh huh, her name is Maria," Ben answered.

Raymond heard only bits and pieces of the conversation. He focused on whether Alex would accept the job. "Alex's mother's name was Maria. She told me that yesterday."

"Maria? Maria was before Tina, and Tina was before Jasmine." Sulie took a deep breath. "Honestly, we can't keep a maid for very long for obvious memory–fucking reasons. Once compelling no longer works they freak out when they see blood and needles all over the house. We had to wipe poor Jasmine's mind so many times I thought her brain would be Swiss cheese."

"Tina quit?" Sterling asked. "Tina was … helpful at times."

Sulie gently smacked Sterling on his arm for that comment. "Tina was the best at cleaning this house. She scrubbed everything so clean."

Sterling took a sip of his beer, "I agree. She was great on her knees." Instantly he glanced over at his father, who appeared to have had avoided the comment entirely.

Raymond wondered if Alex would join their weekly poker game. "Now that Dixon is retiring he won't be in our games anymore. I don't know if Alex plays. We probably should ask her." Raymond announced to no one in particular.

Sneering at Sulie, Ben chuckled, "I thought our maid's name was Sulie."

As a poker chip flew by his face, Sulie left the room to refill her empty goblet. The cards were dealt by the time she returned.

"What are the stakes tonight?" Sterling asked.

139

"Pennies," Ben said, pointing to a jar on the coffee table. "Put your dollar in."

"I'll bring Alex around here tomorrow night to meet you." Raymond said as Sterling got up and stuffed two dollars into the glass, one for him and the other for his father.

Sterling studied his father on the way back to the table. "No way. Am I the only one picking up on this?" he looked around the room as he took his seat. "Sulie, you can sometimes read my father, what's going on?"

Sulie stared at her brother, but then shrugged her shoulders. "Nothing. ... Are you blocking me Raymond?"

He was pulled from his Alex–induced coma. "What? Of course not." He stared around the table at the faces of his team members. He wondered why they were all staring back at him.

"His aura is all red. Damn, I don't even see any secondary colors." Ben commented.

"You've mentioned Alex a couple of times tonight, and you've spent a lot of time with her this week. In fact, you've been smiling a lot more since you met this woman." Sulie added.

"I doubt my father would give up his priestly, celibate status and join the sexually immoral. After all, he holds the world's record for not getting laid," Sterling sneered.

"Enough, Sterling!" Raymond didn't like all eyes on him, but managed to say, "She's pleasant. I like her." He thought about Alex's kind manner and charming smile. He couldn't get the memory of her touch from his mind.

"Does she like you?" Sulie asked. Without waiting for an answer she continued, "My brother in a

140

relationship? After roughly 180 years! Could she possibly have feelings for you too?"

Shocked, and a little embarrassed, Raymond shook his head and looked away from his team, not wanting to make eye contact. "I don't know if she has feelings for me or not." *How can I really know when she's been compelled this entire time not to run from me in fright?* "It doesn't matter even if she does. I'm not interested in pursuing a relationship with anyone," he lied.

"Your aura begs to differ, my man." Ben accused.

Sterling nodded over to his father. "I know you're out of practice, but it's easy to see if a woman is interested in you, Dad. There are many ways, like if she rips off your clothing the first chance she gets."

Raymond fiddled with his poker chips. "Please Sterling. No clothing got ripped," Raymond protested.

"Knowing you, Dad, if you were to get any action, you'd probably fold the clothes as you took them off."

Ben held up his hands to get a word in edgewise. "OK, here is a subtle one. At any point in time, did she giggle?"

Raymond tried to concentrate on his poker hand, but couldn't. "What?"

"Women giggle if they like you. It's the 'giggle factor'," Ben added.

Raymond looked from his son to Ben and then back to Sulie. "Women giggle. It's a fact of life. ... And, no. I don't think she giggled." He then thought for a second and added, "Wait, she may have. I don't remember."

Sulie protested. "I giggle sometimes."

Sterling looked over at his aunt, the woman who raised him as a mother. "No, you don't. You hiss, you sneer, and sometimes when you laugh so hard you snort.

But you don't giggle – at least, not with present company."

Sulie shot her nephew a deadly glance.

"Remember the time she laughed so hard blood came up her nose?" Ben laughed. "That stain on the rug at the bottom of the stairs is still there."

"This proves my point that we need a maid!" Sulie threw up her hands.

Getting back to the original point, Ben took a good look at Raymond's red aura. "It's a fact. Grown women over the age of 30 don't just giggle for the hell of it. They giggle when they like you. She looks about 30. What do you think Raymond?"

Raymond set his cards down in defeat. "She's probably about 30, I don't know. But I don't think she giggled, so it's a moot point. Trust me; I can't really be sure of her feelings right now."

"Wait. You can't read her?" Sulie interrupted.

How did this conversation get so turned around? "I can read her … but, her thoughts are not clear."

"OK, so you're not sure if she likes you or not. But do you like her?" Sterling prodded.

Raymond shrugged. "She's nice, like I said."

Sulie added, "Raymond, if you like her, and she likes you, you should consider asking her out."

"But you can't just date her, Dad. After all, remember your first Corinthians 7:8–9."

Raymond flushed, half in anger and half in embarrassment. "Nobody's getting married. Although it warms my heart to hear you quote passages from the New Testament, Sterling."

"You've Bible–thumped the verses enough around here," Sterling huffed.

Raymond's eyes scanned around the table. "Not that it's anyone's business …" he looked around sheepishly, "… but, even if there was a relationship, which there isn't, it hasn't progressed anywhere near Corinthians 7."

"Yet," Ben whispered.

Raymond was tempted to leave the table, but didn't want to give them the satisfaction. "Besides, I don't know how I feel about her just yet. End of discussion."

Ben leaned closer to Raymond. "Yeah, but what did her hair smell like?"

Raymond closed his eyes, took a deep breath. As his chest slowly expanded and contracted, he quietly said, "Honey almond."

CHAPTER TWENTY–THREE

Alex walked trance–like down the hallway to Dixon's office. She refused to allow her feelings for Raymond to interfere with her accepting the best promotion she had ever been offered.

Her thoughts bounced back and forth as she struggled with her ethics. The adage "You never fish off the company pier," came to mind. The week passed and she meant to ask about the ring on his finger. He claimed to be a widower, so he must be recently widowed if he wasn't ready to remove the ring. Great, she was going to be the new director and Miss Rebound? No. The price wasn't worth the headache to start a relationship.

Speaking of headaches, two of them were walking up to her.

"Can we have a word, Captain?" Brandon asked.

She didn't think she could say 'never' and just run away. "I'm going into a meeting with Dixon right now."

"This will only take a moment," Matt reassured her.

Before she could even say, "Straitjacket for two", she was whisked away to their office. She found herself in the middle of what she would have considered paranoid central if it weren't for the last week of her own world being torn apart.

"Raul Medina was a prisoner down in questioning a week ago. He was involved with some drug smuggling," Matt began.

"That's right. Then Mr. Teal Eyes came in with Mr. Seventies Hair, and things got weird." Brandon unlocked his computer and showed her a video feed.

"This is from the hallway of the interrogation cells. The original video has been erased, but a single frame exists where you can see the two men as they stand at the security check. The man standing with them is Lt. Gallendar. The Lt's name is on the roster followed by two other names, which are fake. At least, we can't find any agents with their names."

"Wait a second," Alex said, looking at the single frame which showed Raymond and the profile of the other man she didn't know, but guessed was a Colony member. She scanned the time stamp, it was just before she was introduced to the Colony. She advanced the video and watched the time stamp jump.

"They're all over the place, but they're also not," Matt said.

Alex put one hand on her mouth to hide her shocked expression. "OK, fast forward."

Brandon clicked on the keyboard and stopped the video once more. "Here is a frame showing the left hand of a man at the door of the Medina's interrogation room. We compared the ring to the ring worn by Mr. Teal Eyes. They match."

Alex took a good look at the ring. It was the one Raymond wore.

"Obviously, these two were entering the room," Matt chimed in.

Brandon slapped his hands together, startling Alex. "And BAM! The time stamp jumps a good five minutes." He paused the video, pointed at the time stamp, and looked at her like the cat that ate the canary.

"And the lieutenant who escorted the two doesn't even remember being anywhere near this room at this time," Matt added.

Alex noticed Brandon rubbing his temple and Matt squinting at the lights. Memory wipes. These two may act like idiots, but they saw, and suspected, a lot more than they should. "Is there any more of this video?"

"They visited two more holding cells. In each case, the video has been tampered with. In one of the rooms, you see their shadows in several of the frames." Matt was about to queue up the other videos when Alex stopped him.

"I have to meet with Dixon. Don't show this to anyone just yet. I'll be back to talk to you about this."

Alex's head swarmed with thoughts as she continued down the corridor to Dixon's office. She needed to warn him of Brandon and Matt's findings. She had already made up her mind; she wanted to know more about vampires and the Colony. She didn't want to be left in the dark like Matt and Brandon.

She was running late now. After just one tap on the closed door, Dixon welcomed her into his office. It surprised her to find another lady, whom she did not know, present. She looked not much more than a child, perhaps eighteen to twenty years old. The woman had a short, professional haircut, which framed her apple–shaped face. She held a coffee mug in one hand, and wore a classic, cream colored tweed, double–breasted, two–piece suit. The long sleeved outfit was fastened with mother–of–pearl buttons for accents. Whoever she was, she had taste.

Alex took a seat next to the woman.

"Have you made a decision?" Dixon asked without introducing the other woman.

"I've decided to accept the position." Alex smiled at Dixon and the woman.

"I'm glad." Dixon gestured over to the woman, "This is Sulie. She is a member of the Colony."

"So nice to meet you, Captain Brennan," Sulie said.

Another vampire. Alex studied the young blond and remembered that Raymond had mentioned his sister's name was Sulie. Of course, there would be females in the group, and good Lord they could pass as human. "Likewise," she said in a cracked voice as she shook the woman's hand. The hand was 'coffee cup' warmed. "Is Sulie going to help with the next step of my orientation?" Alex asked as she turned to face Dixon.

"No. Her services this morning are not needed. She was just leaving." Dixon walked Sulie out the door. Alex noticed a brief pause as Sulie smiled at Dixon and he gave her a slight nod before the door closed.

Once they were alone in the office, Alex asked, "What services?"

"Excuse me?" he said, closing the office door.

"You said her services were no longer needed. What services?"

Dixon cleared his throat. "She was here to wipe your memory if you elected not to take the position."

Alex's face blanched. "I see." Alex felt uneasy as she shifted in her seat. "I suppose I shouldn't be too surprised."

"Don't let the precaution disturb you." Dixon suggested in a reassuring voice.

Alex shook her head. "It's fine. I was told ahead of time what the consequences were." Remembering her conversation with Matt and Brandon, she added, "By the way, Matt and Brandon have some video of Raymond that needs to be addressed."

He reached for his phone. "The process is called a cleanup. I'll text Raymond to come by and talk with the two of them." As he quickly texted he added, "This sort of thing happens a lot with those two."

Alex pursed her lips, understanding what happened during a cleanup. "OK, then. I'm glad I mentioned it."

Taking his seat, Dixon began the briefing. "BTW, your security clearance was confirmed this morning."

Alex smiled knowing exactly what that meant. She had been cleared to talk directly to the President. There was nothing hindering her clearance, but it still was good to know the hurdle had been jumped.

"We have to discuss security measures now that we are alone." Dixon looked grave. "I've known the members of the Colony for decades. All have been working with the government for longer than I've had my career. At no time have any of them ever shown any weakness or signs of treason to this country." He reached into his drawer and pulled out a long thin box. He carefully opened the box and placed its contents in front of Alex. "The members of the Colony can never know about this security measure. Here is a dagger for you to carry with you at all times."

Alex inspected the dagger and admired the beautifully crafted detail. The light from above glinted off the blade and she caught her reflection in it. "And the Colony is not to know I have a dagger?"

"You will be issued your weapons today, but this dagger is for you to carry always. It is to be hidden on your person without their knowledge."

Alex was confused. "They can compel me. How am I supposed to keep a secret from them?"

"All Colony members are required to take an oath not to compel you," Dixon explained. He then took a deep breath. "Actually, the oath doesn't matter because they won't be able to compel you."

She glanced up from the dagger. Her heart skipped a beat. "I'm human," she said in a hushed tone. "Why won't they be able to compel me?"

"As the Director of the team your mind will be altered to not allow any compelling."

Her eyes went wide. "What?"

He took the dagger from her hands. "It sounds worse than it really is. A subroutine, so to speak, will be implanted in your subconscious mind. If any vampire tries to compel you, the subroutine will be triggered. You see, you can be compelled by more than one vampire at a time. But with a subroutine only the one who places it in your mind can ever compel you. This way you'll be safe when you're out in the field."

She crossed her arms in front of her chest. Her eyes narrowed and her jaw locked–in place. "A subroutine. In my mind?"

"It's for your own protection as the director of the team."

Alex thought about the possibilities. "Does this mean the President and the cabinet all have subroutines?"

He shook his head. "No. No member of the Colony is allowed to compel, or alter the mind of the President, the Vice President, the Speaker of the House, and now the Director of Homeland Security."

"So. All other cabinet positions are just up for grabs?" she said defiantly.

Dixon tone grew harsher. "No. Of course not. The Colony Director is the only human to be altered."

"Uh, huh. For my own protection."

"Yes. Like it or not, you are dealing with another species. You, not the President, will be working closely with them. You are the one human that must be the liaison between the President and this team."

Her stance softened. "I see." She took the dagger from Dixon's hand and mindlessly ran her fingers down the hilt. "So the President doesn't actually deal with the team directly."

"He does, if he chooses to do so. The duties vary from president to president, and that is why it is so important the director of the Colony be a human. The last President was too scared to deal directly with them." He pointed to the picture of the President that hung on his wall. "This one likes the team. He doesn't see them as a threat. He actually likes to hang out with Sterling and Ben at times."

"The director is always human then," she stated, letting fact sink in.

"Always."

She played with the dagger, not really focusing on the tiny weapon. "So, this subroutine. What exactly is it?"

"It's a compelling to not be compelled. The only compelling the team is allowed to do to you."

She studied his face. "You …"

He met her gaze. "Yes. Me. All the directors before me. All the directors to come."

Alex remained staring at him. "The procedure is not painful," he added. You won't even feel that it's in place. Raymond will connect with your mind and reprogram your brain so you can't be compelled once it's in place."

She stopped staring and momentarily looked down at the dagger she played with in her hands. "How?" she finally asked.

He shrugged. "How the hell should I know? Raymond is the only one who can do it, or undo it."

Her head jerked back up. "Raymond? Why?"

"He's the only one capable of placing the subroutine. That fact is in his records, which you'll be privileged to."

She hated not knowing, but knew she'd be able to find out. She began playing with the dagger again, careful not to cut herself, as she gathered her thoughts. "Has a vampire ever tried to compel you?"

"Yes." He moved his hand to his temple. "To me it feels like eating ice cream too fast – you get a brain freeze. Some directors say it feels like a sharp headache. You're not compelled though. Either you will hear everything the vampire is saying, you just won't care to follow his commands — or, what they're saying won't make sense to you. The interpretation varies from director to director." He then added, "You can postpone the procedure until I officially retire, but eventually you will need to undergo the procedure. Of course, you could still decline the position."

"No," she said quickly. "I'll still take the job." Now that she knew about vampires, it was nice to know that she could protect herself from being compelled. She felt that she could trust Raymond. "I understand. And, it is reassuring. I think I'll wait then." She held up the dagger, realizing she had been playing with it. "The

151

dagger is for my protection then," she said to change the subject.

"Yes. In case one of them ever goes rogue."

Alex stared in disbelief. "Have there been any team members who have done so?"

"Never."

That was comforting. Alex studied the dagger, understanding its exact purpose. "This is so I can kill a rogue if needed."

"No. Even with your strong physique it's doubtful you'd be able to kill a vampire – at least not without help. It would take a vampire to kill another vampire since they can only die with excessive blood loss. Their bodies are incapable of producing new blood cells, and yet their very lifeline is blood. Did Raymond explain to you their aging process?"

Alex thought back to all the information she received in the past few days. The intel was sizable. "Yes. The more blood consumed the younger they appear."

"Exactly. The less blood they have, the older they appear. If their system has no blood, they age rapidly and turn to dust. So if they were beheaded, they would die due to massive blood loss. Or if they were stabbed in the heart and bled out they would also die."

"What about a gunshot?" she asked.

"No. Bullets are either through–and–throughs or their bodies will expel any logged bullet. They have to bleed out in order to die. That's why it usually takes a vampire to kill a vampire. Humans, as well as half–breeds, don't have the strength to stake a vampire and ensure the stake remains in place until the last drop of blood spills out."

Alex's eyebrow furrowed as she sat for a moment deep in thought. "A captured vampire, subdued somehow, would be vulnerable enough for a human, or half–breed to kill."

Dixon nodded. "True. If you can chain them in silver you would have a chance, especially since silver burns their flesh. But first you'd have to capture them."

Thinking back to an earlier conversation, Alex blurted out, "Or fire."

"What?"

"Fire can kill them as well," Alex explained.

"Yes," he nodded. "But we don't issue you a flamethrower. It's too dangerous of a weapon if civilians are nearby." Dixon pointed to the remaining artifact on the table. "The only alternative is to paralyze them with this." He held up a syringe. "A tranquilizer capable of taking down six charging rhinos. In theory, this shot should paralyze vampires." As Alex reached for the syringe Dixon pulled it away. "This stuff will most likely kill you instantly if you accidentally inject yourself. If you use it against a vampire, it will paralyze them long enough to stake them to the point of their death. Although, it has been untried."

Instinctively Alex pulled her hand back from the syringe of death and watched as Dixon put the syringe away.

The sobriety of the situation sunk in. She handed the dagger back to Dixon. "Do you think all of this is necessary?"

He snapped the box shut. "Nope. Not one bit. My dagger and original syringe have sat in my desk drawer for the last three decades. I never carry them. Well, after the first week I never carried them. Plus I was always afraid that, in the heat of battle, I could accidentally inject the tranquilizer into one of the team members mistaking it for a syringe of blood. I'm only required to give these items to you and prepare you in case you need to use them."

Alex held no qualms about taking a life in combat. And, even though she had only just met Raymond, she didn't like the idea of causing his death, even in the worst of circumstances. "I think I'll be fine. We can leave the box in my desk here at work then."

"That will be off the record. I'm just required to give the weapons to you." He handed her the box. "I have a box, the President, Vice President, Secretary of State, Director of Homeland Security, and now you, all have similar boxes. The President also has a dozen or so letter openers in his office. It isn't because he gets much snail mail. They are daggers hidden in plain sight, but he also agrees there is no danger from the vampires. He gets along just fine with the team." He then added, "Remember, the Colony members cannot know about this talk."

"Of course."

"Now let's drop this box off at your new desk and drive over to requisitions to get your remaining weapons."

CHAPTER TWENTY–FOUR

Alex spent the morning with federal security officials. Retina scans were performed, new picture IDs made, and access codes and files were given to her. Weapons, which included firearms, daggers, and a silver entwined whip, were issued. Now with full security clearance, she reviewed all of the computer files the government held on each member of the Colony as well as operational procedures surrounding them, the mansion in which they lived, and other important factors.

She thought it clever that the Colony had been classified as a private military hospital. She read information about blood deliveries and requisition forms for blood. The vampires lived at Fang Manor for free since it was government owned. Alex chuckled at the nickname as she read through the information. Another file had the security information about the mansion itself, which was very impressive. The place contained a mini-command center with all the bells and whistles, so many in fact that Alex wasn't sure if NASA was as well equipped. The building stood three stories in height (plus a basement) and it also had considerable land acreage.

Alex scanned over another set of files and discovered an entire section on blood and sexual activity. The information noted an increased sexual appetite in the vampires immediately following a feeding of blood. Alex wondered if that was why Raymond shied away from eating in front of her. He had given mixed signals for days and she still didn't know if he was interested in her or not. The files didn't answer her questions; they just perplexed her more. And that angered her, so she helped herself to a glass of wine.

She glanced at the folders and opened the ones for each individual vampire. Over a dozen files existed for each member. She pulled up Raymond's folder first and studied the files. He was born in 1801 ... full transition done by 1828 ... oldest vampire member of the Colony and is the highest ranking senior member ... parents died in a fire ... single parent to son Sterling, also a vampire ... .

Alex jumped ahead and glanced through Sterling's folder for his age. He was born in 1821. So much for Raymond being widowed recently, she thought. She continued reading Raymond's file. "'... older brother to Sulie ... fought in the Civil War ... founding member of the Colony ... vampire sire to Mason Warner.'" So she was right. He had turned someone. Alex wondered why Raymond kept that information a secret. Surely he knew it would be in the files.

A list of aliases for Raymond existed. He owned several different passports and identities, military, CIA, FBI ... at least a dozen different persona were current in the system. A file contained several defunct aliases which dated back over more than a hundred years. The man could literally disappear in a crowd with all his aliases and compelling ability. Of course, that was the idea.

There was no mention of a current wife, fiance, or girlfriend listed for Raymond. At least the files didn't say he had one. Alex sighed. She needed to put Raymond in the do not touch category and get on with her assignment.

156

She noticed not a single picture of Raymond existed in the file except of the images on the IDs themselves. In some of the pictures he appeared as a young man, in others he was quite a bit older. No pictures existed on any IDs before digital photo technology came along. Instead of a picture of Raymond, there was another man's image on those IDs. The compelling ability must prove very helpful in convincing someone the picture was actually who it should be of. The men on the IDs were nowhere near as good looking as Raymond, but then what man would be? He pushed every sexual button Alex had. Sex appeal poured from him like water from a faucet. Probably every woman he met had a similar reaction to him.

She got herself another glass of wine and focused her attention on the files. She discovered that Raymond's work included security with the Departments of the Interior, Treasury, Commerce ... the list went on and included FBI, CIA, even the IRS. Interesting. He functioned as a Federal Jack of all trades. Alex found a file sighting a list of accommodations and awards for the vampire as well.

Impressive. He'd fought in three American wars, took bullets while protecting President Benjamin Harrison, President Calvin Coolidge, and President Ford. What could this man not do?

Alex froze reading the next file of information. It referred to special abilities. Her expectations did not include any of the vampires having super powers. God. Extra sexy and gorgeous wasn't enough? Could the man fly?

She opened the file and read, "'... reading of mental patterns in humans tested at a distance of 40 feet ...

contact not needed to read humans, physical contact for reading vampires required … Thought patterns easily read without the need of touch on some humans … Testing of mental projection not substantiated except within his sister Sulie … can compel humans. Can compel vampires if physically in contact with them …'" The file went on and on.

She gasped. She had held his hand! Not just once but several times. Good Lord, she thought some pretty erotic things of him last night. She read the special abilities again. Did she read that right? "Does not have to be in physical contact to read mental patterns in humans." All she had to be was in the room with him and he might be able to read her mind.

She remembered back to last night as she reclined in her chair. She seduced him over and over in her mind, especially when Raymond looked at her with those dark black eyes. He seemed on board with showing her his eyes, but, damn, could that have just been a reaction to the blood he consumed? Was he reading her mind and thinking she'd be easy to get into bed? Or was he interested in her? Could he have projected those thoughts into her head? Probably not.

She finished her wine, and considered pouring herself another glass but thought it best not to do so. She should remain level headed for her evening. Yes, that would be for the best. Alex knew her threshold was high in terms of alcohol, but didn't want to push the her limits.

Scanning another page of the file, she continued reading about Raymond's mind reading ability. She had spent the entire night lusting after a vampire, and if that wasn't bad enough, he knew it. What was worse, he

158

wasn't even interested! Her face flushed with embarrassment. She lusted for him and as far as she could tell, he may have just been being polite. Damn it.

She then ran across the "No Bite" waiver. "Vampires/Immortals are restricted in biting humans. … Vampires are allowed to bite humans for medicinal purposes when their lives are in jeopardy … or when engaged in consensual sexual activity …" Signed Raymond Metcalf. She guessed there were similar files for all the other members of the Colony.

Alex shook her head. When she asked to see Raymond feed last night, he specifically mentioned that they feed by syringes. If she had offered him her vein, which she was sorely tempted to do, would that be a prelude to sex? OK, her mind did go there and it wanted to camp out … but this paper suggested that he could only bite her if he was dying or engaged in sex.

In the end, it didn't matter anyway. He injected the syringe into his arm and kept his distance from her. But if Sulie hadn't called about an emergency, Raymond might have ended up in her bed. That's where she had wanted the evening to end.

Now that she gave it some thought, she didn't remember the phone ringing. She also didn't remember Raymond talking with Sulie over the phone. Her suspicions of being compelled were confirmed when a slight headache formed. She rubbed her temple. Yup. It was the same feeling as she had before. Maybe Raymond wanted to leave last night before the festivities began. He wanted an out for the evening and gave himself one. And, of course, she had bought it hook, line and sinker.

Plucking petals from a flower with the old "he loves me, he loves me not" was probably a better signal of how Raymond felt than the bits and pieces she was deciphering. The headache worsened and she helped herself to some more wine to wash down some Advil.

She flipped through the other folders and saw similar documents for each member of the Colony. She topped off her wineglass and started reading hours of information on her new team members. She reviewed their super power files so she wouldn't be caught off guard anymore.

*****

Time was not on Alex's side. She was running late and needed to look presentable when Raymond picked her up tonight. She was meeting the rest of the team. She wasn't a vain woman, but she wanted to make a good first impression. She felt like she already knew them all to a certain extent because of the files she had read, but they didn't know her one bit. Showing up looking like death warmed over was not the look she wanted.

She chuckled as she thought about the expression death warmed over. Just a short while ago, she thought Raymond was dead and soulless. Nope. Alive and patriotic seemed a better description. Standing from her desk, she felt dizzy. She took several deep breaths and made as straight of a line to the shower as she could.

After a quick shower, she walked into her closet. What to wear, what to wear? Jeans and button down? A dress? How formal is this going to be? Honestly, what do you wear when you know you're going to meet a

160

group of immortals? Panicking, she picked up the phone and called Dixon.

She dialed his number correctly on the second attempt.

"What should I wear tonight?" she asked when he picked up.

"Just be yourself. Be comfortable. Tonight won't be dressy." After a moment of silence, he added, "It's after hours … think of it as a cocktail party where you will meet the team."

She knew better than to ask a man. "OK. That doesn't help Dixon. I'll see you there later. Bye."

She looked through her closet. Nothing felt right, especially as she remembered what Sulie had worn earlier. She didn't want to be too fancy, but she didn't want to look dressed down either. In fact, after Raymond had probably read her lustful thoughts the other night, and didn't react to them, she decided to put on a dress that didn't look too formal, but looked hot enough so Raymond would know what he was missing. The second part of her plan forbid her to think of anything sexy about him all night. She wasn't sure that was even possible, but she certainly wouldn't want to promote embarrassing thoughts tonight.

She was applying bright red lipstick when Raymond knocked on her door. "Don't think sexy thoughts, don't think sexy thoughts," she reminded herself. "Be aloof and disconnected … and keep him drooling over your body in this dress," she mentally scolded.

161

CHAPTER TWENTY–FIVE

Raymond had offered to drive Alex to Fang Manor for her introduction to the team. He assumed she would have questions about team members now that she had had access to the personnel files. By driving her, it allowed him time to answer them. His plan also had an added benefit. He would have extra time with her during the long ride.

Five knocks sounded on Alex's door before he heard her footsteps approach. Of course, the dogs barked on the first knock. He heard the commands "sit" and "stay" a few times, but finally the door opened. Raymond tried to say hello, but his breath felt taken away. He felt light–headed by her beauty, like he had traveled to a land of perfection with Alex as the Supreme Being.

The dress she wore straddled the borderline of indecent and sexy. It was burning desire red in color — the reserved color of streetwalkers his mother always told him, taboo and to be avoided. It looked inviting tonight with its tight fit that curved Alex's shapely body, including the plunging halter–top bodice. The one thin spaghetti strap, which ran around her neck, strained with the chore of supporting her ample bosom. He looked at her from head to toe, and saw her long legs displayed through a high slit in the form–fitting dress. He blinked a few times before he realized she had asked him a question.

"Am I dressed too fancy?" she asked again as she looked over his blazer and slacks. She then spun around to show him the back.

He murmured a grunt of a reply as his eyes remained glued on her silky, white skin. He managed a whispered, "You look ... lovely." When his eyes finally pulled away from the amazing display of skin, he focused them on her luscious red lips. They were so ruby and plump, almost the same color as the dress. They begged to be kissed.

He realized he stared at her. Christ. He was nearly drooling. "Good evening, Alex," he said in a firmer voice. His lips curled up into a smile as she locked the front door on their way out. "You look lovely tonight," he repeated. Picking up on her mental patterns he noticed her being nervous, but calm. He figured the concern centered more about her outfit than meeting the team members. He escorted her to the car and opened the passenger side door.

"I accepted the directorship for the Colony!" She said, as soon as they sat alone in the car. Her lovely face beamed more radiantly with the smile she now had. Raymond couldn't help but smile back.

Her announcement wasn't exactly a news flash. Raymond received a text earlier that day from both Sulie and Dixon. Still, he liked hearing it from Alex. He realized he wanted to hug her to congratulate her. That would mean touching her ivory colored, silky, smooth skin. He gripped the steering wheel as if it were a life preserver. Damn. He had underestimated her effect on him. He couldn't deny his physical attraction to her.

He read her thought patterns, and found them to be confusing. At times, she appeared emotionally high, like a schoolgirl; at times she became more guarded and putting up walls. It was an odd combination, so he decided to keep his distance for now. It was a shifting–

in–your–seat, uncomfortable car ride back to Fang Manor.

****

Raymond and Alex drove down the two–lane private street which led to Fang Manor. The three story brick house dwarfed the tiny sports car as they pulled up the driveway. A beautiful garden with a fountain stood in the front of the house. The porch traveled along the front side of the home, with chairs and tables for outside use. The home was red brick on all sides, with a chimney sticking out from the top. The sun had set, but the outside lights lit the porch and surrounding areas around the house.

Alex's placed her hand on her mouth as a gasp escaped. "This house is beautiful, Raymond."

Raymond glanced up at the house. "Thanks. The place was built in the fifties. Of course, we've made some modifications, but it's been a great home for us."

She glanced around at the gardens and yard. "Seems like a lot of space."

He parked the car in the garage, and then walked around to open her door. "We built an apartment over the garage. Eventually, we may build a second house. After all, we do have the room to expand," he said as he helped her out of the car.

Next to the Jag sat a Porsche. Alex paused to examine all the cars in the garage. A Ferrari, Maserati, Lamborghini, and a few others were there. She figured without the cost of food and lodging, the team could afford such niceties. Cars had never impressed her too much, but it did look like a private showroom.

164

She walked along the stone path, careful not to trip in the torture devices that passed as her shoes. "What changes have been done?" she asked.

As he spoke, he gestured to the different areas. "We added the sleeping deck on the third floor; converted the bomb shelter under the house into our headquarters, the gardens were extended, a walk in refrigerator for blood storage. ... Just a few changes."

The fresh scent of roses from the garden lingered in the evening air and she inhaled the fragrance deeply. "Sounds like a lot of work," she said as she stumbled on one of the garden stones. Raymond grabbed her by her tiny waist and prevented her fall. She placed her hands on his strong arms as she steadied herself. The high spikes of her shoe took a scuff or two during the spill, but survived. She took a deep breath as she poised herself on them. The shoes hurt her feet, but sometimes a good shoe can make even your ass look incredible. With the tightness of this dress, she felt as though her ass needed all the help it could get.

"Your bio readings were uploaded this afternoon." Raymond gestured for her to unlock the security settings on the door. Once her retina scan, fingerprint scan, and voice commands were recognized, she punched in the security number. The clicks of the alarm sounded disabling the device. "The doors of the house are always locked."

She nodded. "I wonder if this type of system will ever be available commercially." The door opened and something unpleasant smelling hit her nose. They walked into the kitchen and witnessed something as it nearly boiled over on the stove. Alex recognized the woman who stood in an apron before the messy pot. It

165

was odd to see someone wearing an apron over an elegant beige sequin vest pantsuit, with golden accent and scarf. A smile crossed Alex's face as she realized she had dressed appropriately. "Hello Sulie," she said as she entered.

Raymond leaned in and whispered in Alex's ear, "Watch out. My sister is a hugger."

"Captain Brennan! How wonderful to see you again. Please do come in." Sulie placed the wooden spoon she held on the counter. Walking with arms held out to give Alex a hug she muttered, "Be nice Raymond. Hugging is just a hello with your arms."

OK, the hug was a bit too familiar for Alex. She usually did not hug near perfect strangers, but there was something about Sulie that was so calm and friendly. Alex looked to see if perhaps Ben and his mood–altering abilities were afoot, but he was nowhere to be seen. Alex awkwardly returned the hug. "Thank you."

Keeping Alex's hands in hers, Sulie took a step back. "My, what a lovely dress." Glancing over at Raymond she added, "And such a bold color."

"Thank you, Sulie." Alex returned the compliment, "Your outfit is lovely as well."

Raymond walked over to a small bookshelf. Alex watched as he removed his shoes and set them on the top–shelf. She then looked at Sulie's footwear and noticed house slippers.

"If you don't mind, Alex. We don't wear shoes in the house," Sulie explained.

"Except for the kitchen," Raymond commented as he put on his own pair of slippers. "We do this for my son and his reaction to allergens." As he walked to the corner of the room and turned on the air purifier, he added, "There are guest slippers for you to wear."

So much for her ass looking good, but at least it she got a reprieve from the attack of the killer shoes. "Of course I don't mind." She selected a black pair that looked to be her size and then said to Sulie, "You have a lovely home ... and please call me Alex." She placed her purse on an empty counter in the sparse kitchen. Aside from the several different coffeemakers and an air purifier, she didn't see any other appliances. The only items out, other than what rested on the stove, was a bowl filled with avocados and a fork Sulie was holding to mash them.

"Let me get you a goblet of wine." Sulie fetched a goblet from the cabinet. "Here, I'll put this little metal tassel around the base of your wine goblet so you won't confuse it with someone else's."

"I'll go round up the others." Raymond left. Alex figured he was giving her a chance to talk with Sule and get to know her better.

Alex stared at the glass of wine. How much wine had she had earlier? If she had to ask herself that question, then she should say no to wine right now. But, as Sulie held out the glass to her, Alex accepted the goblet. "Thank you, Sulie. I'll keep the tassel in mind. I don't want to accidentally drink blood tonight. I mean, I don't mind if you and the others do, I'm sure it's delicious to you ..." Alex watched Sulie drink the blood from the goblet as she busily made guacamole dip.

"Don't be so nervous, Alex. We rarely bite." Sulie said.

Alex decided to take that as a joke. Overall, the woman seemed harmless, but Alex had read the dossier on Sulie. She was a trained killer, and looked the part now that she held a sharp kitchen knife in her hand. "Can I ask you something before Raymond gets back?" Alex asked.

"Sure. Anything." Sulie said as she cut open another avocado and tossed the pulp into the bowl.

Alex paused to gather her thoughts. She then remembered what she wanted to ask. "I watched Raymond feed last night …"

Sulie stopped mashing the avocados and looked up at Alex. "He fed in front of you?"

"Yes. I read there can be an effect, but you're drinking blood right now and it's not affecting you the same way. At least I don't think it is."

Sulie laughed. "I should hope not. You see, we have to drink blood to sustain our life."

Alex nodded. "Yes. I understand."

Sulie stopped mashing and looked at Alex. "Did Raymond explain that the more often we feed the younger we are?"

Alex nodded as she sipped her wine.

"And you know of the orgasmic pleasure we can get from drinking the blood." Sulie smiled.

Alex bit her lip. "Yes. I read something to that effect." This was the confirmation Alex needed. The blood explained Raymond's yo–yo like affection to her over the last week.

"You see, I'm not married. No live–in mate either. Many of us are single. If we graze all–day, the sensual effects are dulled. However, if we eat meals a couple times a day we have the blood's full affect and we get exceedingly aroused." She smiled when she added, "It's when we skip meals and then feast when you have to watch out for us."

Alex's eyes widened in surprise. She stared at the goblet. "Really?"

Sulie waved her hands dismissively. "Don't worry. The government keeps us well fed. You must have been told of our blood shipments."

"Yes. I read about them." Alex still wanted more information. She took a sip of wine and then blurted out, "Raymond told me he is a widower."

Sulie cut fresh tomatoes for the guacamole. "Yes. Even for a vampire it was a long time ago."

"I figured that much." Alex lifted her arm and waved the fingers of her left hand. "What about the ring he wears?"

Sulie wiped her hands on her apron. "He's never taken off his wedding ring." She opened the refrigerator and pulled out the salsa and added it to the mixture. She offered Alex a chip from a bowl on the counter. "Can you taste this?"

The guacamole looked odd but Alex politely tasted the mixture. It wasn't the worst, but it wasn't good either. She obligingly said, "The dip has an interesting flavor."

"It could be the soy sauce. I was out of lemons, so I substituted."

Her lips pursed as she suppressed a grimace. "That explains the taste." Alex took a large gulp of her wine to flush the food from her mouth. "So Raymond isn't married, shouldn't he sip on blood all–day too? Or does he have a girlfriend?" She bit her lip hoping there wasn't a girlfriend.

"No girlfriend. It's just that he can't be so obvious out in the field. He's too busy and in too much of the public eye to be sipping blood all–day long. Plus, it depends on how old his alias is as to how much blood he needs to consume. Raymond just began a new alias, so he drinks often right now. Sterling has other outlets and prefers the human vein. Same with Ben."

Alex could feel her heart skip a beat. 'Human vein'. Humans existed as food to these people. Of course, she knew that fact going into this den of vampires, but it was a reality check nonetheless.

The slight pause from Sulie caused Alex to wonder if the woman could somehow sense her fright. Sulie smiled and then continued, "Mason and Daniel drink rarely right now and blood lust isn't a big deal for them. William and Jackie are married, so they feed together and keep it under control."

Some deep breaths drove the fright from Alex. Then curiosity took over. "I don't know how to ask this, so I'm going to spit it out. If you sip blood all–day long does that mean you never have certain needs … or, ah, desires?"

Sulie chuckled. "Grazing doesn't block the need. I just don't get crazy when I drink blood. I can control the need. I think the boys have problems controlling the lust at times."

Alex figured Raymond may have eventually made a play for her last night, until Sulie had called him away on an emergency. "They get carried away? How so?"

"Part of our security agreement with the federal government states we can't bring guests into this house, so even with Sterling and Ben's female interests, at least

170

they take the women elsewhere. Let's just say, it's a lot of women."

Alex thought on that last statement, *'a lot of women'.* All the men? Or only Ben and Sterling? Alex had worked with many male co–workers in the past, but was never privy to their personal bedroom business. The topic didn't embarrass her, but it did cause a blush to cross her cheeks.

Sulie had already started to open a second bag of chips when Alex decided to change the topic. It wasn't her place to ask for a head count on the revolving door of these peoples' love lives, so she asked about the home's furnishings and antiques instead. Raymond had been right about Sulie's fondness for antiques. Alex was soon being regaled by Sulie about which items in the kitchen were from which time periods, which ones had interesting stories behind them, and so forth.

****

Alex wasn't much into antiques, and was happy when Raymond returned to the kitchen. "I've rounded the group up. They're excited to meet you Alex."

The three entered the large living room and she saw all the members of the Colony sitting or standing around. Their massive bodies dwarfed the furnishings. Raymond put his arm around Alex's shoulder as he walked her over to the member standing closest to them. "You remember Ben from the other day."

A visible double take was done by Alex as she narrowed her brow and took a closer look at the man. The vampire looked like Ben, but not quite. She thought, surely she hadn't drank that much wine.

171

"I've adjusted my age since you last saw me." He smiled at her as she continued to examine his face.

"Nice to see you again, Ben. You look so much younger … I wouldn't have recognized you." He now wore his jet–black hair in a slightly longer Afro. A youthful glow now replaced the wrinkles of his face. Even his outfit, jeans and a sports coat, seemed a younger man's attire. As she stared at his face, she added, "I mean, it's obviously you, but you look a good twenty years younger."

Ben smiled. "My alias ran its course. Dixon assigned a new one to me so now my name is 'Ben Preston'."

Seeing the change of age amazed Alex. If they could bottle and sell this to humans, they'd make a mint. "Your last alias was mid fifties or so?"

He nodded. "About that, yes."

Alex tilted her head and studied the man's profile. "But your alias could have lasted until retirement. Why cancel it a good fifteen to twenty years early?"

Raymond quickly offered an explanation. "Sometimes a human will suspect something odd about the alias, sometimes humans become immune to compelling and it compromises the alias … there are many reasons an alias will be terminated early."

Ben rolled his eyes and then glanced over at Alex. "I swam in the company pool one time too often. I couldn't perform a memory wipe on my supervisor anymore, and she was beginning to remember my late night snacks on her."

Alex's eyes widened and her jaw fell.

"Delicately put, Mr. Preston," Raymond chided as he put his hand on Alex's shoulder.

172

"It's fine," Alex reassured both the men. "I'm not a porcelain doll … or any doll for that matter. Besides, … this type of predicament is now my job." Alex took note of Raymond's attempt to be sensitive on a delicate matter. A bit old fashioned perhaps, but a sign of something, but of what? Was he protective of her? Was he belittling her? It was hard to determine — especially when he looked so damn hot and sexy. She mentally played the he likes me, he likes me not game to decide Raymond's feelings for her. If he put his arm around her, score one point for liking her. If the hand never travels south, take away the point. She mentally devised a point system and planned to check the score periodically throughout the night.

When Ben left the two of them alone, she focused her thoughts on Raymond and his current age. His hair had some slight gray in it, which made him look about 30 years of age. She wondered when he fed last. She wanted to test a theory, and didn't mind using him as the specimen.

She had read that vamp skin temperature is always cold, which she did feel the other day when she touched his hand. Fresh blood would circulate faster in their system and make their body temperature warm to the touch. All she had to do was touch him. She took another sip of her wine. Would it be horribly unprofessional if she held his hand? Well, since it was for an experiment in their body warmth, she figured it would be okay.

She deliberately rubbed her hand against his and found that it was indeed cool to the touch. Naturally his extremities would probably cool off the fastest. A better test would be to touch his chest, or perhaps his

173

magnificent abs. The white button down shirt would be easy enough to unbutton and slide her hand inside. Would he have hair on his chest? How well–defined were his abs? Were they six–pack firm?

She caught herself. Just like her New Year's Resolutions, her promise to not think sexy thoughts sure didn't last long. She replaced the sexy image in her mind to a body covered in an itchy rash and boils.

Touching his hand was a guilty pleasure she shouldn't have done, especially since he could read her thoughts. Of course, now she was practically holding his hand and giving him signals. She felt like she was losing the 'he likes me' game, and she was the only one playing.

Raymond responded to the touch by gently massaging her fingers with his thumb. It felt nice, and she added five points to her tally to him liking her. His skin felt smooth and inviting. She decided to give his hand a squeeze, and he squeezed her hand back. He gave a gentle tug and led her across the room.

"Alex, this is my son, Sterling."

Before Alex could stop it, a chuckle escaped her lips. This was "Mr. Seventies Haircut" from the videotape, and his hair was right out of the past – and near picture–perfect. The style did suit him though. Alex expected Raymond's son to be a mini–version of him, but Sterling looked nothing like his father. Sterling's hair resembled Shaun Cassidy's hair circa 1976. Sterling's skin was darker than Raymond's too, like an evenly covered tan. Could vampires sunbathe? Raymond certainly didn't prefer to be in the sun, but that didn't mean they couldn't have a tan. Sterling stood slightly shorter than the other vampires and Alex remembered Dixon's

174

comments about half–breeds not having all the same physical qualities of purebreds and full vampires.

Alex noticed Sterling give his father a look of amusement, followed by him moving his lips, but no sound escaping. She looked over towards Raymond and noticed his lips moving as well.

Sterling then turned and noticed her presence. "It's so nice to finally meet you, Alex. My father couldn't say enough nice things about you."

"That's very kind of him," she said looking over at Raymond. She wondered what he had said, and held out her hand to shake Sterling's.

Sterling smiled at his father and then added, "I must say, you are far more attractive than my father had led me to believe." Sterling reached for Alex's extended hand, brought it to his lips and kissed her in a gentleman's greeting.

Alex felt Raymond's hand move to her waist and tighten in what she would consider a protective manner. Yes, more points were added to her tally, but she wondered what was behind Sterling's comment and their private conversation.

"Lovely. But not my type," Sterling announced. He looked at his father, eyebrows raised. Raymond tightened his grip on her waist and Alex noticed Sterling's mouth twist into a smirk and his head nod.

Alex listened to the silence that followed. Raymond appeared angry with his son. "I'm not sure what all is going on ..." she said.

Sterling interrupted. "Oh, don't worry. I'm sure you're someone's type." He stressed the word someone and glanced over at his father.

"I'm sorry. I'm not following." Alex had read about this ability between vampires. They could speak at a high–pitched level. "You're doing that secret vampire whisper thing I read about. If it wasn't so fascinating, I'd be royally pissed," she said with a slight giggle.

Sterling's grin deepened into an all out smile from ear–to–ear as he looked over to his father.

After a long pause, Alex asked Sterling, "You look much older than your father. Do you prefer to be an older age or is it just your alias?"

Sterling shook his head and his 70s style mane glided over his shoulders. "No. My alias is in the mid thirties. I can adjust my age to be in my late twenties, but no younger. Our fangs come in during our early to mid twenties. Just like humans with their wisdom teeth, but your teeth come in during your late teens. The youngest we can look is the age we were when our fangs could completely extend and feed us on their own. My fangs came in when I was 28 years old, so the youngest I can appear is 28."

"My fangs fully extended at the age of 22." Raymond explained. "I can look as young as that."

Alex turned towards Sterling. "Why did your fangs come in so much later?"

Sterling shot a look at his father. "I have my human mother to thank for that. Half–breeds mature later."

Alex noticed Raymond rolled his eyes to the term half–breed. She looked between the two. Certainly there were similarities, but the two were quite different in appearance. "You must take after your mother."

"I look exactly like her, or so I'm told." Sterling's attention shifted over to his father. "My father has a

176

portrait of her. Maybe he'll give you a tour of the house, which would include his bed-chamber."

As Alex admired the word choices which gave her a hint as to their true ages, she heard Raymond clear his throat. She watched as their mouths moved, but no sound came out once again. Of course, Raymond had the decency to cover his mouth in an attempt to hide his rudeness, but Sterling evidently had no issue with offending her. An awkward quiet surrounded them as the two men squared off at each other.

She was going to give them one more minute, and then scream. She took in a deep breath. "Your Aunt Sulie has an elliptic …," Alex caught herself, "… I mean, eclectic taste when it comes to antiques," Alex said to change the subject. "She said you finalize all purchases for the house."

Sterling stopped the private conversation with his father and looked over at Alex. "Yes. I prefer to shop at outlet stores and get new belongings, but Sulie loves her antiques. I always try to approve all purchases because I like for her to buy objects that don't have personal signatures if she can. If they do have signatures I like them to be benevolent ones."

Alex had read Sterling's profile and his ability to sense feelings and images from intimate objects. "How does your ability work?"

Sterling took a breath and explained. "When I touch an object there is always a shadow left on it from its previous or current owner. It's a signature shadow. The more personal the object, the stronger the signature is. Sometimes I can touch a person's skin and get readings as well." Showing his gloved hands, he added "I wear gloves and long sleeved shirts and pants so I can touch

177

objects as little as possible." He lifted an eyebrow and gestured at his hand. "If you'd like for me to touch a personal object you may be wearing, I could show you my special ability. Of course, the more personal the better."

At that remark, her chin hit the floor far faster than her eyebrow raised into her hairline. She even thought she heard a slight growl from Raymond.

"No, thanks. I'm good," she said. Alex took a deep breath remembering something about Sterling's preoccupation with women from his files. So much for changing the subject to a light and pleasant one. She sipped her wine and began again. "Sulie told me the story of some candlesticks she wanted to buy, but you sensed they had been used in a murder. That's fascinating. I can see why you wouldn't want objects like that around."

Sterling snickered under his breath and his face flushed as he looked from Alex to his father. "Heh. OK. I'm not too proud of that one. And you can't tell Sulie this, but I lied about the murder story on those candlesticks."

"Why would you do such a thing? She wanted them for the dining room table," Raymond asked.

"Oh, I know she did, Dad. I just had to tell her something so she wouldn't buy them. Those candlesticks were too damn hideous to buy."

"How manipulative of you, Sterling," Raymond chided.

He shrugged his shoulders, "Hey, better than hurting her feelings." He glanced down at his now empty bottle of beer, and decided it was time for a new one. On his way to the kitchen he warned his father, "Honesty is not always the best policy. Sometimes little white lies can smooth out delicate situations."

****

Alex felt a tug on her shoulder as Raymond guided her towards another team member. This man wore a white t–shirt with a big yellow happy face smile. The smiley face had a gunshot hole in his head, and his eyes were x's. His torn blue jeans finished the ensemble. He looked odd next to the woman standing next to him. She was stunning in a Michelle Obama put together way. She wore a Pepto Bismol pink two–piece suit, and it looked incredible on her, even in its extended maternity state.

"This is William and his wife Jackie. Over there on the couch, digging into the doughnuts, are their children Sinclair and Nicole. … This is Alex, our new director."

"Nice to meet you." Alex glanced at the children. She thought back to the guacamole and figured these kids probably had the right idea. She shook William and Jackie's hands. "My, two beautiful children and another one on the way. You must be so excited."

"Thank you. We are." Jackie said.

Alex chatted with the couple and realized how incredibly human and normal they seemed. Actually, the two of them were very lovey dovey and Alex felt as though she was stuck in a mush pit.

After a few minutes of discussing the needs of vampire children and pregnant vampires to consume human food, Jackie looked over to her children. "Damn. The kids call him Uncle Dix. As hard as it will be for us to let the man go, it'll be harder on them." She directed her next question to her husband. "What's going to happen to Dixon?"

"The man will be fine. Sure, some marbles will be jumbled. He won't remember us, the kids, or working with our group, but he'll remember he had a military career and a good life. We'll relocate him to a nice spot, maybe out in the country, where he can live out the rest of his days."

Jackie glared at her husband. "Baby, we used that excuse on the kids when the dog died. They didn't believe us then either." She started crying. "I loved that dog." William put his arms around her to calm her down. He mouthed the word "hormones" to Alex.

Alex had learned more about vampire children and pregnant vampires, and their food needs, in just a few minutes talking with Jackie than in anything she had read. She found it fascinating, and could have talked for hours. Raymond had already walked away to talk with other team members, and now with Jackie crying, Alex excused herself to mingle as well.

CHAPTER TWENTY–SIX

Alex found her wineglass sitting on the coffee table. Thanks to the little tassel, she recognized it as hers, but she still sniffed at contents to be sure. She took a sip of her wine and enjoyed that it remained chilled. The sweet taste coated her throat. Scanning the room, she noticed Dixon had finally arrived. He came fashionably late and wearing jeans. Men! How hard would it have been for him to tell her this was a casual affair? His denim blue button down shirt wasn't even tucked in.

Sulie seemed to the unofficial hostess of the party. She brought out trays of different types of food, but nothing appealed to Alex. Another member of the team helped Sulie to serve. From the team folders, Alex recognized the vampire as Daniel, a turned human who had joined the group only a few decades ago. He appeared older than the other members of the Colony. While reading his file, Alex took note of the fact there were no past aliases listed for the man. Now seeing his fully gray hair and beard, age spots on his arms, and the wrinkles in his face, she understood why. This tall, lean vampire was still living his first life. She decided to walk over and introduce herself.

"This is hot," Daniel said in a slight British accent. He walked past her and placed the pie on the trivet on the table. It smelled like apple–pie that had been heavily seasoned with cinnamon. "You must be Captain Brennan," he said, holding out his hand.

"Nice to meet you. Please call me Alex," she said as she shook his hand. She watched as his cool blue eyes looked again at his hand. She remembered from his file that he had two sires, Sterling and Raymond. He had once been human. She couldn't stop herself from asking. "So tell me, Daniel, you were turned by Sterling and Raymond?"

He stared down at her from his tall 6–foot 2–inch frame, his cool blue eyes looking as calm as a glacial lake. "That's right. I'm the same age as Dixon, the man you're replacing."

Overall, he looked like a typical history or philosophy professor in his blue button down shirt and khaki pants. His mannerisms, sense of style, and composure were so opposite of Sterling's that she never would have put the two together. "Why do you have two sires? I thought it was a one–to–one relationship."

His cool blue eyes now lacked their luster, and the corners of his mouth turned down. "I don't like discussing the day I died, Captain. Let's just say, I made the most of a bad situation."

Her mouth fell slightly open; a tiny gasp escaped her lips. She had never thought of how personal the experience would be, and it wouldn't necessarily be a pleasant experience. "Sorry. I didn't mean to offend you. I was only curious."

"Perhaps Mason can quench your curiosity," he said dryly. "He was also turned."

She pursed her lips and nodded in understanding. "I didn't mean to be rude." She lifted her wineglass and took a big gulp, finishing her drink.

"Let me collect your empties for you, Alex." He took the glass from her hands before she could say no, or even before she could thank him, and returned to the kitchen. Probably making a hasty retreat from the prying new director.

182

Standing alone, she mentally chastised herself for her lack of common decency. Vampire etiquette. She'd have to write some notes so the next director wouldn't be so confused when she retired. Maybe Dixon had such a book. She then shook her head. Mr. Denim Jeans at a cocktail party probably wouldn't have such a thing.

Looking around the room she didn't see Dixon, but did notice all the lovely antiques once again. The style of the room was eclectic with pieces ranging from what Alex assumed was turn of the century to modern day. The window dressings, wall coverings and kick–knacks all looked old, but it wasn't like she was an Antique Road Show expert, so she had no clue about their origin. The furniture looked more modern, as were the air purifiers she noticed each room had. Bigger and sturdier furnishings filled the room. Of course with the frame size of all the vampires, you would need bulkier furniture.

The lighting was darker than Alex preferred, but she assumed that was because of their exceptional eyesight and ability to see well in the dark. She liked the decor, everything from the lace curtains to the black leather sofa. The exterior wall of the room had a large, stunning fireplace. It was built with stone bricks, not masonry bricks. It appeared more rustic and homey in her mind, plus the hearth was large enough to offer two seats close up to the fire.

"Here Alex," Dixon said, walking up to her and offering her a plate of food.

Now that she didn't hold her wineglass, the plate gave her hands something to do. "Thanks, Dixon." A small grimace crossed her face as she sniffed the food on the plate. The smell wasn't too bad, but she had to guess the brown stuff was hummus. She watched as Dixon ate some off his plate, and even made a satisfying noise like he liked the food. Alex ventured a try. It had a hummus texture, but tasted more like what she suspected gourmet dog food would be like.

"By the way, I was thinking that any notes you may have taken …" Alex began, but was quickly cut short when Dixon told her she had to try a dish called Matador Mania and he left to find her some. Standing alone, she took the opportunity to set her plate down and to take pity on the man for being a bachelor and liking Sulie's cooking.

As Dixon walked into the kitchen, he passed Sterling coming out of it. Sterling's shoulder length, feathered blond hair brushed across his face as he walked towards her. "Here, Alex," he said, handing her a glass of wine. "I believe this tasseled one is yours."

She thought back to the information she read in his file. Playboy. She noticed his seductive smile and the glint in his eyes. Did women really fall for the retro look? Overall he was a good–looking man, … er, vampire, but the look was not a turn–on for her.

His smile widened and showed his fangs. He lifted the wineglass he offered slightly into the air. "Is there something other than this wine you want, Alex?"

She stifled a snicker. Perhaps if she hadn't read of his sexual escapades from his file, his charm may have worked — maybe. Right now he looked transparent. She took the offered glass. She sniffed the offering to confirm it wasn't blood, then took a big gulp of wine to get the dog food taste out of her mouth. "Thanks for the wine."

His eyes studied her, and she felt uneasy.

"I think I offended Daniel," she confessed in a low whisper to give them something to talk about. She then shook her head and corrected herself. "I know I offended him." She took another sip of her wine.

He took a step back and Alex wondered if his new physical stance meant a surrender in terms of playing her.

"How so?" Sterling asked.

She sighed. "I asked about his turning." Alex watched as Sterling's look turned stone cold. She narrowed her brow as she studied the vampire. She may be in his lair, but she wasn't a damsel in distress, and there were answers she wanted. "I'm so new to this entire vampire thing. It's so fascinating to me."

Sterling glanced away, as if surveying the room. "Well, we have purebreds, half–breeds and full vampires in this house. I'm sure Daniel didn't take offense." He then mumbled under his breath, "Hell, you could kill the man and he wouldn't be offended."

She seized the opportunity. "You were the one who turned him. How did it happen?"

He turned his head, looked her straight in the eyes, and said, "That's not my story to share." He took the last sip of his beer. "I'm empty. You need a refill?"

Looking down at the nearly full goblet she said, "I'm good for now."

****

Alex walked over to the fireplace hearth to warm herself. That's when she noticed that Dixon had gathered more food on two plates. She suspected one of the plates was going to be hers. She patted her growling stomach. She was hungry, but there wasn't much of

185

anything here to eat. She found a bowl of tortilla chips and some salsa and nibbled on what she thought was the last of the edible food in the house. At this point in time, the guacamole even began to taste good.

She looked over at Dixon once again. How could he have worked so closely with these people for so long? Secrets definitely lurked about that were not documented. Alex wondered if the man knew the answers, if he didn't care to know them, or if he remained oblivious to them.

Just then, she noticed that Raymond pulled Dixon aside and started talking to him. She wondered if their conversation was information about a case, or perhaps another secret. She didn't want to interrupt. Well, that wasn't true. She didn't want to appear pushy on her first day on the job, so she remained where she was, wishing she had the super hearing vampires had. She watched as Dixon's hopeful expression turned to a saddened one. After a few minutes, Dixon nodded and walked away from Raymond, leaving the plates of food on the table. Alex noticed a look of disappointment from Dixon – like he had just been told that Santa didn't exist. She suspected the conversation was probably on the topic of his retirement. Of course, the men would be sad to say good–bye to each other. After all, they had worked together for decades.

Raymond approached Alex as she continued pretending to admire the fireplace. In truth, she was using her hand on the mantle to steady herself. Hopefully he had not noticed her trying to eavesdrop on his conversation. She took a sip of her wine and told herself to be more professional. After all, this was an official team meeting.

His expression changed from a saddened one to smiling at her as he approached. "We enjoy having a fire here during the winter months." He continued smiling at her as she sipped her wine. "We have no body heat." He offered her his hand and she held it. He slid his thumb back and forth across her hand, his skin temperature picking up her warmth. "The heat of the fireplace can warm us, just like your hand is warming my hand right now."

She cleared her throat and closed the gap between the two of them. "You like feeling warm. Don't you?"

"Oh, yes." He continued stroking her hand.

She took a sip of her wine. She pointed across the room. "What were you and Dixon discussing?"

Raymond glanced over at Dixon and cleared his throat. "His retirement plans. He was hoping for a specific opportunity and, unfortunately, it isn't available."

Alex picked up on his saddened tone. "That's too bad. I hope it doesn't interfere with him enjoying his retirement."

Raymond looked away from her. "I'm sure he'll enjoy the twenty or thirty years he has left."

She felt like another secret was in place, but still placed her arm on his shoulder to comfort him. Obviously the two were close. "I am sorry he's leaving." She sighed, "I am grateful for the promotion, but I know I have some pretty big shoes to fill." She stroked his back and leaned slightly in toward him. "Do you want to talk about it?" she asked.

Without hesitation, he said, "No."

She didn't like secrets, but, after having offended one vampire tonight, she decided not to offend a second

– especially not Raymond. She dropped her hand from his back. "OK," she said.

He grabbed her hand and leaned into her. His breath caressed her cheek, "Thanks for understanding." His hand touched her face, "I will miss him, but I am looking forward to working with the new director."

She glanced down at his moist lips, and then licked her own. The light from the fireplace cast a warm glow across his strong muscular jaw. She took a breath, and waited for his kiss, but he pulled away abruptly, removing his hands from her face. He turned from her and faced the kitchen the exact moment his sister walked through to the living room.

"Yes, Sulie," Raymond said.

"Oh, there you are. I've been looking for you."

He straightened his stance, crossed his arms, and became stoic. "Yes. I heard you calling, but I was busy talking with Alex."

Alex turned slightly away and ran her hand through her hair. What was she doing? Kissing a team member was bad enough, but to kiss him in front of other team members? Exactly how unprofessional did she want to be tonight? Looking over at Raymond she decided she didn't care. He was all sex wrapped together in a handsome vampire, tight body. She felt embarrassed, as though his sister just caught them in bed together, and they hadn't done anything yet. Yet. Now wasn't that the operative word here?

Sulie looked between the two of them. "I thought Alex would like a tour of Fang Manor."

Both vampires looked over to Alex, as if waiting her answer. The moment with Raymond had already been spoiled, so she said, "That would be nice."

Sulie stared at Raymond. "The house is big, so you and Raymond take your time."

****

The tour was just finishing when Raymond saw Sterling leaving by the front door. He excused himself and followed his son outside. "Sterling, where are you going?"

Sterling rolled his eyes. "Out".

"I thought you'd stay and get to know Alex a little more. After all, she is our new director."

"I did meet her. Remember, right over there in the living room we had an awkward moment together when we first met when your arms were around her; we bonded over my lie of a fake murder story. I think we're good."

"It's early. Stay."

Sterling took in a deep breath, as if anger were building inside. "I don't like it when we talk about my sex life. You can only imagine how weird it is to talk about yours, so I'm only going to say this once." Sterling looked his father squarely in the eyes. "I don't fish off the company pier, but if you want to dabble with our new boss, so be it. But I'll tell you what, this acorn sure didn't fall far from the tree."

Raymond could taste the fury in his throat. He fought back the bitter taste. "I wasn't going to tell you this," Sterling said, getting his father's full attention. "You claim you just met her this past week, but she's known you a whole hell of a lot longer."

"Impossible," Raymond challenged. "We met the other day in Dixon's office."

189

"Regardless. She has known you for months. It explains why a career professional woman, suddenly, is flirting like a little slut in front of her new team."

Raymond furrowed his brow, and did his best to ignore the last remark. "How does she know me? We just met."

Sterling smiled. "You really don't know, do you?"

Raymond's anger bubbled inside once again. His hands balled into fists. "Spit it out, Sterling!"

"Usually a human's mind doesn't notice us. We're predators; we slip into the background and fade away. But that didn't happen with her. Her subconscious mind remembers seeing you for months, possibly years."

"That's not possible. I never spoke with her before this past week."

"Maybe you're a little too hard to forget. Nonetheless, the psychic echo is there. But it's even worse than that. When I met her and shook her hand, I read her skin."

Raymond raised his voice, "You are not allowed to touch the director like that."

"She isn't the director until Dixon officially retires, so until then I can fuck with her mind all I want."

Raymond's slammed his son back into the wall. "Never again. Do you understand me?"

The wall gave way to Sterling's smaller frame, and cracks appeared in the brick. Sterling tried to brush his father's hands off him. "Be glad I read her this time, old man. Her subconscious mind even has a name for you. Seeing how you've been staring in all of her wet dreams for months, it's only fitting that she's has given you a porn star name."

Raymond's eyes widened as he let go of his son.

"Oh, yes. Go ask her who 'Butch Manly' is, father. I'm sure all the blood will not only rush to her face in embarrassment, but she'll be flushed elsewhere as well."

Raymond took a step back. "I never touched her mind like that. I swear."

"Obviously you didn't need to. Since you're so out of practice touching a woman in any way, I think she may as well just dream about 'Butch' in your stead. She probably would be more satisfied doing so." Sterling took a good look at his father. "Honestly, here you are hoping for a first date, and emotionally she is on date fifty. Since women tend to sleep with men on the first date, at least in my experience, I'm guessing that she not only has names picked out for your children, I'm betting she has names for your grandkids as well."

Raymond blinked, and then continued to stare at his son.

"Toss on the amount of wine she's put away tonight, and I can't even begin to tell you how entertaining it has been watching the floor show. She doesn't even know how inappropriate she's been behaving. I got to say, everyone thought it was odd until I explained it to them."

Raymond's eyes narrowed in anger. Gritting his teeth, he asked, "Everyone has been making fun of her all–night?"

He watched as Sterling looked through the window in the living room. "Oh, please. Sulie had found every possible angle to get the two of you alone; the woman's nearly giddy with joy. Ben has been adjusting Alex's aura so she wouldn't undress you in the living room. Jackie and William find it charming, which, to me, is nauseating. Daniel kept taking her wine goblet away

191

every time she set it down. Moot point though, seeing how I kept refilling it and handing it back to her. Only Dixon was appalled. He kept trying to get her to eat Sulie's nasty food all night."

Raymond looked through the window at the team members. "Sounds to me like you were the only one not helping the situation."

"Trust me. Getting women liquored up is always a big help." He took a step away from the window and looked at his father. "What I don't understand, is why a man who is as celibate as the Pope would be so willing to hit the sheets so quickly." He held up his hand, "I mean, I can understand the physical need to tear into some female flesh before Mount Vesuvius explodes in your pants, but it isn't like you're the wham, bam, thank–you ma'am type of guy. So why are you in such a hurry with this one, when no other woman in your dry spell ever made you hot and sweaty?"

Raymond sighed and looked at his son, the oddest person in the world he would consider an ally in any discussions of romance. "When you meet someone special, you just know it. In less than two months, I had met your mother, gotten her pregnant, and we were man and wife."

Sterling tilted his head, his mind obviously twisting around past known facts. "Wait, you and mom were married a year before she got pregnant. What's the real truth?"

Raymond cleared his throat and said sheepishly, "It was the 1800s; you were too big to pass off as a premature baby. Your mother was dead. The least I could do was to give her the dignity of a proper timeline."

192

Sterling shook his head and huffed. "I can see how you would find that totally acceptable. In loving memory and all."

Raymond closed his eyes; his shoulders sagged. "Alex is special to me. But it's not even me she's interested in." He let out a huge sigh. "The first woman I've liked since your mother, and it's all fake."

"Here's a tip. If she yells out 'Butch' while you're fucking her, you'll know which one of you she really wants."

Raymond cringed at his son's crass remark, but he never considered a woman yelling out another man's name during an intimate moment. He was the only man Wilma had ever been with. "I can't even imagine the horror I'd feel if something like that were to happen."

Sterling shirked his shoulders. "You get used to it. It's not that big of a deal."

Raymond's jaw dropped to the floor. "It would matter to me!" He raked his hands through his hair. "This was a bad idea. I can't pursue her ... I just can't."

Sterling rolled his eyes. "Christ," he swore. He put a hand on his father's shoulder. "I'm sorry. I shouldn't have been so blunt to such a choirboy."

Raymond closed his eyes and shook his head. "It is what it is."

Sterling's expression softened. "Look, she may have this internal idea of who, and what, she's looking for, but she's still pursuing you. I'm guessing that whatever she has imagined for her fantasy lover ... let's just say, you are fulfilling her dreams. You must be, or she wouldn't still be here and quite literally all over you. Her idea of Butch Manly may have opened the door for you, but she's inviting *you* in."

193

Raymond allowed that thought to sink in. "Perhaps."

In a calmer tone, Sterling added, "Dad, have you noticed her body language? That living, breathing, here–and–available woman couldn't keep her eyes off you. Her bedroom eyes undressed you all–night. Her heart beats faster when she's near you and I can even smell her arousal. You'd be an idiot to miss the signs."

"I did notice them." Raymond smiled slightly as he glanced up at his son. Especially now, with the news that he had left some sort of psychic echo, how could he know her true feelings?

"And I don't need Ben's ability to see that you want her. Your aura must be red with lust, and you can't deny it."

Gazing through the window, Raymond noticed Alex, who had joined the others in the living room. When their eyes met, she gave him a smile that lit up the room. He responded with a smile that flushed his cheeks. "She's different. I can't put my finger on it Sterling, but she's different to me." He eyed her from top to bottom. " … Yes, very, very different."

"And that's a good thing, future boss or not. You don't need me and the others hanging around. You should get her alone and talk to her." He leaned in, tugged his father's arm, and whispered, "Hell, you should take her up to your room and have her fuck your brains out."

Raymond pulled away. "She's not some easy floozy without any self–respect."

Sterling's facial features hardened at the remark. "Women today are just as aggressive as men. After she finishes that goblet of wine, and you are alone with her, she'll probably jump your ass. My advice to you is to

194

enjoy the night, then erase her memory before Dixon steps down."

"I don't use women, Sterling," Raymond said, with emphasis on the word 'I'.

Sterling stared coldly at his father. "I guess between the two of us, we lick the plate clean." He jingled his keys in his hand. "I'm going out. Have a good evening with her, and try not to disappoint her in bed."

Raymond watched as his son walked towards his car which was parked just off the street. He worried that his son might be right. Would he disappoint Alex? Had sex changed? He figured sex was the same as riding a bike, you never forget.

Raymond had just entered the living room when he spotted Alex approaching, her cell phone in hand. From the corner of his eye, Raymond also saw Dixon busy with his iPhone and heading his way.

"The President's Chief of Staff just texted, Raymond," Alex said as she made her way to him. There's been a change of orders. The President moved up the scheduled 'Storm Stop' for the hurricane that hit Florida earlier. We need to tell the team of the change of plans."

Dixon stood by the two of them. "We knew this emergency was coming." He looked down at his text. "Mission 09298 T–10 hours." He glanced over to Alex, "Damn good thing we put your bags on the docket in preparation for you accepting the promotion."

Raymond gave a curt node. All bags were already screened for explosives a good three days before departure. Having her bags already prepared was a good move on Dixon's part, especially now with T minus ten hours remaining. Raymond knew all the Colony bags were already on board, as well as blood for them. "Mason needs to prepare." He gestured towards his eyes and nose suggesting the disguise Mason would need to put on to pass as the President's doppelganger.

"Does Mason really look just like the President?" Alex asked.

Nodding yes, Raymond added, "Usually the Advance Team doesn't have much time to ensure the President's safety in natural disasters. They can't do a complete threat assessment, so most Presidents just do a flyover with Marine One. But since Mason is the President's twin …"

Alex gasped, her hand moving quickly to her mouth to hide her surprise. "No way!" Her eyes widened as she thought. "The President is known as the 'Peoples' President' because he is very open to the public. He is known for shaking hands up on the rope line."

"Mason wears gloves when he shakes their hands."

She let out a small laugh. "He gets full credit, and it's Mason who does all the work."

Dixon's lips curled in a half smile. "The President is safely secured in a hotel, watching the event on television. He'll do the fly over, and we'll have one of our team members flanking his side the entire time. Whoever is on call will flank him, and then stay with him at the hotel while Mason greets the public."

Wide–eyed, Alex asked, "But the human team never knows this?"

"The inner circle does, but that's all. Of course, they think we're human." Raymond shook his head. "I hate emergency trips with the President. The Secret Service will be busy securing the area. Debris usually lays everywhere, and adds to potential dangers. Keyhole satellites are repositioned, federal mailboxes are removed, manhole covers are welded shut, counter snipers are placed on rooftops ..." Raymond sighed, "... well, given time." He began the text to Mason and added, "Mason is super busy. The rest of the team remains in the motorcade out of sight."

Alex looked around the room. "Is any Colony member a part of the Advance team?"

"No," both Dixon and Raymond answered. Dixon continued, "There aren't that many Colony members to spread that thin. If there is a vampire threat, then that would come when the President is available, therefore the team stays close to him at all times."

Raymond felt more sympathy for the humans in these situations. The vampires just had to show up and be on alert. The Secret Service was already securing the University of Texas for the President's visit in a few days. They were being stretched thin with this Storm Stop and it would require the humans to pull an all–nighter on this one.

While Raymond texted Mason, Alex gathered everyone in the living room.

"We've all been watching the hurricane over the last few days," Raymond began. "I know we were all expecting this storm, and the time will be tomorrow at 7am. We need to be at Andrews AFB by 5:30am so we can get through security. The team will be Mason, Dixon, Sulie, Sterling, Alex and me. William, you'll continue to work with Ben on the stolen memory and finding out who hired the dead forger. With the President's speech in Austin Texas on Wednesday about the future of clean energy and Texas oil, we may be doing these flights back–to–back and the State Dinner is fast approaching, so we'll need to divide and conquer."

"I already anticipated that scenario and had a surplus of blood delivered to Air Force One for back–to–back trips," Dixon reported. "Alex, I'm still the lead and the human team is accustomed to me, so I'll check in with everyone on our end."

"I should go with you and observe at least," Alex said.

Dixon shook his head. "I'm not going to throw you into the deep end just yet. Doing two trips, followed by a state dinner, is enough of a learning experience right now. You have months to transition and you don't need to be burned out your first week."

Raymond sensed the disappointment as well as relief radiating from Alex's thought patterns. He wasn't surprised when she acquiesced and allowed Dixon to run the show.

"I'll inspect my medical supplies. Tonight I should examine the President before the flight tomorrow." Sulie added.

Raymond put his hand on Alex's shoulder. "I'll give you a ride home, Alex." She nodded and finished her goblet of wine before setting it down on the table.

William was busy texting. "Sterling is getting the new itinerary as we speak."

CHAPTER TWENTY–SEVEN

Raymond walked Alex to the garage and opened the car door for her. Once he had her comfortably in the car, he helped his sister transfer medical supplies into her Porsche so she could examine the President and refill his prescriptions.

"Thanks for the help, Raymond," Sulie said.

Raymond glanced over towards Alex and then back at his sister. "I need you to do me a favor." He cleared his throat and looked back towards Alex.

Sulie touched her brother's arm; a sly smile formed on her lips as she looked over and intensely studied Alex. "She's fine, Raymond. Enjoy your evening." She hopped into her car and backed out of the garage.

He watched as his sister sped down the drive, then he joined Alex in the Jag. "Would you like to listen to the radio?" he asked.

"Okay."

He turned on the radio and love songs filled the car.

Alex immediately said, "I love this song," and sang along, even though she could not carry a tune. She did so for the next several songs in a row. At times, she confused the words and would laugh at herself. Raymond thought it delightful for her to be so relaxed with him. She had flirted with him during the evening, and her thought patterns had been of an amorous nature all night.

The drive to her home sped by, and they arrived sooner than Raymond expected. As they walked along the stone path to her home, past the beautiful flower garden, Alex miss–stepped and started to fall. Raymond saved her from a header into her rosebush. When his hand touched her bare arm, images flared up from her inner thoughts. Passionate images of them having sex on her bed in various ways. As wild as the images were, they didn't come close to matching what raged through Raymond's head. What stood between them now were not his hesitations or worries, it was only a large wooden door that would be opened shortly.

She opened the door of her home and ran to the alarm unit to disable it. "Close the door, don't let the dogs out."

Raymond shut the door behind him and stepped into the house. He glanced towards the kitchen where Alex opened the back door and let the animals out. She picked up the phone and dialed a number. Thanks to Raymond's super hearing, he heard the entire conversation. She arranged for a neighbor to watch her dogs for the next few days.

Organized, professional, and responsible. Raymond didn't think most men would find these traits sexy, but he did. Of course, he liked watching her on the phone. She leaned halfway over the kitchen island as she talked and her cleavage showed him exactly what he wanted to see. She played with her hair as she hung up the phone. Her auburn long hair draped over her graceful neck, and he found his fangs extending. His manhood grew and hardened just looking at her. It had been so long since he had been with a woman, since he had wanted a woman. His world revolved around this woman, and his body ached for her. He intended to stay the night. This was a huge step for him, but it felt right.

"Get in kiddos." Alex closed and locked the door as she got the dogs inside. Raymond advanced towards her, but stopped when she announced that one of the dogs needed medicine. He watched as she tried to sit on the floor to medicate the dog. She tumbled, thanks to the tight dress, and hit the floor hard with her bottom. Alex paid it no mind and began dispensing the medicine.

His voice was deep and sexy. "I don't think that dress is meant to be sat in on the floor." He thought the garment would look fabulous lying on the floor in front of her bed with her out of it. The idea of diving onto the floor and taking her right there in the kitchen occurred to him. He quite possibly would have done so if he had not heard her giggle just then.

"Oh *(giggle)* probably not. This dress is too expensive and tight to be sitting like this with. But, (*giggle*) I can manage."

And totally revealing with you in that position, he thought. He noticed the "giggle factor" – the second one this evening. The bed would be more comfortable, so he decided to wait and possibly use the floor at another time with her.

Alex fussed with the medicine bottles and finally got each pill out and fed them to the dog. Raymond was about to burst, so he distracted himself. He looked around the kitchen. The room looked nice and clean, organized. It was how he would imagine Alex to keep it. He noticed a strong chicken theme in the room. She had rooster decorations on the wall, on the place mats on the table, salt and pepper shakers … they were everywhere. He counted well over a dozen chickens in her kitchen and could not understand the meaning behind the decor. It would be as if a vampire had decorated their own kitchen with pictures of A+ and O– blood. As he reflected what the chicken theme could mean, Alex finished with the dog.

"Now lay down. Sleep. Mommy has a big day tomorrow."

Like lightning, he moved and stood directly in front of her. He offered her his hand and helped her off the floor. Her high heeled shoes threw her off balance once again. He touched her hand and instantly read her thoughts. They were images of him lying nude in her bed, of her crying out his name over and over again. He became nervous, but her sensuous thoughts strengthened his resolve, as well as other things. He pulled her up close to him so she stroked his body as she stood. His erection pressed against her hips as he leaned in and claimed her mouth with his. He pinned her between him and the island, grabbed her by the hips, and sat her atop the counter. He deepened the kiss and she moaned. He pulled the tight skirt of her dress up past her thighs. He ground his swelled erection into her core and kissed her deeper.

Her thoughts told him she wanted the evening to end here. Well, not the kitchen, in her bedroom. A tidal wave of her thoughts crashed down on him. They were mostly jumbled, but he listened to her. At first she was grateful she had shaved her legs. She also felt embarrassed the house wasn't clean. Between kisses he muttered, "Don't worry about the house. Just focus on us."

"What?"

"Nothing." He fondled her breasts through her clothing. "It's nothing." He continued kissing her as more thoughts came through. Insecurity. She was wondering how her meager sexual experiences would compare with the vast experiences he must have had over his long lifespan. He almost laughed at such a thought. She had no idea how long he had been widowed; he wanted to reassure her. He looked into her eyes. "You're the most passionate woman I've ever held in my arms, Alex."

"It's been a long time for me, Raymond. A very long time."

"It's been a while for me as well, Alex. But I'm sure between the two of us we'll remember where everything goes." He caressed her bare leg, under her dress and up the outside of her panties. Her hands captured the back of his neck and pulled him closer to her body. She sat on the edge of the island. She arched into him and he ached to be within her.

"Tell me what you want" Raymond growled. "Tell me. I want to hear you say the words." He knew what she was thinking, but needed to hear her say that she wanted him as desperately as he wanted her.

A moan was all she could muster.

He carried her to the bedroom and placed her on the unmade bed. "I want you Alex. I'm so ready for you. ... I need to be in you right now." His deep and husky voice echoed his desire. His eyes turned black as midnight and his fangs extended for her vein. He touched her neck to feel the pulsing of her vein, the vein he could hear so clearly in his ears. Her blood racing and pumping frantically for him. His hand caressed her neck and brushed up against her necklace.

Instant pain shot through him. His hand scorched. He pulled his hand away. "Aaaahhh. Oh dear Lord."

"Wha?"

"Your necklace. Take it off."

"Is cross bad?"

"No. I can't touch the silver."

"So sorry. Only the cross is silver, the chain is white gold. I didn't even think about the necklace. I'm so sorry. You told me earlier you couldn't touch silver." She fumbled taking the cross off.

Raymond sat back on the bed and pulled himself away from Alex. She had tested all the stupid vampire lore imaginable, and the one that she got right had left welts on his hand. It may have been an accident, he wasn't sure, so he tried to read her jumbled and disorganized thoughts. Sorrow and empathy existed for what had happened to him. It had been accidental after all. He watched her as she struggled to remove the offensive necklace. She was having a difficult time doing so.

"Let me get you some cream." She struggled to get up, and he pushed her back on the bed.

He examined her carefully. "Alex, how much have you had to drink?"

"Nah much."

Raymond thought back to the car ride and how she messed up the words to so many songs. She had nearly tripped on the stone walkway and had used the island for support in the kitchen. She practically fell over to giving medicine to the dog. She also had struggled with the medicine bottles. She had glassy eyes, and slurred her speech as she now fumbled with her necklace. She was inebriated. He was currently taking advantage of her in this situation. Good Lord. Luck was just not on his side.

"How many goblets of wine did you have tonight?" He pulled the bedspread over and covered her body.

"Uh, … dunno. Maybe four … no, five …"

204

"Goblets are a lot bigger than wineglasses, Alex. That's why my sister uses them." He thought back to Alex's remarkably clean kitchen. She either she was a meticulous house cleaner or perhaps did not eat at home tonight since no dishes were around. Taking a look at the messy state of her bedroom, he assumed it was the latter choice. "When was the last time you ate?"

"Your place."

"Did you have dinner tonight?"

"No time. Busy all–day long" she tossed the necklace onto the floor and put her hand on his thigh. The covers dropped to the side and revealed her body once more to him.

"The only thing you ate tonight was the pasty guacamole my sister made?"

"It was yummy. She's good ... it was good."

Raymond had seen enough humans gagging on his sister's cooking to know that wasn't the case. He started to leave the bed when she threw her hands around his neck and captured him. She grabbed at his shoulders and kissed him, pulling him back on top of her. Her lips tasted of wine. He had noticed it earlier, but didn't think she was half drunk. She kissed him as he pulled away. She was persistent. Her hands pressed him to her and traveled down his back. They traveled over his muscular shoulders, down his spine and into the back pockets of his jeans. Raymond was still fully erect. His erection was not going to simply disappear just because the current situation did. He couldn't make love to her in this condition though.

Her hands managed to untuck his shirt and unbutton the front of his jeans. She slid her hands under the waistband and grabbed his ass. Doing so caused the front zipper to tug itself down and give his sex more room to spring free. He gave in to the moment and kissed her back. His hands went down and cupped her breast through her dress, and she moaned. Her hands had traveled from across his backside to the front of his jeans where the zipper was down. She reached in and grabbed Raymond's manhood through his underwear. He let out a low and seductive growl as he closed his eyes.

This was torture for him. He had to leave, and he had to leave now. He couldn't think straight. As he was about to sink his fangs into her neck, he finally stopped himself. "No. … Stop Alex. …" He pulled her hands off of his body and sat up. "I'm not going to take advantage of you in this condition." He pulled himself off the bed. He trembled for want of her body, but he pulled up his jeans and fastened them.

"It's okay. I want you to stay."

He stood there shaking. He refused to look at her as he gained control of his desires. "I'm going to make you something to eat. Just lie down. Stay in bed."

"Bed is always good."

"Yes. And you need your rest." Knowing he'd have to lock the door behind him when he left, he asked, "Do you have an extra set of keys to your house?"

"Hmm? … ah. Desk drawer." She pointed to the desk in the corner of her bedroom.

"OK. Stay here."

After getting the keys, he entered the kitchen and checked inside the refrigerator. It wasn't all that useful since he had no idea how to cook, plus the only food in her refrigerator was leftover takeout boxes that contained spoiled food. He looked through her pantry and found cold breakfast cereal, but not much else. He selected the cereal and got the milk from the refrigerator and a bowl and spoon from a cabinet and drawer. He brought the food over to the bedroom and found Alex passed out on her bed.

He wanted to stay with her, but still had some last minute preparations on his end with the team before leaving tomorrow morning. He thought it best to cover her with blankets, set an alarm clock on her nightstand for 4am so she would wake up early in the morning. She had no luggage to worry about, just her purse, so she wouldn't need to spend much time getting ready in the morning since Andrews AFB was just ten miles SE of downtown Washington DC.

He sighed as he scanned the room. As opposed to the rest of her clean and neat home, her bedroom was a mess. Her bed remained unmade, her clothes lay on the floor, and her makeup rested all over the counter in the bathroom, with the hair dryer on the floor. A pizza box sat closed on her dresser. The mess probably suggested she didn't entertain in here a lot. He was thankful for that. It also probably meant that she worked so hard that the only time she spent at her home was when she slept.

He went back to the desk and wrote down the schedule for the morning just in case she didn't remember. He left the note, the alarm clock, a glass of water and some Advil he found in her bathroom on the nightstand. He wrote himself a mental note to call her first thing in the morning to make sure she was up and awake.

Alex stirred in the bed and let out a moan. Her thought patterns hit Raymond, and he knew that Alex was dreaming of where they had left off. The temptation was too much, but he reached down anyway and touched her face. He enjoyed the erotic images he saw streaming from her mind. Definitely nice to be starring in her dreams, but he'd rather have a real performance. He waited another minute until the tension within him grew to be too much. He left her home, locking the door behind himself.

CHAPTER TWENTY–EIGHT

Alex drove to Andrews AFB, thankful not to be the last car in the long lineup waiting outside the armed gates. T minus one hour and some change remained before mission 09298 took flight. Not much time considering she still had to pass through security, which included a sweep for potential bombs in her car and on her person. Her White House clearance was checked before she, and some other passengers, were put onto a transport vehicle and led to an unmarked hangar which sat in an off–limit compound deep within Andrews.

She didn't recognize everyone on the transport, but a few she had seen on television by the President's side several times. The press secretary was easy to spot. She assumed the man sitting next to her was the Secretary of Health, but she wasn't sure. Of course, the bigwigs would also have their personal assistants accompanying them. Everyone seemed calm and relaxed with this trip falling into the category of just another day at the office.

As the car approached its destination, she studied the people surrounding the hangar. All were military personnel and, as far as she could detect, all were armed. As the transport rounded the hanger, she caught sight of the most impressive vehicle she had ever laid eyes on – actually, make that the two most impressive vehicles. The VC25 jet and its twin were both parked on the tarmac. One would carry the President and his entourage, the other merely a decoy which would fly empty. Both were impressive with a height of six stories and the massive size of a football field. She caught her breath as she saw the sun gleam off their shinny waxed exteriors, which gave them a bigger than life look about them.

Scanning around, she realized the absence of any of her team members, human as well as vampire. She assumed they had already boarded since she was running late. The sun had barely risen and she had been wearing her sunglasses since leaving the first guard station. Her headache remained in check, but what bothered her more than anything were the mosquito bites she endured while waiting for her car to be inspected for potential bombs.

She scratched at the two bites on her arms as the transport car stopped on the tarmac. She gathered her purse and was led to one of the impressive planes by a Chief Master Sergeant (CMSGT). The professional sergeant took her and two others to the ramp leading up to the plane. She scratched the back of her neck and her left ear as she climbed the steps. She then scratched the biggest bite in the middle of her forehead as she entered the majestic and impressive plane.

An armed guard greeted her once she stepped aboard. Thinking back to the sergeant's instructions, she strode forward searching for her seat. The plane only carried seventy passengers, and, according to the sergeant, each seat was formally assigned in the passenger compartment – and she was one of them! Never in her wildest dreams (well, okay, maybe in her wildest) did she ever dream she'd be here. Walking past the vacant seats, she noticed the higher the rank the closer the seat was to the President's executive suite. She realized she held her breath in awe, so she took a deep breath as she walked past the first few rows of passenger seats. She wasn't sure if she wanted to tear up or cry for joy, but with so many armed guards and officials about, she didn't want to act like a giddy schoolgirl. Mentally though, she jumped up and down.

Moving through the plane she saw her vampire team scattered about, with Dixon and Raymond the closest to the President. She gave a nod to them as she scratched the annoying bite on her forehead once again. What was it? An industrial sized mosquito? One hopped up on radiation? The bite itched like hell. Pulling her hand away from the evil spawn she noticed that she had scratched the bite to the point of bleeding. She mentally cursed as she wiped the blood away with the back of her hand.

She winked at Raymond as she walked past him, but forgot about her sunglasses. Ugh! She must look like some strung out hippy. She quickly removed them and continued back into the plane. After passing several rows, she realized she wasn't going to see Raymond at all during this flight. Last night, as wonderful as it was, didn't quite end the way she had wanted it to end. Then this morning she overslept and had a mind–splitting headache. She had no time to eat and was starving. Breakfast was always the most important meal of the day and she never missed the it. Even with the stupid alarm clock getting her up at 4am, and with Raymond's call at 4:05 am, she still didn't have time to eat.

Her agenda had her being introduced to the human team this morning and then board the plane with her vampire team, and now she was behind in that schedule. Lateness was also an awful first impression to make on her first official day on the job. She'd have to meet with the human team first thing on the plane, or once they land. Thankfully Dixon had been up all night making the preparations and there was little for her to do this morning.

Her forehead itched again. Of all things, she now resembled a Cyclops. She was an itchy mess. Not a morning person to say the least, she felt thankful Air Force One had a full coffee service and was determined to get a cup at her earliest convenience. She suddenly realized that she was going to meet the President for the first time today sporting a third eye where the damn mosquito had left its mark. Stupid bloodsucking bastard!

Her seat sat in front of the rows of fax and copier machines, and just next to some secure phone lines. Of course her seat was the last row. Dixon sat closer to the front and next to Raymond since she was second–string to Dixon this time around. Perhaps next time she would be farther up. Noticing that her seat was next to Matt and Brandon, she grimaced inwardly, but still said a polite 'good morning' to the pair.

She glided down into her plush seat and felt the seat cushion give way. Letting out a comforting sigh, she let it all sink in. The armrest had broadband Internet service. The console in front of her had satellite video feeds. Everything was marked with the Executive/Presidential seal. And down the hall was the executive suite. She would be meeting the President today. Everything was exciting.

One thing did give her pause though. Raymond didn't even say hello to her as she walked past him. He probably had an off night last night as well. Maybe he was upset because she had been drunk. She hoped they'd have a chance to talk once they arrived in Florida. Matt sat quietly sipping his coffee and not paying her any attention, which was nice. She suspected Brandon, who sat next to the window, liked looking out the window when they flew. The man probably wanted to make sure no gremlins attacked the engines of the plane or something else just as ridiculous.

Alex quietly sipped her coffee and listened to one conspiracy theory after another from Brandon, even though his suspicions were trying her patience — and Matt wasn't much of a buffer. That was when the President walked into the cabin, extended his hand, and said hello to her.

Shocked, Alex spilled her coffee on her jacket. Damn it! Toss in the run on her stockings and how the wind had recoiffed her hair this morning and she looked a fright for meeting the President. If she had eaten breakfast she just knew that she'd have had something stuck between her teeth. "Hello Mr. President." she said as she stood and shook his hand.

He smiled a toothy grin, allowing her to see his set of fangs. "Call me Mason. It's a pleasure to meet the new director."

Mason? Oh God, the vampire double. She grabbed a napkin and sopped up the coffee from her blouse as she composed herself. "It's an honor to meet you, Mason. My, you look exactly like the man." Alex did a double take and focused on Mason's facial features.

Mason asked Matt to allow him to sit in his seat for a few minutes, and Matt politely complied. As Mason took the seat, he kept an eye on Brandon. "It's a pleasure to make your acquaintance, Ma'am." He reached over and politely shook her hand.

"Oh please, call me Alex." For looking so much like the President, Alex marveled at his thick southern

213

accent. His voice sounded nothing like the President's heavy Boston one.

Shifting in the seat, he crossed his legs, his right ankle resting on top of his left knee. "Can't imagine a pretty young woman, such as yourself, being named Alex. Must be short for Alexandria, right?"

She smiled. How many times had people asked her that exact question? She had lost track. Of course Mason's question came with a nice compliment, most didn't. "Close. Alexandra, but I go by Alex."

"Alright, Miss Alex it is." Mason glared over at Brandon, who was leaning over in his chair and staring at Mason's face.

"You look older than the President today." Brandon inspected Mason like he was the Lost Ark. "Something isn't right. Sometimes you look younger, but today you look a good ten years older than he does."

Mason waved the comment off. "Nothin' more than stress and a poor night's rest. It's nothin' for you to fret over."

Alex watched closely as the human became compelled. "Now you will please excuse the lady and me while we have ourselves a private talk. You will ignore everything you hear," he continued. Like a robot, Brandon turned towards the window and ignored them, just as if Mason and Alex had disappeared.

"Now that boy scares the livin' tar out of me," Mason said pointing to Brandon. "His mother must have dropped him when he was a wee baby." Mason touched his face, "He notices way too much for my liking."

How cool was this compelling trick? Alex could use this tool in her handbag of tricks, too bad it wasn't a learned ability. She realized she still stared in awe at

214

Mason in light of what he had done. Alex cleared her throat and looked away.

He glanced around and then said in a whisper, "You get used to it. Come soon enough you won't even notice when we compel the humans in front of you. It'll be old hat."

Alex returned her gaze at the vampire. "You have a lovely southern accent," she said, changing the subject.

"Born and raised in Bexar County, right outside of San Antonio. Other than my days fighting Nazis, I lived my entire human life in a small corner of the world."

"Emulating the President's speech must be hard."

Mason licked his lips, and said in a perfect Bostonian accent, "I usually have little to no speaking requirements when I am the President. But I can manage."

Alex laughed. "That's nearly perfect."

He winked. "I've had nearly four years of perfectin' the accent."

She leaned in and whispered, "You hoping he makes it as an incumbent?"

"Honestly Miss. Alex, not in the slightest," he said in still a hushed tone. "Don't get me wrong; he's a good man and all, especially helping the economy, but my poor eyes don't take too well to those darn contacts. I have an inner eyelid, and they sure do hurt when it I'm out in the sun." When she narrowed her gaze deep into his eyes, he added, "The light's not bright enough here, darlin'. Plus those little buggers aren't in right now. You'll only see the transparent eyelids when they try to close down on top of them awful things."

"Sorry," she said as she moved away from his face. "I didn't mean to be too obvious." Actually, she

215

normally would have taken offense to the 'darlin' remark and would have been up in his face for such a sexist comment. She could tell he didn't mean it as a come–on, nor as a degrading title. Somehow, the words coming from a good old southern gentleman, old enough to be her grandfather, didn't bother her. He seemed easy to talk to, and she liked that. It reminded her of when she was a little girl talking with her Paw–Paw all those years ago.

Mason was one of the full vampires in the group, just like Daniel. It meant he was once human, and that piqued her interest. "I read you're a member of the team because of Raymond's actions," she said.

"Yep."

"And you were a fighter pilot before that."

"In World War II," he whispered. "I was on mission, in the wrong place at the wrong time. Raymond gave me the orders and he miscalculated the enemy's position. I knew the truth about him. 'No compelling in foxholes' type of thing. And I begged Raymond to turn me."

"You begged? He didn't want to turn you?"

"I was the first human he turned, and he didn't want to do it. I think his guilt over sending me to my death got the best of him. That, and I told him I had a family that needed me to live."

Alex smiled. "Then the turning worked out. You came home to them."

Mason shook his head and his eyes saddened with pain. "Nah, it didn't work out. My wife rejected me when I told her. She told the kids I had died, and she asked that I never see her or them again."

"I'm so sorry."

Mason looked away. "I am too. It wasn't exactly the homecoming I had hoped for. Raymond compelled them to believe I died in combat, and I spent my entire existence as a vampire away from them."

Alex flinched. "That must have been difficult for you."

He shrugged. "I loved them enough to let them go. Raymond regrets turning me, but he helped me through the pain."

Alex could sense his loneliness. She thought back to Daniel's words of making the best of a bad situation. "I guess I never thought about the negative effects of being turned," she said in a reflective, solemn tone.

Mason shrugged his shoulders and looked away just as Brandon pointed out the window, and announced to no one in particular, "Marine One."

Alex craned her neck to look out the tiny porthole. Not too far in the distance she saw the three marine helicopters, two of which were decoys and one, the real McCoy, approaching. She thought back to when she had boarded the plane. A small contingent of Marines was standing guard, obviously waiting to greet the President so that the Air Force soldiers could escort him aboard the airplane. Everything ran with peak efficiency, and that impressed her.

"I best be going," Mason said just as Matt reappeared looking for his seat.

Saying a quick good–bye to Mason, and allowing Matt access to his seat, Alex stared out the window for any image of the President she could see, but she wasn't able to see where Marine One had landed. Moments later the announcement came over the intercom. The woman's voice sounded confident and firm. "Attention on board the aircraft. The President is on board. We are now Air Force One."

Alex sat straighter in her seat, her head held high, and her lips curled into a satisfied smile. She could get used to this life.

CHAPTER TWENTY–NINE

Air Force One landed in Florida and both the human and vampire teams were busy on security detail. Mason exited with Alex and part of the human team and climbed into the first of the five presidential limos that would drive around Florida. Mason rode in the decoy car; Alex rode in the mobile com center car that linked all five cars together.

Raymond, Sterling and Sulie, plus some humans, made up the President's Protection Detail, also known as the inner circle of protection. The PPD and the President filed into the Presidential limo. The vampires would remain in the car, since they could not afford to have their pictures taken. Thanks to digital technology, they were too exposed now. Of course, in the past bad photography, poor film development … it was easy to explain blurred vampire faces. The press wasn't stupid though. After a while they would catch onto a pattern, and then the team would have to rotate who got out of the car. During one such incident, when a photographer got too close, the team could not risk sitting in the convertible with JFK. It still bothered Raymond that he had not been able to save the President.

The devastation in Florida proved massive. The storm had hit land in the last 48 hours, killing 14, wounding hundreds, and destroying thousands of homes and livelihoods. Many were homeless, many were without electricity, and freshwater was scarce. The President did the flyover in Marine One and allowed Mason to view the neighborhoods and the places of business that were devastated.

While the President remained safely tucked away in a hotel with half the Colony team, Mason gave testimonials on the TV about what he had seen, and to how much federal aid Floridians could expect. Mason did his best to cover his face with his hands often during close up shots, and even wore dark sunglasses.

The vampires stayed in their perspective cars with little to do much of the day, which was truly an exercise in boredom. Between this and the President's schedule to visit Austin, Texas, it was going to be a long week.

Alex felt overwhelmed. Since the original state dinner passes had been forged, a new pass design was drafted and security measures were put into place – which included a change of venue. The team back in D.C. had already compelled the White House Social Secretary, Chief of Protocol, and Chief Usher into believing the White House State Dining Room had experienced a flooding and was unavailable for the State Dinner. Documents were forged from a fake construction and plumbing company which had worked on the room and its nonexistent damage. Even press releases had been made about the fake damage.

The away team worked divided, half with the President, the other half as the decoy. Alex shuffled her priorities between the five motorcade cars. Back home, the dinner's State Arrival Ceremony had to be changed from the White House reception room to a ballroom downtown, the dinner itself was now in an adjourning ballroom. The executive chef, pastry chef, and florists desperately tried to adjust to the change. Alex had spent the last twenty minutes on the phone with the White House calligrapher's assistant who was busy faxing the change of venue invites to all those attending. The calligrapher could not understand why Ben's last name was now Preston. After a series of impressive lies, the invitation was successfully changed.

Alex spent more time on the phone than talking face–to–face with each person, and her voice was threatening to give out. She had another dozen calls to make before she could call it a day and she was ready to relax in a hot bubble bath.

Eventually the motorcade ended their day at the Jamestown Imperial Hotel, a luxury five–star hotel which catered to Hollywood big shots and state dignitaries. It wasn't every day the hotel received such an honor as the president of the United States, but the security was top–notch. The President had already entered through a service entrance earlier that day. Now Mason, with all the fan fair, entered through the same door. If this President had not had the label of being the "People's President" the group may have flown back to D.C., but this one liked reaching out to his people, even if it was his decoy who did the actual reaching.

The top three floors of the hotel were reserved for the President, with Secret Service on the roof, the floor below, the lobby, and every nook and cranny that could be imagined in between.

The Secret Service secured Mason in the presidential suite as the rest of the team found their way to their own rooms. Alex was used to staying in hotels that promoted their rooms as "charming" and "quaint." This room she shared with Sulie was posh. The beds were queens and in separate rooms. She guessed the bathroom and bar fixtures were less than a couple of years old, same with the rug, living room furniture and drapes. The windows were drawn shut, but she could imagine the view was spectacular. She thought the job she accepted was just dealing with the vampires. She had not bargained for her new traveling itinerary, or for the pleasing accommodations. Taking this job really was the best decision of her life.

Security was through with the luggage checks, and she noticed her suitcases in the second bedroom. She unpacked just enough to hang up her suits so they would not be wrinkled, and to dig out her toiletry kit. An emergency blood kit was stored in a secret compartment of her suitcase. The majority of the blood supply for the team was hidden in plain sight – in Sulie's medical supply kits.

Alex ran her fingers over the nearly invisible pocket which held the five small syringes of blood and thought of Raymond. She had wanted to talk with him on the airplane. Once that fell through, she had hoped to talk with him at some point during the day, but he had flanked the President earlier that day, sat on Marine One with the man, and had called it an early day. All while she went from one flooded neighborhood to the other with Mason. Any discussion over last night would have to wait until later.

CHAPTER THIRTY

Raymond and Sterling sat shoulder to shoulder in a cramped security room filled with monitors displaying different areas of the hotel. The President remained locked down for the night, but security always had someone on duty, even into the small hours of the morning.

A knock sounded on the security door, and Sterling grinned from ear–to–ear as he let Alex in. "Look Dad. Alex decided to join us."

It pleased Raymond to see her. There had been no chance throughout the day to apologize for his previous behavior. "Sterling, aren't you due for a break? Maybe Alex could help me for while you take one."

"Actually Sterling, that would be nice. Please give us a few minutes. I have some business to discuss with your father."

"Sure. How about if I get all three of us some coffees?" Sterling suggested.

Raymond watched as the grin on his son's face faded to a look of concern. When a woman said she needed to talk alone for a few minutes, it usually meant a heart–crushing blow was about to happen.

Once alone, Alex apologized. "I am so sorry about last night. It was unprofessional of me to drink as much as I did. There is no excuse."

"It's fine." Raymond became more confused than ever. He should be the one apologizing. "Look, I should never have crossed the line last night. I didn't know how much you had to drink and I never should have … wait, do you remember what happened last night?"

"What do you mean?"

Confusion, thy name is relationship. "You were drunk last night. I got you home, put you into bed. I didn't want to take advantage of you ... hell, I planned to feed you something called Frosted Flakes ..."

Her hand covered her mouth as a gasp escaped. Her eyes widened. "I don't remember any cereal. I drank a few glasses of wine to calm my nerves before meeting the team. Then, at Fang Manor, I lost track of how much I drank."

"What was the last thing you remember?"

A smile crossed her lips. "Pulling you into my bed." Her devilish smile was wicked, her look seductive as hell, but it confused Raymond even more.

"Wait. Why were you so mad at me this morning when you boarded the plane? How did offend you?"

"I wasn't mad at you."

"I heard your thoughts Alex. Who was the 'Stupid bloodsucking bastard' that you were mad at this morning? If it wasn't me, then who else on the team upset you?"

Alex's eyes grew wide in disbelief and she let out a hardy laugh. "I was bitten by mosquitoes this morning, that's all." Watching as the information sank in, she added, "Raymond, you should have talked to me. You went all day long thinking I was mad at you? I'm so sorry."

Raymond laughed. "I'm so relieved." He took in a deep breath and glanced back at the security monitors. All was well, so he focused back on Alex. "Look, next time I'll just talk to you and ask you what's going on. I don't want there to be any miss communication between us."

224

"I agree. I want us to be open with each other."

Raymond hugged her, but after a moment of silence, he said. "I want to share everything with you Alex. I need to tell you about what happened to Wilma."

Alex pulled away from the hug just enough to make eye contact with him. "Who's Wilma?" she asked.

"Sterling's mother. My dead wife. I want you to know what happened and how she died."

Alex's body stiffened, "How did she die?"

"I killed her."

CHAPTER THRITY–ONE

"I don't believe you." Alex shook her head as her chair slid away from him. "You are such a good man. I can't believe you killed her."

Raymond heard the cracking of her voice and noticed her eyes glance back to the closed door. Her heart rate had sped up, and she was now perspiring, which caused her honey scent to fill the tiny room. With widened eyes, she watched him intently.

"No. It wasn't what you're thinking," Raymond quickly said. "I killed her with my arrogance and my pride. Not with …," he held up his hands, "… not by … this." His hands waved around his mouth suggesting his fangs. He took a deep breath, slumped in his chair, and rubbed his jaw with his hand.

Raymond cleared his throat as he felt Alex regaining her calm. He watched as she relaxed in her own chair, her hands gently placed in her lap waiting for him to continue. He never told this story in its entirety to anyone before. Both Sulie and Sterling knew some of the tale, with the rest of the Colony members knowing just hints of what had happened. Only Raymond knew the entire truth. Now, he wanted to share the truth with Alex.

He bit his lip, feeling the tiny prick of his fang as the tooth brushed his inner cheek. "The year was 1820. As a nineteen year old, I had not transitioned. I still ate human food, my fangs had not fully extended, and my blood remained mostly still human in me." He rolled his eyes, "Actually, I was a punk kid who thought he knew everything about life. I lived a waiting game until my

Jahrling Year when I knew I'd become one of the strongest and most enduring creatures to walk the planet." He let out a nervous laugh. "I was such a delinquent back then."

Alex leaned toward him, her voice calm. "Most teenagers are like that. At least they are in my experience. It's called growing up."

He nodded. "And like most teenagers, I became rebellious. Sure, as vampires we mingled with humans. Our neighbors were all humans, I attended school with humans, and ..." He closed his eyes and murmured, "I shared my bed with a human."

Raymond's opened his eyes, but furrowed his brow with a look of defiance. "We are told, very early on, that we do not date humans." He stressed the word human, not paying attention to his current audience. If Alex took offense, it did not show. She sat motionless listening to his story.

"We don't soil our bed with them," he said as tears welled up in his eyes. He took a deep breath, slowly nodded, and again let out nervous laughter. "My father held a seat as head of the Council. He had big plans for me, which included a vampire bride to unite our family line with another one just as wealthy and powerful."

Alex looked confused. "What Council?"

He shrugged his shoulders. "It's nothing to be concerned with. Eventually, on his death, I got his seat on the Council so that I could represent my family line and coven."

"Wait," Alex interrupted. "So the Council is some sort of ... what?"

His hands waved in the air dismissively. "Not important to the story." He cleared his throat and continued, "I didn't want to marry the woman my parents chose for me, and my father would not have approved of me socializing with human women. When I met Wilma, I didn't tell him about her. I didn't share the truth with my mother either. Only Sulie knew."

A blush of contempt colored Alex's cheeks. "So you were embarrassed for sleeping with a human."

"No." He shook his head, "That wasn't it. I fell in love with Wilma. She was as beautiful, and as frail, as a flower." His fingers raked through his hair. "We lived in Milford, Pennsylvania, a small, modest town – even in the 1800s. Wilma was a classmate of mine. She had long golden hair, and she was the sweetest woman I'd ever met. Her freckled face …" He now pointed over to Alex, "… looked much like yours. Her smile could light up a room, and her body …," he paused. Looking over to Alex, he shrugged his shoulders. "Anyway, she was a human. She was *my* human." He glanced up at Alex, "Our budding relationship seemed easy enough to hide from my parents. After our schooling ended, I worked at her father's mill, which was called Sterling Flour and Corn. It gave us plenty of time to be together without anyone knowing."

"Her last name was Sterling?" Alex asked.

Raymond nodded. "Yes. I named our son after her. It seemed proper. Anyway", he cleared his throat, "I loved Wilma; She was everything to me. She was religious and I wasn't sure how she would take the news of me being a vampire." Raymond reflected on that. "Actually I did know in my heart. I was sure she'd take the news poorly, so I didn't tell her my true nature.

"I loved her, and she loved me. One night, out of wedlock, I made love to her. She was so innocent and

228

pure, and she had no clue what it was she was making love to." He slammed his fist onto his knee. "It felt wrong to do that to her, but my feelings of love and lust carried me away. I made love to her within my own lie of omission. And to my heart's greatest joy, she loved me with all of her heart and wanted me as a woman would want a man. Of course, I seemed human. I never bit her because my fangs hadn't fully extended. I wouldn't be able to drink blood for a couple more years."

Raymond leaned forward, and rested his forehead in the entwined fingers of his hands. "I wanted to tell her what I was, but I was a coward. I pretended to be human and thought that perhaps it didn't matter if she didn't know. Then she told me she was in a family way with our son. I asked her to marry me that very day. Her parents disapproved, but we were married within a couple of weeks. Of course, back then, marriage was the honorable and expected thing to do."

Alex leaned forward. "What about your parents? How did they take the news?"

He straightened back into his chair. "Furious. More so when they found out about the baby – a half–breed." He noticed Alex had cast her look downward onto the floor, not making eye contact with him. "My parents did the best they could, but they were prejudiced beyond belief."

She glanced back up at him. "A mixed marriage can be difficult."

"Mixed?" He looked at her. "That's putting it kindly."

A moment passed in awkward silence before Raymond continued. "Anyway, we lived together in our home at the edge of the town. We had a plot of land her parents gave us. We lived as husband and wife while she carried our child. Those months were the happiest time in my life, even though she never knew me for who and what I was."

Raymond paused. His eyes welled up with tears. "I knew she was human when I went into the relationship." Raymond chose his words carefully here. "I loved her for what she was, a human. She never had to be a vampire to own my heart. I gave it to her. I never saw the division between human and vampire like my parents had." He glanced over at Alex, "I still don't, not where it really counts."

"Why not turn Wilma? She could have been a vampire," Alex said.

"Not with her being pregnant. I wouldn't be able to turn her until after the baby came ... so I kept my secret."

"I don't understand."

"We can't turn a pregnant woman or a child. They die in the attempt. A child can't handle the turning and will die during the turn, and that usually kills the mother."

A gasp escaped Alex's throat. "Oh my."

Raymond nodded. "I fully intended to marry Wilma before we had a child together." He shook his head. "I respected her and, well, unplanned pregnancies happen, whether you are human or a vampire — not that I ever regretted having Sterling. I love him dearly. I wanted Wilma to know exactly what I was and to accept me and want my child – a vampire child." He took a deep breath before continuing. "I also wanted Wilma to be turned before we had children so our children would be purebred vampires and not half–breeds. Not that I see anything wrong with half–breeds, but it would be easier on him within our culture."

"But Sterling is a vampire. It doesn't matter that he had a human mother," Alex said.

"I know that. But there is some stigma to being a half–breed." Raymond rolled his eyes. "God. I hate that term."

"I don't understand. I know they're slightly weaker than purebreds, but they are immortal and stronger than humans. What stigma are you talking about?"

He explained. "Half–breeds are usually the result of a male vamp compelling a human woman into his bed without her knowledge, or even forgoing the compelling and raping her. It happens all the time if the male vampire succumbs to blood lust after a feeding." He sighed heavily. "It's not that all vampire men can't control themselves. It just sometimes happens. So half–breeds are generally thought of as unwanted children from their mothers, at least the ones that survive. It's a difficult pregnancy, usually ending in miscarriages. Then if a child is born, most usually die during their transition into adulthood unless they are told what they are and how to … feed." Raymond rubbed his temple. "The children that survive should never be made to feel that they were unwanted or unwelcome in their parents' lives."

"But you and Wilma loved each other. That's different," Alex assured him.

"Of course. Sterling may have been unplanned, but not unwanted. Wilma was very excited about the idea of having a child. So was I."

231

Alex reached out and put her hand on Raymond's shoulder as he continued.

"So the day came, and Wilma called upon a midwife. The birth did not go well." Raymond looked up towards the ceiling. "God, that's putting it mildly." Shaking his head, he looked down at his hands. They were stretched out, as if he were cuddling a baby. "Sterling was a big baby, and also breech."

Her eyes widened as she saw the size Raymond suggested with his hands.

"Wilma tore herself up trying to birth him. She bled so much. She hemorrhaged and I was desperate to save her. I knew I had only minutes until she bled out, so I told her what I was and I terrified her. She laid there dying afraid more of me than of death."

His hand balled and his knuckles grew white as he raised his hand to his mouth and bit at his fist. He glanced over to Alex. "I cut my arm and forced her to drink my blood. She choked on it as I kept forcing it down her throat. The midwife kept working to save the baby and Wilma. I couldn't compel the midwife because I didn't have that ability yet, so she must have thought I was crazy. To her credit, she didn't pay attention to me but focused on the birth. Later I contacted my father and he had to erase the midwife's memories."

Raymond stopped fidgeting with his fist, and slammed it into his thigh. "By telling Wilma the truth, I terrified and tortured her for no reason. My blood wasn't strong enough for a turn, plus she didn't have my blood in her system before the attempt. Of course she also still had Sterling struggling to get out of her."

Alex's face had grown white with the tale. "It sounds awful. But I know you did everything you could," she reassured him.

Raymond tear–filled eyes made eye contact with Alex. "I had never turned anyone before. I was immature and foolish. She kept bleeding and her eyes were wide with fright as she coughed up my blood."

Again Raymond held out his arms and looked at them. "I held her in my arms as she died. Her eyes glazed over and her body went cold as I held her. The midwife left since there was nothing more she could do but leave me to my grief." Raymond cleared his throat. "Even through my pain, I knew I had to at least save the life of our child. Wilma lay dead in our bed, covered with blood. I took a knife and cut Sterling from her body so he would live and that I'd have a part of Wilma with me always."

Alex held Raymond's hand, their fingers entwined.

Raymond sniffed and fought back the tears. "I killed Wilma. I terrified her the last few minutes of her life, and then I tore my knife into her body. My selfishness, and all of my lies in not wanting to lose her, cost Wilma her life and me my love. So you see," he continued. "I'm not the good man you think I am."

"You are a good man Raymond. The best." They hugged for several minutes in silence until Sterling knocked on the door holding a tray of coffee.

CHAPTER THIRTY–TWO

The President finished his business in Florida earlier than expected. With the personal tour done, the federal funding would soon arrive rendering aid. With nothing left to do, the President and his entourage headed back to Washington D.C.

The President would exit by the kitchen, while the decoy Mason would leave by the south entrance of the hotel. Raymond stood with the other agents making up the PPD. He had put on an AMI TAC3S body armor vest, but merely for show. He felt no tingling sensation and the hairs on his arms weren't standing up, so he knew no vampires were about, unless they were half–breeds. Looking at the monitor in his watch, he read the heat signatures of all the people in the area. All was good. Once again, he remained the security officer "no–op" and only existed as a precaution. Not that he minded.

While waiting to board Air Force One, Raymond received a text from his son. Sterling would soon be boarding the plane with Mason and the humans since he drew the short end of the stick. Wishing his son had more tolerance for humans, he read the text and grimaced at the message. Raymond didn't know who "Zippy" was, but figured it was either Brandon or Matt since Sterling never did manage to remember the names of any of the human team. Brandon and Matt were in rare form this trip, and Raymond had needed to do a memory wipe on the shorter of the two humans once already since arriving in Florida.

Raymond typed a response to Sterling which read more of an acknowledgment than anything else, and he entered the plane. The air was stale. Human smelling too. The food from the galley permeated the large craft. If he had to guess, he would say today's menu included some type of fish. He rolled his eyes. He hated pretending to eat.

He walked past the plush seats that were stamped with the presidential seal, the conference room with its monitors and computers, and the President's personal office with the closed door. He felt no tingling sensation, so he knew a vampire was not on board. He inhaled deeply and breathed out a sigh of relief. Mixed in with the smell of food, airplane fuel, and various industrial cleaners, he could also smell the sweet scent of honey almond – which told him Alex was nearby.

Soon after take–off a human Secret Service man came to escort Raymond and Alex to the executive suite. After being given clearance to enter the President's office, they found President Harrimen behind the heavy wooden desk in the overstuffed brown leather chair. His glasses perched on the end of his nose as he flipped through paper after paper. He didn't acknowledge their presence, but murmured comments to various members of his Cabinet who were also in the room. He talked at such an alarming rate that Raymond wondered how the men kept up.

More paperwork was placed on the man's desk, his signature rendered to them, and then the papers were whisked away into folders and briefcases. Raymond noticed Alex's wide eyes as she took in her surroundings. She shifted from one leg to the other, obviously nervous. Raymond looked around, but overall remained unimpressed by the familiar sight. The "Football" was the only item to catch his eye. It was a heavy leather satchel that housed all nuclear security codes and was never more than a few dozen feet from the President at any given time. Mason had a similar one, of course with false codes.

Even the "Football" was old hat to Raymond.

Raymond had just crossed his arms and leaned against the doorjamb when everyone but the President and the Director of Homeland Security left the room, each thanking the President for his time.

The President gazed up towards Raymond, his eyes widened with recognition, and a hint of fear drifted as a mental pattern off the man. Raymond and his team were a favorite of this President — a favorite in the same way that someone would watch a slasher thriller movie, or ride the biggest roller coaster, just to get a rush. The vampires scared the crap out of the President, and he loved it. The man stood and puffed up his chest in what Raymond guessed was a feeble attempt to appear more muscular and manly. He reached out his hand to shake Raymond's, and an all knowing smile crossed his face as he eyed the vampire and felt the absence of body warmth.

Raymond gritted his teeth when the President eyed Alex like she was a prime rib and he was a starving man. Naturally the President was told in his daily briefing, the Presidential Daily Briefing (PDB), that Alex had become the new director of the Colony, but he didn't have to look this god–awful pleased. A lustful smile appeared on the President's face and Raymond had to remind himself that he had taken an oath not to compel, or kill, the letch.

Alex beamed with excitement, and in a breathy voice said, "Oh, Mr. President. It is such an honor to meet you."

"Oh, sweetheart, the pleasure is all mine," he said, shortening all the vowels in a typical Boston accent. The two shook hands, the President clasping her hand with both of his and holding onto the grasp longer than necessary. "I heard you took the caretaker job for these bastards," he joked, his head nodding towards Raymond.

Alex hesitated for a moment, and glanced over to Raymond. "Uh, yes sir," she said returning her look over to the President. "I'm the new Colony Director." She took a seat across from the President when he gestured for her to do so.

Raymond noticed the courtesy was not extended to him, so he remained standing. Just as well. The President's philandering ways put the two at odds on most occasions, especially since he coveted Raymond's sister, and had even asked if the team could find him a "vampire broad" for him to experience. The President's interest in Sulie ended the day she gave him his first annual physical, and Raymond let out a sly grin as he imagined what torture his sister had put the man through.

Alex smiled from ear–to–ear, and proud mental patters radiated from her as she began to talk with the President. Of course, this was to be her first meeting of many with the man. Raymond figured Alex was too intelligent and self–assured to fall for the President's false praises and plastic charm. He wondered how long it would take her, as a human, to see right through the man.

Raymond listened to the President's pleasing words as he talked with Alex. Any time the topic strayed from being professional, or whenever the President told a bold–faced lie, Raymond cleared his throat. Alex and the Director of Homeland Security picked up on the not–too–subtle comments by looking his way occasionally, but the President remained clueless – obviously caught up in the web of seduction he was spinning.

Raymond hated the President, but would more than likely vote for the man again since he had turned around the economy, lowered the deficit, and encouraged businesses to use green resources. It was the President's personal lechery that bothered Raymond more than anything else. Each Colony team member took turns in the "inner circle" of protection to the President. Everyone knew less tension existed when Sterling or Ben pulled that duty.

Alex shifted in her seat. Her body sat stiff and rigid, her jaw muscles tight, and her brow furrowed. Raymond felt emotional walls already forming in her mind in regards to the man. A chuckle almost escaped, but Raymond quickly put his hand to his mouth and held it in.

Unfortunately for Alex, her job was to be the interface between the office of the President and the Colony. Not only was she supposed to confer with the President over any vampire threats against the country, but the job was also to accommodate the President and his comfort level. Some presidents loved having the vampires around, others were scared out of their minds. It was a job that changed with every new president.

Usually when the President said he could give up five minutes of his time, the meeting had less time than promised. However, it was typical for those five minutes to span much longer if a woman was in his company. Raymond looked at his pocket watch. It had already been over ten minutes, which was too long for Raymond's taste. As the President ended the meeting, he placed his hand on Alex's arm. The look she shot back towards him was enough to cause most men to pause and take a step back, but not a man who thought he was the most influential and powerful man in the world. Sure he had great political pull, but he wasn't even the most powerful man in this room.

On his way out of the office, Raymond made eye contact with the President. No words were spoken, just a head nod from the vampire to the human. Raymond allowed Alex to exit first, and then he made sure to block the President's view of her backside as she walked back into the main cabin of the plane. It pleased him to no end when Alex leaned over and whispered into his ear, "What an ass!"

CHAPTER THIRTY–THREE

Alex squeezed into the closet and found the loose panel. Rotating the panel to the left, she revealed the entrance to the Cave and let herself in. The room was not much more than a closet itself, but impressive in size considering the Cave was hidden within the White House residency floor. There were also crawl spaces along the walls thanks to the remodeling efforts of President Truman in the late 1940s when the building's interior had been gutted and then reconstructed with concrete and steel.

The padding along the walls of the crawl space suggested some attempt at soundproofing, but Alex heard the clanking of swords from a computer game she knew all too well. She walked in the Cave to find Mason sitting on a couch with Ben. The large T.V. Monitor buzzed off and she was sure she saw the game World of Warcraft before the screen faded to black.

"Hey, Alex. Come on in. Welcome to the Cave. We were just reviewing transcription logs and watching the surveillance cameras surrounding the house." Ben said.

Alex smiled as she pulled out the papers from her briefcase and ignored the lie. "I need to go over some personal appearance dates the President will have on his calendar with you, Mason."

Ben got off the couch and stretched his enormous body from side to side. World of Warcraft was addictive. You could play the game for hours. Judging his body's reaction to his long stretch, Alex suspected the two had probably been playing most of the day.

"I'm going to grab a bite. The interns should be downstairs."

Alex wasn't sure she heard that quite right. "I'm sorry, Ben. You're what?" she asked.

"I'm hungry so I'm going to find an intern for lunch." Ben turned towards Mason. "Hey Mason, sorry about that."

Mason shrugged in reply.

"I guess I shouldn't have said that in front of you either," Ben said looking over at Alex.

"You can't bite an intern!" Alex scolded.

"Sure I can. My new alias needs me to be younger. Besides, I snack all the time. You want to watch?" He gave her a wicked smile.

"You have bagged blood to eat, you don't need an intern." she insisted. "You're not even allowed to bite for food . It says so in your 'No Biting' agreement." Hah, she got him on the contract details.

He trumped her appeal with the contracts fine print. "Fine. I'll have sex with her afterward and all will be good." Ben pointed at Mason. "Just be glad it's me biting and having sex with an intern and not Mason. We don't need a scandal to rock the White House again." He turned and left the room without another word.

Alex felt like Alice down the hole in Wonderland. She looked over at Mason, horrified that he might answer 'yes' to her next question, but she had to ask. "Do you bite and have sex with the interns, Mason?"

He laughed and shook his head. "Heck, no. I doubt any of those lovely young gals would fancy an old coot like myself. Besides, I can only eat one syringe of blood every few weeks, and I fed yesterday. Until I'm out of the White House I need to control all of my urges. So don't worry none."

Alex was relieved, but confused. "How can you eat only one syringe of blood every 6 weeks and only age about 8–10 years during that time? Raymond misses a day of feeding and he's aged a good 5 years in only 24 hours."

"To appear young takes a lot of blood, and Raymond and the others gorge themselves. You have to understand Miss Alex, we are always hungry. The Colony is blessed to have a lot of blood at its disposal to help our cells keep us young. But a lot of blood is needed to maintain our youthful appearance. Plus, the more you eat, the more your body expects the blood. If you wean yourself a bit at a time, and you choose to look older, your cells get used to having less. Of course, the hunger never goes away. The stomach cramping, the nausea … I'm not one to complain, Miss Alex, but appearing old is no picnic. My body is used to this age, it only needs a little blood right now. Besides, …" he smiled at her, "… it won't be forever. Four more years at the most."

Alex's anger and anxiety calmed down. "I'm so sorry that your hunger hurts you so much."

"Shucks. It ain't nothing I can't deal with."

Alex pitied Mason. He did not ask to resemble the President, and now he hurt every day when the other team members didn't have to endure the same pain. There was a moment of silence between the two of them as Alex thought about their eating habits. Her curiosity needed satisfying. "So Mason, can a vampire consume too much blood? If so, what happens?"

Mason cleared his throat. "Blood brings about something we call blood lust. If there is plenty of blood to eat, our biological clocks kick in … if you get my meaning." Alex noticed Mason look away as he rubbed the back of his neck. "Now, that type of information should be in our paperwork. At the very least, perhaps Raymond could explain it to you."

Alex felt herself blushing. She found his dismissal of the topic incredibly old fashioned.

"I'll make sure to ask him," she said, smiling back at Mason.

"But, overall, I don't think there is such a thing as too much blood in our system," he continued, now making eye contact once again. "Our spleen processes the blood and stores any excess so having too much shouldn't be a problem. Of course, if you didn't have a spleen I guess you would have to be careful not to consume the blood, but rather inject it directly into your bloodstream. I reckon you'd have to inject blood often since it can't be stored."

Alex had never understood what the spleen did in humans. No better time than now to ask. "What exactly does the spleen do?"

"For you humans it's a visceral organ that doesn't do squat. For us, the spleen stores and processes the blood we consume. It routes the blood from our digestive track to our circulatory one and stores any excess blood. My guess is the two species evolved in parallel, and there are some minor differences in our organs. But don't worry about my feeding at the White House. It's only Ben and Sterling who go after the interns and the press, not me."

"The press?!?!? Oh, this is so not good Mason." She sat down on the couch and just knew there possibly were some scandals to avoid. No wonder Dixon was ready to retire at the young age of sixty–five.

"Don't worry Miss Alex. William is here a lot, he's the one that usually pulls White House duty with me. He's married and doesn't touch any of the White House gals. If need be, he feeds from syringes while he's here." Mason pointed out the small refrigerated and small warmer that rested on top. "If you don't believe me you can check the White House trash. All empty blood bags and broken syringes get tossed."

"I see."

"You have something you want to talk to me about?" He pointed to the files and schedule book in her hands.

"Yes. Yes, I do. But first, were you playing World of Warcraft when I walked in?"

Mason glanced away. She had caught him red–handed. "Yes, Ma'am."

"Which realm?"

Mason looked back towards Alex. "Tanaris."

Alex gave an all–knowing smile at Mason. "My character Zelfin exists in that realm." She went to the Ben's laptop and logged into the game with her userid and password. "I can only play for a few minutes, and then we need to discuss the schedule because I have an appointment I must keep later today."

CHAPTER THIRTY–FOUR

Raymond watched his sister cross the living room of the mansion. She carried two boxes of poker chips in one hand and a goblet of blood in the other. He watched as she skirted her way around the love seat and coffee table, and made her way to the green table that sat in the corner of the room, opposite the bay window. He thought about offering to help her, but didn't want to incur her wrath. She had been moody as of late. Raymond suspected it was because of Dixon's decision to retire.

She sat the chips down on the hexagon shaped green velvet, spilling a drop of blood from her goblet in the process.

"Damn it," she cursed, and then quickly licked the side of the glass to prevent more spillage. She reached across the table and grabbed a coaster, which was inches from Raymond's hand, and placed the challis safely down. She took a seat and pulled out a tissue from her pocket and dabbed at the stain. "Raymond, did you ever ask Alex if she played poker?"

Raymond shirked his shoulders. "The game didn't come up."

"Where is she tonight? Maybe you could see if she wants to come by and spend some time with us tonight." Sulie's smile was obvious. "I know how much you like her. I like her too. She does fit in with the family."

Raymond smiled. "She said she had plans this evening — something about an appointment she had to reschedule due to the Florida trip." Raymond thought of his schedule. He was not on the away team to Texas, so he would not see her tonight, or even tomorrow. His shoulders slumped, and a frown crossed his face. "Probably for the best really. I need to think a few things over," he said, trying to convince himself that more time was what he needed.

"What's to think about?" Sulie asked. When Raymond offered a sheepish look, she rolled her eyes. "You both like each other. It's destiny."

Raymond picked up a poker chip and tapped the chip back down at the table, like it kept pace and allowed him to think. He looked down at the chip in his hand. "She's human, Sulie."

"Most of the world is human. So what?"

He stopped tapping the chip on the table and looked up accusingly at her. "You, out of everyone, should understand. For God's sakes, you helped me raise Sterling."

"And Sterling is a half–breed," she quipped back.

Raymond's face hardened as he stared at his sister. He tossed the chip aside. "Yes, damn it. He's a half–breed. Do you know how hard it is for me to see his pain? To know that I can never arrange a marriage for him? It kills me to know that I am useless when it comes to helping him."

Sulie rolled her eyes. "I don't think Sterling is hurting for female companionship."

"He hurts for female *vampire* companionship. There are times I can sense his thoughts, and I know he'd be happier with a mate of his own kind." Raymond looked away and no longer made eye contact with Sulie. "After his Jahrling Year, when he left home for a short while …," Raymond swallowed hard, "… part of me was

246

happy to see him go." He placed his hand over his mouth, shocked the confession came out.

Shock, and then rage flared in her eyes. "That is so not true! I know exactly how much you suffered when he went rogue and shunned our bloodline. Not knowing where he was, or how he was doing. His absence was one of the hardest times in your life, and you know it!"

"Yes, but part of me was happy not to see the pain in his eyes every day." Raymond shifted nervously. "I've never admitted that to anyone before." He turned back towards the table and focused on another poker chip, playing with the tiny disk with his fingers.

Sulie reached over and put her hand on his arm, stopping the little dance of the poker chip. "It's okay. Watching loved ones suffer is always difficult."

"He'll never marry a vampire woman, well, maybe another half–breed, or he could marry a turned human — of course he treats human women with no respect, so I don't see that last one happening." Raymond took a deep breath, "He'll never have a seat on the Council or represent our bloodline."

Sulie smacked his hand with hers. "He doesn't want to be on the Council, and since he's the only child either of us has had, he basically *is* our bloodline." She paused a moment. "Wait. This isn't about Sterling. This is about you and Alex," Sulie accused, her finger-pointing at him.

Raymond nodded. "Yes, and I'm only a member of the Council because my human wife is dead. You know yourself the Council does not recognize marriages to humans. They only accepted me as a Council member, and as the Coven Master for our group, because I'm the oldest purebred among us, and I'm male. And even then

247

I had to be 100 years old to even ask that we be considered our own coven." He rolled his eyes. "If the Council wasn't in awe of my ability to compel other vampires, they never would have granted us that much, and you know it."

Raymond looked at Sulie. "If I take a human to my bed, and its public knowledge, I don't think the Council will be so forgiving this time around." Raymond then added, "Especially if a child is produced."

Sulie gave her brother a questioning look. "The other night. Things didn't go as planned?"

Raymond shrugged his shoulders. "Not in the slightest."

"You're getting ahead of yourself, Raymond." She patted him on the arm. "Dating a human is not the same as marrying her. Plus, there is no child as of yet."

"No. Of course not," he replied.

"You also don't know if Alex would want to be turned. Maybe you're worried about nothing."

He sighed and feigned renewed interest in his poker chips. "She can't be the human director for our team if she's turned. It's part of the job requirement that she be human, and I know how much this promotion means to her. Plus, … I care about her. I wouldn't turn her unless she was to be my wife, and we're not even dating, at least not yet." He put his hand to his temple. "It's just so confusing."

"It's no longer the 1800s, Raymond. The strict rules of yesteryear have softened. Sometimes I think only the Council members care about the Council rules and procedures."

He pursed his lips. "We still need a seat on the Council so we can voice our needs and opinions as a society. If I lose my seat, we lose our ability to represent ourselves, we lose any negotiation leverage to secure marriages for the kids of the Colony ..."

"I honestly do not see the Council as playing that important of a role in our every daily routine," Sulie said, cutting him off. "But, I do not want to be classified into another Coven. I like our little group and don't want to answer to anyone else," she said taking a sip from her goblet.

"I like being separated from them as much as possible as well," Raymond confided. "And, even though we work for the government, the kids might not want to follow in our footsteps. William's kids, or any other kids the team might have, may want to join another coven elsewhere. We don't need them blacklisted." He let out a deep sigh. It wasn't enough to care for this generation of team members, the little ones needed his protection as well. A vampire who wasn't protected by the Council was a starving vampire, or an exposed one. How could he knowingly risk their future?

"You fret too much. Besides, it's okay to love a human. You just need to take things on a day–by–day basis," Sulie said.

Raymond allowed her words to sink in, but they weighed heavily on him. He was being selfish to put his wants above his team members. Deep down he believed everyone should be allowed to find a wife or a husband and live happily – lifespan after lifespan. He looked over at his sister, someone who had never known such joy. "I know I ask you this periodically, so I'll ask you again," Raymond said, changing the topic. "I can contact the Council about arranging a marriage for you again."

She held up her hand. "Thank you, but no. Never. I'm fine as I am."

Raymond knew of Sulie's nickname of 'Old Maid' around the Council. Many of the available bachelors had their eyes on her as she looked the other way. He suspected Sulie never knew how much of a catch she was. "You shouldn't be alone, Sulie. You could have a family of your own."

"I'm happy with my life as it is. So, no thank you."

Raymond made eye contact with his sister. In a lowered voice, he said, "The Council voted against turning Dixon."

Sulie glanced away. "I'm aware of their decision," she curtly replied. She began stacking her cluster of chips in stacks by color.

"I would look the other way if you turned him," he whispered. Her eyes quickly made contact with his. They both understood the risks of an unapproved turning. Sure, Dixon would have the blood from the government because of the Colony, but his family line would be unprotected. The Council had connections with the Red Cross, other blood banks and hospitals across the nation. A vampire under the protection of the Council did not have to hunt for food, and thereby not run the risk of detection. There was a seedy underground for blood supplies, but usually at a high cost, so many unprotected vampires lived as scavengers, eating from humans, and always on the run so no one would discover their true natures. They also lived meagerly, unable to arrange marriages in family lines which had massive amounts of wealth through literally generations of accumulation. To be an unprotected vampire meant pain and hard work, and possibly death if your activities

250

to survive caught the notice of the Council. Raymond watched as Sulie shook her head. She did not want that future for Dixon and his descendants, and neither did Raymond.

He reached over and held his sister's hand. "Tell Dixon you love him. The Council will approve his turn if you choose to marry him."

Sulie took a deep breath, and then wiped away a tear. "Dixon isn't in love with me. I check him medically when I'm with him. He never gives off any signs of love."

Raymond shook his head. "The man loves you, Sulie."

"Even if that is true, he doesn't know it."

Raymond sighed. "Perhaps you declaring your love will be the catalyst he needs to consider his true feelings for you."

Sulie frowned. "Or he'll turn and run." She bit her lip. "I still have time before you wipe his memory, right?"

Raymond raised his hand as though taking an oath. "I swear not to touch his mind without your knowledge."

"Thank you." She accepted the handkerchief Raymond offered. "So? Alex, huh?"

He drew in a deep breath. "I'm starting to have feelings for her. I actually miss her when she's not around." Raymond smiled, but then added, "She wants children though."

"You're a great father, just look at how wonderful Sterling turned out. Plus, you get along beautifully with William's children. You love kids. There's nothing wrong with having more."

He grimaced. "As a human she would only be fertile for just a short time more; we'd have to have children soon. They would be …," he paused briefly, "… they would be half–breeds."

"Half–breed or purebred … What difference does it make anyway? A baby is a baby."

Before they could continue their conversation, they heard Ben's heavy footsteps in the kitchen. Sulie hugged Raymond's hand within her own hands, ending their private conversation. The winner of tonight's game not only had to do laundry for the house, since they still didn't have a housekeeper, but also got to choose the team names for the Austin trip. Raymond hoped the names would be livelier than the last set, which was Team A and Team B.

CHAPTER THIRTY–FIVE

"Thank you so much, Micki, for rescheduling me this past week." Alex said as she sat down on her usual spot on the white couch. With Alex leaving the next day for Austin, Texas, this was the only chance she would have to talk with the doctor.

"No problem." Micki closed the door, tossed her keys into her handbag, and placed it on the table. She then opened her drawer and pulled out a notebook and pen before finally taking her own seat. "I don't mind working the occasional evening when it's needed. You sounded stressed on the phone. Did you take the promotion?"

Alex sat on the edge of the couch cushion. She wasn't sure when the transition occurred, but she now was a full believer in therapy. She hated being here, hated spilling her guts to a total stranger, but she felt she needed to talk to someone about recent developments and was so relieved when Micki said she could be available this evening.

"Yes, I did take the promotion," she began, "but that wasn't what I wanted to talk with you about. ... Well, it kind of is. It's a new environment. Different than what I'm used to." Alex chose her words carefully. "I just hope they can accept me as the new security chief."

Micki jotted down the information. "Why wouldn't they accept you? You'd be one of them, right? A member of the team?"

"A member of the team, yes. One of them? ... Not exactly." Alex purposefully sidestepped any details of any differences that existed – the obvious one being human vs. vampire. "I wanted to talk to you about the man I work with." Alex paused, thinking what would be the best way to discuss her situation. "His name is … 'Michael'." She felt that she shouldn't use Raymond's real name for security reasons, even though Micki had assured her several times over the years that everything shared would be confidential. "He's wonderful. He's tall and muscular, good–looking. He has a sweet nature about him too and I love spending time with him." She bit her lip. "I want to date him, Micki."

Micki narrowed her eyes to study her client. "Whether you have a relationship or not, you'll be working closely with this man. Long hours. Evenings, weekends." Micki leaned in toward her patient. "How do you feel about that?"

Alex took a deep breath. "I'm okay with that. He's … well, he's different. Honorable. Trustworthy – and I'm not just saying that because I have access to his private files and know a lot about him."

Micki nodded, obviously taking it in. "The problem is that you work with him."

"Oh, yeah." When Micki just stared at her, Alex continued, "It is a conflict of interest. If I date him I could lose the promotion." She inwardly groaned. It was more than that and she knew it. Relationships usually only ended bitterly or happily ever after. A break up would probably lead to her being dismissed eventually as the Director, and her memory zapped. Happily ever after sounded great, unless she became a vampire and could no longer be the human liaison for the team. Dating Raymond led down just one road – and it would be a bad career move.

"I want to see him romantically, but it's a bad career choice," she admitted.

"There are often several risks when it comes to love — if we are talking about love and not a fleeting encounter."

Shaking her head, Alex confessed, "It would not be fleeting."

"It is your career, and your choice, but just last session you made the observation … ," she flipped back a page in the notebook, "that you always put your career first. 'It's what I do', you said."

A slight smile crossed Alex's lips. "That does sound like me."

"Love is a leap of faith, Alex. There are no guarantees when it comes to the heart."

Alex realized she did want a guarantee. Even a crystal ball of some sort that could see into the future would be welcomed. She leaned forward and rubbed her temple with her fingertips. "Michael is perfect … Simply perfect in every way. But … ," Alex sighed. " … I don't know how to say this."

When she noticed Micki slyly glace at her watch, Alex began. "Let's say I did start seeing him, and it works out. Michael is … a different religion than I am."

"Oh?" Micki opened her notebook and started taking notes again. "Tell me about him and what his religion is. You're Catholic, right?" Alex nodded. "Is his religion a denomination of Christianity?"

"Let's just say that his religion is different from mine. … Overall I don't mind his religion. I find it quite sexy. … I can see myself with him for a very long, long time. The thing is, what if he asks me to convert?"

Micki set her pen down. "When you say that you see yourself with him a 'very long, long time' are you thinking possibly of marriage to him?"

"Sure, if the relationship works out," Alex said, sitting more pensive on the couch.

Micki set the notepad in her lap. "Alex, you just met the man. I think you need to examine what you're feeling and understand that this relationship is really only in its infancy."

"I know. I know." Alex wrung her hands. She hadn't realized she had been sweating. The office was normally a cool temperature, and yet she felt the need to wipe her hands on her pant leg. "In the best scenario, let's just say that he is the one I marry."

"Would that be the best scenario?"

"For the sake of argument, let's say it is. I don't know how I feel about converting. Another team member told me that he converted and lost his family in the process."

Micki sighed. "OK. So if this man, who you currently are not dating, were to ask you to marry him, he may never ask you to convert."

"Oh, I think it is important to him," Alex said.

"OK. What else is important? Does he want children? You always told me you want children one day."

"He has a child already. I think he'd be open to having more children."

Micki's eyebrow rose under her bleached bangs. "Is he divorced?"

"Widowed."

"I see." Micki said in a hushed tone. "Is his child young?"

256

The question took Alex a bit by surprise. She didn't want to focus on any elaborate lies. "He's older. Out of the house. Really a non–issue."

"Children are not so easily dismissed, Alex. I assume his son is very important to him."

"Yes."

Micki simply nodded. "If you and Michael had children, what religion would you raise them as, Alex?"

Alex thought back to the conversation she had with Sterling the first time she had met him. "Oh, they'd definitely be his religion. No question about that."

"They'd be your kids too. They don't have to be his religion. This would have to be negotiated by the two of you before any marriage and definitely before any planned pregnancy."

"I wouldn't mind them being his religion. Actually, it'd be great if they did have his religion and lived such long happy lives."

"So your husband would be this religion, your children would be this religion, your household would embrace this religion. I'm curious. What issues exactly would prevent you from converting to this religion as well?"

Alex bit her lip and sat deep in thought. Finally, she said, "That is an excellent question, Micki."

"But I want you to understand something. You're putting the cart before the horse. You said you were not dating him at the moment. And are you willing to risk this promotion over him?"

Alex focused on that and took a deep breath. "I don't know. Maybe."

CHAPTER THIRTY–SIX

Dixon walked Matt and Brandon down to his office. "I'm so glad you boys were using your head and keeping your eyes open. This is a good find. Could be a security leak."

Brandon and Matt shared a triumphant look with each other as Dixon led them down the hallway. They had found an abandoned janitor uniform at the State Dinner's new place, and thought the outfit could be part of a plan to harm the President.

The uniform contained no embroidered name tag, but that was standard issue at the hall and not alarming. Being stuffed in a cabinet in one of the first floor's mens rooms was what made it suspicious. Another worry for Dixon was the size of the uniform. It fit a large man, one over six feet in height, and a very lean one at that. The accompanying shoes were size fifteen mens.

A database search had already been conducted to find out how many custodians in the employ of the hall would fit the suit. Surprisingly, three men had the correct build – and they were all human. None of them could account for the lost, or perhaps stolen uniform. Raymond had already questioned the three men, but found them to be hard–working men with no qualms about the President or his administration.

Forensics inspected the items. Any prints, hair, or DNA they retrieved were dead–ends in the system. The items were now in Dixon's office, lying in a box on top of his desk. Any story they may have would have to be told by Sterling's special ability.

The three entered the office where Raymond and Sterling waited. Sterling was already touching the article of clothing, carefully reading the fabric, the buttons, and zipper. His eyes were closed in concentration, but opened when the doorknob turned and the men entered.

"Smith. Jones," Dixon said to Raymond and Sterling, "These are the men that found the uniform. I told them you wanted to talk with them."

Even before Dixon closed the office door, Raymond recognized the two men.

"Oh, hell no!" Sterling furrowed his brow and shook his head. Raymond knew that Sterling had wiped the shorter man's mind so many times over the last several years he wasn't sure if the man's mind could handle much more. Hell, Sterling had wiped the man's mind just yesterday morning.

"Hey, Detective Smith! Nice to see you again!" Brandon, the shorter human, said.

Raymond's eyebrow rose as he looked from the human to his son. "Interesting," he said. "You remember working with Detective Smith before?" he asked Brandon.

Brandon glanced over to Raymond, then back to Sterling. "Um, yes. I guess," he stammered. He studied Sterling. "We worked together on ... well, the case was a while back on ... something." He shook his head, not remembering any specifics. He looked over to Matt for help.

Matt held out his hand to Raymond. "It's a pleasure to meet both of you. I believe this is the first time we've met."

Raymond shook Matt's hand. Matt stood taller than Raymond at a height of six foot five. For a human, he was quite tall. The mental patterns from Matt were even and calm, like a glacial lake. There was no recognition from him as to the vampires' true identities. The two shook hands, "I'm Agent Jones. Nice to meet you."

Focusing now on Brandon, Raymond read his thought patterns. They were confusing to say the least. The man's thoughts were clear, but his patterns were choppy like a record that had been scratched too many times – which was a sign of having been compelled too often. Raymond sighed. Brandon's mental record was not broken, but he was nearing the point of not being able to be compelled anymore.

Sterling continued inspecting the clothes. His bare hands ran up and down the sleeves, and around the back and collar. In the high–pitched vampire speak, he talked with his father. "The little one is a problem. His mind is nearly Swiss cheese." When his father merely nodded a reply, Sterling added, "Either we should offer full disclosure or transfer him to another department." He reached for the boots in the box, "I don't like the man, so you can guess which choice I prefer."

Raymond put his hand to his mouth to hide his moving lips, "Sterling, full disclosure is not an option. Not until we can't compel him anymore. His security clearance is not high enough." The protocol was clear, and his son should know it. Only the President, the Vice President, the Speaker of the House, Colony Director, and now the Director of Homeland Security were privileged with the knowledge of the vampires. A few others knew, but only because it had been a last resort due to their mind's inability to handle a vampire's touch.

Matt and Brandon watched intensely as Sterling reviewed the boots. Sterling's fingers worked down the

260

laces, swiped over the tongue, and felt the sole and heel of each boot.

Brandon lacked expertise in evidence preservation, but obviously guessed that this was not a standard technique to preserve evidence in a case. "Excuse me. Smith? Shouldn't you be putting on gloves to touch evidence?"

"And shouldn't the gloves be rubber?" Matt added, noticing the cloth ones on the desk. He and Brandon exchanged knowing head nods at each other like they had both seen the same episode of CSI.

Sterling ignored all the questions from the humans.

"What are you hoping to do with those boots?" Brandon asked.

Sterling's jaw tightened. he took a deep breath and now bothered to look at the humans. "I'm going to scour the kingdom looking for the foot that it fits. … Dad, wipe them!"

Raymond's face flushed red. The look from the two humans questioned as to why he was being called "Dad" by a man clearly older than he was.

Before the two could ask any questions, Raymond said, "Fellas, I'm going to need you to look at me for a moment." As they did, their faces paled and their eyes grew dim. "You two found nothing unusual at the hotel for the State Dinner."

"We found nothing," they said in unison.

"And as always, you can trust that Dixon will get to the bottom of everything. So, please contact him if you notice anything out of the ordinary. Now get back to work." Both Brandon and Matt looked around the room. "We should be heading back to work." Matt said.

"Ya, think!?!" Sterling snarled without even looking at them.

Dixon opened the door and let the two men out. "I'll be here in my office if you need me. Thanks for coming by."

Now with the privacy of Dixon's office restored, Sterling set the boots back in the box, sat in Dixon's chair and placed his hands on the armrests. His hands tightened and his knuckles whitened. His breath grew even as he took slow and methodical breaths.

"Are you in pain?" his father asked.

"Not more than usual." Sterling raised his hand and pointed towards the box. "There's nothing on these clothes. They're old, at least a couple of years." He stood and grabbed his gloves from the desk. "This isn't evidence. All I'm getting is a headache from touching them."

As he and his father left Dixon's office, Sterling looked back at Dixon. "Keep an eye out for 'Bert and Ernie' there Dixon. We don't need them turning up any vamps on their own."

CHAPTER THIRTY–SEVEN

The next morning Fang Manor was quiet. Too quiet for Raymond's tastes. Sulie and her team left early for the trip to Austin, Texas with the President for his energy speech to the University. Raymond remained in D.C. to take care of security at home because of the upcoming dinner, but he'd rather be seated next to Alex aboard Air Force One. Being separated from her pained him, even for a day. It was hard for him to even comprehend that it had only been a week since he first met her.

He had fallen hard.

He sat alone in his bedroom and reached into his small refrigerator to retrieved his breakfast. He stretched out on the bed while his breakfast sat in the warmer and his thoughts went to Alex, which didn't help the current flagpole situation where his manhood was concerned.

He fed himself the blood and enjoyed the warmth of it as it entered and surged in his body. This morning however, when he closed his eyes and allowed himself to get carried away with the bliss of the blood, his thoughts were of Alex, the way she felt, and her scent. It was her name he growled as he came.

****

Visions of Alex consumed Raymond's thoughts, and he found it difficult to sit idle just missing her. He busied himself with work in an effort to keep his mind occupied. With the team separated, he volunteered to work a double shift and spent the day with William and

Ben at the White House. The three hid away from prying human eyes by sitting in the Cave. Ben sat at the small table, the other two on the hideous green couch. The large panel screen on the wall buzzed with nine monitor feedbacks in what looked like a White House Hollywood Squares.

The video feed the Colony received split off from the monitors the human team viewed. The human team watched the visitors down in the W16 security room and relied on facial recognition programs to detect potential threats. The vampire team filtered their incoming images with an infrared scanner. Today the team performed two tasks—their daily task of checking for vampires trying to infiltrate the White House, and also monitoring for the woman whose picture was on one of the forged security pass they had retrieved only days earlier.

Raymond and William sat side–by–side, dwarfing the small couch and causing its springs to buckle in the middle. Each worked on a laptop and typed away on their keyboards as Ben sat at the desk viewing bank and phone records for Verna Foiles. Raymond had just signed into a secure vampire database, one in which he was allowed to access as a member of the North American Vampire Council, and searched for a woman matching the picture from the security pass. The computer slowly did its magic as it scanned all the database entries. Again he found himself sitting idle, and again he thought of Alex.

Waiting for any response, and doing his best to keep his head in the game, Raymond looked up at the video tick–tack–toe board showing him the nine different views of rooms within the White House. The images were a light green hue, standard for infrared sensors.

"Has the intern, Verna Foiles, come in for work today?" he asked.

William stopped typing on his keyboard. "Woman isn't supposed to be here today, not according to the schedule anyhow. Lady's been out the last few days though. She missed her last two shifts. If she's a vamp, she's dust by now. Else she's swimming with the fishes somewhere. That's my guess."

"No." Raymond shook his head. "Her image was on one of the passes. I'm betting she's still alive. With the President out of residence today it's a good time for whatever they may have in mind."

Ben glanced over at the two, "She should cover her tracks better. Not calling in about her missing work just sent flags up to the humans. They'll be on alert the second she logs in for work."

The changing screen on Raymond's laptop caught his attention. He looked down and saw the results of his search. No female vampire matched the facial recognition from the ID pass on any vampire database he searched – which included the family line database, the eligible bachelorette vampire database, and the known missing rogue database. Of course, she could be an independent and not registered anywhere, or perhaps she was registered in the European, Asian, or other vampire databases. Unfortunately, he had limited access to those databases.

William noticed a message on his computer. He clicked a button and focused on the computer display. "Wait up. The badge reader just signed her in." William adjusted the image on his computer and shot it up to the big display on the wall so Raymond and Ben could see.

265

"This is the feed from the kitchen entrance. She's not coming in through her normal door."

Raymond stared at the image. "No infrared heat signature. She's no longer human." Newly turned — it confirmed the lack of results he got from the vampire databases.

Ben added, "She also got a bleach job to disguise herself. Which department does she normally work in?"

William pulled up a second window to the large screen to view the work schedule. He scanned back and showed the schedule for the last three months, her name highlighted in the roster. "Speech writing, some work with the environmental groups — grunt work mostly." He brought the camera images to the forefront of the computer screen. "Woman is heading towards the Oval Office."

"Let me guess, she's never worked in that wing of the White House before," Raymond asked.

"Nope. And I don't think she's there to work today," William said.

Ben had been overseeing the human team's activity on his personal laptop. "Human guards are on the move," he said standing up. "I'll get them first. She may be newly turned, but she can still wipe them out easily enough." He ran out of the room at vampire speed, the papers on the small desk he was using picked up in the breeze.

The display on the wall monitor was of the cameras in the West Wing. "I have her passing the Oval Office," William said into the com unit. "I think she's heading to the Situation Room downstairs."

"Stay here and monitor her." Raymond adjusted his earpiece. "Ben, I'm heading to the Situation Room right now."

William texted all Colony members the status.

****

Raymond received a text from Sterling indicating he was minutes away from joining the party. Raymond texted back, "solo fem vamp blond in Sit Rm. W8 4 me. No hostility so far." He sped down to the basement of the West Wing to catch Verna, taking three to four steps at a time at super speed. He caught the scent of another predator once he neared the Oval Office and pulled out his silver flex whip and his SBC Launcher, also known as a silver bolt cannon. Through his earpiece Ben said that another set of human guards were already in the Situation Room and were now in jeopardy.

Sterling started receiving the audio signals on his secure com link once he breached the White House perimeter. "I'm outside on the grounds," Sterling announced. "I tripped the underground sensors. It should keep some of the guards busy. William, make it look like an equipment error in a few minutes."

"No problem," William replied in the com link.

Raymond descended the stairs to the basement. A group of human guards lay unconscious on the floor in the hallway just before the Situation Room. He knelt next to one of them and noticed they were still alive, only asleep. He breathed a sigh of relief as he looked into the President's personal command center, or Sit Room, as it was often called. Verna wasn't in the main conference room area, but the glass to the Director's Office was fogged, signaling the motion sensor had been triggered. "She's in the President's private office," he said into his earpiece in a whispered voice. He watched as she left the small room and entered the main conference room, with no knowledge that Raymond lay in wait for her.

Her focus remained on her task at hand, or she would have noticed another predator so close by. She walked to a painting which hung on the wall, and place what looked like a bug within its large wooden frame. She did the same with the other two smaller paintings in the room before looking closer at the heavy wooden desk which took up most of the space in the room. Its dark red varnish was reflective, and Raymond could see her look of concentration even though her back was to him. Next she pulled out one of the black leather chairs and began to inspect it for what Raymond thought would be another place to hide a bug.

Overall, her plan was ridiculous. This room had built-in sensors to detect bugs. Of course, the general population wasn't privy to such information. Hiding the bugs on picture frames? Raymond didn't even want to think of how obvious that was.

Sterling appeared at the bottom of the stairs with Ben, just a few feet away from the unconscious guards and the entrance to the Sit Room. They approached the room with caution, but they must have affected Verna's senses because her eyes darted towards the door. Her focus was no longer on the bugs she planted, but probably on escaping and perhaps hurting one of the team members on her way out. She looked towards the door away from where Raymond hid. He had a good shot of her and took it. He discharged a silver bolt from his SBC Launcher and the bolt passed through her body without harming her. She dodged behind a chair on the far side of the large conference room table and pulled out a gun, taking two shots at Raymond.

Raymond ducked into the Director's Office for shelter, and the now clear glass fogged once more. "She's armed," he announced even though the team members would have heard the shots and, by now, smelled the gunshot residue. He felt confusion and apprehension from her thought patterns. She wasn't expecting vampires to be protecting the White House, and she wasn't sure what to do next — which was why the Colony and their mission were always kept secret.

When Raymond heard another bullet whiz by the door, he knew that even through her confusion she was willing to kill to get what she wanted. She had spared the human guards' lives, but obviously she came prepared to use force.

Raymond surveyed the small office for any strategic advantage against his opponent. The room was a basic office, although with sound resistant padding and expensive furniture. It had a wooden desk, comfortable brown leather chair, and computer equipment – and everything was stamped with the presidential seal. There was nothing out of the ordinary. The room had exactly one exit, and that was not to his advantage. He needed to make sure the confrontation with her did not capture him in this small area.

He walked to the President's desk and tugged at the first drawer, which broke the lock. Pens, cell phone chargers, and what looked like a generous number of letter openers lay inside. Raymond also noticed an ornate box, so he opened it. He was surprised to find a small dagger inside, but wasn't going to question the perfect timing of the find. He touched the hilt to remove it from the box. His fingertip sizzled when his hand contacted with the silver. Dropping the box back into the drawer he let out a slight curse. He then collected the sharp metal, non–silver, letter openers to use as projectile weapons if necessary.

Ben lurched his body into the room and took refuge behind a conference room chair. He inched closer to where Verna hid. When she rose to take another shot at Raymond, Ben fired a silver bolt directly at her back. The bolt burst through her clothing and splattered her purplish–red blood on the conference room desk and the wall. She yelled in pain as she dove towards the plush carpeted floor. Turning her attention towards Ben, she fired two rounds in his direction, one of which hit him in the shoulder. Ben let out a grunt as his purple blood spilled out onto his shirt, and he ducked down out of the way of fire.

Raymond saw the action and flung five letter openers through the air. Verna's cries as she ducked for cover told him that they hit their target.

Sterling seized the opportunity and jumped up on the conference room table, soiling its fine varnished finish. From Raymond's vantage point, he could see Verna pulling the daggers from her quickly aging body. Her long, now white hair, was being stained with deep purple blood as she fought with the letter openers. Sterling whipped his Flex Whip. As the weapon sliced through the air, the leather unveiled itself and revealed the silver flex strips. The whip coiled itself around the woman's body, burning her where it touched her flesh. Her remaining golden locks turned to gray as she visibly changed from mid forties to her late fifties. Her life–

sustaining blood stained the plush rug below her and she moaned in agony. The whip restricted her movements, and she fell backwards onto the silver bolt that still ratcheted itself deeper and deeper into her flesh.

Raymond approached her first, with Sterling jumping off the table directly beside him. Her gun had fallen from her hand and out of reach. Raymond stood above her in the tight corner of the room. Ben slid the conference room table out of the way so he too could join the team.

She resembled the young woman Raymond had viewed on the monitor only moments ago, but now she was aged. Her appearance exceeded the age of 60. Her blood spilled onto him, soiling his clothes. She was going to bleed out before the team could get their answers. She was completely immobilized, so he began questioning her.

"I've got her." Raymond said as he held the now frail body to the ground. "Sterling, start scanning. Ben, check for humans."

Blood covered Ben's shirt, but his shoulder was healing itself already. He searched the hallways to check for humans and William assured him that none were around according to the monitors. William sent stilled pictures to the guard stations and had disabled the motion sensors before Verna even crossed the hallway to the Oval Office.

Raymond focused his attention on Verna and compelled her to answer all of his questions. "What did you plan to do here today?"

Her face flinched in pain. "Bugs. I was planting bugs."

"For what purpose?" he pressed.

She licked her lips and murmured through the pain, "Presidential decision on Supreme Court nomination to replace Justice McCade."

"Justice McCade isn't retiring." Sterling said as he removed his gloves and began touching the woman's clothes. Her body flinched in pain the second he touched her. Her eyes shut as a moan escaped her lips. "Shit," Sterling cursed as he read images from her jewelry. "He isn't retiring. He's being murdered."

Raymond tightened his grip. "Is Justice McCade your only target on the court?"

She struggled to shake her head, and finally said, "No. There are others."

"Who?" Raymond asked. His hands now applying pressure to her wounds to slow her death. Her blood oozed through his fingers, staining them a deep purplish hue.

"I don't know," she moaned. "Please help me." Her hands reached out towards him, her eyes beseeched him.

Raymond held his ground. "Who are you working for?"

Blood spat out of her mouth as she replied. "His name is Zmiya. Groyki Zmiya."

"Who else are you working with?" Raymond looked at Sterling and mouthed the word 'blood'. Raymond grabbed Sterling's glove and did his best to remove the silver bolt which was draining the life out of his prisoner. The bolt was just two inches long, and half an inch in diameter, but it ratcheted deeper and deeper into her flesh with the barbs along its sides. Her skin sizzled in response to the silver.

"I only know Zmiya," she gasped as death tightened its grip. She closed her eyes as her breathing slowed.

Sterling injected three syringes of human blood into her, giving her a burst of momentary energy.

Her eyes opened once again. "Blood. Please ... More blood." Now red human blood spilled from her wounds. Raymond could feel the increase of bodily fluid as the new blood poured over his fingers and mixed with the darkened purple which had already spilled to the floor.

He struggled, but eventually Raymond successfully removed the bolt and tossed it onto the floor, his hands burned in the process where the bolt touched him in his haste. "After you answer my questions you'll get more blood. How are you going to kill Justice McCade?" He interpreted her thought patterns. She was merely a pawn in Zmiya's game — a scared pawn who didn't want to die, but was so in love with the creep she would not give him up unless she was compelled.

"Poison. He's being killed with poison," she choked out.

"Are other Justices in danger?"

"I don't know," she shook her head.

Adding more pressure to her wounds, Raymond asked, "Is there an antidote?"

She closed her eyes and whispered, "I don't know"

"Where is Zmiya?"

"… Don't know," she sobbed.

"What is Zmiya's plan?"

"… d'know." Her eyes tightened and her lips pursed in pain. Another injection of human blood was performed by Sterling.

During the questioning, Sterling continued his tactile search. He touched her clothing, the contents of her pockets as he emptied them, which included the bugs

273

she was planning to plant, and he even touched her skin. "I've got all I can from her."

Ben stood above the three of them. "Hallway is clear."

Verna's blond hair was all white, her bones frail, and her skin an ashen color. Raymond loosened his grip on her and began to lick her wounds. "She's dying," he said between licks.

"Let her die," Ben said.

Raymond glanced up, but continued sealing the wounds.

Without offering to help, Ben simply said, "Last time I checked, treason was punishable by death."

He now looked to his son for aid. "Help me Sterling. Other than misplaced loyalties she isn't a bad person." Her blood now pooled faster onto the floor. The two began licking her wounds, but she turned to dust before their eyes.

The three soldiers stood in the puddle of blood and dust which was once Verna. Raymond shot Ben a look of disgust.

"The bitch shot me! She was only repentant at her end. If she had survived, she would have still been a traitor to this country."

"We could have gotten more information from her, or even have used her to lure Zmiya out," Sterling said. He put on his gloves and retrieved the bolts which now sat among the scattered ashes.

"She had the ability to faze her body so objects could pass through." Raymond admired. "Nice little trick."

"That still didn't save her." Ben fiddled with the leather band of Sterling's whip until it caught in the leather casing. Without touching the silver, he wound the chain up within the leather until it was safe for him to hand the weapon over to Sterling.

Fastening his gloves Sterling thanked Ben for the whip. "She was food for Zmiya for months until he recently turned her." He shuddered. "She was in love with the man. She thought by helping him she'd prove her worth to him."

"Sad, but an enemy of the state nonetheless. I'll search for information about Zmiya from the Council database." Raymond knelt down and collected Verna's dust and some blood samples. "Officially we'll have to classify her as EKIA and her COD a stabbing. Unofficially, her human family won't understand what happened to her, so we'll have to list her as a missing person." Pocketing the remains, he added, "Sulie will want to review her DNA for information about her transparency ability." He walked down the hallway removing his phone from his pocket to dial his sister.

"That's odd," Sterling said as Ben surveyed the mess in the room.

"What is?" Ben asked.

A puzzled look appeared on Sterling's face. "She said his name was Zmiya."

"Yes. Do you know the family?" Ben asked.

"Back when I worked with the United Nations I did some work with the Russian ambassador, who was an ass and his men hated him. They called him zmiya behind his back."

"Could he be related to our Zmiya?"

Sterling shook his head. "I doubt it. The word zmiya in Russian is an old slang term."

"For what?" asked Ben.

"Serpent."

CHAPTER THIRTY–EIGHT

Raymond rejoined William in the Cave as he kept vigil on the monitors. Fortunately, no other vampires tried to gain entry into the White House. With no more threats, the West Wing needed a cleanup job.

Dark purple blood spatter had run vertically down the beige colored walls when Verna had ducked for cover, making a horrific display which now needed to be cleaned up. The short wooden filing cabinet stood against the wall draped in blood as well, but at least it was locked shut, so no blood had ended up on the contents inside. The plush dark brown carpet had taken most of the damage. A sticky mess of blackened blood and dust combining into a paste lay thick and heavy on the rug. With his arm now fully healed, Ben scrubbed the corporal remains of Verna from every surface, leaving everything looking as good as new.

Ben's injury was not a through–and–through. He caught in his hand the brass bullet as the object made its way out of his body. The other bullets fired by Verna were wedged into the walls and furniture. They needed to be dislodged, the walls puttied over, and the chair upholstery fixed. After the final scrubbing with bleach was done, Ben joined Sterling in the M16 room to help wipe the memories of any guards who may have witnessed the event. Thanks to the surveillance monitors having been hacked into by William, not much work was needed.

Raymond glanced over from his computer screen when Sterling and Ben rejoined them in the Cave. Once again, "no match" came up on the monitor when he searched for the name Groyki Zmiya. He figured, with a foreign sounding name, any reference to him may be in a foreign vampire database, and not at his disposal.

"Where is Justice McCade? And what protection do you suggest for him?" Ben asked.

Raymond closed the search screen on his laptop. Of course, he needed to search for Justice McCade. In the rush to find Zmiya he almost forgot about the man's targeted victim. He logged into an internal government website and used his mouse to click the necessary links. "I'm trying to download the Justice's calendar." Raymond pointed to the large display screen that hung on the wall showing William's current task. "William transferred the images from the cams to our server so we can do a review. He also erased the footage from the main feed."

"Human guards are now clean," Sterling said as he sat on the green couch. "They all think a computer glitch caused the security sensors to go haywire."

Looking at his son, Raymond asked, "What about the guards that were attacked by Verna?"

"Awake and fully refreshed. They think their shifts just started." Sterling wiped his hands together in a spic–and–span manner, suggesting that everything needing to be done had been done.

"The last White House tour has finished and the place is shut down for now." Ben watched the security monitors. "West Wing staff is shutting down for the night. No stewards are in the kitchen since the President isn't in–residence."

William adjusted the cameras to show the West Wing, Residential Hall, and the kitchen. Employees were leaving, lights were turned out, and all was quiet.

"Ben, I want you and Sterling walking the grounds. Coms stay on. William will watch the monitors for any activity."

Sterling nodded over to Ben, and the two left the Cave on their assigned task.

Raymond had contacted the other Coven Masters of the American Council during his search for Zmiya, but the task proved fruitless. A Google search produced nothing as well. Without an image, fingerprints or DNA, it was near impossible to track the vampire down. Zmiya was definitely a vampire since he turned Verna, which meant that somewhere out there a family line existed, unless he was an independent and didn't live in a coven. More than likely, he was rogue and his family line had disinherited him. Since the American Vampire Council turned up nothing, Raymond had placed a call into the European, Canadian and South American Vampire Councils and was waiting to hear back from them.

The schedule for the Justice showed nothing out of the ordinary. Raymond checked the list of meetings the man had had for the last several weeks, and there were no mystery meetings on his calendar. All names, dates and places checked out. He pulled up phone records for the man, but everything looked fine.

Raymond reached for his phone. "I need to update Dixon and Alex on what happened," he said to William. He glanced down at the phone in his hands. This was the first time he had thought of Alex in a while because of all the excitement. *This is a hell of a way for her to start her week, and it's only going to get worse,* he thought. He began to dial her number when his cell phone rang. Looking down at the secured line, he realized she was calling him.

Ring–ring! Ring–ring!

Raymond answered his phone, "Go."

"'Team Kick Butt calling in with status," Alex said from the other end of the line.

"'Team Fairy Dust acknowledges." Damn full house beating his four–of–a–kind last night.

William let out a soft chuckle in the background; Raymond ignored him.

"What is the status Alex?" Raymond asked.

"All is well with nothing to report. How is the house?"

"Secure now. How are you doing in Texas?"

"Oh, Texas is fine. I sent the report you wrote about the camera malfunction to the human team. They're now all a buzz and doing diagnostics on all their equipment and have no clue a vampire entered the Sit Room. The President is in his private quarters and tucked in for the night. He was told the truth and feels fortunate not to have been home today. Sulie and the team are running a perimeter check here at the hotel and will be gone for a few hours. What about you?"

"Situation is normal around here, finally. White House tours stopped the minute Sterling tripped the outside alarms."

"Sounds good," Alex said.

"With this second breech, I'm glad the setting for the State Dinner was changed."

"Me too," Alex agreed.

"The President has hosted affairs in this new ballroom before, so that makes it easier for the human team to quickly assess the dangers. The Advance Team is already running security checks as we speak. It'll be a headache to get everything changed, especially with it being your first week on the job, but at least everyone knows their part." Raymond heard a pause on the phone. "You still there Alex?"

"Yeah, yeah. I'm fine. Nothing like a trial by fire to get me up to speed. At least the speech tonight at Greggory Gym at the university went well."

"That is good news."

"I'm in my hotel room. Sulie is my roommate again."

Raymond smiled. "I hope you like my sister, considering that she's probably always going to be your roommate." Raymond hated talking on the phone instead of in person. He wanted to have a long talk with her about something other than business. Sighing, Raymond realized just how much he missed Alex.

"How is Ben's shoulder?" she asked.

"He's fine. The bullet expelled itself. He keeps a jar of bullets at Fang Manor for all the times he's been shot."

"Really?"

Raymond cleared his throat. "We all do."

Alex lowered her voice. "You know, I was really worried about you."

Raymond could hear the concern in her voice. He looked down at his blood soaked clothes. "I'm fine."

"… So are you alone?"

"No. William is here. We're held up in the Cave at the White House checking out surveillance cams and reviewing the footage. Why do you ask?"

Alex giggled. "I was just going to ask you what you were wearing."

Raymond wondered if her question had to do with the bloodstains on his clothes, but she couldn't have

281

known about them. "My clothes have some blood on them, but none of it is mine. All the blood belonged to Verna."

"That's not exactly what I meant. Just skip it. Since you're working I'll let you go."

"OK. I'll talk with you at the next check–in time. Bye." Raymond hung up the phone still wondering about the clothes. "William, please text the team the latest checkpoint was cleared."

"Got it." William looked over at Raymond. "What's wrong?"

"It's just odd. She couldn't have known about my stained clothing, and yet she asked me what I was wearing."

William smiled in disbelief. "Dude! She asked what you were wearing?"

"Yes. Why?"

"Duuuude!" William said, lengthening the vowel. "You know you're older than dirt, right? Ay'ight, this is what I've been talking about. You and the boys, your sister included, just don't keep up. You can text and shit, but you don't know the lingo. I beg y'all to just get online and surf a little, or hell, watch a little TV or something to keep up. You're so out of touch you didn't even see this fly lady wanting your ass and askin' for phone sex."

Raymond took a seat next to William. "She wanted to have sex with me over the phone?"

"Sounds like it to me. "

Raymond gazed down at his phone, and he shook his head. "Sounds a bit impersonal. Plus, we have work to do," Raymond said as he put his phone away. He wondered if phone sex was what the phone option *69 meant.

CHAPTER THIRTY–NINE

The plates clinked against one another as Alex set the heavy tray outside her hotel room. She winced at the sight of leftover food. Leaving the French fries didn't bother her since she hadn't eaten the grease–ridden things in years, but the leftover extra large sandwich proved too much for her to eat. She noticed the security guards placed up and down the hallway like live tin soldiers, but these were dressed in black suits and wired com units – with guns holstered under their jackets. Feeling a bit self–conscious, she placed the tin cover over her dinner plate to hide the waste. She had asked for a small salad instead of the fries, but, after waiting over an hour for room service, she decided not to complain and ate the club sandwich, which wasn't that tasty.

She walked back into the posh hotel room, making sure the door securely locked behind her. The small room was extravagant with the details. A beveled mirror hung in the bathroom just above the two large basins and what she guessed were marble sinks. The double beds had beautiful bedspreads on them which looked freshly laundered, at least to the point where Alex didn't feel germy after she sat down on one. Even the drapes and furniture appeared spic–and–span, clean and neat in every way.

She entered the bathroom and washed her hands, drying them on the plush white hand towel. Reaching into her pocket, she checked her handheld monitor to read the latest Secret Service announcement. "P.O.T.U.S. Lock Down." She knew the President was secured in his hotel suite, leaving her with nothing to do tonight since she had already eaten dinner and had showered. As she lay down on the bed, her thoughts instantly overflowed with images of Raymond, the sound of his voice, and the feel of him. Perhaps Micki was right. What held her back? All these years she sat on that same damn couch, spilling her guts. Micki always told her that she was holding herself back in the romance department. Alex always sought out safe passages through the valley of love, and here was the proof.

Alex suspected she was falling in love with Raymond. He shared the story of his dead wife with her, and that touched her more than anything any man had ever done to her in the past. She fluffed the pillow under her head. Why hadn't Raymond picked up on the phone sex idea? She had gathered her courage all day just to suggest it, and the idea fell flat. God, she wanted to be with him so much. She wondered what his touch would be like, how soft his kisses would be. Her thoughts were interrupted when Sulie entered their room.

"I prefer presidential flyovers to personal visits and hotel stays," Sulie said as she let out an exhausted sigh. Sulie placed her room key on the wooden dresser that sat across from the two beds. "My shift is finally over. Looks like we're both in for the night, with a very early start tomorrow." She sipped from a water bottle as she sat on her bed.

"Let me guess. Not water, right?" Alex pointed at the metal container Sulie carried. The metal of the bottle hid the liquid inside.

A smile crossed Sulie's face, revealing her fangs. "You guessed it. Nothing is better tasting than human blood."

Alex blushed, and her hand went instinctively towards her neck. "Good to know."

Sulie raised her hand toward Alex and shook her head. "I'm sorry. I didn't mean to scare you like that."

Alex swallowed hard and removed the hand from her neck, steeling herself. She took a deep breath and pushed her shoulders back. "I'm not scared."

"Grossed out?"

"No. I'm fine." she laughed feeling more at ease. "I'm glad you can be yourself around me." She watched as Sulie took another sip. "What does the blood taste like?"

Sulie made a dramatic smacking sound with her lips. "Hmmm, thick and syrupy. Sometimes the blood tastes sweet, sometimes it doesn't. I think it mostly depends on how the human lives. Mostly though, it's all delicious. It tastes like watered down vampire blood. Our blood is more concentrated and it's always sweet."

There had been no mention of them drinking vampire blood in the documentation Alex had read. She hated how incomplete the files had been. "Do vampires drink vampire blood?" OK, it sounded like a silly question, but she wanted to know, plus she wanted to document the answer for the next director.

"Oh, we don't feed off each other. We taste the blood more than anything else. Lovers bite one other like humans would kiss. So, it's more like a taste than actually eating."

Alex smiled back at the vampire. "You told me you weren't married. Were you before?"

286

Sulie shook her head. "No. I know what vampire blood tastes like because our tongue can seal wounds on our skin. Our saliva stops the bleeding almost immediately. It's why our fangs are so sharp" She sat up on the bed. "If you're curious, I could bite my arm and show you?"

She quickly shook her head. "I'm good. Actually, I experienced that ability with Raymond when I had cut my finger and he sealed the wound for me." She inspected her finger. "See? It didn't leave a scar."

Sulie barely glanced at the offered finger. "Never does. Coagulants in our saliva do the trick. As the Colony doctor, I treat all the team members. Every once in a while one will be wounded. Blood will heal them, but a deep wound needs a lot of human blood to heal. Licking the wound to seal it first is usually best."

"Outside of healing, how much blood do you need to drink each day?"

Sulie shrugged. "The amount depends on how young we want to appear, or if we've been recently hurt in any physical way, and on how much blood is around. We crave the stuff."

There was a moment of silence, and Alex realized just how much she enjoyed talking with Sulie. She looked younger than 22. She could pass for a teenager almost. She suspected Sulie would answer any question she may have about vampires, and more importantly about her brother. Alex had several questions about Raymond. Alex cleared her throat. "I saw Raymond's blood the other day. He explained that vampire blood turns purple over time, but his wasn't purple. His blood looked mostly red."

Sulie's eyes narrowed as she quickly sat up on the bed. "Why was my brother bleeding?"

Alex held her hands up in a calming manner as she shook her head. "It was an accident. I think I may have broken his nose, but he healed quickly."

"Oh." Sulie relaxed on the bed. "Well, if you're with us long enough you're bound to see everything. This business does come with its dangers. You'll get used to it all. The blood deliveries, the keeping of our secret, the extracurricular feedings …"

"What extracurricular feedings?"

"Oh, if one of us is injured in the line of duty and dying we can drink from a human. It's considered extracurricular on the books. It basically means a lot of clean up to make sure the human's mind is properly erased. Any feeding that isn't government sanctioned, or part of a personal mating, is supposed to be reported to you. You then confirm that the necessary precautions have been done to protect us. It's what happened with Ben recently and his superior."

"I see." Everything fascinated Alex. She pondered over what Sulie had shared, and finally asked. "What kind of feedings are government sanctioned?"

"There are none anymore, but they were the feedings from our Offering Parties decades ago. The government stopped the practice a while back."

Alex had seen files mentioning "Offering Parties" when she reviewed the Colony paperwork a few days ago. Mostly the information she saw just referred to them but gave no detail. Almost as if the government wanted to erase them from existence, like they never happened. She wondered what could have been so controversial at those parties that the government would try to erase them from the records.

Sulie offered an explanation as she prepared for bed. "The Offering Parties fed us before bagged blood came along. God, I hated those parties because I felt trapped in my body. You see, back then we were all older looking. We only fed every two to three months. I hated looking that old." Sulie took another sip from her water bottle as she glanced at her blurred reflection in a mirror. "The government would allow us to have these parties and they would maintain a guest list, which consisted mostly of whores who worked the streets. They were never told the true nature of the parties and were paid more than money for their services."

"The government paid for their blood?"

"The fellas would drink their blood and have sex with them," Sulie said reaching for her nightgown.

Alex's face turned white. "The government used to pay for hookers for the Colony and then allow them to feed off their blood? What about the OIG?"

Sulie shook her head. "The Colony isn't subjected to the Office of the Inspector General. We have our own office of professional responsibility, and the person in that role is now you."

Alex stared in disbelief. "But prostitutes …"

"I know. The idea sounds horrific, especially when you say it like that." She brushed out her hair. "But what are you going to do? Allow all these vampires to eat free range over the population? The parties allowed the government to control our feedings. The prostitutes were recorded so the government knew exactly how many times and on what dates they were invited to the parties. You can't have one attend them too many times in a row since it's hard to compel and erase memories if it becomes a habit. So the prostitutes would be brought to Fang Manor for a two–day stay and my job was to check for diseases and whether the women were fertile."

She remembered a medical detection ability from Sulie's file. "Your gift. You have the ability to see medically what might be going on with a human or a vampire's body."

"That's right." Sulie undressed and slipped on her nightgown. "I would medically survey them and take note of any medical needs they had. The government would see to their needs with medicines, antibiotics, whatever they needed. Personally we can't pick up any human diseases, but it was still nice to leave the women in better health than when they came to the party."

"Very charitable of you," Alex said curtly.

"Hey, it was a way of life. We would give medicines to the fertile ones too, even though they would be rejected and not gain access to the party." She sipped her bottle and continued. "The government didn't want us procreating with the women since they were being lied to about the party."

Recognition appeared on Alex's face. "I see. You can detect if a woman is ovulating."

"Actually, I can tell when she ovulated and if she's currently fertile." She eyed Alex. "You, for example, ovulated seven days ago. You stopped being fertile just before you came to our home."

Alex thought about that for a moment. It was another missed chance at having a child; of course she had no husband either – so moot point. You can't miss out on something when it just won't ever happen. She focused back to the party information, "And everyone had sex with the prostitutes?"

"The blood drives us crazy. You have no idea. Going months without blood and finally being able to feed again makes you *insane* for sex. And we would feed until we would appear to be in our twenties again. The parties turned into blood and sex orgies."

Alex had to ask. "Even your brother would …"

Sulie's eyes widened. "Oh, I'm so sorry. Look, it wasn't like that. The first few parties he struggled and could resist, but over time he did give into the temptation. Honestly, blood lust is just a part of our makeup. That's all. The sex he had with them meant nothing to him, and he agonized over it in since he felt like a filthy user of those women. When he finally did give in to the temptation, he must have showered a dozen times after the party. Afterward, he was surly towards everyone for at least a week. But don't worry. We have bagged blood now. No need for those parties anymore."

Alex sat deep in thought and her face paled as she felt a twinge of a headache. She wanted to phrase her next question just right. "Sulie, the other night, did you call Raymond for an emergency when he drove me home?"

Sulie thought for a moment. "No. I don't know what you're talking about. Maybe the call came from one of the guys."

Right. Alex didn't remember hearing a phone ring that night. So Raymond could sleep with a ton of prostitutes but for some reason had to lie to get out of sleeping with her, even with the effects of new blood in his system. She didn't know what it felt like to be compelled, but she had read enough examples of the process in the Colony documentation to see the signs. A lag in memory and perhaps disorientation were at the top of the list. For memory erasing, a headache usually followed. She didn't have a headache after Raymond left, but she really didn't remember a phone ringing. He had shared with her a very intimate part of himself when he told her the story of Wilma's death while they were in Florida. She had felt special to him when he shared the story. So was he repulsed by her body maybe? Why were men so confusing?

"I shouldn't have said anything. Especially knowing how he feels about you."

Alex's eyes widened and she turned quickly towards Sulie. "He's told you how he feels?"

"I can read his thoughts at times. Lately he's been pretty open with them. Ben has told me that Raymond's aura contains bright red in it, which usually means he's in an amorous mood. He's been in one about 24/7 lately when you've been around. Your aura had red in it the last few days as well."

Alex blushed. "I didn't think my attraction to him was that obvious." She looked up at Sulie and wondered if Raymond would man up and tell her himself about those awful parties.

CHAPTER FORTY

Raymond dressed casually in a white polo shirt and khaki pants. He glanced quickly at his watch and realized he ran late. No time to shave, but he was only meeting Dixon for another early morning breakfast meeting where he would watch his best friend eat.

He started down the stairs and noticed Sterling on his way up, who reeked of blood, alcohol and sex. Sterling had obviously not spent the night at Fang Manor, and he appeared well–fed from his nocturnal activities. Raymond tried to hold his tongue, but the slight pause was enough to give Sterling concern.

"What?" Sterling huffed. He stopped walking up the stairs and barely looked at his father.

Raymond stopped mid–step and stared at his son. His eyes narrowed and his nose wrinkled. "You smell like human females."

Sterling didn't even blink. "I'm half human, thanks to you having cavorted with one."

Raymond's cheeks grew red. His hand tightened on the hand railing. "Sterling!"

Sterling allowed the reprimand to go unnoticed. He now looked his father squarely in the eyes. "What offends you more? That I was with humans? Or that I was with women?"

Raymond leaned against the banister. He had not expected the question. He replied honestly, "Both."

"Since vampire women ignore me, and I detest human men … I guess you're shit out of luck."

Raymond didn't have the time to get into this again with his son, but he still began a protest. "Sterling," he said softly, "It's not just the company you keep." He took a deep breath. "If you could find yourself a wife …"

"A wife? Right. I'll ask the Vampire Council to arrange that when they have a moment. Oh, wait, we already tried several times. They don't want me. Nobody does."

"The Council serves a purpose."

Sterling closed the distance between the two of them. He got up into his father's face. "Fuck the Council. I don't need their services, or their blood bank to keep me in check."

Raymond's face tightened as he prepared for the shouting match, but his son finished their conversation by filling in the words for both of them.

"Why don't we skip to the end, Dad? You tell me the merits of finding that special vampire someone; I blow you off because, being a half–breed, I'm a genetic reject. You then launch into how a human woman of quality and worth could be turned into a vampire. I tell you that there's no way in hell I'd want any of the human women I've been with turned. They'd just be raging bitches as vamps tormenting me for eternity, or even reject me because they're full vampires and I'm only half. Of course, the conversation can't end there. I then have to lie and promise to take your words under consideration. You would pretend to believe me. And then the two of us would go on about our lives until the next time you feel the need to nag me." He looked at his father, "That sound about right?"

Raymond's shoulders sagged. "Yes. I think that just about covers it," he sighed.

"Good talk, dad," Sterling sneered as he slapped his father on the shoulder. "I'm going to bed." Sterling continued up the stairs, not looking back at his father.

It was the same lecture. Raymond was tired of it. After all, at a certain point in time, how do you parent a child who is almost 180 years old? Sterling wasn't living the life Raymond and his late wife had wanted for him. Raymond had sat with his dead wife at her grave site the day he buried her and had promised to raise their son to be an honorable man. Somehow Raymond knew that his late wife wouldn't approve of Sterling's love life, and it hurt Raymond to think that he had failed her. He continued down the stairs and gave his son the win for the argument.

The house was quiet. Evidently, everyone had already started their day. He was running late. He grabbed his car keys from the key rack on the wall and headed out.

******

The GPS had to be wrong. The Mexican restaurant was in a part of town where anyone would be worried about parking a Jag. At this morning hour, the streets were clear, but Raymond suspected that mere hours ago the streets were filled with teenagers hanging out on the street corners, with prostitutes hoping to turn a quick buck, and drug deals going down.

The restaurant was painted an ugly canary yellow. Chunks of paint were missing from the sides of the building, but the graffiti covered up most of the remaining paint. The only thing nastier than the sight of the place was the smell. It reeked of burned beans and heavy cheese. The few letters that were left on the broken marquee suggested they had the best breakfast tacos in town, so this must be the place.

Dixon could never show up for anything on time, and this morning was no exception. Tardiness was one of the human's less endearing qualities, but it was pure Dixon through and through. Even now, Raymond still had the courtesy of showing up on time. He just had to wait, like always. Three decades ago the bad habit irritated Raymond, but now … well its strange how you can forgive such quirks when you care for someone.

The two had forged a strong bond over the decades. Each had saved each others' lives at some point during the friendship. Dixon was well integrated in the vampire lifestyle, and Raymond had learned a lot about living in modern times from Dixon.

Raymond never had a friend that was such an open book. Everything was a good topic of conversation, not just about sports and how careers were on the right track. Maybe everyone had such a confidant in his life, but for Raymond, his didn't come until he met Dixon. And now the man was leaving.

A covered wooden bench was next to the restaurant, so Raymond took the opportunity to sit in the shade as he waited. The morning sun wasn't too taxing, but it made him appear more human to have a seat. The old bench gave way and creaked under his weight. He pulled out his pocket watch and noted the time. Five minutes late – not late by Dixon's standards. Taking a deep breath, he settled more on the bench and thought on the passing of time, wincing at the thought of Dixon's retirement. As excited as Raymond was about having Alex as the new Director, it bothered him to see Dixon go.

A car entering the parking lot caught Raymond's attention. He turned, hoping to see Dixon's red BMW, but it wasn't him.

Dixon drove a red BMW—the newest sport car in a line of several Dixon had owned. The man was in the middle of a mid–life crisis when he had joined the team, and had gone through his third divorce just after coming on board with the Colony. He was a playboy want–to–be with a romantic heart who just wanted to find the right woman, but failed at every turn. Watching Dixon's failures was one reason Raymond never wanted to put himself out there again. There was always too much pain where love was concerned.

And meeting women had certainly changed over the years. Through Dixon, Raymond learned about such things as speed dating, Internet dating and online porn sites. How could Raymond blame his son for living a modern life in a time when sex is only a few clicks away on your keyboard? Dixon always proclaimed that he wanted to find the right woman and settle down, but what was love anymore to this generation of modern man? Maybe Raymond felt just too old fashioned.

Another car entered the parking lot, and this time it was the car Raymond knew so well. Seventeen minutes late. Typical. Dixon quickly parked and offered the usual excuses of work and bad traffic. It was so typical of him. Raymond made a passive hand gesture to dismiss his tardiness.

Raymond took another good look at the restaurant before they entered. "You sure you want to eat here?"

Dixon opened the door, its handle the shape of a burrito. "People who don't eat shouldn't judge. I discovered this place last week. Best breakfast enchiladas in town." He paused as he entered the building, "You'll have to take my word for that."

Raymond nodded in agreement and followed his friend. The place had a few empty tables in the back, so they found the one with the least number of crumbs on the table. The breakfast crowd was sizable, so maybe they did have good food here. They sat down and the table tilted to one side. The folded paper coaster under the leg did little to level the table.

After sitting down Dixon asked, "So, what do you think of the captain as the new Director? I mean, I know she just started, but what is your gut telling you about her so far?" He grabbed a napkin and slid the crumbs onto the floor.

"Alex is nice. I like her." Raymond then decided to add, "It does take a bit to transition into any new job and I think she's doing great so far."

Dixon added a second coaster to the table leg. "OK. So she's handling the differences of the team?" No need to say "vampire" or "immortal" here and draw attention to themselves.

"Yeah, she can handle weird well." Raymond paused while Dixon ordered a breakfast enchilada and two coffees for them. He always did the ordering when he could, allowing Raymond to blend in.

Raymond handed his unopened menu back to the waitress before she left the table. "Alex is asking all the right questions, she's not just interested in the job, but us as a people. I think she'll do well."

"I know Sulie likes her."

Raymond smiled. "Sulie likes everybody. But, yes. I do think they get along quite well."

Dixon took a deep breath. "There was one incident, a few years back," Dixon began. "It involved a stalker."

"Alex told me."

Dixon's eyebrow rose. "Did she mention she is seeing a psychologist?"

Thinking back, Raymond remembered his private conversation with Alex. She had said she was working on getting past her fear. "She eluded to it, yes. Will that be a problem if she accepts the position?"

"Usually you don't want a high-level individual seeking counseling, but Alex took all the necessary precautions. The plus side of it is that she's nearly invisible."

"How so?"

"Well, for one thing, she drives to and from work at different times. She also changes her route making her drives very random. She switches gyms often and varies her workout routines. She's also not a regular at any restaurant, bar, or store. She blends right into the background, just like you all do. In fact, … she's perfect for you."

Raymond felt some odd mental patterns from Dixon. He knew the human well enough to know something was up. "What's on your mind?" he asked.

Dixon's eyes shifted back on Raymond's. A smile spread across the man's face. "There was a list of candidates for the position. I had already been leaning towards selecting Alex for the job, but Sulie was the one who picked her."

Raymond took a deep breath. The smell of the food filled his nostrils and was nauseating. "My sister chose our new Director?"

A slight chuckle escaped. "Sulie thought Alex was a good fit."

Raymond leaned in. He sensed something odd in the mental patterns coming from his friend. "A good fit for what? Being the Director?"

"Mostly. She told me afterward that she pushed for Alex because she thought you might be attracted to her. Thought it might get you back into the game of life."

Raising his voice, Raymond asked, "Game of life?"

The coffees arrived, and Dixon waited for them to be alone before continuing. "She's worried about you. Wants you to be happy and find someone."

Raymond's jaw tightened. "Sulie has no right to interfere."

"Hold on," Dixon said, his hand waving in front of Raymond like a stop sign. "Family gets to interfere. It's what makes them family. Besides, it isn't the first time she's tried to set you up with someone. It's only the first time you've been interested."

First time? Raymond thought of all the times he had promised his sister that he would never tell Dixon of her love for the man. Now to find out that she had been playing matchmaker all these years was too much of a violation. She had known the intense pain he had gone through over the loss of his wife, why would she match him up with another human?

"She has your best interest at heart, Raymond. Just remember that."

Best interest. Raymond thought about that, then began saying, "Dixon …" All he had to do was betray Sulie's trust and tell the man of her undying love for him. Just break his word. After all, it was in Sulie's best interest. He looked at his friend as he sat patiently waiting for him to continue. "Sulie ... chose well."

"Obviously," Dixon smiled. "You look happy. You deserve to be happy."

Raymond thought back to the day he met Alex. "You warned me she was off–limits. Now you're suddenly happy to have me cross that line? That doesn't make sense. You should be furious with me."

"Forbidden fruit."

"What?"

Dixon surveyed the room, making sure no one was paying attention to their conversation. "People always want what they can't have. I was actually concerned about Sterling taking an interest in her, but I didn't see him as her type. Sulie and I both thought you would like her. Nothing makes a woman more desirable than her being unattainable, or another man wanting her."

The waitress came, set down Dixon's order, and asked, "Can I get you anything, Sugar?" She stared at Raymond, but he dismissed her with a simple nod and a shake of his head, doing his best to avoid any eye contact.

Dixon inhaled deeply smelling his food. He then unwrapped his fork from the paper napkin it was bound in. "Best breakfast in town," he said, taking his first bite.

Raymond looked at the enchilada. Eggs and sausage stuffed in a cooked tortilla smothered with salsa. How could humans eat such food? It smelled terrible, but looked simple enough to make. It was just a tortilla with food and baked. Any mistakes would be covered up by the sauce. Sulie always complained about how hard it was to cook the simplest dishes. How hard could it be?

To Raymond it looked like humans would eat just about anything anyway.

"My sister is monitoring your cholesterol, isn't she?" Raymond asked as a string of hot cheese draped around the fork and hung off the man's mouth.

Dixon nodded a response as he finished the bite. "Alex did well in Florida and I heard she did well in Austin. So that is a good sign," he said, changing the subject.

Raymond looked around the restaurant, took a sip of his coffee, and finally said, "Yes, Dixon, I think she'll make a great director for us. I'll miss you, but ..." he smiled slightly, "I also enjoy her company and am very attracted to her. She's ..." Raymond searched for the right words. "I don't know how to describe it. It's like I lived this long just so I could know her." He took another sip of the hot coffee, hoping that Dixon would fill the silence, but he didn't. "Dixon, is it so terrible that I'm falling for our new director?"

"Life is about taking risks and putting yourself out there, even if it means getting hurt along the way. It's high time you started living again." He took a sip of his coffee and then added, "Besides, if you were going to fall for your director, I'm just glad it wasn't me."

CHAPTER FORTY–ONE

That evening Air Force One landed in D.C. Alex stretched and politely covered her mouth to hide a huge yawn as she stood to exit the plane. The night wasn't very late, but traveling always wore her out.

She traveled with Mason and the President back to the White House. A quick pass by her office revealed a stack of paperwork for the upcoming dinner. She frowned at the stack, but noticed some of the information needed to be given to Raymond. She smiled realizing she now had an excellent reason to drop by Fang Manor and visit him tonight. By the time she walked to her car, and began the trip over, she had gotten her second wind.

Driving up to the mansion, she noticed only the light in the kitchen was on. Her stomach growled, and she realized that she should have eaten before coming over. She was hungry, but couldn't stomach the idea of eating Sulie's cooking again. She pulled her car up to the closed garage and parked. After providing a code and a retinal scan to the back door, she walked in. Jackie greeted her from the other side of the door.

"Hey girl," Jackie said. "I didn't know you'd be coming by tonight." She grabbed the bottom edge of the blue apron she wore and dried off her hands. A bowl of chocolate chip cookie batter sat on the island in the center of the room, and the air was filled with the sweetness of whatever was in the oven.

Alex closed the door and took a few steps into the room. The chimes on the door sounded, showing the door was once again locked and secure. "Good evening, Jackie. Sorry to just stop by."

"Oh, please. This house is always open to you. You just stopin' by? Or were you looking for a sugar fix?" She smiled as she pointed to a rack of cool off cookies on the counter behind her next to the coffee pots. There were also two tins overflowing with mini–cheesecakes.

"What's with the bake–a–thon?" Alex asked as she heavily sniffed the air.

Jackie took a deep breath and used the back of her hand to wipe her forehead. "Bake sale. Both classes. And those kids tell me about the sale tonight." She shook her head. "Last minute rush. I'd have them help, but they're off doing their homework."

Alex's stomach growled again, loud enough for Jackie to hear. "Everything smells wonderful."

"I know, right? It makes a difference when you can actually taste." She picked up a semi–warm cookie and offered the treat to Alex. "You're hungry. Here — made with dark chocolate, not that sissy milk chocolate nastiness. Makes a huge difference."

Alex smiled. "Thanks, but I haven't had dinner yet."

She still held the cookie up as an offering. "Life's too short, girl. Eat dessert first." She nodded at the sealed tins on the counter. "I have mini–cheesecakes in the red tin over there if you'd rather eat one of them."

"Thanks. This is fine," she said, taking the cookie.

As Alex munched on the cookie, and moaned contently, Jackie asked, "So what does bring you around? Is it Raymond?"

"Mmm hmmm," Alex said as she nodded a yes.

"The man's not here. Left a while ago saying he'd see us tomorrow." Jackie now gave a devilish grin. "I thought he might be picking you up and treating you to an evening of romance."

The blush on Alex's face was immediate. She quickly swallowed the cookie; crumbs from her mouth fell to the table. "I haven't talked with him in a while." She held up the paperwork in her hands. "I needed to talk to him about something with the state dinner."

Jackie looked at her watch. "I get you. Your plane lands, you skip dinner, and rush over here to do even more work on an event that's still days away." Jackie raised a questioning eyebrow. "Are you stickin' to that story?"

Alex held up the paperwork once again and brushed the table crumbs with her other hand. "I just wanted …"

"A booty call," Jackie finished. When Alex's face grew even more red, Jackie added, "It's all good. He's a fine man. You're entitled to get yours."

Alex couldn't make eye contact with Jackie. "I needed to drop this paperwork off for Raymond. It's some forms from the human team."

"Now, don't get all embarrassed. It's all story book, and you need your happy ending too. Now, how about some tea? I was just going to have a cup." She took the documents from Alex and set them on a clean portion of a counter.

Alex's stomach twisted, but not from hunger. She bit her lip as apprehension nearly overcame her. "The mansion looks empty. Where is everyone?" she asked in a desperate need to change the subject.

"Most are out, either work or on a date, I guess. William is down the hall in the gym; I think Ben might be with him." She paused a moment and then added, "Yep. Two treadmills. My man likes to work out in the

305

evenings. Probably takes the edge off since I'm rarely in the mood to rock his world in the bedroom these days." She rubbed her large belly. "Baby will be here soon enough though."

Jackie walked over to the tins sitting on the back counter. She took them, along with two plates she got from a cabinet, over to the kitchen table and sat down. The red tin was opened showing the results of Jackie's hard work. "I do love cheesecake. Truly God's gift to the world," she said, pulling out two of the mini–cakes and placing them on the plates. "I'm so happy to taste again now that I'm pregnant. Thank God, once I go back to blood full–time I'll have my figure back."

"Why is that?" Alex asked. She picked up a mini cake and took a bite. The creamy cheese filling coated her tongue and lips, leaving a velvety, smooth taste in her mouth. Her eyes closed for a moment and she enjoyed the wonderful taste. Cheesecake and many other desserts were typically not in her diet plan.

"A blood exclusive diet rocks. You get the perfect body weight for your frame." She did a 'Vanna White' move across her body. "This will all be what it needs to be again. I went through two pregnancies without the magic wand of being a vampire, and now, I'm loving it." She took a bite of the mini–cheesecake; her manicured nails became coated with graham cracker crusts in the process.

Alex's lips twisted in disgust. The file the government had about the vampire culture certainly had holes in it. There was no mention of pregnancies and children other than Jackie's two kids existed. Maybe the information wasn't important until Jackie had joined the team. Maybe no one was particularly interested in the subject. Either way, the lack of information upset Alex. She made a mental note that she would append all documents with additional information.

"The Colony has been established a long time. Are you and William the first team members to have children?"

Jackie took a deep breath. "Other than Raymond's son Sterling, the members just don't have kids. Daniel raised his younger sister, Sulie raised Sterling, Mason had a family when he was human … I guess everyone feels that they already raised their kids."

"What about Sterling and Ben?"

"What?" Jackie let out a deep chuckle. "Those two are bachelors through and through, girl. I can't imagine one of them changing diapers and running after a rug rat or two. Although, they are both fond of my babies. They get along just fine."

Alex took a bite of her dessert. "Your youngest looks to be about eleven. Your turn must have been recent. Within the last decade I guess?" Alex pried.

"That's right," Jackie said as she reached for another mini–cheesecake to set on her plate. "Five years ago," she held up her hand with her fingers all splayed. "William and I wanted more than just a few decades together … so viola."

Alex took a sip of her tea. The files did have some information about turnings. She wondered if the info was accurate. "But being turned meant that you died." She paused briefly to judge Jackie's response. When the vampire just shrugged her shoulders she asked, "Were you afraid to go through it?"

Jackie took a large bite of her pastry and set it down. She paused to answer while she finished the bite. "A

307

little. You know, it's a big change. But I knew when I married William that my turning would happen eventually."

"May I ask what made you decide to do it five years ago?"

"Oh, sure," she laughed. "All you got to do is ask and I can't help but to share." She licked her fingers clean and focused on the timeline "After Nicole's seventh birthday, Sulie come up to me with some bad news. She detected pre–cancerous cells in my ovaries." Jackie shook her head, "Girl, that ain't news you ever want to hear. My mama died of ovarian cancer years ago. I only had her and my father growing up, and I saw the toll it took on him watching Mama die. So, I chose to go through the change because … well, let's just say that no one ever chooses to die or chooses to have a loved one die." Jackie sighed. "I didn't like watching Mama die and I figured as long as I was human, William would be watching me die each day as I grew older. I love him too much to have him go through my loss."

"Oh," Alex said and then let the silence creep in.

Jackie wiped her hands on her napkin. "Now, don't be like that."

Alex looked up, "Like what?"

Jackie's finger pointed to Alex, but not accusingly. "That brain of yours is having a hard time wrapin' itself around all of this. One minute human, the next vampire." She pointed at the untouched pastry on Alex's plate. "You're even too much in your head to enjoy your second cheesecake."

Alex glanced down and noticed the uneaten dessert. "It's hard to think about dying and being an immortal."

"That's because you're thinkin' with your brain, not your heart. The brain is good for crunchin' numbers, for focusing on the tough issues and such. But your heart tells you your path."

"You still die."

"OK. Think of turning like this. A new vampire is born, right? It's just another way of having a baby. It's the vampire way, that's all. You need to stop thinking like a human and embrace something different."

"But it's a big transition," Alex protested.

"Drinking blood is an easy transition. Hell, you end up lovin' the stuff. Giving up food isn't a big deal, except for cheesecake." She chuckled, "The night before I turned I ate an entire meal of it. I had plain cheesecake, strawberry cheesecake, chocolate cheesecake ..." She started laughing. "Anything cheesecake was great for dinner that night."

Alex joined in with laughter. "I think I'd have a meal of chocolate. And wash it down with a mug of cocoa!"

CHAPTER FORTY–TWO

Raymond waited patiently in the rain for his sister Sulie to arrive at a downtown high–rise. Water streamed down his jacket as he stood under the green awning which led to the main door. The home belonged to one of the Supreme Court Justices, and Raymond needed Sulie's medical expertise to determine whether the Justice had been poisoned.

Justice McCade was the first name on the list of nine Justices to check. Raymond glanced down at his phone. He pulled up the list and asked his GPS map finder to plot out the addresses of all the Justices. He grimaced at the map, with its red flags scattered across the DC and surrounding areas. This was not going to be a one–night job. The rain picked up and thunder sounded in the distance. That's when he noticed his sister's Porsche turn down the street towards him.

He watched as Sulie parked her car across the street and ran through the puddles to join him. Droplets of rain matted down her blond curls and a drop of rain dripped off her nose. Once under the awning she shook the rain from her jacket and rung the water from her hair. "Which one is this?" she asked.

Raymond pointed towards the top of the building. "This is where Justice McCade and his wife live. We'll start with them because we know he has been targeted," he told her.

"This building has underground parking," Sulie said. "Is his car here?"

Raymond shook his head. "His secretary told me that his calendar was empty tonight, so he should be home. His wife is out of town."

Sulie smiled. "The secretary *told* you that, did she?"

Putting the phone back into his pocket, Raymond grinned. "There may have been some charm and compelling involved, but yes. She did tell me." Raymond reached for the door handle just as the heavyset doorman leaned forward and opened it for them. The gold tassels on his sleeve shifted when the breeze from the outside pushed on the door.

"Evening," he nodded to them as he stood sideways in the doorway to allow them to enter. "Who are you visiting today?" He led them towards the locked inner door, not reaching for the key, waiting for their answer.

Raymond stared into the man's eyes. "Justice McCade is expecting us. I'm sure he instructed you to allow us in."

The man's eyes dulled. "Yes. Of course. He's been expecting you." He reached in his pocket and hit a remote control that unlocked the inner door. "Fifteenth floor," he said as he ushered them in. "The elevators are right this way."

"We can find them," Raymond said, allowing the man to resume his initial position and give them privacy.

Once alone, they walked down to the bank of elevators, finding the one that had access to the penthouse. "Two for two. And I'm sure the compelling isn't ending here, Raymond. You're on a roll tonight for someone who doesn't like to interact with humans," she said as they entered.

311

Raymond sent for the elevator, not commenting on the remark. "After you," he said when the lift finally arrived.

On the fifteenth floor were the penthouse suites A and B. The elevator opened to a small foyer, with the penthouses located one on each side of it. Raymond cleared his throat as he turned from the security camera and got Sulie's attention.

She looked squarely into the camera. "If the feed is live, and if they archive the footage more than just a day, we might be able to make use of that."

Raymond knew Sulie would need to see the Judge in person to make a ruling about his physical state, but if a vampire were seen coming and going from this apartment, it could give them a lead. "Too bad the camera is just visual with no heat signature," he said.

"It's something though." Sulie rang the doorbell, and a moment later a voice came across the intercom.

"Yes? Please identify yourself by looking into the camera and speaking into the com," the male voice said.

Raymond paused before he pressed the intercom button, "He sounds too young to be the Justice."

"Butler?" Sulie guessed.

"Only the Justice and his wife live here. No children, so maybe." He pressed the button. "We're here to see Justice McCade. Personal business."

A moment later the man replied, "Do you have an appointment?"

This time Sulie spoke into the com in a sexy, breathy voice. "No. He asked that I be discrete."

Raymond pitched his voice so only Sulie could hear, "What?"

Sulie's rolled her eyes and replied in the same vampire pitch. "These guys all have mistresses. I'm hedging a bet that he is no different."

"The man is seventy–six years old," Raymond replied.

Sulie didn't comment. Instead, she pushed the com button again. "He said I could come by tonight since his wife would not be in," she said in her normal pitched tone.

The door buzzed them in just as she finished her sentence. They were greeted by the man who had spoken to them through the com. By the way he was dressed, Raymond suspected he was not the Judge's butler. He was more than likely McCade's assistant.

"You're a bit early. Come in," he said gruffly. Taking a good look at Raymond he added, "Payment was made in full."

Sulie followed the man into the tastefully furnished penthouse. "I'm early?" she asked.

"You must be new. If you're asked to come back, you need to wait outside until I escort you into the building. You can't be let in by the doorman again. Have a seat."

"Young man," Raymond said, getting his attention. "Why do you think we are here?"

"As far as I was told, she is here for some secretarial services." He glanced over at Sulie, "Have a seat miss." He smiled as he visually inspected her body. "You on the other hand," he said turning towards Raymond, "I have no idea why you are here … but you are excused."

Raymond's eyes squinted at the man and his hands balled into fists. The man was done ogling his sister, even if it meant that Raymond had to close his eyes

313

permanently. He grabbed the man by the shirt and got his attention. "You're done. Do you understand me?" He peered into the man's eyes, "Where is Justice McCade?"

The man paled. His eyes went distant. "He's in the study."

"Fetch him," Raymond growled.

The man left the room right as Sulie began to giggle. "Honestly Raymond."

"What?" he asked.

"It's nothing. Just let it go." She gazed over to a desk and noticed a picture of McCade and his wife, family vacation photos, and some pictures of their grandchildren. "The man is obviously a pig," she added as she pointed down towards the photos.

"Nonetheless," Raymond said as he paced the room and studied more pictures on the adjacent wall.

The door opened and McCade stepped in. He wore a red housecoat and held a glass of whiskey in his hands. "Well. Hello, there." He eyed Sulie from top to bottom. "You're not in a dress. My standard order is for dresses only." He licked his lips. "But there's nothing wrong with the occasional exception." He crossed the room quickly, but stopped mid–stride when he noticed Raymond.

Raymond grabbed a picture of his wife from the wall and held the photo up. "How is Mrs. McCade this evening?"

McCade's face reddened in anger. "Who the hell are you?"

"Good Lord! Where is your sense of decency?" Raymond glared at the letch and compelled him. "First, you are going to fasten your robe. I don't want to see

314

you." He nodded in Sulie's direction and added, "Plus, a lady is present."

Sulie nodded at the recognition.

The Justice did as he was ordered, and Sulie asked. "How long have you been married?"

"Forty–eight years this May," he said in a dull tone.

"You're not trying to make it to fifty?" Raymond sneered at him.

McCade stood there, looking confused in his compelled trance.

"Do you love your wife?" Sulie asked as she took the picture from Raymond and rehung it on the wall.

"Yes."

Raymond rolled his eyes. "Did you take a vow to be faithful when you married her?"

McCade's face was pale as he nodded the vow was taken.

"Of course you did." Sulie snapped. "Do you believe your wife has been faithful to you?"

"Yes. She would never betray me."

"Really?" Sulie asked. She took a good look at the balding, portly man.

"Yes."

"There is no accounting for taste," Sulie said.

Raymond crossed the room and stood closer to the man. "This woman is a doctor. She is going to give you a full physical. You will let her. To you she is the most repulsive woman you've ever set eyes on. You feel no attraction to her. Do you understand?"

He turned his head towards Sulie. His eyes squinted and his mouth grimaced in disgust. "Yes. A physical exam."

"There will also be no talking except for answering my questions," Sulie commanded. She then looked at her brother and said in a vampire high–pitched tone. "After this is done, we need to pull a limp noodle on him."

Raymond chuckled as he walked towards the door. "I'll let you handle that. I'm going to find the assistant to see about the camera."

"Don't forget to check the pantry. If I'm done before you I'll check the bathrooms," Sulie said as she began touching the man's face. She stared into his eyes and began to read his physical state.

****

The camera was a dead end. It wasn't even hooked up with real wires, yet it wasn't a wireless. Raymond hit the jackpot though with the assistant, whose name was AJ. He had been with the couple for the last five years and was well informed about the daily ins and outs of the home.

"The kitchen is down this hallway," AJ said. "We have weekly food deliveries for the staple items, like milk, breads and such. I go every two weeks for any additional items. Of course, the McCades eat out a lot."

Raymond glanced inside the refrigerator, but unless the poison was continuously being put in the fresh groceries, the poison would not be in there. More than likely any poison would be in an item the couple ate daily, or at least stayed in the house for a long period of time. He looked in the pantry and started inspecting the cereal, the flour, and the sugar containers. Most of the packaging of the soup mixes, gravy packets and bottles were all freshness sealed – so would probably be unlikely suspects.

The salt, herbs and seasonings were next. Other than finding some old supplies, they checked out okay. Raymond then tore apart the water purifier. He wasn't a plumber, he had no tools, but his sheer strength ripped the filter. "Damn," he cursed. There was nothing here. Overall he should have been grateful the kitchen had no poison, but he strongly suspected he had missed something. He was in the middle of sniffing the dish soap when he heard his sister calling him. He set the soap down and walked towards the sound of her voice.

"I found it," Sulie exclaimed. "It was here in the bathroom."

Raymond glanced around the tiny room. "Where is McCade?"

"He's sitting in the living room, rethinking his lecherous life." She picked up the shampoo bottle and handed it to her brother. "Here is the culprit."

He unscrewed the cap and took a sniff. His eyebrow rose questioning his sister.

"Taste it."

Pouring a drop onto the palm of his hand he took a small lick of the lotion. His lips smacked together as he pondered the taste, so he read the label. "Just plain dandruff shampoo, but it tastes salty."

She took the bottle and cap from her brother. "Your tongue will tingle for a few minutes. It's a sodium based poison. A lab will have to tell us which one. More than likely it is fast acting if given in large amounts." She held up the half empty bottle. "The balding lewd wonder out there will probably have this same bottle for a good year."

Raymond considered that idea. "What about Mrs. McCade? If she also uses this shampoo, we could be looking at a shorter period of time."

Sulie shook her head and pulled back the shower curtain. A collection of body washes, fruity shampoos and conditioners lined the tub. A pink shaver sat next to the many bottles. "I'm guessing this area here belongs to her." Sulie then pointed across the tub where a cracked bar of soap sat. "This here is his pile of hygienic cleansers."

"How long?"

"Until he croaks? He may not. The poison is a low dosage. I'm guessing McCade probably only washed that patch of hair on his head once a week. Our perp probably didn't count on that."

Raymond breathed a sigh of relief. "Regardless of what we think of him, he is a human being."

She picked up the deadly shampoo bottle. "I'll make sure new shampoo is purchased." Sulie walked out of the bathroom, her brother turning off the light. "Let's release these two and check out the other Justices. We now know what we are looking for, so if you want to go spend some time with Alex …"

"I can see her later," he quickly said. "This is important enough that …"

Now Sulie interrupted him. "I'm the only one who can detect physical ailments in humans, and I don't need help. Just go and visit Alex."

He paused, but then said, "Only if you're sure."

"Yes. Let's just finish here and you can give me the names and addresses of the others."

Raymond found the assistant and released him of the compelling, giving him a credible tale as to their visit.

When he rejoined his sister in the living room, he waited while she released the Justice as well.

"You will suffer bouts of impotence when you are with anyone other than your wife," Sulie told McCade. "If anyone other than your wife, or a doctor, touches your penis, you will have the sensation that your balls are falling off for the next twenty–four hours. The only way to have sex again is with your wife, until death do you part, or unless your wife divorces you. Do you understand?"

Instantly his hands went to his crotch as he whimpered, "yes."

A knock sounded on the door and the assistant entered. This time a young woman in a dress accompanied him.

Raymond smiled as they left the room. "Have a good night Justice McCade."

CHAPTER FORTY–THREE

The car windshield wipers sloshed from side to side as Alex drove home. The sun had set a good hour ago, and her headlights pierced through the downpour leading her safely home. Her stomach rumbled in protest at all the sugar she had consumed. She regretted not having picked up some fast–food, or anything else, for dinner. After these back–to–back trips, she wasn't sure what she had in her kitchen in terms of anything edible. She'd have to make a grocery run during the day tomorrow at some point, but for tonight she'd have to rely on a protein shake.

She turned down her neighborhood street; her thoughts still on her time spent at Fang Manor. Alex enjoyed talking with Jackie. It had been a long time since she had had any 'girl time' with a friend. Even though she had just met the woman, she felt close to her. Jackie was easy to talk to, and Alex had not realized she had spent hours at the mansion. Of course, the two of them had baked two pans of brownies and had made some fudge … so that should have been a good indication of the time, but it wasn't. The truth was, Alex envied Jackie. She was living Alex's dream — the love of a good husband, a family, a child in her womb, and … Alex stopped just shy of saying vampire.

She sighed heavily. With one hand, she rubbed her temple and considered that thought. A lifetime with the man you love, and then some. What would it be like to live forever? To be with someone for centuries? It was hard to wrap her mind around the idea. If given the chance, would she make the same choice Jackie had?

And, what would such a decision mean for her career? She couldn't be the Director of the Colony if she were to be a vampire. The description "human liaison" was reality enough for her to know being a vampire, and keeping the promotion, wasn't an option. Her career meant everything to her. She took in a deep breath and let it out slowly. She had always said a husband and family were her priority, but she never lived up to that self–made promise. She knew being a bachelor was not what she wanted, and she could visually imagine her eggs being depleted and menopause looming around the corner. If only there could be a sign.

She pulled into her neighborhood and drove down the familiar streets. The evening grew late enough that the small children were inside their homes being safely tucked in by their parents. Families filled the neighborhood, and she had originally bought her home believing she would one day fit in. If only.

Driving past her mailbox she made a mental note to get the mail tomorrow during the daylight hours when rain wasn't pouring dow. She kept driving until she reached her driveway. There she noticed a familiar Jag parked out front. The car sat empty, and her house lights were on. Perhaps the dogs' caretaker was here later than usual and she had let Raymond in. Of course, she wasn't allowed to let people into the house. Maybe Raymond compelled her to let him in? She shook her head. No. That didn't seem likely. In any event, he was here, at her house – and neither of them had a flight to catch the next day. They had the whole night for one another. She pulled her car slowly up the driveway.

She turned off the headlights and pulled the key from the ignition. Was she really excited about the prospect of an entire night, especially when the prospect of centuries lingered in the air? She gripped the steering wheel until her knuckles grew white trying to gather her thoughts. One word kept coming to her mind – "centuries." Only a short time ago she didn't even know vampires existed. Now, she had not only fallen in love with one, but she was actually considering becoming one and living forever.

Was she in love?

Yes. She did love the man, but would that love be enough? She thought back to what Micki had said –love comes with no guarantees. Alex's stomach ached, and she wasn't sure if it was because of hunger, too much sugar, or just butterflies.

She took a few moments in the car to gather herself. The windshield filled with raindrops now the wipers no longer swished them aside. Alex could barely make out the front door of her house through the soaked windshield when she unlocked the car, pulled on the door latch and exited the car. Rain sprayed into her eyes, and soaked her jacket. She pulled the hood over her head for protection and walked down the curved walkway to her house. She had walked this path countless times, but tonight each step felt momentous. Raymond was in her house, and she was comfortable with that. It felt right.

She unlocked the door and her dogs welcomed her by barking loudly. She carefully pushed them aside with her legs so she could escape the rain and come into the house. Before she even closed the door, she had reached down to pet the furry family she had assembled. "Hey guys, Mommy's home." She patted each one of them as she closed the door behind her. Once each was greeted, she took the jacket off and draped it across the back of a chair. The dogs sniffed the jacket and her footsteps on the floor, and then followed her into the living room.

Alex looked around for Raymond. The unopened mail still lay on the coffee table where it had sat for most of the week. A basket of laundry still sat in a corner waiting to be folded and put away. A few stray dog toys were strewn about on the floor bringing the point home. But no Raymond.

Her stomach rumbled again once she realized the smell of Mexican food lingered in the air. She took in a long, hard whiff. It was definitely Mexican food, and that was her favorite. She crossed over to the kitchen where she discovered Raymond trying not to burn something in the oven. He looked so out of place as he focused on his cooking. With a great big smile, she asked, "Raymond, what are you doing here?"

She caught him off guard. It was late enough that he should have been expecting her, but he must have lost track of time.

He set the steaming casserole dish on top of the stove burners. "I'm cooking." His smile gave way to a slight frown as he closed the oven door. "What? Am I doing it wrong? The food doesn't even look edible does it?"

There was a smudge of food on his forehead, as if he had wiped his brow with food covered hands. His dark hair was tussled in such a school–boyish way, it made him look hot and sexy – in a domestic kind of way.

She glanced over at the three bowls which sat on the island. The largest bowl contained brown rice, with chopped tomatoes and guacamole in the other two. Next to them sat a cutting board with what looked like finely sliced lettuce and onions. Noting that only four food

323

items rested on the counter, she wondered why her sink overflowed with dirty dishes. Pots and pans claimed most of the space in the sink, utensils and dirty bowls lined the countertop, and why was her blender out? He gave her a sheepish grin as she inspected the place. "It smells delicious," she finally said. She grabbed a towel hanging off the refrigerator door and took a step closer to him. "I'm starving, and I appreciate you cooking for me. But, how did you get in here?" she asked wiping off his forehead.

"Your key."

"My key?"

"I borrowed your spare key the night before we flew to Florida and accidentally neglected to return it. I didn't even realize I still had the key until this morning when I saw it in my change holder in the Jag. That's what inspired me to surprise you tonight." He gave her a huge smile as he pointed out all the food.

She set her purse down on the cluttered counter, making sure to avoid a spill of some kind. "How'd you get past my alarm? Did the dog walker forget to set it?"

He shook his head. "The alarm was set."

"But how? Did you compel her to tell you the code?"

"Of course not. I didn't even see her. I don't think humans realize that about 90% of the time when they punch in access codes, or unlock a combination lock, that they mentally say the numbers in their heads. I simply heard you say the access code mentally when we were here last. I didn't mean to overhear your thoughts, but when a human focuses on something specific, and routine like that, thoughts do tend to be loud."

Alex tilted her head and thought about that. She did always say the numbers in her head.

He turned off the stove. "You're in time too. I just finished." He moved the contents over to the table, which was set for one. "Please eat."

A single red rose, probably from her garden, was in a bud vase on the table. "I have to get my stuff out of the car. I left everything when I saw the lights on."

"I'll get your bags. Just sit and relax."

As he pulled the chair out for her, she leaned in and claimed a kiss. "I've missed you, Raymond."

His smile excited her. "I missed you too. I'll bring in your bags."

Even though it rained, she let her dogs out for a bathroom break. She then gave her dog Gracie her medicine as she surveyed the kitchen. Could a kitchen get messier than this? Probably not. She smiled as Raymond walked back into the kitchen. He looked adorable wearing her hot pink apron with the slogan, "Kitchen Diva." His hair was now drenched, the apron dripping wet by the rain. If his car hadn't been blocking her garage she would have parked in its dry shelter, possibly even had unpacked the car tomorrow morning. She looked at his broad shoulders and suspected that he had gathered all of her bags in just one trip. Big. Strong. Chivalrous. Desirable.

He gestured back towards the dinner table.

"You know you didn't have to cook me dinner, Raymond." She walked back to the breakfast nook. The man wasn't just drop–dead gorgeous, he could also cook. Whether or not the food tasted good, he deserved an A+ in the wanting–to–please department. He was ranking a high score in all the departments that mattered to her.

"I didn't know when you'd be home, but since it's past the dinner hour I thought I'd make you something to eat." He served her an enchilada and some rice, placing the cut vegetables and guacamole on the table as well.

She sat down and took a deep sniff of the food on the plate in front of her. "You didn't have to make all of this from scratch. They do sell frozen dinners." She eyed the mess on the countertops once again. "It would have been easier than using up every dish in the house."

Sheepishly he responded, "This *is* a frozen dinner."

"Oh." Alex laughed. "I appreciate the food. I really do."

He removed the apron and set it on the back of one of the dining chairs to drip–dry. "You don't want to see my earlier attempt. The dogs wouldn't even eat it to dispose of the evidence. It was bad." He smiled at her. "So please, Alex. Eat. The words on the box indicated this was gourmet Mexican cuisine."

"Oh? You found a gourmet one?" she laughed. She suspected Raymond didn't realize that all frozen dinners claimed to be gourmet. Overall the food did look tasty. With her fork, she sectioned off a small corner of the enchilada and scooped up some rice. She blew on the food before she took a bite. "It's good. Thank you."

"I have no idea what wine goes with Mexican food." He held up a blue bottle with a fancy label. "This one is red. And the label is in Spanish."

Enjoying her second bite, she covered her mouth and murmured, "I'm sure it's fine."

Raymond poured the wine while Alex talked about her trip. The conversation stayed on a professional level until Raymond finally said, "I should explain about the Offering Parties." He watched as Alex's body stiffened.

She shrugged her shoulders. "You don't have to explain. You had to eat." Focusing on her plate of food she quickly stuffed another bite into her mouth, not making eye contact with Raymond. She had wondered if he would ever tell her the truth about those parties. She so wished that she had never even heard of them. She had a mental image of his naked body pressed up against another woman, one after the other. The thought made her want to scream.

"Alex," he said softly.

Alex finished off the rice and non–burnt area of her enchilada and decided to leave the rest. Raymond remained silent as he watched her push the food around on her plate. "How did you know I knew about them," she asked.

"Sulie told me. She thought I'd be upset that she told you about them."

"Oh." Generally, sex with other women might fall under full disclosure when you enter a relationship with someone. At least Sulie had told her the truth. "Are you upset with her for telling me?"

He reached across and gently touched her hand. "I care that this information might have upset you. But, no. Sulie was fine in telling you about them. I see it as tantamount to any sister sharing embarrassing stuff to her brother's girlfriend. I have no nude baby pictures lying around, so what else was she going to share." He shook his head and glanced up at her.

327

Girlfriend? That sounded nice. "I wasn't upset by them. Not really." She did her best not to mentally project any hurt feelings that Raymond might pick up on. She suspected she wasn't completely successful.

"I planned to tell you."

She looked into his soft teal eyes and nodded. He was a good man. She believed he would have eventually told her if Sulie hadn't beaten him to the punch. Taking a deep breath, she glanced down at her mostly eaten meal. She bit her lip, wondering what to say next. Should she say that she was hurt? That she wished he had had better restraint? The man needed to eat … even if it was from truckloads of hookers that were wheeled into Fang Manor occasionally by dear old Uncle Sam.

"Alex, I never made love to a single one of them."

Alex remembered Sulie's exact words. "She said you had."

"I used those women, Alex. I felt filthy while with them, but I had to feed. And yes, I did have sex with them. But, I never made love to them." His hand still rested on hers. Now it gently caressed her soft skin. "Not like how I want to make love with you tonight."

Alex fought back a tear. This wonderful man, someone that she had been waiting for all of her life, wanted her. The butterflies returned and mentally she could feel the conscious decision as the pieces fell into place. Her career was on the bench this game. Love was the star player, and love was up to bat. She was never one to move this quickly, but it felt so right. It was a leap, but she was taking it with Raymond, so she knew she'd be all right. She licked her lips slowly and then bit down on her lower lip. In a deep husky voice, she said, "I'm done with my dinner. May I be excused?"

328

"Absolutely. But, I hope you saved room for dessert." He eyed her hungrily as they both stood from the table. Her heart raced. The distance between them disappeared as she wrapped her arms around his neck and he picked her up so she would straddle his waist. She kissed him hard and he leaned her against the wall of the dining room. He thrust his tongue in her mouth and tasted her as his hands tore into her clothes. Her fingers wrapped in his hair as she moaned into his mouth.

Raymond kissed her cheek and then Alex felt him move over to her neck. She noticed his eyes were pitching black and his fangs were fully extended. He kissed her neck. Using his tongue to find her vein, he licked the length of the vein up into her hairline. She felt the lick all the way through her. Her body was eager for his touch and she caught her breath. "My bedroom is down the hallway."

Raymond whispered in her ear, the sound of which was dark and husky. His voice drove her crazy.

"Alex. I know what you want. I want it too. But first, we need to talk."

CHAPTER FORTY–FOUR

Raymond sat down on the couch with Alex in his lap. She kissed his forehead and along his temple as her hand traveled south. "Alex. We need to talk."

"Don't stop." She ripped open his shirt and dove her hands in to touch his bare chest.

He wanted to give in to the temptation, but what he had to say was important. Her mental patterns felt strong, which made concentrating difficult for him. "Everything with Wilma was based on a lie. I need you to understand some things before I take you into that bedroom."

"You want to talk? If I'm not naked and writhing under you in the next 15 seconds I'm going to scream." She leaned in to kiss him, but he turned his head to stop her.

"You're not going to have a human man in your bed, Alex. … Look at me." He touched her hand as it made its way down his chest to his abs, stopping it mid–path. "You're going to have a vampire. I'm bigger and stronger than a human man. I don't want to hurt you."

"You won't hurt me." She peered into his eyes, which he knew had changed already to a deep black. "I'm going to have you in my bed and I know exactly who and what you are." She freed her hand from his and allowed it to continue its journey south.

Raymond groaned as he tried to stay in control. "I'm a lot stronger than a human man. I don't want to crush you when I hold you. I don't want to hurt you as I lay on top of you. As a human you are so frail to me. Promise me you will tell me if I hurt you in any way."

She stopped undressing him. "You slept with humans before, Raymond. Did you hurt any of those women?"

"No. But, I kept as much distance between me and the prostitutes as physically possible. I want to hold you close."

"OK, I promise." She shifted her legs so she now straddled him. Her sensual efforts told him that if he didn't get her into the bedroom soon, that they would end up here on the couch, or even the floor.

"Are you okay with me biting you while I love you?" Now sitting in this new position he felt her rubbing against his rock hard manhood.

"Oh, yes. You can bite me." She grasped his head in her hands and made direct eye contact. "Bite me!"

Raymond growled and bared his fangs. His length strained against his pants in an effort to find freedom. "I will probably bite you multiple times. In multiple places," he said breathlessly. "Are you okay with that?"

She gave him a devilish grin. "I might even bite you." She claimed his mouth and kissed him hard.

Just what he wanted to hear! He lifted her effortlessly and carried her to her bedroom. He surprised her when he opened the door and revealed what he had spent the last couple of hours working on. Over fifty lit candles surrounded the room; soft music played in the background and rose petals lay on the bedspread. On the nightstand sat champagne chilling in a shiny new bucket. As she shrieked in delight, he carried her over and placed her gently on the bed. "Are you surprised?"

"Oh my! I can't believe all of this." She took a good look around the room. "I can't believe you cleaned up my room. Ug! This place was such a mess and you cleaned it. My bedroom looked worst than some of the places in Florida we visited."

His lips curled up in a smile, revealing his fangs. "Its' okay, Alex. I wanted the room to look nice for us tonight."

"It does look good, but where is everything?"

"Let's focus on us tonight. Tomorrow you can peek in your closet and view the damage. I'll tell you now, the mess is not pretty. I had to clean at vamp speed to get this room and the dinner done in time. You probably won't want to be alone when you look inside the closet. It's pretty gruesome." He kissed her passionately on the mouth. She tasted sweet, like honey. His tongue dove into her mouth devouring her sweetness. He began to undress her. "I want to see more of you. I want to feel and caress more of your soft skin."

"Undress me. Please undress me … please."

He undid the tiny buttons down the front of her blouse. With each one, he kissed the skin revealed by his efforts. "You're so beautiful. I'll cherish you forever. Forever." He kissed down the top of her bra and was delighted to discover a frontal opening. He had never seen one before. He freed her breasts from their confinement. "You are absolutely beautiful. So round. So pink. You're perky for me, honey. So very perky." He caressed one with his hand as he suckled the other with his mouth. She arched in response and her fingers slid down his muscular shoulders to his back. She tugged at his shirt and he halfway sat up and took it off. He settled back down and he eyed her neck. It had been so long for him, both sex and feeding from a vein. He wanted her much more naked before he drank though. Much more naked.

332

He unzipped her skirt and tugged the garment down past her hips, past her knees, all the way to her ankles and off her body. She wore red panties. Hot, red panties. Silk. Red. He caressed her thigh and was about to remove the panties when he noticed they had no backing. He assumed they were meant to be this way, because damn, she looked so hot in them. He admired them momentarily and then slid his finger underneath the band on top and tugged them down as well.

"You have too many clothes on," she said.

He removed his clothing and watched as her eyes grew wider and she bit on her lower lip. "Oh, my. You are so beautiful Raymond. So strong. So muscular. I want to feel you inside me." He removed the last of his clothing and his erection sprung forward. His huge swollen sex throbbed for her touch.

Raymond saw her reaction to his size, but it was her mental pattern that told him what she was thinking. He smiled seductively at her and kissed her as he brought her back onto the bed. He loved his ability to read minds. It came in so handy at times. He knew what she was thinking, knew what she wanted. And that was him inside her now.

The last thing he wanted to do was to hurt her with his size during the most intimate of moments. She had confided that it had been a while for her, so he had to prepare her for him. Her hands slid down his back and her nails were digging into his backside. He gently touched her face and kissed her neck. He could smell her blood coursing through her veins and could hear her fast beating heart. She rolled her head to the side to make it easier for him to have access to her neck at the same time she spread her legs wide to welcome him in.

He lay down on top of her and tested the weight of his body on hers. A growl escaped his throat and he felt her shudder beneath him. With his body flushed against hers, he could read her thoughts as anxiety filled her mind. He had pinned her down and, even with the erotic thoughts of her mind, he sensed her panic. He leaned into her ear, "I want to make love to you more than anything else in the world, but if you are having second thoughts, we can stop right here."

She turned to face him, "No. I don't want to stop. I really am fine, it's just that … I wasn't expecting you to growl, that's all."

He stroked her hair knowing her reaction was more than just his growl, "Would you rather be on top?"

She rolled her neck to the side, "I want you exactly like this." She stroked his back with her hand and pulled him closer. "The growl was sexy."

He leaned in and licked her vein on the side of her neck. Her breathing got more labored, her head tilted back and her back arched onto the bed. Raymond's breathing grew shorter and quicker. His body tensed as he lowered himself to her vein.

Alex grabbed his shoulders and pushed him away. "Wait … we … ah, do you have …"

"What? I'm sorry. What's wrong?" He couldn't understand any of her mental images now since her mind was currently incoherent.

"No, no. We need …"

He lifted himself off her, but she held him in place. "No. You're fine. But, do you have a condom?"

He smiled, relief washing over him. "We don't need one. I'm not a carrier of disease and besides, you're not fertile right now."

He leaned in and stroked her neck once more with his tongue.

She turned her head to look at him. "Wait. How do you know I'm not fertile?"

"I had Sulie check days ago."

Her eyes widened. "Really?"

"It's what I asked her just before I took you home the night you met the team. I didn't want to impregnate you." He gently nudged her head back down on the pillow, and continued licking her neck to prepare her vein for his fangs, but sensed something odd from her mental patterns. He pulled away once again. "Honey, what's wrong?"

"You wouldn't want to have children with me?"

This was exactly why Raymond wanted to talk in the other room before they got to her bedroom and naked. Of course, this topic had not been discussed yet, and boy, it was a big topic. It definitely needed to be discussed since he was never letting her go. She belonged to him forever. He just hoped he'd be coherent in his current aroused state to even talk.

"No, Alex. It's not that." He waited for her head to turn so he could face her. "It'd be wrong for me to contribute to a pregnancy when we hadn't first discussed having children – especially if I could verify your condition ahead of time. I would see that as being irresponsible. That's all."

"Oh," she said, and then paused before asking, "Would you want to have another child one day?"

He lifted himself up with his arms so he wouldn't crush her beneath him. He gazed into her shining emerald eyes. "Alex, do you want to have my baby?" He could sense a maternal need in her from her mental

335

patterns, but was it his baby she wanted? A vampire baby? Would a human ever want that?

"One day, yes. Very much so."

He didn't know how he deserved such a beautiful woman in his life. His heart swelled with love for her. "Then I absolutely want to have more children."

He laid her back on the bed as she tilted her head to the side and opened her legs so she could create a cradle for him. His tongue licked up the side of her neck and he felt her shudder beneath him. His breathing became short once again and his body tight. His length hardened for her. He smelled the blood which flowed in her veins just beneath the surface of her beautiful creamy skin. Type A+ positive, his favorite. Thick, rich, and delicious. His fangs ached in expectation. But not quite yet would he satisfy his needs. He was tempted, but wanted to savor the moment. He slid his finger through her wet folds and stroked her nub. She was so wet and close to coming already, her nerve endings there on fire.

Kissing his way down her body his lips felt her warmth. She smelled of fragrant body wash mixed with her sweet passionate sweat. He paused at her breasts, and suckled one while his hand splayed across the other and rubbed its nipple. It pebbled at his touch. Her fingers were entwined in his hair and she let out a deep moan.

All those years. He had forgotten what it felt like to hold a woman who truly wanted him to make love to her. To be desired, to have a woman touch you, to have a woman want you so desperately — it was pleasurable on such a base level. This time was different though. He was a fully transitioned vampire. He could hear her quickened heart beat, could feel the heat of her skin as she warmed him. He couldn't believe that it had taken him this long to find Alex. She was all he wanted, all he needed.

He continued his journey south so he could taste her. His length throbbed in expectation, and he wanted to dive into her slickened heat, but first to taste her precious honey almond arousal. His nostrils flared as he inhaled deeply. She lay wide open to him as he touched her auburn curls. Alex wasn't scared or repulsed by what he was. She wasn't afraid of his fangs and that they were inches from her delicate womanly parts. She was engorged and reddened, glistening with moisture for him. His tongue found her core and circled around her nub, causing her body to tighten and her back to arch. Raymond thought it was the most beautiful sight. Quickening his pace, he lapped up greedily what she offered. He listened to her panted breath and her love murmurs as she called out his name repeatedly. Her thought patterns were focused on just the pleasure her body enjoyed, and it heightened his desire for her. She exploded under him, flooding his mouth with her cream.

A low guttural growl escaped his throat. Her body shook in the aftermath of her orgasm. She lay there catching her breath as Raymond kissed his way back up to her neck. Raymond lowered his head to her throat. The scent of her skin, and the blood just beneath, nearly sent him over the edge. His fangs tingled with pleasure as he gently scraped them across her skin and found her vein. He licked her neck once more, and then slowly inserted his fangs into her. His mouth filled with her warm, crimson, life–giving blood. It had been such a long time since he had bitten anyone. His inner vampire needed this, and the taste was perfection. He swallowed.

His body warmed from the new blood in his body and from her body heat beneath him.

Blood lust was fully upon him when her blood filled his mouth once more. He needed to be inside her. He wanted to pound her and explode within her. Quickly he sealed the two small puncture wounds on her neck. Her response was to arch her back and cry out. He licked her neck repeatedly until she was brought to the brim of a second climax.

He slid his hardened shaft to the portal of heaven, teasing her in its path. He placed both of his hands on her thighs and held them. He pushed her legs further apart and slowly entered her body. Slowly at first to stretch her out, to prepare her body to accept him. She moaned and dug her nails into his back. She was tight and hugged his sex within her. He slowly slid himself in, inching his long length into her. He desperately wanted to plunge himself entirely within her, but could tell she had not had a lover in a while. She moaned and he tilted her hips slightly forward so he could sheathe himself all the way inside of her. She shifted her body, welcoming him in.

Her slick body tightened around his manhood as he retreated and reseated himself deep within her. Her moans filled his ears as he repeated the movement. She was tight and muscular, and he quickly learned to appreciate the athletic build. Being within her was the most pleasure he had ever felt, and he wasn't sure just how long he could last. Even without the blood lust, he would still have had a hard time controlling his urges. His urges needed to be reined in. As muscular as she was, she was only human.

He retreated nearly his full–length, and drove into her slowly once again. He repeated the movement again and again until she lifted her knees higher and again arched her back. She exploded under him. By reading her thought patterns he would be able to read any signs of pain, so he allowed himself to drive into her. He felt nearly out of control as he read only pleasure from her mind. Each time his full–length pounded into her exploding body he read only pleasure from her.

Her raspy voice cheered him on. Her body may be human, but her stamina allowed him to ride her hard. He pumped his length faster and faster into her muscular body, her hips in perfect time with his. His body tightened with imminent release.

When his release came, he growled her name. The pleasure rippled through him as he filled her with his hot seed. His manhood spasmed over and over as he held her tightly. He closed his eyes and worked to catch his breath.

He lifted his head to look into her eyes. His face had been pressed against her hair as he had come. She was out of breath and feeling weakened. "You okay?" he asked.

Alex took a deep breath and nodded. "Yes." With another deep breath she said, "I'm fine. You?"

He nodded and gently kissed her pert little nose. "I love you, Alex."

Her hands gently massaged his back. "I love you too, Raymond."

He shifted his weight off her and rolled her on top of him with the two of them still connected. "You feel so good, Alex." A ringlet of her hair and slid down and hung over her face. He stroked the hair and gently placed it behind her ear. "I'll love you forever."

She nuzzled against his now warm body. "Your body temperature is warmer after you make love." It wasn't a question, more of a statement.

"Yes. It won't last. It's your body warmth and blood that warmed me. It will fade soon."

"I see it as my personal duty to keep your body warm." She giggled.

He had to laugh inside as he heard her giggle. Maybe there was such a thing as the giggle factor. "Alex, I'm going to make love to you all night."

CHAPTER FORTY–FIVE

Alex called a morning meeting to go over the last minute details. The smaller of the two ballrooms at the hotel would serve for the Arrival Ceremony of the State Dinner; the larger ballroom was for the dinner itself. The perishable flowers would arrive tomorrow, but the tables in the large room were laid out and set with the best linens, silverware and china – all with the White House insignia. Video cameras were positioned within the rooms, the entryway of the building, the driveway to the building, and throughout the parking lots. Most guests would arrive by taxi, but there was a valet service for those who chose to drive themselves.

The hotel preparations kept her busy throughout the day. Raymond wanted to spend more time with her, but her schedule wouldn't allow for it. The vampires were not needed until the actual event, but the humans were busy checking all entry and exit points and every cubbyhole imaginable.

The humans were already in place when the Colony gathered at the new venue at the Capital Hilton and did a practice run–through, simulating everyone's roles. Sulie and Ben would be part of the kitchen and wait staff, so they would be busy in the kitchen and in the hall itself looking at table placements, exit doors, and any hiding places assassins could use to their advantage.

Sulie also had one other task. The call from the lab had indicated the type of poison which had been used against Justice McCade. Thankfully, an antidote existed, and she had already administered the medicine to him this morning under a compelling. She had checked five other Justices and those who had been poisoned were also given the antidote. The remaining three would receive their spot–check physicals tonight if they attended the dinner.

Mason would be representing the President. In an earlier meeting with Homeland Security, Dixon, Alex and Raymond, it was suggested the President remain behind because of the vampire threat. Held in a secure location, Daniel would be the President's bodyguard tonight.

Raymond would work the front desk. He stood in position at one of the security stations that visitors would have to pass to gain entry into the ballroom. Not only were the monitors working to ensure heat signatures from each guest, but Raymond would also be able to sense another predator in the room. An added benefit to his position was that he would help the Colony members enter with concealed weapons.

Sterling would oversee the perimeter of the building and the grounds, which included the parking lot. He dressed in black so he would not be detected by the human team or any arriving guests. He would also run a check on random license plates as a precaution.

William would be the eyes and ears of everyone. His position would be a remote location with video and audio feeds from both the vampire and human teams.

Both Dixon and Alex, the only two humans who could eat human food, posed as guests for tonight's event. Their reserved seats sat only one table over from the President — close enough to see him chew his food.

Tonight's com link units were ear buds. They sat low in the ear canal and were small enough to go virtually undetected. The entire team would be in constant communication with one other, with William in tonight's command seat. The men had mini–cameras within their buttons, glass brims, or even on their neckties; Alex hid her camera in her corsage, and Sulie had hers hidden in her waitress cap. Each video was sent wireless to William, who kept an eye on what everyone else was seeing.

Alex had been briefed about the dead forger and the four forged passes into the dinner. Of course, new passes were issued, as well as announcements of the change in venue. With the death of Verna at the White House a few days ago, there were still three deadly vampires on the loose. It was all going to come down in a few short hours. All she could do now was go home and get dressed.

Alex dressed in a designer knockoff. The black and green gown brought out her emerald eyes and her long auburn hair. The beautiful dress featured a knotted breast, laced waist and fell three–quarters in length, which allowed her to wear her SBC holster on her right thigh. The weapon felt a bit bulky, but the extra fabric of the dress proved very forgiving. The dress seemed a bit short for such a ritzy affair, but she needed access to her SBC Launcher. Her whip was strapped to her back and covered by a black wrap that matched the dress. The dress accentuated her strong athletic build. She accessorized the dress with a black beaded handbag with thin spaghetti straps. The bag contained blood syringes, her identification, and extra bolts for her canon. Tonight she wore her hair down and curled. She strived to attain gorgeous and deadly and felt it was a shame the dress was going to wasted at a State Dinner they'd be working instead of a romantic outing for just her and Raymond.

Of course, she enjoyed looking at him in his lightweight mohair wool tuxedo. The man had taste. The tuxedo was single breasted, single button with besom pockets and side vents. It accentuated Raymond's powerful build. The fine garment wasn't as forgiving for concealing an SBC Launcher, but since Raymond was part of the security staff, people would expect him to have a holstered weapon.

Raymond drove her to the event, and they arrived early enough for all the team members to rendezvous and get into their prospective locations. The valet took the keys to the car, giving Alex the ticket to put into her purse.

On their arrival, Raymond walked into the ballroom to man his security station. Alex, wearing her weapons, walked in without detection thanks to Raymond. As Alex passed through to the first of the two ballrooms, she noticed Dixon approach Raymond's station. Dixon dressed in a classic black, double–breasted tuxedo and fit nicely in with the rest of the crowd.

Once inside, Alex surveyed the room. She noticed Sulie and Ben in their striped red shirts suggesting they were part of the wait staff. "Sulie, I see you at my 2 o'clock; Ben, you are at my 11 o'clock. We still have to wait for Mason to arrive as the President. We have less than an hour until the Arrival Ceremony begins." They acknowledged her appearance and she approached some of the human team members for a status update.

Dixon now entered the first of the ballrooms. Speaking into his earpiece he announced, "I have a visual on Alex, Sulie and Ben. I'm making my way to the second ballroom."

344

"Video and audio strength are good. You're all coming in loud and clear," William said from his remote location.

"If anyone cares, I'm here too. In position with nothing to report," came Sterling from his position outside.

Alex checked her secure com panel. The message read, "P.O.T.U.S. Beast on route." She whispered into her com unit that the President was on his way to the dinner in the Beast, the presidential limo, and everyone needed to be on guard. The President of France and his wife had just arrived, and the Secret Service remained on alert.

"I'm not sensing any vampires in the ballroom," Ben said.

"There are none," William chimed in. "All guests are giving off heat signatures."

The team waited a few more minutes as guests filed in; then the loud speaker announced the President was entering the ballroom. The State Dinner would begin after the Arrival Ceremony, which consisted of drinks and appetizers. Guests milled about talking and drinking. Ben and Sulie walked among the guests carrying either cocktails or appetizers.

Each of the Colony team members positioned themselves strategically along the exits of the room as the President, or more to the point, Mason, entered. So far, everything was picture–perfect.

The President was introduced to the President of France and his wife while the press snapped pictures. Afterward the President talked with department heads, senators, and others. Everything seemed pretty tame. But that was just before the vampires crashed the party.

345

CHAPTER FORTY–SIX

Raymond took his position with the human security team. The human stench hit him immediately as the humans took their posts. Most of the guards had eaten an early dinner in preparation for working the late evening hours. He could smell the lingering stench of their food on their breaths.

His station stood at the far end of the entryway, but even so, he could also feel the anxiety in the air from the newer guards who felt excited and worried about security procedures. The mental patterns were hard to bear, but at least the two humans assigned to Raymond's station were used to security procedures. They saw the assignment as just another work day. Unfortunately, the humans were the last two Raymond wanted to work with.

Four stations existed in total. Three neighbored one another at the main entrance, but the fourth station, where Raymond would be working, was singled out. It still remained in the main entryway, but a stone pillar forced a separation of it from the others. Thanks to the Secret Service, the stations had been secured by magnitometers to detect guns, knives, and bombs. All guests would have to walk through one of the four devices before gaining entry into the hotel and its secured area where the President would be. Three men staffed each station. One ran the conveyor belt where purses would be scanned, another would walk the guest through the magnitometer, and the third guard would manually inspect the purses and look through them.

Matt sat down at the scanner for the conveyor belt, while Brandon set out plastic bins for the guests to put jewelry and small metal objects into before he escorted them through the magnitometer. A third agent joined them. He stood at the end of the conveyor belt at a small table where he would perform the hand inspections. This was quite possibly the young man's first time pulling security for the President. He was nervous, and Raymond could sense it. Of course, the perspiration from the man showed as a dead giveaway to Raymond's strong vampire sense of smell.

Raymond would rather compel Matt or Brandon away, but he approached the young man instead. Keeping his back to Matt and Brandon, Raymond compelled the third human to take another position elsewhere because of a change in scheduling.

Not wanting to draw attention to himself, Raymond hung around in the background, hoping to blend in, but it was to no avail. Brandon stood next to the pillar and had watched the compelling and was already questioning it. The human stared at Raymond, at first not recognizing him. But then, Brandon rubbed his temple and said, "I know you. Are you supposed to be at this checkpoint tonight?"

Matt remained busy testing the conveyor belt and had missed Raymond taking the guard's place. Now he looked up at Raymond when he heard the conversation.

Raymond glanced into Brandon's eyes. Brandon's thought patterns overwhelmed Raymond as he tried to compel the man to accept his answer that he worked the same security desk that they did. Brandon's thoughts were sincere, patriotic ones. The man was loyal and trustworthy, but the compelling did not take.

"What do you mean you're at this station?" Brandon asked. "Where did Curtis go?"

Raymond reached into Brandon's mind and noticed a wall firmly planted within the man's brain. He had seen this before, it was a locked compelling, a subroutine, just like the one he had given Dixon all those years ago.

"I don't see you on the duty list," Matt said to Raymond. He held up a work chart and looked over at his partner Brandon. Matt began to rub his temple and Raymond suspected he too began to recognize him.

Raymond turned his attention to Matt. He stared into the man's eyes. "Curtis was reassigned. Don't you remember? You were told I would be his replacement."

Through dim eyes, Matt said, "Oh, right. Hey, sorry about that. I must have forgotten. This is Brandon and I'm Matt."

"Nice to meet you both," Raymond said. He watched as Matt went back to work. This human was clean, but Brandon was another matter.

"You're not supposed to be here," Brandon said.

"Last minute change," Raymond announced.

Matt glanced up at Brandon, "It's cool, man. He's replacing Curtis tonight."

Brandon looked over at Matt, then he held his hand once again to his temple. He visibly shrugged and set back to work on the magnitometer.

It had been a long time since Raymond felt fear, but here it was. Brandon had been compelled, and it wasn't by a member of the Colony. The compelling was done by a vampire strong enough to implant a compelled subroutine, which meant the vampire was as strong as Raymond. Brandon was now a liability, an unknown

348

security risk. He quickly whispered into his ear piece for Ben to join him in the foyer.

Raymond then looked over at the magnitometer, the section Brandon would be checking. The detector had a series of small LED lights that ran down the right side of it. They were amber in color, so faulted and not functioning. He glanced over at the other three similar detectors at the other doors. A series of green lights were lit on all of them. Suspecting that Brandon had faulted the sensors, Raymond studied the wires and information panel on the detector.

"It's in order," Brandon said. "I already inspected the scanner."

Matt glanced over to Brandon. "What's wrong?"

"Nothing," Brandon said, his face pale.

Stopping the conveyor belt, Matt looked over at Raymond.

There were a dozen security personnel in the foyer, and another eight outside the door. A good twenty lives hung in the balance, and Raymond could hear each of their heart beats. Perhaps it was Raymond's stone–like stance, but Matt stood up and walked over to the magnitometer. He must have suspected something was wrong because he reached up and touched the amber light of the panel.

"This isn't right," he said. Matt quickly flipped switches back on to enable the sensors. Brandon pulled his gun and held it closely to his body to avoid detection. He aimed the weapon at Matt as the LED lights began to glow green. Brandon stood securely behind the pillar, with the rest of the security team unaware of his actions.

With widened eyes, Matt's hands quickly went straight up. "What the fuck, Brandon!"

"Quiet," Brandon ordered. He disabled the detector once more. His face was pale, his eyes dim. "This detector is to remain off. It is of the utmost importance."

Raymond took a step closer, and Brandon pointed the gun in his direction. Raymond didn't care about getting shot; he just didn't want anyone else hurt.

"You don't look so good Brandon," Matt said. "You look pale and ..." he paused. "Do you know who I am, Brandon?"

Brandon looked around the pillar at the other stations. No one was aware of what he was doing. He shifted the gun in Matt's direction.

"Brandon," Matt said again. "Who am I?"

Shaking his head and pointing the gun back at Matt, Brandon said, "I don't know."

"Put the gun down," Raymond ordered. In response, the gun was now aimed at him.

"Jesus," Matt said. "You were right Brandon. Look at you. You're under mind control. It wasn't just in your head. There is a threat at the White House brainwashing people."

Raymond rolled his eyes. Good Lord, had it gotten out of control this much? How many times had this human been compelled to know that he had been under the influence? His mind was Swiss cheese and he was telling others to be on the lookout. Raymond's fear grew and he could feel it in his tightening chest. There was no way he could compel Brandon to put down the gun, and there were lives at stake.

Matt calmly said, "Brandon, did I tell you that Elvis was spotted in Germany? You know he loves the place. He met Priscilla over there."

Raymond raised a questioning eyebrow in Matt's direction. The poor human must have been scared witless having a gun pointed at him.

No response came from Brandon, except he pointed the gun in Matt's direction.

Matt's then said, "Skynet could never happen."

No reaction came from Brandon. The two stood there locked in a quiet one–sided dual. Raymond realized that Matt was trying to reach out to Brandon, but he had no idea who or what Skynet was and why it would be important to Brandon.

Finally Brandon spoke, "Don't make me shoot you, Matt."

Matt's eyes widened, obviously as a response that Brandon recognized him. "Astronauts really did land on the moon, Brandon. It's a fact."

Not even an eye flutter came from Brandon to that accusation.

"Most people agree that 'The Phantom Menace' was the superior of the 'Star Wars' movies, with 'The Clone Wars' a close second."

Raymond mouthed the words "Star Wars" and looked from Brandon to Matt, and back again. How could this odd conversation help? But then Brandon sighed. Whatever Matt was doing, it seemed to be working. He noticed Ben enter the foyer. With just a tilt of his head, Raymond signaled to the vamp to remain where he was, and to see what the next step would be.

Matt's eyes lit up. Defiantly he said, "Greedo. Shot. First."

"Han was the only shooter," Brandon turned and stared at Matt. "You know that Han shot and killed Greedo, what are you talking about? Greedo never even fired." The color returned to Brandon's face and his eyes had light in them once more.

Raymond moved at his top speed and grabbed the gun from Brandon's hands.

Brandon's eyes widened, his heart raced. "What happened?"

"Let's just say I now believe you about mind control," Matt answered.

Brandon looked at his partner. "They got to me."

"Who are *they*?" Raymond asked.

Turning to Raymond, who now held his gun, Brandon's gasped. His eyes nearly popped out of his head and he had to hold on to the marble pillar for support. He pointed an accusing finger towards Raymond and said, "Mr. Teal Eyes!"

CHAPTER FORTY–SEVEN

Alex and Dixon walked among the other guests at the reception. Guests clumped together in small groups, each drinking wine or champagne and nibbling at the tiny hors d'oeuvres. Alex held a glass, but only for the sake of blending in.

They navigated the room, carefully walking in front of each guest so their hidden cameras could pick up a clear image of each person's face, as well as any infrared heat signatures. The recognition software William used had so far not detected any known vampires. Alex also knew what the four people on the fake security badges looked like. There were two women and two men on the fake badges. With one woman killed a few days ago by the team in the Sit Room, there were still vampires on the loose.

"Facial recognition affirmative," came William's voice over the com unit.

Alex shot Dixon a quick glance, and then replied, "Where?"

Sulie's voice, from back in the kitchen, came over the com. "I have the second female cornered in the kitchen. Ben was paged by Raymond, so I need backup."

Dixon and Alex quickly walked past the bar stations and through the side door, which would gain them access to the kitchen. When the security officer on the other side of the door tried to stop them, Dixon flashed his badge and they were allowed to continue.

The smell of dinner was strong in the large kitchen, and Alex's stomach twisted at the smell. Her nerves remained on edge, and eating was the last thing on her mind. They walked past the cooks and the heat of the stoves and found Sulie in the corner of the room, with another woman sitting on the ground at her feet.

Alex took a cleansing breath as she walked towards Sulie. Another vampire, an evil one, was nearby. How many times in her life had she been so close to such a deadly creature? Ignorance may be bliss, but it can't protect you. She took a good look at the vampire and recognized the woman's face from one of the forged security passes. The vampire did not appear to be a threat since she sat crouched down in the corner of the kitchen. None of the kitchen staff paid any attention to her. Alex assumed that the vampire had compelled the kitchen staff to leave her alone, but for what purpose? Or had Sulie done that? Alex and Dixon both stepped closer.

Sulie noticed the two team members and nodded in their direction. Now with backup, she approached the vampire with caution.

The cries of the vampire told Alex of her agony. That's when she realized the woman had not been subdued. She had been hiding in the corner just beyond the chopping station of the kitchen where butcher block knives lay on the shiny metal table.

Sulie shook her head, and then whispered into her com, "Her medical reading is off. She's dying and I'm not sure why. I haven't even touched her yet."

The vampire groaned and ordered Sulie away. When the vampire looked over at Alex, Dixon pulled her behind him so the vampire could not make eye contact with her. The vampire again stared at Sulie and tried to compel her away.

"She doesn't know what we are. She's dizzy and confused," Sulie said.

Sulie carefully placed her hand on the vampire's arm, which startled the woman. She tried to sit up, but her equilibrium seemed off. She hit the wall and yelled in pain.

"What's your name?" Sulie asked.

The vampire's eyes had rolled to the back of her head. Chances were great the vampire could not see clearly and the room was spinning. Vertigo. Sulie grabbed the woman tighter to give her some balance and then asked again for her name.

"Angelina. My name is Angelina." The vampire spun her head around. "Who are you?" Her eyes twirled around in their sockets. "Where am I?"

"I'm a doctor, and a vampire like you. Tell me what is wrong." Sulie now touched Angelina's head. Perspiration wetted Sulie's fingertips when she did so. Sulie looked into Angelina's eyes as she medically checked for any signs of a concussion.

Angelina's arms flailed out, trying to gain more balance. Sulie subdued the arms and held the woman down. "You're dizzy. Do you understand me? You are not falling. You are on the ground and safe."

Angelina moaned her reply as Sulie scrambled for a better medical reading. Sulie looked over at Alex and Dixon, "Help me keep her still. She's going to experience full onset dementia shortly as her mind is being destroyed." Angelina was covered in sweat, her heart rate was elevated, and her breathing was labored.

"Am I going to be all right?" Angelina pleaded, obviously not hearing Sulie's diagnosis.

"You will be," Sulie lied.

Alex gasped as she noticed Angelina's skin. There were scales on her arms which trailed up to her shoulder and over her collarbone. Sulie tore Angelina's blouse and inspected her neck and found what looked like more scales which made her skin now resembled that of a reptile.

"Angelina. Listen to me," Sulie said as she shook the woman. "Who did this to you? What did they do?"

Angelina vomited. Human blood, as well as insects, now splayed across the kitchen floor. Sulie read the vamps DNA by touching her scaly skin. "I'm not a herpetologist, but I suspect her DNA had been fused with some sort of lizard or other amphibian."

Dixon held the woman's arm and steadied her. Alex, who was now squatting on the floor next to Sulie, shifted positions to get a better look at the skin.

Sulie examined Angelina's back and noticed black blotches forming.

"Oh my God," Alex said, covering her mouth in horror. She pointed down towards Angelina's eyes. They were now reptilian slits. Sulie moved her hand over the woman's back and noticed her vertebrae fusing together and being altered. The woman's hips hinged out, just like a lizard.

"She's not the only victim here. She's pregnant," Sulie said to Alex and Dixon. Then looking down at Angelina she asked, "Who is the father of the baby?"

The vampire was now writhing on the floor in torturous agony, but managed to bellow out, "Groyki Zmiya. Please save me and my baby."

"Did Zmiya perform experiments on you, Angelina?" Sulie asked sharply, trying to get Angelina to focus.

Angelina grabbed Sulie's hand. Her voice was no longer human sounding. She hissed, "Please, help me."

"I'll end your suffering, Angelina." Sulie noticed a dustpan in the corner. She reached up for a knife from the butcher block and ended the woman's pain.

CHAPTER FORTY–EIGHT

Raymond compelled Matt to continue with his task, during which Brandon babbled on about not wanting to be taken to the mother ship.

For cleanup, Ben compelled the team lead to find two replacements for this station, one for Brandon and one for Raymond. Matt was compelled to be fine with the switch.

Raymond pulled Brandon towards a back wall, out of hearing by the humans nearby. He held the man tight in his grasp, but not in an alarming way as to give the other humans in the area concern.

"I don't have access to the President," Brandon said. "I'm only a pawn in the government, with no real power."

Raymond could understand the man's integrity, even if he was currently lying to save the President. "Brandon, calm down." He tried to compel Brandon, but the task proved to be a moot point, so he glanced over at Ben for help.

The human's heart raced. "You know my name. So tell me yours, Mr. Teal Eyes," he choked out.

"My name is Raymond. I'm not the enemy. I'm trying to save the President."

Brandon studied Raymond's face. "I know you." He gazed deep into Raymond's eyes. "I mean, I don't know you, but I've seen you before." He swallowed hard. "I've seen you plenty of times."

As calmly as he could, Raymond reassured the man. "Yes. We've worked together many times. You were forced to forget."

Brandon's eyebrow rose. "Forced? How?"

Raymond sighed. "If I have to explain every detail to you right now we won't be able to save the President."

In a rehearsed voice, Brandon methodically spit out, "Brandon Wyatt. Serial number four three ..."

Ben kept tabs on the other humans in the room, the ones he compelled to continue with their assigned tasks and to ignore what Raymond was doing. He now focused on Brandon. "I got this, Raymond." Ben looked sternly over at Brandon and the human visibly relaxed. His shoulders sunk down, his eyes were no longer wide with fright, and his stance seemed more at ease.

"We're the good guys," Raymond announced as he released his grip.

Brandon gave a sly smile towards Raymond. "Good guys don't brainwash federal employees."

Raymond stared deep into Brandon's eyes. Then he sensed what had happened. Like trying to use a dry pen to write on unlined paper, Raymond tried to write onto Brandon's mind ... but could not. The man's mind would no longer succumb to compelling.

Brandon took a good look at Raymond. "We've worked together before."

"Yes," Raymond agreed. "I work for the President. We both do."

With discerning eyes that studied Raymond from top to bottom, Brandon asked, "What are you?"

Shit. Raymond had no time for this. In his com unit, he could hear the conversation William was having with Sulie. Two vampires remained, and the night was young.

Raymond decided not to answer the question, but to ask one of his own. "Brandon, I need you to describe all the strangers you've dealt with in the last twenty–four hours."

"What?" Brandon shook his head. "I don't know."

"We're looking for two more people that we believe are trying to hurt the Supreme Court Justices and possibly even the President. I believe you have met at least one of them," Raymond explained.

"I don't know what you are talking about." Brandon eyes squinted in pain and he let out a small grunt. Raymond was there to support him.

"There was someone, a man," Brandon continued in a hushed whisper. "On the Metro last night … he started talking to me. I remember a cold numbing pain, but then we arrived at my stop and he was gone. I didn't see him leave."

Of course, he didn't. That would have been part of the compelling – to forget the meeting of the vampire and what you were being asked to do. Raymond could not compel Brandon to forget, so he now needed a baby–sitter for the human. Or, at the very least, a closet with a locked door.

The best choice for the task was Sterling. Being a half–breed, he was the weakest link in their group. Raymond always saw to it that Sterling played the lesser of the roles when his team did missions such as this, much to the chagrin of his son. At the moment, he had Sterling at a remote distance out in the parking lot checking license plates and looking for suspicious behavior from any of the guests entering the hotel. It was an obvious ploy to remove him from the more imminent danger of the dinner itself being overrun with dangerous vampires, but it gave Raymond piece of mind.

But before he could send for his son, he heard his voice–over the com unit.

"My Spidey senses are tingling," Sterling announced from outside. "Looks like we have an intruder … definitely vampire. He's making his way through the south door. He's well over six foot, blond hair, dressed in all black."

Raymond glanced over to Ben, who still adjusted Brandon's aura to make him calm. "How many?" Raymond asked.

"How many what?" Brandon asked.

Lifting his hand to his ear and turning slightly so Brandon would know the conversation didn't include him, Raymond again asked, "How many?"

"Just the one. Could be Zmiya" Sterling repeated.

Ben shook his head as he also listened to the com unit. "There are two male vampires left. We can't confirm that this is Zmiya."

"Vampire?" Brandon said in a hushed tone. "Oh, man. I knew it. I just knew it …"

"Hush," Raymond said to him, half smiling when he noticed Brandon cover his neck with his hand protectively.

Sterling then added, "Secret Service snipers on the rooftop across the street must be dead."

William's voice filled the com. "They checked in ten minutes ago according to the Secret Service broadcasts. They could just be compelled."

"Either way, the snipers are looking the other way. I'm following the perp in through the same door. That way he can't back out," Sterling said.

For the second time this evening, Raymond felt the hairs on his arms stand on end. He had to get his son out of the kill zone. "Sterling, I have another task for you. Come to the main foyer and let Ben handle the perp." He motioned over to Ben, a turned vampire, to meet with Sterling. Ben nodded and left at top speed.

Sterling didn't respond. But at that moment another pressing need presented itself. It wasn't fear that sickened Raymond's this time; it was another predator at close range. *Another* vampire was nearby.

****

Raymond spun his head around and saw Zmiya, but not before the vampire detected him as another predator as well. Zmiya had dressed to fit in well. No one standing near the vampire would have guessed the danger they were in. Not even Matt or the other two guards at the security station gave him notice.

Zmiya sneered at Raymond, as though he knew the game was on. Raymond turned and faced the vampire, quickly recounting the lives that were at stake in this room. Even if the tally had been one, it was still too high of a price.

Brandon too had turned to see what Raymond was watching. "I know that man," he whispered to Raymond. "He and another man were the ones who approached me on the Metro."

"Stay put, Brandon." Now with Ben gone, Raymond sensed strong mental patterns of fear emanating from Brandon. He wasn't sure if it was fear of the unknown, or fear from what this vampire and his counterpart had done. Raymond knew memories of the attack were flooding Brandon's brain, and that was information the team needed.

Zmiya looked around the room, and settled on his next victim. An elderly husband and wife stood near the vamp. Raymond recognized the man as Justice Maddox, soon to be retiring from the Supreme Court. Not a frail man, but a good hostage with much clout. He watched as Zmiya quietly grabbed the man's arm, looked him in the eyes, and compelled him to obey every order he gave.

"Next," Matt called. "The Justice's wife took a step forward. She placed her purse on the conveyor belt and walked through the functioning magnitometer. Her husband did not follow. Instead, he was pulled out of line by Zmiya and led quietly back towards the door.

"Here," Raymond said to Brandon as he removed the com unit from his ear and pulled the video button from his jacket. "Use these. Tell Dixon I'm going after Zmiya."

Taking the items, Brandon gave Raymond a confused look.

"Tell Dixon the situation. He'll take care of you," Raymond said. With that, he followed Zmiya and his unsuspecting victim outside. The voice of the Justice's wife asking what was going on was the last thing Raymond heard as he left the building.

****

"What did you just say?" Alex asked into the com link. Her eyes grew wider as she listened again as William relayed the information back to her.

Dixon and Sulie were busy dispensing with Angelina's ashy remains. "We have a situation," she began as she walked up to them.

Before she could begin to explain, she heard Dixon talking into his com. "Who is this? ... Brandon?" He looked up at Alex, but she shook her head and walked over to Sulie. She didn't have time to wait, so she grabbed Sulie's arm.

Sulie nearly dropped the bag of Angelina's DNA, but managed to get it into her purse and snapped the clasp. "Zmiya?" she asked.

"Yes, and Raymond ran out after him." Alex was already walking towards a back door to the kitchen. "You and Dixon find Sterling. He's chasing the third vampire," she shouted back to Sulie. When Sulie began to protest, Alex added, "Ben should still be with Raymond. Sterling needs the two of you. I'll be Raymond's backup."

Alex ran out the kitchen and into the side parking lot. There was no sign of Raymond anywhere. She would have to run to the front of the building just to see him. Unfortunately, the Secret Service would probably stop her before she could make it that far.

Pulling her phone from her purse she pulled up an app to locate Raymond's phone. When the device pinpointed his location, she let out a slight curse. The man was already several blocks away.

"William," she said into the com link. "Did Raymond hijack a car?" She reached into her purse and pulled out the valet ticket for the Jag.

"Not sure," he answered. "He's no longer wearing his com link or camera." There was a slight pause on the line, and then he added, "Raymond is alone, Alex. He sent Ben to help Sterling. I'll send Ben to help you."

She looked down at her phone. "Raymond is near the Farragut North metro line," she said, walking over to the valet station. "There's no time. I have his coordinates. I'm going after him."

"Zmiya has a hostage. Male. Elderly. No other information. Be careful, Alex."

Alex quickly walked to the valet station and the attendant took her ticket. She pressed the urgency with her badge and ID, causing the man to run off and fetch the car.

William's voice filled the com once again. "The other team members are engaged with the third vampire in the basement of the south wing. He's a bad ass, Alex. I can't send anyone to help you just yet."

Alex looked around to see if the Jag was on its way, but didn't see the yet. "Do what you can. I'm tracking Raymond by his phone's GPS," she replied back. She glanced down at the phone. He was still only a few blocks away, so obviously they were not yet on the metro line.

The sound of a moan from behind her caused her to nearly jump out of her skin. Her hand shook as she held the phone. She heard another moan, and this time saw an elderly man that she recognized as one of the Justices of the Supreme Court. He looked shaken, but steady.

Guessing this was Zmiya's hostage, she approached the man. He merely dismissed her concern with a wave of his hand and mentioned he didn't know why he was outside when he knew his wife was in the hotel waiting for him.

Alex watched as the man rounded the building towards the front of the hotel. That's when she saw the valet return with the Jag. There was no time for pleasantries or a tip, she jumped into the jag and pulled out of the hotel's parking lot. She was careful not to exceed the speed limit. She didn't want to call attention to herself. She knew just how many snipers from the President's counter assault team had their guns trained on her.

CHAPTER FORTY–NINE

Zmiya ran into the Metroline Park and Ride with Raymond in pursuit. Fortunately, the hour was late, and not too many trains with passengers would be arriving or departing.

A train pulled up to the stop. Zmiya fired three shots in Raymond's direction as he entered the car. Raymond ducked for cover. The few humans that waited for the train now ran in all directions, scurrying away to safety. Just as the train doors began closing, Raymond jumped from his secure location and ran at top speed to the train. He made it inside as the doors closed.

It didn't take long for Zmiya to get a hostage. He held a woman at gunpoint. The passengers were panicking, but the woman Zmiya held remained calm, obviously compelled not to struggle.

Raymond needed to isolate and contain Zmiya. He walked the distance of the train, allowing the passengers to take haven behind him. An exit door stood within reach of Zmiya, so if he decided to leave the train, he could. Raymond didn't have good containment, but would have to make do. Raymond stood before Zmiya. "What do you want, Zmiya?"

Zmiya tightened his hold on the woman. She gasped, but didn't show any signs of concern.

"Yes. I know who you are," Raymond said. "I just don't know what you want. Let the woman go and we can talk."

Zmiya held the gun to the woman's temple. "Don't move, vampire. I know what you're doing and your plan won't work. I'm not some idiot you can manipulate!"

The mental patterns of the passengers bombarded Raymond. Strong emotions about their families and lives assaulted his mind. The train wasn't that full, but there were enough humans to be distracting. With any luck, none of them would try to be a hero.

"It's late, Zmiya. Why don't you tell me what you want so I can help you?" He took another step closer.

Zmiya cocked the gun. "One more step and delicious red splatters on the walls."

Raymond stayed his ground. He felt he could take the vampire down in a physical fight, but he would need to touch the vampire to compel him with his special ability. "What were your plans at the State Dinner?" Zmiya ignored Raymond's question. "I know you want to be a Justice. Tell me about it."

Zmiya narrowed his eyes. "You figured that out all on your own? You must think you're fucking brilliant."

"Listen …"

"No," Zmiya cut Raymond off. "You listen. I'm going to be the most powerful vampire in the country." He tightened his grip around his hostage.

"I'm sure you see yourself as powerful, Zmiya. But you threatened the President and several Justices. I'm not going to let you get away with that."

"President? Oh, please. People in this country vote for the candidate they hate the least, not for the person they want to be President. I could do a better job than that asshole."

"Let the hostage go, and we can talk about what you would do differently than the current President."

"Shut up!" He studied Raymond. "That bitch Verna was weak. Omar couldn't even get a drop off time and place right. Even though they were idiots, you couldn't have killed them all by yourself. You must be working with, or for, someone." He tightened his grip on the hostage. "You and your group of idiots make me sick." Zmiya glared at Raymond; Zmiya's look resembled that of a madman. "When I'm done, my family line will be vampire royalty. Every last one of you will pay for what I've been through."

Raymond took a small step closer. "What have we done to harm you?"

"I'm only doing what I have to do! Human laws are beneath us anyway; we're the top of the fucking food chain!" Zmiya leaned in to bite the neck of the woman he held. Her blood ran down his chin and over her shoulder, staining her dress. The train pulled into another station, so Zmiya took the opportunity by throwing the woman at Raymond and then ducking out the sliding doors. The woman laughed as she fell into Raymond's arms. He barely made it out before the train took off again.

Raymond heard the fast paced footsteps of Zmiya as he ran from the station. The chase was on, with Raymond matching Zmiya's fast speed with every step. The chase led from the row of office buildings, down past storefronts, to a less populated area of town about four miles from the station. The area was vacant of pedestrians and the directionality of the chase was sporadic. Raymond suspected Zmiya was not familiar with this end of town and was possibly looking for another hostage. The chase took them to the warehouse district, which was in a seedier part of town. Raymond could hear stray cats in the background and the rats that they chased. Car noises emanated from the nearby streets, but no humans on foot were nearby – which was a good thing.

Raymond turned down a dark alley to follow Zmiya when a familiar car pulled up along the docking bay of one of the warehouses. The hairs on Raymond's arm stood up as he realized who was driving.

He ran to the Jag just as Alex exit from the car. She shouldn't be here. The situation was much too dangerous. "Get back in the car, Alex. Zmiya is down this alley."

Alex furrowed her brows. "I'm your backup."

He gritted his teeth. Even as athletic and as strong as she might be, both physically and fearlessly, she was still a human. Too frail and too easily killed. He couldn't lose her. "He's already taken two hostages tonight; I'm not letting him take you as well."

Alex looked down the dark alleyway. "He has a hostage with him?"

"No. Not right now."

"But you said …"

Raymond cut her off as he opened the door of the Jag. "Please, I don't want you in harm's way. Get back into the car."

She closed the door. "Sorry, but back down. We do this together."

"It's for your own safety, Alex. Now get in." He gestured back towards the car once again.

Her body stiffened as she stood her ground. "I'm *your* Director and this is a direct order."

Raymond couldn't let her go down that alley, at least not mentally unprepared as she was. A moment of silence existed as Raymond thought out what to do. He had always allowed Dixon to face off the enemies, although never directly on the front line if a vampire team member could fight in his stead. "Dixon told me you wanted to wait for the mental subroutine," Raymond said. "The only way you're going in is if I can force your mind not to accept any compelings." He had considered just compelling her to drive off and leave him to fight alone, but he suspected she'd never talk with him again if she discovered the truth. His oath not to compel her had already been sworn in by Dixon just before the State Dinner, and that also wasn't in his favor at the moment.

"Fine," she said defiantly "Do what you need to do."

It wasn't his oath that caused him to do what he did next, but a wish to respect her as a soldier wanting to do her duty. He had her sit in the Jag as he leaned into the driver's side. "This won't hurt, but it isn't going to be pleasant. If I had more time, I could be more gentle."

"Get it over with," she demanded. "We don't have the time."

He put both his hands to her temples and began the process. His mind met her mind. Soon she entered a trance–like state and he began whispering into her ear, forming the subroutine, and completing the bond. He placed the subroutine faster than he would have normally done it, but the compelling was done nonetheless.

Alex scrunched up her nose and held her eyes tightly shut. "Ugh, brain freeze."

He looked her in the eyes, "Bark like a dog."

"What?" As she moaned again he kissed her on the forehead. "Good. It's properly in place." He helped her from the car. "Let's go."

****

Now that the sun had set, Alex struggled with her vision in the fading sunlight. She walked cautiously down the alley in the back of the warehouse. Raymond walked beside her and the two traversed the alley from one secure location to another, hiding behind dumpsters, air–conditioners, and anything else that would provide them safety. She tossed off her high heels in an effort to keep up with him. His keen sense of vision and hearing allowed them to track Zmiya as he led them further and further down, what Alex hoped, was a dead end alley.

"He's still here. Holding his ground hoping to kill us," Raymond said. "I can feel him."

There wasn't much of a breeze. Alex hoped they weren't downwind to Zmiya.

Raymond's speed was much faster than Alex's. He left one secure location and immediately was snug in another. Alex felt exposed and vulnerable as she scurried at her top speed. Her fingers tightened on the SBC Launcher in her hand. The fact that she was an excellent shot kept her feet moving forward.

Instinctively the two ducked as a shot rang out in front of them. Another two shots came, and this time Alex could tell Zmiya was aiming at Raymond. She thought it could be a tactical advantage and fell back even more from Raymond's position.

"Surrender, Zmiya!" Raymond yelled. "You won't walk away from this. You have nowhere to run."

Raymond placed his whip on the ground and unholstered his SBC Launcher. Alex watched as he took aim and fired at Zmiya. Her tight hold on her SBC Launcher grew slippery wet with perspiration as fear crept over her. She had been in gunfire before, but not with a weapon she had such little experience using. The SBC Launcher felt bulkier than she was accustomed to. The silver whip across her back weighed her down.

"Never," Zmiya replied to Raymond's earlier demand. Two more shots sped towards Raymond's hiding place behind the dumpster. The sound of a cat screeching marked Zmiya's movements. If Alex detected the movement correctly, Zmiya was circling back and headed in her direction. Perhaps it was the garbage in the alley that masked her human scent, Alex wasn't sure, but he headed straight towards her. The narrow alley wouldn't offer much room for a confrontation, though. Alex noticed doors several feet ahead of her. She figured he was making a run for that building.

Raymond must have picked up the sounds of Zmiya's movements as well, because Alex was aware he was doubling back and approaching her location. She didn't have much of a vantage point to take a shot at Zmiya if he did reach the doors. She ran towards some boxes further down the alley that would give her a better shot. She didn't get far when gunfire rained down on her.

At least one of the bullets hit her, but her silver whip strapped to her back protected her like a bulletproof vest. She ran faster and managed to reach the side of the building, but unfortunately there wasn't much cover. Cardboard boxes were now her only shelter and she was wide open to Zmiya's attack.

Her sense of vision played in slow motion. She was aware of Raymond's position as he double backed. He ran at top speed, but it was all dream–like to her as she took in the entire scene. By focusing on Raymond, she had lost the position of Zmiya, until she heard a noise from above her. Zmiya now stood on a fire escape, and not on the ground. He must have jumped! It was a rookie mistake in assuming he couldn't reach that height. He was so close to her now. Even in the darkened shadows of the alley she could make out Zmiya's face. His fangs were bared, his eyes wild, and he looked every bit as scary as any vampire from the horror movies.

When Zmiya aimed his gun at her, she froze like a deer in headlights. He told her to shoot Raymond — like that was ever going to happen. She suddenly felt a sensation like brain freeze. Her focus was on her own stupidity of letting herself be trapped against a wall with a killer who would take her life so easily. She felt stupid to have left the dagger and tranquilizer in her desk, especially during her first encounter with these monsters. She knew this was the end, and she was going to die like a damn coward.

Again he ordered her to attack Raymond, and once again she felt brain freeze. Zmiya cursed in what Alex guessed was Russian and aimed his gun at her head.

She waited for death and squeezed her eyes shut. Her back smashed into the wall as the bullets sounded, but the pain of bullets tearing into her flesh never came. The world seemed to go in slow motion again as she opened her eyes she saw Raymond staring at her, his chest covered in blood. He had thrown her towards the wall as he blocked the bullets that were meant for her. He spat up blood, and she noticed he had aged. Wrinkles now marred his face and his hair had grayed. His body sagged and he fell to the ground at her feet.

No thoughts existed. No reflections. No processing what her next move was. Alex was only vaguely aware of herself screaming the word "No!" as she watched Raymond take the bullets meant for her. Instinctively, she lifted her weapon and shot three silver bolts directly at Zmiya. The vampire screamed in pain and fell from his perch with a thud. As she reloaded her weapon, Zmiya cursed in Russian and stood. The blood from the wound on his chest suggested at least one of the bolts hit their target, but she suspected that all three had not.

Before she could fire again, he was on top of her. The SBC Launcher fell to the ground when he picked her up and flung her like a rag doll. The impact to the ground was the hardest blow she had ever felt. Her chest felt on fire making it hard for her to breathe. Blood oozed down her forehead and she felt dizzy. She rolled to get her feet under her and stood up. She eyed her opponent, who stood directly in front of her. No. She would not be his next meal. The bastard was going down, or at least going to have one hell of a battle on his hands. She wished she had not dropped the SBC launcher, but she would make–do with what she had available. If she had to, she'd tear him apart with her bare hands.

Zmiya cursed at her again.

The only weapon she had on her was the whip, a weapon she had only used once, unsuccessfully, in practice. She ran towards a dumpster for protection, but Zmiya beat her to the haven. He kicked her with a roundhouse kick and sent her flying backwards further into the alley.

Pain. She was sure she either had several cracked ribs or a collapsed lung. She labored to breathe as she stood up. The silver bolt she shot in his side still ratcheted itself deeper and deeper into his flesh, thanks to the silver barbs it had. She noticed him trying to remove the deadly weapon, but the silver burned his flesh as he touched it.

She unhooked the whip from her back. She may be coming to her end, but she knew a few things. First, he was toying with her, like a cat playing with a mouse before its demise. Second, she suspected the pain affected him more than he would admit. All the curses in Russian were probably him voicing his pain. And lastly, she wasn't going to be a hapless victim again. The man that attacked her all those years ago was human; she had no doubt about that. Her current adversary may be immortal, and the biggest villain she ever fought, but he wasn't going to win tonight. This battle may claim her life, but it was going to take him down as well. The bolt was tearing more and more into his flesh. Soon it would shred the organs in its path as it worked itself out the other side. The bolt would kill him long before it worked itself out.

With all her strength, she flexed the whip in the air. A snap was supposed to occur, but her feeble attempt didn't even come close to doing so.

He pointed at her whip and laughed. His laughter intensified as he neared her. She noticed how much he aged in just the last few minutes. A pool of purple blood stained the alley where he stood. She only had to survive a few more minutes. She looked past Zmiya and saw Raymond still lying on the pavement. Perhaps she still had time to save him, if she could somehow kill Zmiya.

His laughter continued. His endless, evil, maniacal laughter enraged her. She was done being toyed with.

She took a deep breath and clenched her teeth. She flexed the whip again through the air. This time a snap sounded and the leather separated from the silver. The whip coiled around Zmiya's neck and sizzled on his skin. Alex's palm burned as the whip's handle was whisked from her hand and flew into the air. As the thought of her only weapon, and her only hope, left her, the whip flew into an air–conditioner and caught in the fan. Zmiya was thrown back as the whip lapped around the fan blades and tightened its hold on his neck, subduing him.

There was no time to lose. Alex quickly recovered her SBC Launcher and ran up to Zmiya, swearing at him with her every breath. Zmiya's hands and feet were still mobile and she dared not get too close. She aimed the SBC Launcher at him as she approached him and shot three silver bolts directly into his chest from point–blank range.

Blood spilled from her opponent, but there was something else that she noticed. The dim lights from the building reflected off a shiny surface from around the Zmiya's neck. A necklace. A violent yank on the necklace snatched it from his now frail and aged neck.

"Come here!" he bellowed at her. Blood spat from his mouth as he choked out the words.

She felt the pain of him trying to compel her. "Nyet!" was her reply.

He screamed at her, but the words were weak as they left his mouth. She took the SBC Launcher in her hand and smacked him in the jaw to get him to shut up. She watched as he turned to dust where he stood.

CHAPTER FIFTY

Dust was all that remained. Even having read how vampires died, it still shocked Alex to see it with her own eyes. The son of a bitch had barely died, and his ashes had just touched the tops of her shoes, as she turned and ran towards Raymond. He remained still full bodied and alive. He would not be turning to dust if she could help it.

She watched as Raymond struggled to regain consciousness. As he sat up, he stumbled, aging a few more years. He fell back down onto his back just as Alex reached him.

"Raymond. We got him. We got Zmiya." She ignored the pain from her ribs and helped Raymond sit up.

He wrapped his arm around her shoulder. "Call the team. Have them send out help."

Alex had heard four shots and had seen bloodstains on Raymond's shirt. She ripped the suit jacket and tore the shirt. She noticed four entrance wounds, but only two bullets exited his body. Wasn't his body supposed to regenerate? Bullets shouldn't have this much effect on him. She retrieved six syringes of blood from her purse and administered them. With each syringe, she noticed a surge of energy from Raymond, followed by red human blood pouring from his wounds. She helped him to stand and struggled maneuvering him down the alley and into the Jag.

Now that Raymond wasn't lying on the cold ground, she dialed Ben's number and instantly the vampire gave status. "All is well at the hotel," he said out of breath. "We got the third one, finally."

"Raymond was shot," Alex blurted out as she got herself into the car.

There was a moment of silence on the other end of the line. "There should be blood in his pockets and blood in his car. Bullets come right out Alex, don't worry. Bring him back to the hotel. We have more blood here too." He took a deep breath, "Get back here, Alex. We need to regroup."

"OK" She hung up the phone. This was normal? Raymond's body oozed blood all over the place. Blood now pooled on the seat of the Jag. She could see why Dixon wanted to retire. It was only her first week on the job, and already her nerves were shot.

Just then, Raymond collapsed into a convulsion.

CHAPTER FIFTY–ONE

The four syringes of blood from the car and the two from Raymond's pockets were fully exhausted. Raymond's convulsions stopped and he was aware of the situation. He gasped, "We have to go, Alex. I need more blood."

Alex slammed on the accelerator and sped out of the alley. She wasn't all that familiar with this area of town. It had been neglected for years, and certainly not a place she ever visited, so she had no idea exactly where she was. No one was on the streets, which was good since she was running all traffic lights and speeding like crazy.

Could she convince Raymond to feed off her? Did she even have enough blood to give him? How could she drive and feed him at the same time? Her mind raced as she turned down one street and then another, trying to find a way out of this area.

She ran several red lights as she sped towards any familiar street, trying her best to remember which way she had come. She didn't know how to use the GPS in Raymond's car, but felt relieved when she turned the machine on and found her address pop up as the last address punched in. She let out a sigh of relief when the device showed they were not far from her house.

Raymond slid in his seat as she careened around a corner. She hadn't taken the time to buckle herself in, let alone Raymond. She looked over at him and realized that he now appeared older. She needed to call for help.

"Ben! The blood isn't working!" she said the second he picked up his phone.

"Where are you?"

"I have him in the car. He's been shot." Alex took her hand and balanced Raymond as she made a quick turn to get onto the interstate.

"How many bullets did he take?"

"Four. Two looked like through–and–throughs … so he still has two in his body … in his chest actually. I don't know what to do."

In a calm voice, Ben said, "Relax. The Jag has extra blood in the glove compartment. I need you to give him that blood. Once he has it in his system, the bullets should work themselves out, even if they've fractured. It's only two bullets, he'll be fine."

"I gave him the four syringes of blood from the car already, plus what he had in his pocket, and the six I was carrying on me. They don't seem to be working!" she screamed into the phone.

"Okay. Relax. Let me talk to him."

"You can't. He's unconscious."

"What? Alex, vampires don't just lose consciousness. Two bullets shouldn't be this critical. Where exactly are you?" he growled.

"I have more blood at my home. I got a shipment this morning. I'm taking him there now." She hung up without giving Ben another chance to speak. Raymond's aging had not slowed down with the twelve syringes of blood in his system, and now his beautiful black eyes were shut and he was unconscious. She pulled the car over on the shoulder of the interstate. She had to get more blood into him and right now. She opened her car door and rushed to his side of the car. "Raymond! Wake up!" He lay motionless. Alex put her wrist up to Raymond's nose. "Smell. There's more blood. Here."

381

There was no response from Raymond. His fangs were fully extended, so she took her finger and pierced her fingertip. She had to put her finger in his mouth so that the blood could drip down on his tongue. Hopefully, this would be enough to stir him back to consciousness.

She felt his tongue move against her finger. "That's right Raymond. There's more blood. Wake up and feed." His eye lids opened. He was weak and his aging was showing once again. He looked about seventy years old. She brushed her forearm against his fangs and cut into her skin so he could see and smell the offering. Even as weak as his body was, his impulse to feed took over. He pierced his fangs into her arm, in an almost savage manner. His fangs ripped into her flesh and searing pain swept over Alex. This was so unlike the dozen or so other bites he had done to her earlier all over her body. This one hurt like hell. She resisted the urge to pull away, as well as the urge to scream out in pain.

Raymond recoiled from her arm and Alex realized that even as weak as he was, he was picking up her thoughts. He could sense her pain. She shoved her arm back onto his lips and concentrated on just one word over and over again. "Drink. Drink. Drink. …" He responded and bit into her arm again, he drank deep and swallowed over and over. His eyes half shut as he did, but as more blood entered his body the more aware of his surroundings he became. He opened his eyes and looked at Alex, immediately pulling her arm away from his fangs.

"I'm taking too much. I could kill you." He gasped. Her blood trickled down his lips and onto his chin. "Leave me. I don't want to kill you."

Alex ignored his plea. "Drink more, Raymond. I want you to drink more blood right now." She positioned her arm directly under his fangs once more, but he refused to drink again from her arm.

Alex started to feel weak from the blood loss, but she had to get him to her home for more blood. She pulled her arm away which caused her skin to tear even more. "There's more blood at my home. We'll be there soon. Hang on." She closed his door and ran towards the driver's side of the car. She tore a strip of cloth from the hem of her dress and wrapped the makeshift bandage on her wound to halt the bleeding. The fabric sopped up the blood and was soon drenched. She added another strip with pressure, and then started driving.

She sped down the road with her blood dripping down her arm and staining her clothes and the car.

"I love you Alex." It was the last thing he said before convulsions hit him again and he lost consciousness once more. That's when she screamed.

CHAPTER FIFTY–TWO

"No," Alex screamed. "This is not Raymond's day to die." After racing past other motorists and running more red lights, Alex found herself back in familiar territory. The Jag sped down her street, and she screeched to a halt half in her driveway and half on her front lawn.

She reached for the door handle that was slick with her own blood. She pulled at the lock and then hurled herself from the car. Her arm dripped with blood on the pavement as she ran to Raymond's side of the car. She managed to open the door and pull him half out, but knew it would be a struggle to get the man inside her home, to where more blood would be.

"Raymond," she said forcefully, "Wake up." She placed her left arm around his waist, her right under his left armpit, and gave a tug. The wound on her arm ripped open even more causing blood to gush out, and the pain from her cracked ribs felt agonizing. Her blood splattered on Raymond's shirt, the leather seats, and down to the floor. Alex felt dizzy. She took a deep breath. She knew she was losing too much blood, and she needed help.

Her purse was now stained in crimson red, and the bag lay on the floor by Raymond's feet. She bent down and stretched herself over his body and reached for it. Her right arm felt too damaged to do much, so she tugged at the zipper with her left fingers until the purse finally gave way. She groped for her phone, but couldn't find it. She pulled at the purse to bring it closer, but the bag was now pinned under Raymond's foot.

Sitting halfway up, she searched Raymond's coat pocket. Inside she found his phone.

"Come on … Come on … ," she said into the phone as the listened to the rings of the number she had just dialed.

"Dad, are you okay?"

"Sterling!" she yelled into the phone.

"Alex?"

"Your father's been shot. He's dying. You need to come help me. I'm at home. I have more blood in the house."

"Sulie and I are on our way. Ben said my father has bullets still lodged inside him. They will work themselves out. Don't panic Alex."

She ripped away the rest of Raymond's torn shirt. His thick purple blood had matted with the hairs on his chest. She ran her hand up and down inspecting him. Something was wrong, and when her finger grazed a raised bump in his abs, she bent down lower to get a better look at it. "There's a bullet coming out!" she yelled.

"Good. That's very good. Once it's out he should heal. There's a bag of blood in the trunk of his car."

Alex removed the bullet. Its mushroomed head was blunt. She tossed it onto the dashboard, untangled herself from Raymond's lap, and ran to the trunk of the car. There she found a pint of blood. Bagged, not syringed.

"I got the blood," she said as she scurried back to Raymond. Sweat dripped from her face, matting her hair onto her cheeks.

"It's Sulie, Alex. Sterling is driving. Is Raymond still unconscious?" Sulie asked.

She looked inside the car. Raymond's head hung down low, his eyes were closed. "Yes."

"OK You'll have to put the blood into syringes and inject it into his bloodstream. Can you do that, Alex?"

Alex nodded, and then in a low voice replied, "Yes. I can do that."

The used syringes were strewn about on the floor of the car, so she hunted one down. The plunger of the syringe was difficult to pull with her injured arm. Her hands shook, but she pulled at the plunger and watched as the syringe filled with the blood from the bag. She plunged the needle into Raymond's leg and gave the full dose.

"How much?" she asked into the phone.

"All of it, Alex. Give him everything you have. Sterling told me the bullet is out, so he should come around soon."

Alex plunged syringe after syringe into Raymond's body. He remained aged, his hair white, his skin wrinkled. The blood on her arm was no longer dripping with fresh blood, but she still kept putting her arm up to his non–responsive face and hoping against hope that he would be enticed by the smell.

With each emptied syringe, she kept a tally and announced the number into the phone for Sulie to hear. With each count, Sulie encouraged her to do more. It wasn't until the bag was nearly empty that Sulie took over the count and kept Alex awake by talking to her about the teams triumph over the third vampire at the dinner.

Alex passed out before the bag was done.

CHAPTER FIFTY-THREE

Alex was aware of being moved. The sensation reminded her of childhood when her father would carry her to her room and put her to bed. She wanted to sleep. Yes, sleep would be good.

When her head hit the pillow, she finally opened her eyes. The room was dark, but with the street lamp outside shining through the window, she could make out the layout of the room – the nightstand, dresser, and closet door. This wasn't her childhood home. She forced her head up to look at the man standing over her. The man wasn't her father. It was an older man, in torn black clothes. His face was burned and stained a dark purple color. His face looked familiar but hard to place.

She knew she lay on her bed at her house. The soft pillow nestled her head and felt good. She shifted into the comforter and realized how much her body ached. Her back felt like it had been twisted into a pretzel and her legs felt like limp noodles. She was sore all over.

"Good, you're awake."

She stared at the familiar face of the man. Alex didn't know if she needed to scream, ask a question, or just go back to sleep. She liked the idea of sleeping.

"Stay awake, Alex," the man ordered. He sat on the bed beside her and her weakened body swayed as the mattress gave way to his weight.

Her mind swirled with images. Images which seemed not all pleasant. She remembered a fancy dinner. Yes, a dinner where she was all dressed up. She glanced down at her clothing. The torn dress was dirty, not resembling its earlier beauty. She swallowed hard, trying to remember how she got back to her room.

She watched as the man held up a syringe. The street lamplight glistened off the empty vial. She remembered syringes. She was doing something with syringes, but what?

"You were attacked. But you're going to be fine," he assured her.

"Who …?"

She watched as the man studied her. He took a good look, deep into her eyes. "It's me. Sterling."

Sterling? She took in his facial features. Yes. It was him. He looked older than she had remembered him, but it was definitely him. His face was marred by wrinkles, bruises and burns. The events were all coming back to her. Sterling. The Colony. The mission.

"Raymond!" she yelled as she desperately tried to jerk her body up.

He placed his hand on her shoulder and held her back down to the bed. "My father is fine. Sulie is seeing to him." He stuck the empty syringe into his arm, and she watched as he filled it with his own purple blood.

She looked towards the door of her bedroom. "The car. He was in the car," she said.

Not looking at her he replied, "Yes, he was. He's now in the living room being healed by Sulie."

Her eyes turned quickly to Sterling, "He's alive?"

"Yes. Evidently the vampire fled after attacking you both." Sterling picked up her arm and showed it to her. Her smooth creamy skin looked flawless with only the exception of dried blood around her hand and upper arm. "Zmiya tore into your arm. He must have brutally fed on you. You lost a lot of blood, but I sealed the wound for you."

She looked at her arm and remembered back. "No. Raymond fed from me."

Sterling studied her, then looked back towards the bedroom door as though looking past the walls and at his father. Turning back to Alex, he asked, "My father did this to you?"

Alex cleared her throat and laid her arm back down on the comforter. "I gave my vein to him. He was dying. Not enough blood in the car to save him."

Sterling placed his hand on her arm where the wound had been. "Thank you for saving my father's life." He slowly rubbed the area where his father had fed. "I've never come close to losing him before, and he means the world to me." He gazed her in the eyes, "I'm glad he's found you, Alex. You make him very happy."

Taking a deep breath Alex felt the pain in her chest. "Thank you." She tried to smile, but there was more pain. "Zmiya ..." she began.

"We'll find him. Don't worry."

"No," she protested. "He's dead. I killed him."

Sterling's eyes grew wide. "It's okay Alex. You're just disoriented. Relax."

She felt the tug of sleep weighing heavy upon her. She licked her lips and asked, "What am I doing here? Why are you here?"

"I'm here for you, Alex." Just before she passed out, she watched him poke the needle of the syringe into her arm and injected his blood into her.

****

Alex awoke in unfamiliar surroundings. The deep hue of the hardwood floors, the style of the crown molding surrounding the doors and windows, and the outdated windows that opened outward told her she was in one of the bedrooms of Fang Manor. The bedroom was huge, and she stretched out in the king-sized bed to rouse herself from sleep.

The room itself was nicely decorated. The oversized nightstand matched the dresser and full-length, standing mirror. The matching lamps were tall with drum shades. The green curtains were drawn, and the room was dimly lit. She could tell it was daylight by the small amount of light that snuck in through the edges of the window frames. She sat up and turned on the lamp closest to her.

With more light, she was able to get a better look around the room. The decorations were sparse. Even the bedspread was just a solid brown in color. There were no pictures on the dresser, no artwork on the walls, and no knick–knacks strewn about the room. She did notice a square discoloration on the wall opposite the bed, with a nail above it. No painting hung there now. She wondered if this room had been made vacant for her.

The last thing she remembered was Sterling turning her. Maybe now that she was a vampire she was expected to live here at the mansion, and this was to be her room.

She looked down at her arm. Of course, it had been healed. Not only had Sterling sealed the wound, but as a vampire she would no longer have any concerns over cuts and bruises. Her hand went across her rib cage, then traveled down to her hips and legs. Everything was here, and not broken or in pain. Even her back, which had always given her grief, felt just fine.

The full-length mirror across the room gave her pause. Why even have a mirror if you appear fuzzy in it. Perhaps that was why it was full-length. Obviously, as a vampire you could still see your clothes and how your overall appearance looked, even if your face remained unclear. She considered getting up to look into the mirror when she heard the creaking of the stairs outside the closed door.

She watched as the door handle rotated slowly. It occurred to her that her eyesight wasn't better than when she was a human. Maybe it took time for a person's body to acclimate to being a vampire. The door creaked open, and a familiar face poked in through the narrow crack.

"Oh, good. You're awake," Raymond said as he opened the door wider and walked in. He had barely closed the door when Alex ran across the room and threw her arms around him.

"You're alive!" she said.

He smiled at her, his fangs showing slightly through his lips. "I'm fine, honey. How do you feel?"

"I'm fine," she said looking into his eyes. "Especially considering everything that has happened." She smiled at him as he lifted her into his arms and carried her back to the bed. He set her down and sat next to her.

"You definitely went through a lot." He touched her arm, then raised it up to his lips and gently kissed it. "I am sorry for feeding from you like I did. I wasn't even aware of how ..." He looked down towards the bed, away from her. "Sterling told me how he found you. And I am sorry."

She placed her hand on his cheek and turned his head to face her. "I'm not. You were dying."

He smiled. "And you saved my life."

They remained silent, looking into each others' eyes, until Alex asked, "I saw the bullet come out, but you were not growing younger with the blood I had given you. Was it not enough blood?"

Raymond shook his head. "Normally, it would have been enough blood. More than enough actually. The problem was the bullets were silver tipped. One had fragmented and the silver tip became lodged in one of my ribs. My body was healing itself by growing bone over the silver, which was burning me from the inside and killing me."

Her hand rose instinctively to her mouth as she let out a gasp. "It must have been very painful."

"Sulie detected the bullet the second she touched me. It only took her a few minutes to cut open my chest and dig the bullet out. After that, I healed with additional blood and was fine."

"Silver tipped." She shook her head. "I guess I'll have to be careful of such things. Especially now."

"It's just a hazard of being a vampire." He brushed a strand of hair from her cheek and tucked it behind her ear. "I do have a question for you."

"Anything," she smiled back.

"Fill me in on what happened after I passed out."

She took a deep breath and thought back. "He tried to compel me to attack you."

Raymond touched the side of her head. "The subroutine."

Alex nodded. "He was angry. He kept swearing in Russian."

"Russian was his native language," Raymond interrupted. "Through the Council, we located his coven in Russia. He went rogue decades ago. His family issued a statement this morning denouncing him from their family line. His half sister has been designated as his replacement as heir to their bloodline."

Alex raised her hand to stop Raymond. "She's the heir of what? The coven? What's the Council? You never really told me what that was."

"No. A coven is a group of vampires living together. A coven master is responsible for the group and has a seat on a Vampire Council – our ruling body, so to speak. I am the coven master of the Colony and sit on the Council."

Alex narrowed her eyes as she sat up. "None of that is in the documents I read."

"I know. We don't share everything with the government. The Vampire Council is not violent in nature. It governs us and provides us a network of communication and access to blood, not that the Colony needs the blood. We protect ourselves and humans from vampires who go rogue, we control our population growth by limiting our heirs, we can locate other vampires through their covens, arrange marriages between bloodlines, and much more."

Alex took it all in. "So Zmiya is out, his sister is in?"

Raymond nodded. "His death allowed for it, yes. She's an upstanding member of the human community, so the change was for the better." He reached in his pocket. "I want to thank you for picking up this." He held up a chain of dog tags.

She reached for them. "I took this from Zmiya just before I killed him." She inspected the writing on the tags. "It's in Russian."

"We found them on the floor of the Jag. They told us quite a bit, thanks to Sterling's ability."

Alex quoted from the documentation she had read about Sterling from the government files. "The more personal the object, the more information he can glean from it."

"Exactly. And these tags were very personal to Zmiya. We found out where he lived and uncovered quite an interesting laboratory of sinister intentions."

She handed the tags back to Raymond. "What do you mean?"

"I investigated his bloodline. His family has no special abilities. Most bloodlines don't, so it isn't surprising. That's why many purebred families arrange marriages and try to gain abilities for their future generations, as well as to secure their future financially. Zmiya's family was unsuccessful in locating a woman from a prestigious family line willing to marry him, that's why he went rogue. Since he was the only son, his father kept him as the heir of his family line. Zmiya was desperate to not only sire children with abilities, but he also wanted those abilities himself. He felt entitled to them, so he experimented with newly turned vampires by fusing their DNA with animal DNA and then impregnating them. He was filled with delusions of grandeur, and we discovered a sandbox filled with vampire ashes from his failed experiments. He forced dozens of humans to suffer at his hands by his experiments, and then he would turn them so they would have abilities. Sterling discovered a male vampire at the

394

dinner who's DNA must have been fused with an electric eel. He was probably a lab rat to Zmiya to see how the DNA would work."

"Sulie dealt with a pregnant female vampire who had amphibian DNA in her," Alex said.

"Yes. From what we've discovered, the DNA modifications are not viable. The vampires die shortly after turning. Sulie found several newly turned, pregnant vampires who were either dead or dying in Zmiya's lair. We suspect he had access to a considerable amount of blood for these women to even conceive. Sulie put an end to their suffering and removed all the computers and notes on his experiments. She'll probably spend the next several months reviewing them."

Alex rubbed her temple. "Good Lord. That's so sinister. But why attack the Supreme Court?"

"Zmiya wanted to control the Supreme Court in an effort to rule favorably towards environmental violations that he had perpetrated over several decades, which had included the importation of several exotic and rare species of animals and insects. He wanted to first control the Supreme Court, then the Senate and Congress to make rulings in court cases to pave the way for his unsafe medical experiments."

Alex shuddered. "All that just to muck with DNA and to torture people."

"Shh. Don't worry about anything. The Supreme Court Justices are recovering; our team is home and we're all safe." He inched his body towards her to delicately hold her. "I love you Alex. I love you very much."

"I love you too."

Raymond kissed her gently. "Tell me. How did you kill Zmiya? The GPS on the Jag allowed us to go back to the warehouse district. There we found bloodstains, mine and his. He lost a considerable amount of blood, but there were no ashes around. It's been windy the last couple of days, so they must have blown away. The huge blood stain is what tells us he must have died there, plus you had told Sterling you killed him. How did you do it?"

She shrugged her shoulders. "I had luck on my side." She looked up at Raymond. "I was more concerned about you." She glanced around the room once more, "You said a couple of days. How long have I …"

"Just two days. Your body needed time to adjust, so I brought you to my room. I hope that is all right."

Her smile widened across her face. "Your room?"

He moved a pillow to the head of the bed and lay down with her. "You had several broken bones, including some cracked ribs when the team found you. Plus you had a lot of blood loss. Sterling told me he took care of you."

She took a deep breath. "Yes. He gave me his blood and … took care of everything." She moved her tongue over her teeth, but did not feel any fangs. Her stomach growled in protest and she realized how hungry she was. Shouldn't her fangs be out if she was ready to eat? Maybe there was a trick to get them to pop out. Of course, the idea of eating blood didn't sound too appealing. What she really wanted was a cheeseburger with all the greasy French fries, but she knew that was in her past. She wasn't sure if she was ready for her new diet.

"You're worried about something, Alex. Tell me," he said, turning his body to look her more directly.

She had never been fond of needles, but the idea of drinking someone's blood … as hungry as she was, that didn't sound very tasty. She looked into Raymond's eyes. "I'm hungry."

He smiled back at her. "I thought you might be. That's why I came upstairs to wake you. Sulie has something downstairs for you."

Something? Or someone? she thought. "For a first feeding I think I'd rather not have an audience."

He gave her a puzzled look. "First feeding?"

She now felt embarrassed, and she wasn't sure why. It was called a feeding. Maybe she wasn't saying it right.

Raymond's expression turned grim. His jaw clenched, and he grabbed her by the shoulders sternly. "What did Zmiya try to do to you? Did he try to turn you?"

Her eyes widened and her mouth gaped open by the sudden concern. "No. Your son did."

His grasp on her loosened. "My son?" he asked. "Sterling tried to turn you?"

She looked down at her arm where the injection took place. "I must have been dying. He injected his blood into me."

Raymond reached for her arm and stroked it gently. "No, honey. Sterling injected his blood into you to make you stronger – so you could heal quicker. His mother was human, so his blood isn't strong enough to turn a human."

Alex took a deep breath; a blush came over her face. "I thought … I mean … it was vampire blood, and all."

She shook her head, "I didn't realize half–breeds," she paused, "… vampires with mixed parentage could not turn humans. I thought he turned me." Her face grew red with embarrassment.

Raymond held her closely in his arms. "No, Alex. You're still human. Still a mortal. Still the same woman I fell in love with."

"The information I read about turning did not mention anything about Sterling's blood healing humans."

Raymond paused a moment before continuing. "If your child were able to cure humans, would you tell the government and risk him being bled dry?"

Alex swallowed hard. "Of course not."

"There are certain secrets we keep from the government. All to protect ourselves, not for anything violent."

"I understand," Alex said. "And it explains why Daniel is listed as having two sires. I'm guessing Sterling tried to turn him but failed."

Raymond bit his lip, and then let out a slight sigh. "Daniel was a young man, about twenty–five years of age. He attacked Sterling and nearly killed him with several gunshots directly through his heart."

Alex's eyes widened. "That's terrible."

"Sterling fought back, and Daniel bit him in the process. The fight couldn't have lasted long, and Daniel was drained dry as Sterling fed on him."

She covered Raymond's hand with hers and caressed. "Sterling was dying. He had no choice."

"Well, because Daniel bit him, he had some of Sterling's blood in his mouth. He wasn't killed in the attack, but he also wasn't healed afterward either. Daniel was left in a coma, with very little options. He could have lived the extent of his life in the coma, we could have released him from this life, or I could turn him."

"Sounds like you opted for the best choice."

"Daniel did not have a choice in the matter. I thought it was best, so I did what I had to do."

Alex nodded in agreement. "Why did Daniel attack him?"

Raymond's face reddened. "Sterling was having sex with Daniel's teenage sister. He walked in on them and surprised Sterling."

Her chin hit the floor. "OMG!"

"I lied on the report and said I was with Sterling at the time. For years after the turning, I was worried that Daniel, as a full vampire, would seek retaliation against Sterling, but none came. Daniel adjusted well into our culture."

"So Daniel just woke up and discovered he was a vampire," Alex said softly. Her eyes looked away from Raymond and focused on the spot on her arm where the blood had been injected.

Raymond studied her while she was deep in thought. "Alex?" he asked.

"Yes?"

"You're disappointed." He touched her face and read her thoughts. "You thought you had been turned, and you're disappointed that you're not." His eyes widened as he spoke. "Do you want to be turned?"

Alex felt her heart skip a beat. Another woman, in the same situation, once told her to listen to her heart, not her head. Alex looked into Raymond's beautiful, teal eyes. She knew the answer. She knew what her heart wanted.

****

Raymond was thrilled that Alex wanted to be a vampire. Alex had agreed to be turned immediately, but Sulie insisted she needed one more week of rest. It was a big decision, and Raymond was grateful that his sister gave him a buffer of a couple of days.

He walked up the stairs to the room he shared with Alex in the mansion. Halfway up the second staircase he heard an all too familiar ring tone from his phone. A text had come in. He refused to look at it. There was something he needed to do first.

Even though the bedroom was also his, he knocked before entering. "Honey? You here?" He looked around, but the room was empty. The sound of the shower turning off told him where she was.

His phone chirped telling him he had a text. Again he ignored it. He knew who it was, and didn't want, or need, their answer for his decision. This was about him, his happiness, and a life he craved with Alex.

He gently knocked on the door before opening it. The moist, hot steam from the shower had filled the tiny room, making it warm and inviting. Alex's skin was slightly pink from the heat of the hot water and her hair drenched. Noticing that he had entered the room, she reached for the fluffy brown towel that hung on the rack beside the shower. She tantalized him by using it to dry her hair, leaving her body naked for him to view. "Were you looking for me?" she asked, her lips plump and pouty, her eyes seductively sexy.

He removed his suit jacket and tossed it to the ground. It landed with a weighty thump. "All my life," he replied. He began to unbutton his shirt when Alex

400

started to dry herself. She leaned over and dried her feet with the towel. Quickly he closed the gap between the two.

She laughed as he picked her up and moved her over to the bed. Her wet body dripped cooling shower water onto the sheets and especially to her pillow where her head was lying.

"Alex," he began. "I'll turn you either way. I promise." His blackened eyes took in her beauty. "Make me the happiest man alive. Marry me."

The smile was quick upon her face. Her reply almost deafening to his ears. "Yes! Oh, yes!"

Raymond kissed her repeatedly until he realized that with the removal of his jacket, he had left the ring in the bathroom in the front pocket. "One second," he said as he ran back to the bathroom. In his rush to retrieve the ring, his phone slipped out and hit the ground. He picked it up and glanced at the text. It was the Vampire Council. The text only had one word, "Yes."

He ran back to the bed to put the ring on her finger.

CHAPTER FIFTY–FOUR

Raymond and Alex walked down the hallway of the White House to Brandon's new office. It had been two months since their wedding. Dixon was still on the team in an advisory role, but the new director, Brandon, was catching on quickly to his new duties.

Raymond opened the door and allowed Alex to enter the office first. They found Brandon busy on his computer, but he was expecting them.

"Hey you two. Come on in," he said taking a good look at Alex. "How was the honeymoon?"

"It was very nice," Raymond said.

Alex blushed slightly and gave a hint of a smile. The tips of her fangs were slightly noticeable.

Brandon's eyebrow lifted, obviously noticing. "You look good, Alex. Married life certainly suits you." He swiveled his chair and moved over to the printer. He snatched the printout and handed it to Raymond. "Since Alex has decided to remain in her former position and live out her first life; I have created a new alias for you, Raymond. Your ages now match. That sheet is a summary of your background."

"Thanks, Brandon," Raymond said as he glanced at the paperwork. His hair had a touch of gray and his eyes looked more aged in preparation for this transition.

Unlocking his desk drawer, Brandon pulled out a large envelope. "These are your birth certificate, passport, Secret Service badge and the other usual things. We can go over it if you want."

Raymond accepted the envelope. "Unless you need to review it, I'm fine. I've gone through this dozens of times." He glanced down at the last name. "Soloman?"

"Human resources. Diversification being a good thing and all," Brandon quipped back.

"Mazel Tov," Alex said giggling.

A knock sounded on the door, and Brandon walked across the room to see who was there.

"Hey Brandon," Matt said, poking his head in. "I wanted to see if you were free for lunch today."

"Lunch would be nice, buddy," Brandon replied, not introducing the couple in his office.

Matt leaned in and whispered, "Hey, I heard of some additional information about those police reports I told you about."

"Which ones?" Brandon whispered back.

"The ones where an entire Metroline train of passengers swears they saw a vampire attack a woman. A new witness has come forward. This one says he got the entire incident on his cell phone."

"You don't say. Maybe during lunch we should head over and talk to the witness," Brandon said as he patted Matt on the shoulder. "I'll swing by your desk in a few hours and we'll head out."

"Great. See you then," Matt said as he left the office.

Brandon closed the door and turned to Raymond. "That guy's going to be a problem. You free for lunch?"

THE END

About the Author

Dear Readers,

I hope you enjoyed reading my novel, **Eternal Service** *(Book One of the Colony Series).*

Please visit my website (http://www.reginamorris.com) for more information about the other novels in the Colony Series. Feel free to contact me through my website, through my social media sites (see my website for the list) or by email at regina@reginamorris.com.

I live in Austin, Texas with my husband and two children. I graduated high school in Germany and I attended the University of Texas at Austin where I received a degree in Computer Science with a minor in math. After enjoying a career in software engineering, I discovered that writing is in my blood, and had to put pen to paper!

The opinions I express in my novels are my own. My stories are my own intellectual property. Copyright (c) 2012, Regina Morris

Sincerely,

Regina Morris

Other Books in the Colony Series by Regina Morris

Vampires exist among us. They can be our neighbor, best friend, our child's teacher ...

They alter their aged appearance based upon the amount of blood they consume. They move to a new area, drink a lot of blood, and appear young. Slowly they limit their intake of blood and age, right in front of our unsuspecting eyes. After decades, they fake their death, move, and do it over and over again.

Most live quiet lives in an effort to blend in.

Some however want power and control.

The Colony is an elite group of vampires sworn to protect the President of the United States from these rogue vampires.

Eternal Service (Book #1)

When Raymond, part of a covert special ops team of vampires who protects the President of the United States, teams up with a federal operative of the human female persuasion—who has no idea that vampires even exist—will his mission or his heart be compromised first?

Career military woman, Alex Brennan, is being offered the promotion of a lifetime – and with it a romance that she has desperately been seeking. Does she dare accept the position as Director of the Colony, an elite group of deadly creatures of the night and risk a dangerous romance with a man who isn't even human?

United Service (Book #2)

Available Fall of 2013

Sterling, a half–breed vampire who works with a covert team of vampires to protect the President of the United States, is the weakest link in the chain for his team, and he knows it.

Having the special ability to glean information from inanimate objects, he spends most of his time in the FBI evidence room suffering from painful side–effects of his ability. His current case involves the kidnapping of vampire children. He teams up with a purebred vampire, Kate, who is the nanny of one of the kids, to rescue the kidnapped children. Would Kate ever consider a relationship with a half–breed who is constantly in pain? Insecure in his own ability to woo the lovely Kate, Sterling travels across the country on a journey of self–discovery where he realizes he is a person of value, truly deserving of love, forgiveness and happiness.

Kate has led a sheltered life and is considered handicapped by vampire standards since, like Sterling, her vampire ability has horrific side effects. She creates a symbiotic relationship with Sterling, who helps her to discover that she is able to have a normal life, with all the joys and sorrows that it brings.

Enduring Service (Book #3)

Available in 2014

Sulie has been in love with the same human man for nearly thirty years. The object of her unrequited love is her boss, Dixon — the only human Sulie has come to truly know in her nearly 200 years of existence. As Dixon's retirement looms near, and his memory of Sulie and the last thirty years of his life is about to be erased, will she confront her fear of intimacy and take a leap of faith before it's too late?

Dixon has decided that it's time to retire and enjoy what time he has left. When Sulie is kidnapped during a medical emergency, Dixon realizes that retirement means giving up everything, and everyone, he's known for the last three decades. Will he risk his life, and his heart, to save her?

Reliant Service (Book #4)

Available in 2014

After retiring his first, and only, alias with the Colony, Daniel Brighton discovers the mandatory sabbatical to be less than exciting. He chooses to do a favor and act as a security guard for a fading pop-singer, Lorilei Austyn, whose career is winding down. He travels across Europe with her and discovers her past to be one of deception and intrigue with a past leading directly back to the Colony itself.

Lorilei Austyn is struggling to keep her career alive, and is willing to do what is necessary to save it. Even though she believes she is deathly ill, she travels across Europe on a relief tour to revitalize her career. On the journey she finds the truth behind her past and realizes that the one man who can save her is the handsome security guard she fought so hard not to hire.

Acknowledgements

Special thanks to my husband and our children for their love and support; to my sister for believing in me and encouraging me to follow my dreams; and to my critique partners for being with me every step of the way: Tracy, Kelly, Sue, Alma, & Salli.

I would also like to thank my content editor Erin, my line editor Sue, and my Street Team of supporters – For the Love of Fiction team.

The cover art photo of the couple, entitled "Love Struck", is by Jess Ellis Art (http://fallinginsane.deviantart.com).

UNITED SERVICE
Colony Series Book #2
Chapter One
Available Fall 2013

Gentle rain drizzled onto his nude body like healing kisses renewing his sense of self–peace. Even his headache had subsided a little, but in truth, it always persisted. It just seemed to be more manageable right now. Sterling lay on the patio chair, his body dwarfing the small size of the furniture as he stretched to wake up in his solitude. Feeling slightly sunburned, his skin chafed against the chair. He opened his eyes to a cloudless sky and cursed as the sun blinded him ... no more relief would come today.

As a half–breed vampire he didn't have the protective inner eyelid the purebreds had, so he closed his eyes against the sun. Thinking of the day's schedule, he knew he would spend most of his time down at the penitentiary. He groaned because every time he visited the place his body ached. It wasn't being around humans that did him in, but rather the physical touching of evidence. His ability to glean information from inanimate objects was always helpful in solving cases, and he was happy to help, but his body always paid the price, and he detested the side effects.

Sterling's touch would tell him everything he needed to know about the item's owner, what it was used for, and the feelings and emotions surrounding the item. Each touch made his skin crawl and itch, and the more he touched, the more his skin would scream in agony.

After a few hours his head would pound with a migraine.

But the pain meant nothing; it was just one more damn thing about his human half he had to deal with. Most vampire abilities had good side effects, but it was just his lot in life to be cursed. Fortunately though, it did allow him to bring some of the sickest and most depraved criminals to trial, and that was the justification he needed to keep living his lonely life.

He squinted at the sun again as he reached for his sunglasses on the ground beside him and sat up. The private sleeping porch of the mansion was his little oasis, and his alone. No one would disturb him while he healed and sat in his solitude.

Solitude and loneliness were only separated by a thin line. A very thin line – and he knew it all too well.

Sterling inhaled deeply, taking in the crisp morning air. He could hear the chirping of the songbirds nearby and the wind chime down below swaying in the breeze. Cursing softly to himself he realized he could also hear his father and new wife stirring in their bedroom, next to his sundeck.

It was time to get up. Fang Manor's walls weren't soundproof, and he now tried to block out a conversation which had changed into more intimate noises. *"Newlyweds,"* he thought as he rolled his eyes. No way was he listening to an encore of last night. It wasn't anything Oedipal in his distaste of the noise, just that it reminded him how powerless he was to find a wife of his own. He had failed to secure an arranged marriage, and his own attempts to find a purebred vampire mate had proven unsuccessful, many times.

He stood, scooped up rain pooled on the chair beside him and splashed it on his face. Shaking water from his shoulder length hair, he moaned contently at the soothing touch. He knew it would be the last time he would feel good all day.

Checking his rain catchers, he poured the collected rain into bottles to be used later. He then walked through the few puddles of rainwater which sat on the stone floor of the deck; he opened the glass door and entered his private bedroom. The room was beautifully furnished, with the decor specifically chosen by Sterling himself. The cherry wood king–sized bed with matching nightstand and dresser filled the room. A hunter green duvet, with burgundy and gold pillows, in various sizes and shapes, were placed at the head and the foot of the bed. An old gold cross, which he had inherited from his human grandmother, hung on the wall above it. As nice as the room was, Sterling spent very little time here, even though this house had been his home for too many decades to count.

He lived here with his father, step–mother, aunt, and several team members, making up "The Colony", a special operative team of vampires employed by the federal government to protect the President and the American way of life. Sterling was one of the founding members of the Colony when it was established in 1866, after the assassination of President Abraham Lincoln. It was the only life Sterling knew. The job had benefits and perks, but also pitfalls. But what job didn't?

Sterling looked around the room. It was a gilded cage with free room and board paid for by Uncle Sam. Sure, he loved his family, and Fang Manor was a far cry from 'slumming it', but due to security measures he could never entertain guests at the place. A wife could live here with him, not that he had one. A girlfriend? Hell, he never dated a woman longer than, well, an hour tops. And even then, the women were humans.

Speaking of human females, he was hungry, and there wasn't one in his bed at the moment. This is exactly why he maintained an apartment in the city.

Damn. His fangs were already extended, expecting to eat. It was time for plan B. He shook his head as he walked across the room. Next to the air purifier on the floor sat a small personal refrigerator. He opened it and pulled out a bag of AB negative blood. Bagged blood. Not his favorite, but at least it was free. He poured some into a mug and warned it in the microwave which sat atop the refrigerator. It took only a minute for him to down it all after the microwave beeped. There was no reason to savor bagged blood. Honestly, no reason at all. The packaging, for starters, was all wrong.

The dried rain still clung to his skin. Not wanting to wash it off, he skipped a shower. In his private bathroom he stared at his blurred reflection in the mirror. One corner of his mouth turned up in a half grin as his reflection reminded him of the vampire lore that Hollywood just messed up in their movies. Hollywood did get the mirror reflection right though. Thanks to the silver in the mirror, and even the silver in the old fashioned photography, vampire images were always obscured.

As he brushed his shoulder length dirty–blond hair, he took a good look at himself in the mirror. He spent time last night at the mansion's private gym lifting weights with his father. Sterling's muscular physique was well formed, and even the poor reflection could show his ripped muscles. He took great pride in this lure since it worked so well where human women were concerned.

He paused and leaned into the mirror. Was that a gray hair? Yep, but just one or two. Next, he studied his eyes. Wrinkles had formed over night as well. Looking down at the medallion of the Patron Saint of Rain, Genevieve, he noticed a gray chest hair. Guessing his age was now in the late thirties he continued to brush his hair as he waited for the effects of his breakfast on his body.

The wait wasn't long. He felt the warmed blood course through his veins and his cells began to regenerate. His hair gained more color, his wrinkles ironed themselves out, and he had a healthier glow about him. He took a deep breath and looked back in the mirror. His fuzzy reflection showed him at the age of twenty–seven again. It was his age during his Jahrling Year, when he transitioned into a full vampire and his fangs lengthened to their full–size to allow him to eat from a blood–only diet. His fangs came in late because he was a half–breed. If he had been a purebred vampire, he could look as young as the age when most humans got their wisdom teeth, their early twenties. It was just one more thing to thank his long, dead mother for, not that he ever had a chance to meet the woman.

The blood lust from his morning's breakfast finally hit him. It would come quicker if he had injected the blood directly into his veins. By orally consuming it, his spleen had to process the blood from his digestive system to his circulatory system, which took time. The first drops of blood acted as a fountain of youth, then eventually affecting other areas of his body like liquid

Viagra. With no woman to satisfy him, he ignored his aroused state and decided to get dressed. He was used to feeling miserable, so it really didn't bother him to remain uncomfortable.

He opened the top drawer of his dresser and pulled out a pair of socks and underwear. In the middle drawer he pulled out a set of skin coverings. They resembled long–johns but were made from a light cotton fabric. They covered him from neck to ankles and prevented most of everything from touching him. They weren't a great fashion statement, but they worked well. He walked to his closet for a pair of jeans and a shirt.

He had just finished dressing when his cell phone buzzed. It was another Colony member, Daniel, who was working downtown, and the one vampire in the world that Sterling avoided as much as possible.

The phone rang again, and Sterling stared at it with a grimace on his face. When it rang a third time he answered it. "Yes, what?" Sterling huffed.

"Good morning to you too, mate," Daniel said in a slightly faded British accent. "I'm with the police investigating a bloody murder, quite literally. I think you ought to see this."

Sterling cursed under his breath. Miss Manners never covered the social protocol of how to behave when dealing with a man you murdered in cold blood, and then had turned into a vampire against his will.

He could understand the need to exact revenge, but Daniel forgave him for what he did. On top of that, Daniel was nice to him, which made no sense to Sterling. He gritted his teeth, "Text me the address."

ENDURING SERVICE
Colony Series Book #3
Available 2014
Chapter One

Watching the apartment window from where she was seated in her parked car, Sulie let out a huge yawn. She couldn't help it. Her insane schedule was taxing her body. Between her shifts at the hospital and her responsibilities as a member of the Colony, the secret vampire task force for the White House, she needed a break. She wondered how human women could keep up. It wasn't like she had a career and a family, but two careers were enough — at least for now.

She had awakened before dawn to give the President his yearly physical before leaving for Camp David. As the President's private physician she would be accompanying him once again. She cringed at the thought. The man was a letch when it came to women, especially blonds. Sulie looked all of twenty–two and had long blond hair, curled in locks. She inwardly cursed herself for not cutting and dyeing her hair before the trip.

It was all routine. Her packed bags had already passed through security checks and had been loaded onto Marine One, the President's private helicopter. The trip was not business related, and should—in theory—be relaxing, but she always hated going to Camp David. Again she would have to dodge the President's advances, or ignore the man's parade of women. The Secret Service would be discrete, as always, and Sulie would be asked to compel any humans to forget

i

anything less than proper. She hated doing that. She was a trained professional doctor and soldier, not the man's personal clean–up crew.

Sulie sighed heavily as she again glanced up to the apartment window. These presidential trips used to have a silver lining – a silver–haired lining named Jonathan Dixon. He was the retiring Director of the Colony and had always accompanied her when she traveled with the President. The Director was the human liaison between the President and the vampire team that had protected all the presidents since Lincoln's assassination. Dixon had served in that role for thirty years. Sulie liked the new replacement Director, but he was no Dixon.

Nobody was better than Dixon. He had been the best Director the team ever had, and the one person in the world that Sulie trusted, depended on, and loved with all of her heart. She felt the pain as her stomach twisted at the thought of his retirement.

With his retirement, Dixon's memories of their last thirty years together would be wiped away. She, and everything they did together, would be forgotten by Dixon. He had known the outcome when he had accepted the assignment and was willing to fulfill his last duty with the team. She couldn't let that happen. At least, not before she told the man how much she loved him. Even if he didn't love her back, at least he would know how she felt.

This was the time. This was the place. She looked down at the now empty bottle of scotch lying in her lap and felt the slight buzz of its effects. It had taken the whole bottle for her to muster the courage to do what she needed to do, to say what she needed to say. There was no turning back.

Grabbing her purse, she opened the car door. The glass bottle tumbled to the concrete street and shattered. She clung onto the car door and took several deep breaths. Other than wine, she had never been much of a drinker. And even then, she never allowed herself to get tipsy.

The two flights of stairs challenged her, but she got her second wind when her foot hit the last step. Apartment 26E. It was an apartment she was very familiar with. As she approached the door, she again felt the butterflies in her stomach.

She rotated her neck and rolled her shoulders before knocking on the door. When she heard Dixon approaching, she took in a deep breath and remembered to smile, her fangs slightly showing.

The door flew open and she gazed into Dixon's panicked eyes.

"I'm glad you're here," he said. "I need you."

CHAPTER TWO

Sulie quickly walked into the small, sparsely furnished apartment. Immediately her nose wrinkled at the scent of stale food. "What's wrong?" she asked, glancing at a stack of empty pizza boxes and take–out containers on the dining room table.

Dixon closed the door and walked past her to the kitchen. The mortal man was in his mid–sixties and more than a century younger than Sulie. Over the years, his salt–and–pepper hair had grayed. His waistline had widened slightly, but his 6'1" frame carried the extra weight just fine in her opinion. He wore bifocals, but still had the most beautiful green eyes she had ever seen. She inhaled deeply and took in the subtle scent of his aftershave as he walked past. The man had aged well, just like a fine bottle of wine.

Fumbling through his medications in a cabinet, Dixon pulled out a small, empty bottle with a dropper top. "I'm out of Devolixion," he said reading the label, his voice nearly breathless. "I called the pharmacy, but even when I spelled out the medication they said they couldn't fill it."

I slight smile crossed Sulie's lips. "It's fine," she said reaching into her purse. "I brought you a three–month supply." She handed one of the bottles to Dixon and stored the other two in his cabinet.

She watched as Dixon smiled and let out a sigh of relief. The man had no idea how adorable he was. He could lead the team of vampires when it came to missions with the President, but ask him to keep track of anything personal and he was a mess. Sulie thought the man needed a woman in his life. She knew Dixon had been married several times, and had suspected that he had given up when it came to matters of the heart.

Now was the time. All she had to do was confess her love, but why were her knees suddenly shaking? The butterflies had also returned to her stomach. Feeling queasy from the scotch, she decided to have a seat in the living room.

There was a couch, a chair that did not match, and a huge television in the room. In the middle was a table, stained from years of abuse, which desperately needed coasters. The dry cleaning she had picked up for him days ago was still in its plastic bag and draped over the overstuffed leather chair. As she shifted the laundered clothes aside so she could sit, she caught her reflection in the small mirror that was hanging on the wall. Her reflection was fuzzy because of her vampire nature, but clear enough for her to recognize the image as her own. In preparation for this day she had spent all of yesterday at the spa. The hair extensions were an easy choice to have done, especially since she knew Dixon liked long, flowing hair. The manicure and pedicure would probably go unnoticed, but were pleasant, and the facial had been nice.

She sat down and noticed Dixon yawning as he squirted some Devolixion into his coffee cup. He stirred the drink as he walked to the couch, leaning heavily on the armrest as he took his seat.

"Dixon, it's nearly eleven o'clock. Why are you so tired?" she asked.

Slouching, he rubbed his eyes. "I don't know. Maybe because I'm late taking the Devolixion?" he asked looking down into his coffee mug.

"No," she said quickly. She moved onto the couch and, taking his hand, she used her special ability to read him medically. A simple touch was sufficient for a good diagnosis, but she ran her hand up his arm and allowed it to travel to his face. Caressing him tenderly she continued diagnosing him.

He closed his eyes as her fingers danced along his brow. "Your hair looks nice. Did you do something different to it?"

"It's springtime. I figured it was time for a new look," she lied. She wanted to admit that she changed her look just for him, but she wasn't quite ready for that discussion. She needed to find out what was wrong with him first.

"It's nice. I like the bouncy curls."

She smiled as she accepted the anticipated compliment. Dixon had a fondness for the Farrah Fawcett look from the show "Charlie's Angels" in the '70s and Sulie had changed her hairstyle a few times to mimic the woman's tresses. Sulie did the same thing in the '90s when Dixon commented on Rachel's hairstyle in the "Friends" show. Each change in hairstyle had earned her a compliment from the man, but unfortunately, nothing more.

After a brief pause he added, "I liked the short hairstyle too, like the hairstyle you had over a year ago at Easter. This is just … different. It looks real nice."

Sulie loved how attentive to detail Dixon was. His photographic memory allowed him to remember many fine points. "Thank you, Dixon. Now hush so I can finish giving you your exam." Her hands dove into his lush hairline.

After another moment of her caressing the nape of his neck, she announced, "You're anemic." She studied his tired face. "How long have you been this tired?"

"What? Um … I guess I've been tired for a while now. I don't know." He motioned with his hands over his body. "I'm falling to pieces. I did do some training exercises with Brandon yesterday, which wore me out."

"Brandon is less than half your age," Sulie said about the man replacing Dixon as Colony Director. "Your anemia could be a result of the ulcer you have. Probably a lack of iron in your blood. I better taste it so I can be sure." Her fangs were not fully extracted, but she rubbed his fingertip across one of the two sharp points in her mouth. A drop of blood pooled, so she licked the small wound and quickly sealed it.

The sample was small, but enough for an accurate reading – even better than having lab work done. At the very least they got the answer immediately without having to wait.

She grimaced as she tasted his blood. "It's weak. Not much hemoglobin." She licked her lips clean. "You have a lack of iron in your system. Let's go have some lunch. I suggest you order a steak and I'll prescribe some supplements for you."

"You're treating me like one of the babies you deliver," he laughed as he wiped her saliva off his hand and onto his pant leg.

"More gentle than a heel prick for a newborn." she said, noticing his actions. It wasn't like he had brought out antibacterial gel and sanitized his hand, but the gesture still hurt. During the exam she had picked up no signs of love from the man. No raised heart rate. No increase of   perspiration. No elevated endorphin level. No sexual arousal. No nothing.

Sulie looked away to hide her teary eyes. Human beings were easy to manipulate with a simple compelling, but she wanted Dixon's love to be genuine. Other than her oath to the President which forbade her from compelling select government officials, including the Colony Director, she couldn't compel Dixon – not even in a moment of weakness. His mind had been altered when he had accepted the office of Director. No vampire could compel him.

She was just a friend to Dixon. A well trusted friend. Perhaps declaring her love would be the catalyst for him to see her in a new light. Unfortunately, professing her love was not something she wanted to do once they were at a crowded restaurant. She also didn't want to rush the subject. The man was sick, and he needed to eat. It could wait until after the President's Camp David trip. But after that, she would tell him. There would still be plenty of time.

"Steak probably isn't a good idea. You know I avoid red meat because of my cholesterol. You're the one who prescribed Devolixion to me in the first place."

"I prescribed Crestor for your cholesterol," she corrected him.

Looking down at his coffee mug, he said, "I thought Devolixion was also for my cholesterol."

"Don't avoid red meat today," she said, changing the subject. "This afternoon you'll enjoy a steak and we'll talk about your diet. I want you eating foods that are rich in iron for a few days."

He finished his coffee and stood up. "I'm feeling a little better. Let me grab my coat and then we'll head out."

She wasn't surprised that he was feeling better. That was a nice side effect of Devolixion, and one reason she made sure he took it every day. Thankfully she had anticipated his need for more and was able to mix–up another batch of the fictitious drug before heading over. Medically speaking, what she was doing was unethical, but no one ever said love was fair.

RELIANT SERVICE
Colony Series Book #4
Available Fall 2014
Chapter One

Daniel surveyed the huge crowd with a cautious eye. The amount of onlookers had more than doubled over the last hour and the people had begun to push against the rope-line that marked off the safety zone. The near breach caused the posted agents to forcibly hold them back.

Even though the crowd stood a good distance away, Daniel suspected it still posed a threat. The President had just finished a speech at a public auditorium. Daniel's job was to get him safely to the Beast, the presidential limo which waited out back near the kitchen dumpsters. The decoy limo, with its own agents, protected a fake president at another exit.

From the corner of his eye, Daniel could see the Beast, but he remained steadfast on watching the crowd. The President would be safe once again inside the car with its bulletproof glass, its reinforced armor, and its antiterrorist safety features. Daniel counted off the President's footsteps. Four more and the human would be safe.

With his vampire hearing, Daniel heard a bullet enter its gun chamber. Fearing for the President's life, Daniel sprung into action. He was unsure of the direction from which the bullet would come, but he did know the exact location of the President, and that's all that mattered. Daniel pushed past the two human Secret Service agents nearest the Beast and stood directly behind the

I

President, wedging the man between the opened car door and himself.

A moment later Daniel heard the shot and the bullet streaking through the air.

The crowd screamed. The agents quickly pulled their guns and surrounded the President.

Daniel stood tall and held out his arms to block the President from all angles. The bullet whistled past the line of defense and continued its path. The hot lead missed its mark, but hit Daniel in the jaw where it traveled through to his neck and lodged in his spine.

The pain caused Daniel to cry out. His purple blood sprayed from the wound and covered one of the nearby agents, the cement sidewalk, and the inside of the still opened car door. Involuntarily, his head flung back, and any hope Daniel had of seeing the shooter disappeared.

A mass frenzy of agents jumped the shooter as Daniel felt his knees grow weak. He took a step backwards, towards the President. In the com unit, he heard the orders for the Beast to leave. Evacuate. Keep the President safe.

Daniel stumbled, turned, and pushed the President into the car. He noticed an agent from within the Beast grabbing the man and pulling him to safety as well. It caused Daniel to further lose balance. A Secret Service agent, standing on the sidewalk and covered with Daniel's blood, pushed him the rest of the way into the Beast in an effort to close the car door as quickly as possible.

His head hit the President's knee and caused more searing pain. Daniel lie on the floor of the Beast as the car sped from the auditorium and entered the streets under police escort. His blood poured from its wound onto the President's pants, and soiling the floor. He had only detected one bullet, but still didn't know if the President survived.

The President pulled himself into one of the seats. "I'm fine," he said repeatedly. The man's face whitened with fright and Daniel heard the man's speeding heart rate. He heard all the heart beats of the human's in the car. His eyes blackened and his fangs extended their full-length. He needed to feed. Feed, or die.

Again Daniel listened as the President proclaimed he was fine. Relief washed over him. He had done his job. But if someone didn't remove the President from within his reach, the President would be his next meal.

Sulie inspected the President and then declared him healthy. She had been the President's private physician for his entire tenure, just like she had been for all the presidents since Lincoln. She was another member of The Colony, the covert team of vampires who protected the President. She was also a vampire, just like Daniel. She moved from the President and now sat next to him on the floor. "Daniel," she began, "I need you to look at me. Focus on me."

Daniel's initial aged appearance had been in his late sixties. His purple vampire blood gushed to the floor of the car. The blood darkened each moment as the cells of his body aged. In the moments since he had been shot, he had aged ten years.

Sulie leaned over and licked his wound to seal it, but Daniel knew the wound was bad. The determined, yet saddened, expression on Sulie's face told him as much.

"You can see his jawbone from his chin," Brandon said.

Daniel's eyesight began fading, but he looked over to Brandon, the Colony Director. He was human. He had blood in his body. Blood that Daniel needed.

"It will heal," Sulie insisted. "The bullet is lodged in him. It'll work itself out soon."

Brandon injected a syringe of blood into Daniel's thigh. The hiss of the syringe was slight compared with the sound of Brandon's beating heart.

Daniel counted the number of syringes Brandon injected into him. He felt the human red blood pouring out his wound and knew it was mixing with the dark purple pool on the floor.

"We need more blood," Sulie cried out.

Weakness overpowered Daniel and he could no longer see. Before he lost consciousness, he managed to say, "I really loved my life."

Books by
Silkhaven Publishing, LLC

Due Out 2013

Eternal Service by Regina Morris

Growing Up Lately by Sue S Morris

Facebooking with Mona by Sue S Morris

United Service by Regina Morris

Due Out 2014

Time Historian: Mystery at Preston Hall by Lillian Kendall

Enduring Service by Regina Morris

The Story of Jane by Sue S Morris

Reliant Service by Regina Morris

22359319R00254

Made in the USA
Charleston, SC
17 September 2013